D0342261

An
Affair of Honor

The Honor Series
by Robert N. Macomber

At the Edge of Honor
Point of Honor
Honorable Mention
A Dishonorable Few
An Affair of Honor

An Affair of Honor

The fifth novel in the Honor Series
following the
exploits of
Lt. Peter Wake
United States Navy

Robert N. Macomber

Pineapple Press, Inc.
Sarasota, Florida

Copyright © 2006 by Robert N. Macomber

All rights reserved. No part of this book may be reproduced in any form or by any means, electronic or mechanical, including photo-copying, recording, or by any information storage and retrieval sys-tem, without permission in writing from the publisher.

Inquiries should be addressed to:

Pineapple Press, Inc.
P.O. Box 3889
Sarasota, Florida 34230
www.pineapplepress.com

Library of Congress Cataloging-in-Publication Data

Macomber, Robert N., 1953-
  An affair of honor / Robert N. Macomber.— 1st ed.
      p. cm.
  ISBN-13: 978-1-56164-368-4 (alk. paper)
  ISBN-10: 1-56164-368-8 (alk. paper)
  1. Wake, Peter (Fictitious character)—Fiction. 2. United States—History, Naval—19th century—Fiction. 3. United States. Navy—Officers—Fiction. 4. Americans—Europe—Fiction. 5. Americans—Morocco—Fiction. 6. Americans—Caribbean Area—Fiction. 7. Europe—History—1871-1918—Fiction. 8. Morocco—Fiction. 9. Caribbean Area—Fiction. I. Title.
  PS3613.A28A35 2006
  813'.6—dc22
                                                            2006007505

First Edition
10 9 8 7 6 5 4 3 2 1

Design by Shé Heaton
Printed in United States of America

This novel is respectfully dedicated to

Sidi Goudimi Ahmed,
my incredible Berber driver/guide on the long trek
along the coasts, through the mountains, and down to the
desert of Morocco,
a good man, a wonderful teacher, a patient friend, and an
outstanding ambassador for his people, his nation, and his faith.
Salaamu 'lekum, Sahbi. Shukran bezzef.

and to

**the magnificent and ancient
people of Morocco**

We are *all* the children of Abraham....

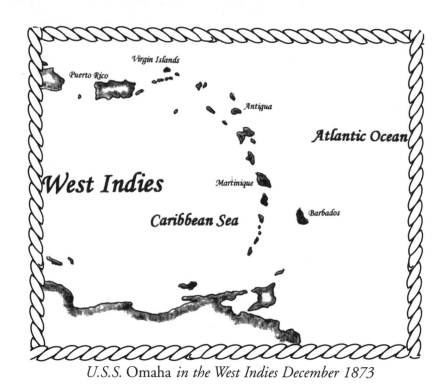

U.S.S. Omaha *in the West Indies December 1873*

Ashore in Italy Winter 1874

Ashore in Spain January 1874

Northern Africa Spring 1874

Foreword

As with all of my novels, I have tried to accurately portray the times and locales that Peter Wake encounters. I picked 1874 for this novel because of the tremendous amount of dynamic change going on around the world. What a time for Wake to head east!

America was recovering from her self-slaughter the decade before. In the South, the military occupation of the Reconstruction was ending, the Democrats were returning to power, and the newly won freedoms for African-Americans were about to evaporate. Nationwide, the financial panic of 1873 had devastated large parts of the economy, the U.S. Army was fighting Indians out west, and the technological revolution was in full swing.

The U.S. Navy was a sad, weak shadow of its Civil War strength—neglected by Congress, pitied or laughed at by other navies, and struggling to fulfill its squadron commitments around the world. The most powerful navies were the British, French, and German. Naval technology was advancing rapidly, but American sailors still had to *sail*.

The Caribbean had become a fetid backwater of the European empires—sugar values were in decline and the mother countries were concentrating on expanding their holdings in Africa and Asia. The West Indies had become a drain on the empires and were no longer a prestigious posting.

Europe in 1874 was full of intrigue. The French had been humiliated by the Mexicans in the mid-1860s and by the Germans in the Franco-Prussian War in 1870. Napoleon III had been ousted, another republic proclaimed, and the nation was attempting to reestablish its confidence at home and image abroad. The victorious Germans had unified under Bismarck and Wilhelm I, and were becoming global players, expanding their military and naval power rapidly. The Italians, unified by Garibaldi and Cavour for the first time in sixteen centuries, were beaten by the Austrians in the war of 1866 and abandoned by their French protectors. The Spanish, having removed the corrupt monarchy, were trying to start a republic but falling back into the chaos of their perpetual civil war. The Austrians had united with the Hungarians and their empire stretched across much of central Europe and was now facing the Muslim Ottomans. The Ottoman Empire was beginning to crumble, but remained large and very dangerous. The Russians were desperately trying to modernize and keep up with the Germans, unsuccessfully. The smaller countries aligned themselves with their biggest neighbor or proclaimed a neutral stance and hoped for the best. Great Britain's empire was in her glory, economically sound and protected by the most famous navy the world has known, but even she was watching the new German nation with close attention.

Africa didn't have many independent nations, but Morocco was one of them. Even the Ottomans couldn't conquer the Magreb Arabs and Berbers. The French had a large economic influence there and the Moroccan leadership walked the tightrope of political reality. It was (and still is) a mystical land, in most ways ancient and completely alien to a European or American in 1874. Marrakech and Fez were the fabled cities of the caravan trade routes, the stuff of dreams and legends.

Peter Wake ends up seeing all of this—a wary American naval officer suddenly adrift in Machiavellian Europe and mysterious Morocco. The dead-eyed oddsmakers of Monaco probably wouldn't back him one *centime*, but my money's on our hero.

He has the wonderful American habit of beating the oddsmakers.

Onward and upward!
Bob Macomber
Marrakech, Morocco
Northwest Africa

1

Déjà Vu

20 December 1873

San Juan, Puerto Rico
Spanish West Indies

"More sangria, señor?" asked the waiter.

Lieutenant Peter Wake, United States Navy, nodded and shifted his lanky frame back in the chair, reveling in the warm sea breeze. Seated at a stone patio table at the Café Réal, overlooking the jade-colored waters of San Juan's bay, he savored the aromas of salt air, white frangipani flowers, and citrus-marinated grouper cooking on coals. Downing the drink in one long swig, he glanced over his shoulder, and immediately the waiter refilled the fruit wine that was enhanced by strong dark rum.

The mold-covered, faded pink buildings of the declining Spanish empire were the same on this visit, but Wake felt a new air about the place. And not just because the ominous annual *huracán* season was ending. No, a momentous event had occurred just months earlier—slavery had been ended forever. Wake smiled at the thought of it as he drank the sangria, slower now, for he didn't want to get drunk.

The waiter's dark face, leathered by time and toil, crinkled into a sly grin. "You are perhaps waiting for a beautiful lady to arrive, señor?" he asked.

Wake laughed and answered with a mock sigh. "No, Jorge. I am expecting only a man. But it *would* be nice if a beautiful woman were with him." Wake waved his hand around. "And yes, Jorge, it would complete this scene as a perfect memory for my old age."

"Sí, señor. A day like today should include a woman. And *that* memory," the waiter sighed also, "would make you warm on a cold night when you are old, like me."

"Yes, you're right. Please tell me, Jorge, just how did your English get so good?" Wake had wondered that since the waiter first greeted him at the café.

"My original master was a British man in St. Augustine, up in Florida, señor. When the Americans bought it from Spain, he sold me to a Spanish family that was moving to San Juan. Then they sold me to this café owner's father, who bequeathed me to his son. I was twenty years old when I left Florida all those years ago, but I never forgot my English. My master here used me as a translator with American sailors in the port."

Wake did the mathematics and realized the man would be about seventy-three. "But now you are free," he said.

"Yes, señor. God has allowed me to live long enough to be a free man. I still work for my master here at the café, but now I do so willingly."

"And, of course, now they pay you for working."

"Oh no, señor. My master has no money to pay me, but he lets me stay in my old room and still lets me eat in the kitchen." Seeing Wake's reaction, the waiter shrugged, paternal softness coming into his voice. "Slavery is a state of mind and heart, señor. Money does not matter—my mind and my heart are now free."

As the waiter went back to the kitchen, Wake remembered the former slaves he had seen in Pensacola after the recent war in his country. The Republicans were trying hard to assimilate them into society as freedmen, but the problems of that lofty endeavor were far more difficult than anything a legal proclamation or the recent Constitutional amendment could overcome. Politics had a way of slowing the best of intentions and Wake wondered how much longer the effort would continue before the Democrats in Congress would grind it to a halt. In addition to all of that, corruption was widespread in the Reconstruction, with a lot of people—except the new black citizens—getting rich off the government. The thought of the whole mess depressed him. A lot of men, some of them his friends, had died in that war. Liberating the slaves was the one tangible outcome he could point to with pride.

"You are looking very pensive, my old friend."

Wake turned around. Standing there was a slender, handsome man in his late forties, silver hair flowing over his collar. The man moved easily and could pass for a local, for he was wearing a guayabera, the Latino white shirt of the tropics that was so much more comfortable than Wake's wool coat. His smile was accented by crinkled eyes and one eyebrow cocked high in a mien of mock concern. This was the man who had sent Wake the invitation for lunch.

Jonathan Saunders was a former Confederate blockade runner and wartime foe turned friend. Wake had chased Saunders for two long years in Florida, the Bahamas, Mexico, and Cuba—catching him twice and thinking him surely dead once, but the devious rebel always escaped. Both had developed a grudging respect for the other, and after the war, in January of 1866, Wake had conducted an official naval visit to Saunders' colony of former Confederates on the west end of Puerto Rico. The two men finally became friends and had stayed such in the years since.

"Just thinking of the old days, Jonathan. It's good to see you," replied Wake. They shook hands and he beckoned

Saunders to sit. "Been far too long. Now, how in the world did you know I was here? We just pulled in yesterday."

"Whenever I come to San Juan for business I always check the harbor to see if any American naval vessels are in. If they are, I always ask for you. But lately there haven't been any, what with the war scare and all. Then this morning I saw the *Omaha,* asked, and heard you were aboard. It's been, what, two years? You were just coming home from the Panamanian jungle then."

"Ah, yes, the Selfridge Survey Expedition. I was damn near dead from the fever when I saw you in seventy-one."

Saunders nodded at the memory. "You did look pretty bad. I was worried about you. It's amazing, Peter—you managed to avoid yellow fever all those years in Florida, but it nailed you good in Panama."

"Enough of that story, Jonathan," said Wake with a visible cringe at the memory of the pain endured while nearly dying from what the Royal Navy called the "black vomit." It was time to change the subject. "Tell me, how's your colony at Por Fin doing?"

"Well, the sugar cane's doing fine. Of course, people'll always drink rum, so we're making it through the money panic without too much trouble," said Saunders, referring to the economic depression caused by the failure of financier Jay Cooke's Northern Pacific Railroad three months earlier in September. By November, the panic that devastated the United States' banks had spread worldwide. "We didn't use slaves anyway, so emancipation hasn't hurt us like it did some planter folks. As far as socially, the people at Por Fin have settled in with the surrounding towns pretty well, I think. You know, the west coast is a world away from the bureaucrats here in San Juan, so we just don't have the same problems as many of the immigrants on the island."

"Then a toast is called for to celebrate continued success in your new life, Jonathan," offered Wake when his friend's drink arrived.

"Thank you, my friend—"

Saunders was interrupted by a Southern-accented feminine voice from behind Wake. "Oh my Lord, I *do* declare! If it isn't my heroic savior, in the flesh and blood. Peter, my dear, how *are* you?"

Cynda Denaud Williams swept onto the patio and caressed Wake's right arm as she leaned over and embraced him, her bosom, mostly exposed by her low-cut dress, only inches from his eyes.

Saunders tried not to laugh as Wake recovered from the shock of seeing the woman he had rescued from enemy territory near the end of the war. At the time he had fallen for her damsel-in-distress portrayal, even briefly starting to fall under her sexual spell until he came to his senses. She was a woman who could make men believe—and do—anything, and Wake couldn't imagine that she had changed. Even though it had been eight years since he had last seen her in Key West she looked exactly the same—a beautiful blonde with a perfect figure and a honey-dipped voice.

"Ah, hello, Mrs. Williams," Wake said. "It is truly quite a surprise. I knew you had gone to Por Fin but didn't expect to see you here in San Juan."

"Oh, Peter. We know each other far too well for such formalities." She brushed away a lock of his brown hair and touched the scar on his right temple. "If you call me anything other than Cynda I do declare I shall *cry*. You don't want to make me cry, do you, Peter?"

Saunders held up a hand. "It's my fault, Cynda. I forgot to tell him you were here in San Juan and would be with us for lunch. Now sit down, dear, while I explain. By the way, Peter, Cynda is no longer named Williams."

Wake wondered whom she had hooked. "Oh?"

Saunders laughed. "Yes. Her divorce came through last year and we married in October. Her last name is Saunders now."

"Oh . . . well, Jonathan," stammered Wake, stunned by the news and worried for his friend. "I certainly am surprised yet again. You never mentioned this the last time we met, or in your letters."

"Yes, well," Saunders chuckled, "we just became serious this last summer, Peter."

"Then another toast is in order," said Wake as the old waiter poured the lady's wine. "To your life shared together. May it bring health, wealth, and love, and all the time to enjoy them."

"Oh, Peter, that was so very beautiful. Thank you," gushed Cynda, clutching both Wake's and her new husband's arms as she sat between them. "Now, you simply *must* tell us how your life has been going for the last few years. Please start with your lovely wife, Linda."

"Linda's doing just fine with the children in our house in Pensacola. Sean is growing up fast and learning all kinds of new things, and Useppa is having fun playing the big sister. She's eight years old now, almost nine, and actually becoming a real help to Linda. Sean is six."

Saunders asked, "How is little Useppa's leg doing? Were the doctors able to help her?"

It was a subject that broke Wake's heart. His little princess had pain in her lower right leg, making her limp and also causing some of the other children to make fun of her.

"We've had her to several doctors, but they can't determine what's wrong, much less how to correct it. One suggested a heavy brace, but the others said that would make it worse. Linda and I are really worried for her."

Cynda squeezed his arm with obvious empathy. "Oh, Peter. I'm so sorry."

"Thank you, Cynda. The good news is that Useppa's young and strong. So there's still a lot of time for her to get help. Say, how's your little sister Mary Alice doing?"

"She married a man named Pickett, of the famous family, and lives in Virginia. You heard about those scamps, the Yard Dogs?"

Three former soldiers who had formed a minstrel troupe in

Key West, the Yard Dogs had been friends of Wake during the war. They had been playing during the infamous tavern brawl of 1864, which was inadvertently started by Wake while defending the honor of his squadron. He escaped, seriously hurt, and was nursed overnight by a prostitute—he couldn't remember her name—but the Yard Dogs had ended up in the Key West jail. It was a fact they later used to get rum out of him. "Come to think of it, I didn't see them in Key West when I was there lately. What's happened?"

"Run out of Key West for a while by the Monroe County sheriff." Cynda shook her head. "Those boys got into one bar fight too many at Schooner's Wharf. Now they're reduced to playing at fish camps along the Gulf coast. More their style, if you ask me."

Wake laughed. "Kip was always a good one at rousing the crowd, no doubt on it. Of course, Charlie and Brian were no slouches either. They'll be back once the sheriff calms down."

"So how's the naval career going?" interrupted Saunders. He was an old seaman and always interested in naval matters. "I hear the American navy's going downhill fast. Is that true?"

"The navy? Well, it's surely not what it was during the war, or even doing well compared to the Latin American navies now."

Saunders sighed. "Peter, I've got to let you know that the Spanish leadership around here is joking about the American navy. They're upset that Madrid backed down last month and are saying the *yanquis* don't have the strength anymore to push them around. Heard some ugly stuff coming from them. Guess they thought I'd be sympathetic, so they were very candid."

"Well, they're right about our fleet," Wake admitted. "But you know, that mess in Cuba at Santiago last month where the Spanish government shot our merchant seamen got the attention of some of the leadership in Congress when they found out how ill prepared we are. The president sent Admiral Porter down to Key West for a while, gathering up ships from the Med and the local squadron for a battle fleet, but fortunately the Spanish *did* back down.

"I was with the fleet at Key West and I admit I was scared

when I saw what we had to work with, Jonathan, but I really think we would've won in the end. I'm just damned glad we didn't have to try. The sailors didn't want a war—it was the politicians. Nobody's gloating though because it was a damned close-run thing. Hell, this is the first official visit to San Juan since it all got defused. But everybody here's been nice so far."

"They're trying to smooth it over, but I'm telling you—be careful with 'em," Saunders said. "So, will Congress make you stronger now?"

"Word is that Washington's going to fund some new ships for us, but that'll take years." Wake shook his head. "Congress screams for us to do something to protect Americans around the world but hasn't funded us even the fuel budget we need. Been that way since sixty-seven. Maybe it'll change now. Time will tell."

Saunders leaned forward. "What about you? Any word on promotion?"

"Been a regularly commissioned lieutenant now for eight years, but it's hard to tell, Jonathan. I'm executive officer of *Omaha* and think that at the end of this ship assignment, in June next year, I may have a chance at promotion and/or command."

"So how's *Omaha*? What's she doing? Any chance for glory?" Saunders asked.

"She's assigned to the West Indies and a pretty good sailor. Her engine's in good shape, but of course we're prohibited from using it except for entering and leaving harbor. She's got coal bunkers for only about a hundred fifty tons, which limits her anyway. We've been busy at the Spanish islands since September, so now we'll sail around the other islands, show the flag, help the diplomats and merchants, keep the peace, that sort of thing. Glory part's over now. Just routine patrol."

"How about Sean Rork, that wild Irish bosun of yours?"

Wake laughed. "Ah, old Sean! Last I knew, he's still aboard *Alaska*. They were here for a while during the war scare, but are in New York for repairs right now. Saw him in October. He told me he damn near didn't survive the sinking of *Oneida* at Yokohama when that Brit steamer ran her down and fled the scene a couple of years ago. Wrote that he used up every one of his Gaelic oaths, but still lived through it. Floated on a plank and got picked up later."

"And the old gunner's mate? I forgot his name."

"Durling. He's ashore at Newport at the new torpedo station there. They took some of the gunners and made them specialize in the new torpedoes they're working on, figuring that they already knew more about explosives than anyone else. But I hear he's not happy—misses his beloved guns!"

"Gentlemen, I hate to interrupt all this talk of guns and death, but why don't we order lunch and talk of something more tranquil?" said Cynda. "It's far too pretty a day to talk about the navy."

Exactly what Linda would've said, thought Wake. Linda had gotten to the point where she despised the navy and its cloud on their marriage, causing an unspoken rift to grow between them. He put that out of his mind and smiled. "I bow to your wisdom, ma'am. Let us talk of the future and of peaceful things, Jonathan."

"Quite right, Peter," agreed Saunders. "The war is over. Thank God. Let's talk about making money from rum!"

"I do believe I'll drink to *that!*" said Wake. He downed the sangria and signaled for more.

2

Future Plans

Two days later *Omaha* steamed east from San Juan into a twenty-knot wind and rising seas. Her nine-hundred-fifty-horsepower, horizontal-return-connecting-rod engine was pushing her at twelve knots, assisted a bit by her jibs and stay sails, but the senior engineer was warning of the fuel consumption and unaccustomed strain on the boilers. When Wake arrived on deck for his noon watch Captain Gardiner was already there, examining the northeast point of Puerto Rico through his binoculars.

"Mr. Wake, Cabezas de San Juan bears to the southwest about fifteen miles or so. What say you? Should we bear off and steer so'east? I've already used too much coal to get to this point, but I'll be damned if I'll let my ship get caught on a lee coast."

Wake checked the bearing of the point, barely visible on the horizon, then the chart on the binnacle table. "Yes, sir. The wind is nor'nor'east to nor'east, so I would recommend that course." His finger traced the projected route through the islands. "It should take us comfortably to the windward of Culebra's reefs, through the Virgin Passage, around to the east of St. Croix, and down to Pointe de la Grande Vigie at Guadeloupe. I'm sure

Omaha'll be able to lee bow the current to Guadeloupe and we'll be able to carry topsails and make at least eight or maybe even nine knots of speed. Once we make Guadeloupe we can tack back north into English Harbour at Antigua."

"I see. About three days."

"I concur, sir. We should be entering the harbor in the late afternoon on Wednesday."

"Very well, Mr. Wake. Steer so'east, set topsails, and stop engine. Make it so," Gardiner ordered as he turned to go to his cabin.

Ten minutes later the pounding rhythm of the engine slowed to a stop and the twin stacks blew off the remaining steam pressure, ejecting soot all over the sails and decks, which caused the deck division sailors to groan. They would have to clean it up right away. If left where it fell the soot would get tracked onto everything. But first the captain's order to set topsails had to be implemented.

Omaha bore off to the southeast and the topmen raced aloft to set the topsails as other sailors on the main deck slacked the sheets and hauled away on the topsail halyards. Soon the ship was sailing up and over the long beam swells, coming alive with the wind humming in the rigging, the bow wave swishing past, and her timbers and bulwarks creaking.

Wake stood on the canted teak deck loving every minute of it, feeling the power of the wind as it made the rigging hum. Looking around, he saw the helmsmen were grinning and aloft the topmen were shouting with glee. He took a deep breath of the thick sea air and slowly exhaled as his legs swayed in time with the motion of the ship.

It was one of those moments that only a sailor knows—the kind that never failed to exhilarate him.

~~

Omaha's captain, Lieutenant Commander Lewis Gardiner, was pleased as he sat in his upholstered chair in the dimming light of his great cabin. He was on independent duty and his ship was well provisioned, topped with fuel, and had an experienced crew. They were bound south on a routine patrol of the West Indies in the dry season and would stop at Antigua, Martinique, and Barbados before turning west and running downwind to Panama and then up to Jamaica. In four months' time they would return to Key West, and then sail on north to New York before the fever season in the tropics started. Gardiner fingered his beard and thought about that. With luck he would be at home with Josephine in Philadelphia on final leave by mid-May.

Veteran of African coastal anti-slave patrols, battles against Chinese pirates, and Porter's squadron on the Mississippi, Gardiner was getting ready to leave the navy after twenty-four years. He was tired, and the navy's deterioration in stature, ships, and equipment after the war simply accelerated his desire to get out. Gardiner thought he might try his hand in business back home and turn over the navy to younger men like Wake, who weren't quite so pessimistic. He liked Lieutenant Wake, thought he was a good officer, and had recommended him for promotion and command of the *Omaha,* but knew that wouldn't happen.

Wake had several things going against him. He was not a naval academy graduate, he had no influential relatives, and most of all, his record was marred by his involvement in that unfortunate *Canton* affair back in sixty-nine when he had forcibly relieved his captain of duty. Through some sort of legal mumbo-jumbo the court in effect had cleared him of wrongdoing, but Gardiner knew that naval officers were still divided in their opinion of Wake's action in that case. Some said he was a hero for saving the ship from a drug-addicted, lunatic commander; others said it was mutiny and he should have been hanged. Either way, it made him *controversial,* and controversial officers usually didn't get promoted.

Controversy makes peacetime admirals uneasy, Gardiner

told himself bitterly. Better to ignore problems and let them fester for years than to confront them. That's why I'm leaving. We've lost the warrior ethos, he grumbled to himself.

A knock came from the door to his cabin, followed by Wake's voice. "Sir, watch has changed and all's well."

"Very well, Mr. Wake. Come in and sit awhile. Relax."

The sunset sent golden shafts of dusty light swaying across Gardiner's spacious stern windows as Wake entered and took the offered seat at the gallery bench. A moment later Gardiner's steward silently entered, carrying a tray of coffee.

"Mr. Wake, would you care to share a coffee with me?" asked Gardiner.

"Yes, thank you, sir."

After the steward poured the coffee and left, Gardiner held up his mug of coffee.

"So, Peter, how is everything going?"

Wake respected Gardiner's professionalism and liked his personality. Occasionally the captain would invite Wake for a cup of coffee in his cabin and they would talk of the ship's officers and men, and of their own families back home. Wake knew, as a former ship commander himself, how very lonely it was for a captain and that the executive officer was usually the only man aboard a captain could confide in, or even relax with. It was obvious that Gardiner needed to talk.

"Everything appears to be going well, sir. The coal needs to be rebunkered and they are starting on that. We used about four tons getting to windward of San Juan and the rest hasn't really settled down yet. I want to make sure it won't shift in the bunkers and—"

"I know that, Peter. I was talking about *you*. How's it going for you?"

"Me? Well, sir, I guess it's going well for me. I have no complaints."

"I want you to know that I've recommended you for promotion and command. In fact, I recommended you to command the *Omaha* after I go ashore in May."

Wake was touched. He knew Gardiner was leaving and it meant a lot that the man's last promotion recommendation would be for him. "Thank you, sir. I am very honored by your recommendation. But I wish you wouldn't leave us. We need good leaders, especially these days."

"No, I've had enough of the political pantywaists in Washington, Peter. Can't take it anymore. Time for dinosaurs like me to leave while there's still someone who wants me to stay. What's that old saying from the stage? Always leave 'em wantin' more."

Wake didn't know what to say to that, so he uttered the age-old safe reply to a superior. "Yes, sir."

"Well, I'm sorry to say that my recommendation may not be enough to make it happen. You've had a tough career and you'll need more than merely my good words to get promoted up. But, by God, I still have five months to go. And in that time I want to try to get you noticed by the diplomatic types in the Caribbean so they'll send back complimentary reports on you to the secretary of state, who will hopefully pass them along to Secretary Robeson at the Navy Department."

"Thank you, sir."

"Don't thank me yet, Peter!" Gardiner's face transformed into a mischievous grin. "I'm going to send *you* to all the fancy-pants parties ashore so that you can deal with those pompous fools. I just don't have the patience anymore. I might hurt one of those two-faced, pin-striped, Froggie talking, diplomatic bastards."

Wake laughed. "I'll do my very best not to hurt them, sir!"

Gardiner's grin faded as he brought up a difficult subject among naval officers. "You do want to stay in, right? What about your wife and family?"

"Linda wants me out. She doesn't mind me going to sea but doesn't want me in the navy. She thinks the navy's treated me badly. Says I have no future here and should go back to the merchant fleet." He shrugged. "One of her arguments is that the pay is better."

"Aye, a disgruntled wife weighs heavy on a man's mind. You need to solve that dilemma, Peter. Get her aboard with you for your career or you won't have the right attitude even if you do stay in. Don't get into a situation where you have to choose between her and the navy. You lose either way on that kind of deal."

Wake understood completely. He had seen other men go through that and they were miserable afterward, no matter what they decided. "My leave comes up in June, sir. I'll go home and be with her at Pensacola for about two months while *Omaha* is in Philadelphia on refit, so we'll have time to work it out then."

Gardiner smiled and raised his coffee mug. "Aye, then we'll have a rumless toast to your wife and your navy, Peter Wake. May the two live in peace."

"Thank you, sir." They drank to the toast and Wake raised his mug again. "And here's to your last cruise, Captain. May it be your best."

Gardiner started to raise his mug, then stopped, his eyebrows cocked and the grin back. "We're in the West Indies, Peter. I don't know if it'll be the *best* cruise of my career, but I do know it won't be a dull one!"

3

Antigua

Her Most Britannic Majesty's customs cutter *Hudson* rounded up into the wind off the *Omaha's* starboard beam and a speaking trumpet brought forth the word that *Omaha* was not to enter the Royal Navy station at English Harbour, but instead to sail around to St. John's, the capital of the colony of Antigua. No explanation was given.

"Damn Limeys," muttered Gardiner as Wake yelled out an acknowledgment to the British cutter. "The sun'll set in two hours and I wanted to have the hook down and secured. It'll take at least that long to get around the island to St. John's, and we can't enter at night through those reefs. Mr. Wake, we'll sail around under the lee of the island, heave-to until dawn and enter then."

"Aye, aye, sir," said Wake as he checked the chart. "We should be off Fullerton Point by sunset. That'll be a good place to loiter for the night."

Gardiner shook his head while watching the cutter sail back toward English Harbour. "They've allowed us to enter English Harbour before. I wonder why not now?"

When *Omaha* let go her anchor at St. John's Harbour on the northwest coast of Antigua the next morning, it wasn't five minutes before the governor's launch arrived at the port side with a message for the captain. The officer of the deck, Lieutenant Laporte, brought it to Gardiner in his cabin where he had just started to go over the monthly supply reports with Wake.

Gardiner tore open the envelope and read the note, then looked at Wake. "It seems that His Excellency, Governor Gilford Habersham welcomes me to Her Majesty's Crown Colony of Antigua and would be delighted if I and one of my officers could attend dinner tonight at the governor's residence."

Wake was surprised, not by the invitation—it was routine for local leaders to invite visiting naval officers to dinner—but by the timing. They had just dropped anchor and the local American consul's greetings to the ship hadn't even arrived yet. "Something odd's going on, sir. Why were they in such a rush to get a standard dinner invitation to us?"

"Perhaps embarrassment over denying us entrance into the naval station at English Harbour? Who knows, Peter? I understand that culturally they're our cousins but I'll be damned if I understand them sometimes."

Wake shook his head. "I don't understand that denial or the timing of the invite, sir. Coincidence? I think not, Captain."

Laporte knocked on the door again, walked in, and delivered another envelope, this one with an embossed eagle on the front. It was from the American consulate. Gardiner nodded for Wake to open and read it aloud.

Captain Lewis Gardiner, Lt. Cmdr, U.S.N.
Commanding Officer
U.S.S. Omaha
West Indies Flotilla   22 December 1873
Home Squadron

My Dear Captain Gardiner,

    Allow me the honor of welcoming you to Antigua. I fear I must impose upon your valuable time and request that we meet at my office at 107 Long Street, here in St. John's. There are matters of national interest that we should discuss and due to factors beyond my control I cannot visit your ship this morning.
    The mail for your ship, and also some for other consuls in the area and for Panama, is here and ready for your custody when you come by.
    I regret the appearance of impropriety in this request, but assure you that upon your arrival you will conclude this unusual missive is justified.
    Please acknowledge via the courier that brought this note.

                                Respectfully,
                          Gustavius Williams
                   Consul in Antigua for the
                       United States of America

    "Well, that's a bit unusual! What do you make of it, Peter?" asked Gardiner.
    "I have no idea, sir. But this is getting very curious. Do you want me to go to the consul's office?"
    Gardiner slyly nodded. "Yes, I think I do. Go to both of these events and tell them I'm indisposed. Report back to me what you find. In the meantime I'll finish my letter to Josephine."

Wake made his way through the confusion of St. John's congested waterfront, then through the market and up St. Mary Street. At Market Street he declined a tout's gentle invitation to enter a tavern and forty feet further refused a courteous offer to "parlay with a lady" in an upstairs room. Continuing on while marveling at how sophisticated the vice-purveyors were in this British colony, he crossed over to Long Street and made his way along the narrow sidewalk until he found the office of the American consulate.

It was just down from the massive government building constructed a century earlier, when the legendary Nelson had been on the island. The government building was out of scale with the rest of the town, except for the magnificent Anglican church atop the hill that dominated the landscape. The town of St. John's impressed Wake as clean and neat, with even the usual seaport ne'er-do-wells being polite.

A small emblem was all that identified the door as the American consulate. Once inside he found himself in a small room with a harried woman who introduced herself as the consul's wife and apologized for her husband being late and the place being unswept. Wake took the offered tea and sat down to wait as the woman alternately yelled at unseen children upstairs and banged pots and pans in a back room.

Minutes later the room's rear door burst open and a thin disheveled man with anxious eyes strode in, fixed his gaze on Wake, and announced he was Gustavius Williams.

"I am Lieutenant Peter Wake, executive officer of the U.S. naval ship *Omaha,* Mr. Williams. I am here in response to your note this morning."

"You're not the captain? I wanted the captain!"

"I regret to report that he is indisposed and couldn't make it.

I am here in his stead, sir. Now, how can we assist you? You alluded in your note you had important information to discuss."

Williams glanced around the room. "I told the captain to come to this office, not send someone else."

Wake clenched his jaw. He had met many consuls in various ports, but never one this strange. Or rude. It was time to explain who was who in the pecking order. "You don't get to *order* a United States warship captain to do anything, Mr. Williams. You are allowed the privilege of *asking* them to assist you. Captain Gardiner sent me, so you'll deal with me, or I'll leave this office right now."

Williams huffed and sat down at the plain desk, then riffled through some papers in a valise. "I suppose you'll have to do then, but I hope you don't fail to act properly." Williams sighed. "I wanted the captain."

"What in the hell are you talking about, Mr. Williams?"

Williams hunched down and leaned across the desk. "Secret warship—that's what I'm talking about, Lieutenant. I know what's going on at the naval station. When I was sent here last year they told me to be on the lookout for anything that could assist our country. Well, I've seen what they're doing over there on that side of the island at English Harbour." He winked at Wake and whispered. "And *they* don't know that I know."

The man in front of Wake looked and sounded to him like a fool that had read too many of the cheap adventure novels currently the rage in America. Nonetheless, he wondered if the man could actually be telling at least a particle of truth.

Wake leaned forward in his chair. "I see. What exactly did you uncover?"

"They got HMS *Inconstant* over there and somehow have her steaming at eighteen knots. They're doing time trials off the station in deep water. One of the dockyard workers told a friend of mine that they are trying for twenty-one knots and think they can reach it within a week."

Wake knew *Inconstant* was one of the Royal Navy's newest

and best ships. He had heard she was the fastest in their navy at over sixteen knots. But eighteen? And trying for twenty? Only light merchant ships could do that. "Eighteen knots? Really, Mr. Williams, no warship has done that speed. The fastest is sixteen. When did you get this information?"

"This morning. I went over there to talk to him because I knew our navy would want to know."

"Yes, well, if true, this is indeed intriguing information. But please remember, Mr. Williams, that we are friends with Great Britain and not supposed to be spying on them. I don't think it would bode well for you if the local authorities found out what you've been doing."

"You don't want to know what they're doing?"

Wake thought for a moment. Yes, he did want to know, but without spying. It felt so *unseemly* to be doing that to the Royal Navy. Since the end of the war he had always considered them close allies. But eighteen knots? Hmm. "Yes. Send us the intelligence, but don't use illicit means to get it. It's not worth creating an incident over. Now, is there anything else going on, Mr. Williams?"

"Just the reception tonight at Government House," said Williams, dejected. "I'll be there too."

"Very good, Mr. Williams. We are not in need of any harbor supplies or services so we won't need your assistance on anything. This is merely a courtesy call, so tomorrow we'll be weighing anchor. I'll see you tonight at the reception."

"Be sure and tell the captain what I told you!"

"With pleasure, Mr. Williams. I've got to go now. Please have the mail delivered aboard as soon as possible this morning."

That evening Wake and Laporte attended the governor's reception. It was an excruciatingly boring affair—until moments before the Americans were about to leave.

"We absolutely insist you stay over Christmas here with us, Lieutenant Wake. Give your crew some liberty, relax for a while. We are a very friendly island," proclaimed a slightly tipsy Governor Habersham in a voice that could be heard well outside the building. Captain Stansell Warner, commandant of Naval Station Antigua, stood next to the portly governor, nodding his support.

"I'll pass that along to my captain, sir," replied Wake. "We are honored by your very kind offer. He will send a note ashore with an officer in response tomorrow morning."

"Yes, really, Lieutenant. There's no reason for you to go anywhere during this holiest of weeks," said Warner. "In fact, I'd like to invite you and two other officers to a dinner at the naval station tomorrow night at five o'clock. We'll provide carriage transportation to that side of the island from here at St. John's."

"Thank you, sir. I'll pass that along as well. Oh, sir?"

"Yes, Lieutenant?"

"I heard *Inconstant* was at the naval station, sir." Wake thought the moment opportune and decided to press it. "I was hoping to see her but the excise cutter told us not to enter and to come to St. John's instead. I hope she's all right and not in need of serious repairs."

Warner looked him in the eyes and said, "No, she's not there, Lieutenant. Your information is incorrect. You were asked to go to St. John's because the dock water at the station is fouled with a sunken barge. I hope to see you tomorrow evening. Now I must beg your leave."

He walked out of the room leaving Wake standing there perplexed. Five minutes later a steward delivered the official invitation, addressed to Gardiner.

As he sat in his easy chair in the great cabin looking out over the anchorage at St. John's, Gardiner's curiosity was piqued. Maybe the Brits—past masters at subterfuge—really were developing some new type of engine. What better place to work on it than in a sleepy backwater of the West Indies.

"Well, Peter, I admit this whole thing is getting curiouser and curiouser. Go tonight and take Laporte and an ensign with you. According to the invite, they are arranging lodging, so stay there and return tomorrow morning. I want a full report of all you learn in writing by noon. We'll send it off in Williams' diplo' pouch."

"Aye, aye, sir. But this Williams fellow worries me. He seems unstable. I'm not convinced his information is true and not sure what his motive is."

"But what if it's true? If they have a ship that can go that fast, Washington will want to know. See what you can find by just quietly asking around."

"Aye, aye, sir."

"And Lieutenant Wake . . ."

"Be careful."

4

A Moonlight Stroll

The ride was long and bumpy. Wake, Laporte, and Ensign Kevin Brogan sat crammed together in a carriage that had seen far better days, apparently in the seventeen-hundreds. The driver proudly explained that it had been the carriage Admiral Lord Nelson used on the island eighty-six years earlier when he was a young captain commanding a frigate. Brogan, a fresh-faced young man of Irish descent, quipped that he hoped the springs weren't as bad then, "for the sake of Nelson's sainted arse." Laporte, the ship's gunnery officer and resident ladies' man, brushed a brown curl of hair back in place and retorted he couldn't care less about Nelson's arse, he was worried about his own.

After a two-hour ride through the interior hill country they arrived at the village of All Saints, in the geographic center of the island where each of the pie-shaped parishes joined. A change of horses later they were once again on their way, arriving at Falmouth on the south coast at mid-afternoon. The driver pointed out sights along the way, but the dust and jarring dampened the passengers' enthusiasm for such tourist chatter. Then the driver swung left off the road onto a path that went straight up a high hill, saying that he had a sight to show them they would appreciate and they would return to the main road later.

Horses exhaling loudly with the strain, the carriage made its way past Clarence House, where the Duke of Clarence once stayed, and onto the rounded top of Shirley Hill, near a decayed fortification. There the driver stopped the carriage and suggested that the Americans might want to disembark and stretch their legs, taking a moment to walk to the edge and look down to the west at a little cove.

Laporte was the first to do so and whistled in surprise. Wake and Brogan joined him afterward, standing there stunned as the driver sauntered over and said he *thought* they would enjoy the view.

Spread out four hundred eighty feet below them was a hidden cove, off the main bay of English Harbour. At the entrance were three forts and around the cove was clustered the famous naval station of Antigua, commonly called Nelson's Dockyard ever since that icon of the Royal Navy was stationed there. It was an unexpected, startling, and magnificent sight.

"Perfect defensive position. Look at the interlocking gun bearings," observed Laporte.

"And completely hidden from seaward," observed Wake as he scanned the cove and English Harbour for any sign of *Inconstant* or any other large warship. All he saw was the excise cutter and a small gunboat.

The driver described the various forts and villages in view, adding that there were even more defensive positions that couldn't be seen and that Antigua had never been captured. He also added that most forts had not been manned since 1850, and that only a small remnant of the 29th Worchester Infantry Regiment was still on the island. Most had been shipped home the year before.

Wake thought about what he was seeing. And not seeing. The driver was a civilian employee of the naval station who had taken them out of the way to get a bird's eye view of the station. No large warship was in sight. If there was anything to be hidden the man wouldn't have taken them there. He scanned again, paying close attention to the docks.

Evidently nothing was there, he decided, then paused, wondering if it was all part of an elaborate ruse and the speed ship was there, simply camouflaged?

$\sim$

Wake bowed slightly to Captain Warner as diffused late afternoon sunlight came through the open doors of the dining room from the verandah. "Thank you again, sir, for the very kind invitation. Captain Gardiner sends his most sincere regrets that he cannot attend."

"It is we who regret that Captain Gardiner was not able to come, Lieutenant. We were looking forward to making his acquaintance," said Warner smoothly. His executive officer, Commander Stark, stood next to him with a grim face that Wake realized was apparently his usual appearance. Stark, like, Warner, was an older man and didn't have the tan of a seagoing naval officer, one of the first things a sailor looked at when meeting another professional. They also seemed soft, with rounded stomachs one seldom saw on officers who were on active duty. Wake's impression was that their positions were a reward for past services, possibly long past.

The dinner was held at the station commandant's home, located in the center of the facility. It was surrounded by storehouses that held cordage, sail canvas, pitch, lumber, spars, and every manner of equipage needed by a sailing navy. During a brief tour of the station Wake saw that the padlocks on the shed doors were very old and some looked rusted shut. The volume of supplies that could be contained in the buildings was impressive, but they all were for sailing ships. Wake noticed that other than a small blacksmith shop and boiler engine, there were no large mechanical shops capable of engine repairs or iron work. His trust in Williams' mystery speed ship was dwindling rapidly.

After dinner Warner led the guests upstairs to the second-story verandah where a delightful sea breeze cooled the air and the sunset glinted off the surrounding hills. It had been hot while walking around the station and at dinner on the first floor, making him sweat and his uniform coat clammy, but in the shade of the jacaranda and mahogany trees the second-floor wind washing over him felt delicious and he closed his eyes for a moment.

"—I said, Lieutenant, are you staying for Christmas services at the cathedral tomorrow?"

Stark stared at Wake, who realized he must have been dreaming and appearing idiotic to the others. "Oh, I'm very sorry, sir. Yes, we are staying. I was just thinking how nice it is up here with this wind. I'm afraid I was lost in thought, sir."

"Yes. Nelson thought so too. He loved to have his tea here overlooking the bay and the station." Stark swept a hand around. "You can see it all from here."

Wake followed his hand and saw that indeed, he could see even more of the station. In the dim light, a shed caught his eye by the outer capstan dock. It looked newly built and he hadn't seen it on the tour he'd been given.

He pointed in that direction. "Sir. That looks like a new shed. May I ask what you've got there?"

"Just some maintenance supplies, Lieutenant. If you are of a mind, I can have someone show them to you," Stark replied coolly.

Wake knew he had gone too far. "I am sorry for being too intrusive, sir. I meant no disrespect or offense."

"None taken, Lieutenant, of course. Please have another drink of port. We have plenty," intoned Stark before walking away to speak with another guest.

Laporte was talking to a pretty girl, daughter of the mayor of Falmouth, and Brogan was chuckling at a British midshipman's joke. Others on the verandah were engaged in conversations about the recent Franco-Prussian War, the unification of Italy, and the relative merits of various types of rum. Wake stood alone in a dark corner as an idea suddenly entered his mind.

Asking a steward where the officers' head was located, he was directed to an outbuilding behind the commandant's home. He made his way there and afterward went to the east, through a row of hibiscus and around the back of the officers' quarters, the sick bay, and the apothecary shop, toward the rope walk. The tropical sun had set rapidly but fortunately a full moon was rising and gave Wake some light beyond the few dim lanterns scattered about.

Pausing to get his bearings, he walked behind the rope walk toward the dock and saw the shed. It was bigger than he originally had thought and there was a large sturdy wagon parked in front of the double doors. The padlock on the doors was new and solid. Walking around the shed he saw only one small window. Moonlight illuminated the interior enough that Wake could see a long crate on a table by the window.

He strained his eyes to read some lettering on the side of the crate, gradually making out the words. It was a shipping address and a warning:

> *To: Commander J. Fisher, RN*
> *Woolwich Naval Arsenal*
> *Woolwich, Great Britain*
> *From: Robert Whitehead, Presidente*
> *Stabilimento Tecnico di Fiume*
> *Fiume, Austria*
> *15 Agosto 1873*
> *Pericolo—Esplosivi Navali*
> *Danger—Naval Explosives*

In the moonlight he saw ruts and wheel marks from the shed to the adjacent dock. Peering around the water in the dim moonlight he could see no wreckage of a barge, but lying on the dock he did see a new life-ring with a ship's name painted on it. HMS *Invincible.* Wake knew that name—she was a new ship assigned to the Royal Navy's West Indies Squadron. He also remembered the name on the crate from somewhere: Whitehead. There was something odd about the *Invincible* he had heard, but at the moment couldn't remember what.

The unmistakable stamp of a military boot and click of a rifle's hammer was followed by a tin whistle blowing loudly.

"Sir! Stand fast and identify yourself!" boomed the order from a Royal Marine standing thirty feet away, his white cross belt glowing in the moonlight and Enfield rifle with fixed bayonet at the port arms parry position.

"It's all right, Marine. I am Lieutenant Wake of the American Navy, attending the commandant's dinner and just taking a stroll after using the officers' head over there."

The Marine did not relax. "Sir! This is a prohibited area. I have summoned the sergeant of the guard. Please stand fast right there until the sergeant arrives."

The sound of heavy boots running made Wake's heart sink. He needed to get out of there before the sergeant arrived. "Marine, this is ridiculous and insulting. I'm returning to the commandant's party," he bluffed. It didn't work—the Marine moved to block him.

"I said 'stand fast,' sir. Do not move."

The Royal Marine sergeant's arrival resulted in quick words with the Marine that Wake couldn't hear. Other boots were running toward them as the sergeant approached Wake and boomed out, "Lieutenant, I am Colour Sergeant Lithgow of the Her Majesty's Royal Marines. This is a prohibited area and you are far from the officers' head and the commandant's dinner party. I have the officer of the guard coming and he will speak with you directly. Remain in position until his arrival, sir."

Wake realized that it was now or never. "I have been insulted, sergeant, and I'm informing the station commandant right now about the behavior of his men. I certainly expected better of a veteran such as yourself." He started walking to the main street and called over his shoulder, "And you can have your officer of the guard meet me at the commandant's home, straight away."

Behind him Wake heard the rifle being brought up to fire, then the sergeant quickly telling the Marine, "For Christ's sake, put that weapon *down*. He's just a damn fool Yankee."

Wake walked back toward the rope walk, momentarily relieved, but he knew that now he would have to explain it to Warner and Stark. Five minutes later he was back on the verandah and walked up to Warner, who was talking with the Falmouth mayor, just as an agitated Marine subaltern arrived at the doorway, looking around the crowd for the senior officer.

Wake plunged in. "Captain Warner, pardon me for interrupting, but I have the unfortunate duty, sir, to report a breach of naval respect toward me by one of your Royal Marines a moment ago. I knew you'd want to know of it."

Warner turned to Wake with an annoyed look. "What, you say? Disrespect by a Royal Marine?"

The subaltern was making his way through the crowd as Wake went on. "Yes, sir. I was accosted by a Marine sentry as I made my way back from the officers' head to the party. The man held me prisoner at *gunpoint*. Of course, once the sergeant got there cooler heads prevailed. But I did think it bizarre, sir, that a Marine would do that to an allied naval officer."

Wake knew that, technically, the American and Royal navies were not allies, but by this point everyone on the verandah could hear the conversation and he saw that the mayor and several other guests were shocked at the allegation. He also saw Laporte and Brogan come up and stand behind him, their jaws set and eyes leveled at Warner.

"Sir! I have to report that one of our sentries just discovered this American officer in a prohibited area," announced the subaltern to Warner.

"Oh? And where was that?" asked Warner.

"At the capstan dock, sir."

Wake cut in. "Captain, this is ridiculous. The only thing there is a maintenance shed and the old capstans used to warp Nelson's ships into the dock. I was taking a walk back from the head, sir, and those men obviously went way over the line of respect and discipline."

The civilians were nodding their heads in agreement and starting to voice objections when Warner held up his hands. "Yes, Lieutenant. Perhaps they were a bit overzealous. After all, it's just an old dock and shed there."

"Thank you, sir. I was certain you'd understand and rectify the situation."

"Oh, yes, Lieutenant Wake," Warner growled low so that the others couldn't hear it. "I believe I understand *exactly* what happened. . . ."

"But, sir!" protested the subaltern. "This man was—"

Warner held up a hand. "Enough said. It was a misunderstanding. Send a report to my office in the morning."

Then he turned back to Wake. "Lieutenant Wake, quarters for you and your officers are ready. The dinner and party are concluded. Thank you for coming. I'll have you escorted to your quarters by an officer so you won't get *lost* in the dark again. Tomorrow after breakfast you will be driven back to St. John's."

The British officer spoke that part loud enough that the other guests and officers started to file back into the home and descend the stairs. Wake, following inside, was unnerved by the look in Warner's eye and his tone—there was no doubt he knew what Wake had been up to. This whole situation was out of control, Wake thought, worried about the consequences of his getting caught.

"Why thank you, sir," he tried to say nonchalantly. "We are much obliged."

Warner stopped on the stairwell. "I will see you at the church service tomorrow, Lieutenant. Please make sure your captain is there. I need to speak with him and I'd rather see him ashore than have to go out to your ship."

"Aye, aye, sir."

5

Nelson's Ghost

The Christmas Eve service at the Anglican Cathedral of St. John the Divine started at four in the afternoon and ended two hours later. Everyone who was anyone on the island was in attendance within the massive church. It had been devastated by an earthquake in 1843, but the island leaders had rebuilt it even larger in 1847, with a structure of coral stone and façade of gray cement wash on the outside. Dark pitchpine paneling covered every inch of the interior to provide additional protection against earthquakes and hurricanes, lending an Old World ambience. The open side doors allowed the breeze to cleanse the air, unlike so many damp musty churches in New England that Wake had known as a youth. He had never seen anything like it and could appreciate why the islanders were exceedingly proud of what they had built.

The somber ceremony began after the governor and senior imperial staff members arrived and sat in the first pew, with clergy and second ranked civil leaders behind them. Gardiner, Wake, 1st Engineer Grimsrud, Ensign Chisholm, and Consul Gustavius Williams sat in the third pew, next to the senior Royal

Navy officers. No mention of the incident the night before was made to Gardiner or Wake, but Captain Warner's demeanor was anything but friendly, his cold gray eyes staring ahead. Wake, who grew up Episcopalian in Massachusetts but attended the Methodist church when in Pensacola, remembered the mass service from his youth and attempted to ignore the cold looks from the Royal Navy and instead focus on the meaning of the rector's message. He was unsuccessful. The swirl of the last two days' events dominated his thoughts.

That morning he had reported to Gardiner all that had transpired at the dockyard the night before, including Captain Warner's insistence that Gardiner come ashore and speak with him. Gardiner had laughed when he heard of Wake's incident and his bluff out of it. His impending retirement allowed Gardiner a certain degree of freedom from anxiety, though he counseled Wake to be very careful and expect some sort of repercussion once Washington finally heard about this situation three months in the future.

Sitting in the great cabin they pondered what it was that the British were hiding. "Whitehead" was a name that rang a bell in both their minds. Then Wake remembered.

Gunner Durling, a gunner's mate who had served under Wake in the war, was currently assigned to the U.S. Navy's new torpedo development station at Newport, Rhode Island. In mid-1873, Durling had told Wake in a letter that he was working with a Lieutenant Commander Howell on developing a better version of the *Whitehead torpedo* and that they were getting close. The Whitehead torpedo was fourteen feet long and Howell's newest "automobile torpedo" was almost twenty feet long—bigger and faster, with a more powerful explosive than any other torpedo in the field, with a range of over 3,000 feet.

Wake also remembered why *Invincible* was familiar to him. He had heard from a Royal Navy officer at Nassau in August that she had just come out to the West Indies from the Royal Navy's Portsmouth Naval Base, home of their new torpedo base, HMS *Vernon*.

Gardiner added that he now recalled reading in *Harper's Magazine* that a man named Whitehead, presumably the very same one, was an Englishman with a naval ordnance factory in Fiume, on the Adriatic Sea. He had developed, then sold, torpedo technology to the Royal Navy and other European navies. Gardiner remembered that an officer named Fisher was the Royal Navy's lead man on the controversial project. The same article mentioned that *Inconstant* had been fitted with experimental torpedo carriages and that other ships would be also.

One more thing bothered Wake that morning in Gardiner's cabin. The crate he saw through the window at the dockyard was far longer than fourteen feet. It appeared more than twenty feet long. The wagon's bed was also that long. An uneasy question emerged.

"Sir, do you suppose Whitehead could have gotten a copy of the American plans, built his own version and given it to the Brits?" he had asked Gardiner.

"Ill-gotten gains? Hmm, I think that's a possibility, Peter. A very real possibility. Otherwise, why would they go to such great lengths to hide it there?"

"Precisely what I was thinking, Captain. And the information about the speed trials was a deception? The real work is on torpedoes!"

"Hmm, yes. Could very well be." Gardiner exhaled loudly as he folded his hands under his chin. "Quite the situation we've landed in."

As the rector droned out a prayer from the pulpit before them, Wake remembered that after thinking for a few minutes that morning Gardiner had begun to grin. "You know what, Lieutenant Wake? This is the most fun I've had in years. I'm going to enjoy our little religious opportunity ashore this afternoon."

Wake hadn't shared Gardiner's enthusiasm at the time, and sitting there in the church he worried about what would happen next. He was sure there would be a confrontation at some point, a feeling reinforced by Warner's behavior in the pew next to him.

After the service a traditional Christmas dinner was served in the rectory. So far, nothing but the obligatory courtesies had been exchanged between the two senior naval officers. That ended after dessert when Warner and the governor asked Gardiner to step into the rector's study, away from the crowd. Once inside, Warner quickly closed the door and turned to Gardiner.

"Your man Wake was spying at our naval station, Captain Gardiner," Warner began without preamble. "I don't know why or on whose orders, but I do know it was deliberate and very foolish. This is a minor naval station and there is nothing of real value here except the legacy and memory of Admiral Lord Nelson."

"Yes, Captain Gardiner, and in addition, your country's consul here has been soliciting inside information regarding the station from local workers," chided Governor Habersham, his double chin shaking. "That too has been deliberate and foolish and an insult. I am sending an official complaint to the Foreign Office in London, requesting your consul's immediate expulsion and official censure against your Lieutenant Wake. Do you have anything to say about that, sir, before I send it?"

Gardiner walked slowly to a window, then looked back and smiled at the two Englishmen—they had done exactly as he had expected and prepared for. "Well, gentlemen, I'm glad you brought that up. And yes, Your Excellency, I have these few things to say about *that*. . . .

"Lord Nelson, that greatest sailor of the Royal Navy, must have quite a ghostly power here at Antigua, for he makes ships disappear. Ships like the *Invincible,* which just arrived, and like *Inconstant,* your new torpedo ship. And speaking of torpedoes, how are they working out for you down here? Especially the big new American prototype design you got through Whitehead—how's that coming along in your secret tests? You know, gentlemen, the one from the United States Navy's Newport Torpedo Station.

"By the way, how exactly did you get that design, gentlemen? That's a question that I think Washington—particularly President Grant—will want to know, since it hasn't been put into production and Commander Howell, the designer, hasn't got the patent just yet. Forget your little old foreign office bureaucrats, Governor—these are all things Prime Minister Gladstone himself will most definitely hear about. From the highest levels of the government of the United States of America."

Captain Warner was about to speak but stopped when the governor shook his head. Habersham's eyes never left Gardiner, who went on in an even stronger tone.

"Now, Mr. Gladstone of the Liberals is having a rather difficult time in Great Britain these days, isn't he, gentlemen? Something about his being weak on foreign policy in Europe, according to the British papers. In fact, as everyone knows, he's fighting for his political life and the Tories under Mr. Disraeli are breathing down his neck. And what effect would this torpedo espionage on *your* part, against one of Great Britain's greatest supporters in the world, have on the current government's future? Especially when many in both countries are trying to put our past differences away. And while the *Alabama* Claims Commission is assessing damages against American shipping caused by your building of ships for our enemies, in violation of your supposed neutrality during the war. Yes, I think it would make Prime Minister Gladstone's high moralistic posturing about being such an honorable and religious man seem to ring a bit hollow, don't you think? Why, my goodness gracious, gentlemen, what would those Fleet Street editors say about all this?"

Gardiner paused a moment, sighing. "Now why don't we all take a step back and calm down here, shall we? Let's remember that we are cultural cousins and naval professionals and stop playing adversarial roles. This was just curiosity on the part of a naval officer. Nothing more. So why don't we just work together and share our information on torpedo development? That is the message I will send to Washington. I suggest you send the same to London."

Gardiner spread his hands out, palms upward. "Let's just end this silliness and let Nelson's ghost in Antigua rest in peace."

Gardiner walked to the rector's chair behind the desk and sat down, deliberately leaning back in a relaxed pose, waiting for an answer. Warner stood by an elegant wingback, grimly looking at Habersham for guidance. The governor paced twice across the office, then stopped and smiled at Captain Warner.

"Well, Stansell, I do believe that Shakespeare would say we've been hoisted upon our own petite petard. Our American self-styled *cousin* here has put forth a valid political point, though I'm sure it does not negate his man's unauthorized reconnoitering. The reality is that a public blathering about who has done what to whom would not serve the interests of either of our nations. I believe you can understand that evaluation of the situation, can you not?"

Warner barely controlled his anger. "I don't take orders from the foreign office—or the governor of some colonial island for that matter—and I don't discuss British imperial policy in front of foreigners. And I also don't consider Americans our cousins, brothers, or any other sort of relative. That is *my* evaluation of this situation, Your Excellency."

He followed with a "Merry Christmas, Your Excellency" and walked out of the study without closing the door. Habersham sat down in the vacated chair and shrugged.

"I would suppose that American naval officers think the same of their civil leadership and diplomats, Captain Gardiner. However, the ultimate factor is that the Lords of the Admiralty *do* take orders from the Prime Minister and this will be handled quietly on our side. Captain Warner just needs a bit of time to shed some embarrassment."

"And I will suggest it be done the same on our side, sir," said Gardiner as he got up from the chair. "I believe it is time for me to go, sir. May I sincerely wish you, your islanders, and the Royal Navy, a merry Christmas and a peaceful New Year. Good night, Your Excellency, and thank you for your wisdom in this matter."

Omaha spent Christmas at anchor in St. John's Harbour, with all hands taking the day off except when on watch. The ship had been cleaned and polished the day before and at noon on Christmas day Gardiner read the obligatory passage from the Bible to the assembled crew and afterward declared the start of the holiday. The cooks had been preparing a sumptuous feast and with the captain's tacit approval had marinated several of the dishes with rum, getting around the navy's prohibition of issued grog for the crew, in effect since 1862. The galley's aromas had been teasing everyone all morning and all hands were ready for the celebration. Wake thought it a wonderful day, not only from Gardiner's description of the previous night's de-escalation of tensions, but from the magnificent sunny weather and warm winds. He didn't miss the white Christmases of New England at all.

Gustavius Williams and his family joined the island's American residents aboard the warship for the dinner. Gardiner decided not to tell Williams about what Wake had discovered at the dockyard and what had transpired later with Warner and the governor. The man was just too unsettled in nature for them to trust his judgment or ability to keep a secret. They did tell him, to his obvious disappointment, they saw no sign of the ship he had information on and to stop trying to recruit informants.

Dessert was followed with entertainment by the amateur musicians and thespians in the crew, highlighted by a satirical rendition of dinner in the petty officers' mess. It brought forth an uproarious response from the audience and afterward the guests departed the ship. That evening little groups clustered along the decks, talking in hushed, contented tones about the day and home and future ports, a quiet foreground for the tropical display in the sky to the west.

Wake longed for Linda, her green eyes and silky auburn hair, the soft touch of her hand, her Irish-lilted Southern accent, the smell of her jasmine perfume. He imagined her in bed, beckoning him demurely. . . .

As the sun gloriously set behind Sandy Island at the mouth of the harbor, Gardiner broke Wake's trance by slapping him on the shoulder and raising his ever-present mug of coffee, making a toast as they stood on the afterdeck. "May our friends never love our enemies, whoever they may be!"

Wake replied quietly with a toast of his own. "May Nelson's ghost in Antigua finally relax."

Gardiner nodded and solemnly held up a finger. "To our wives and our sweethearts, Peter. May they all have good health, tranquility, love for us . . ." A sly grin emerged on his face. ". . . and may they never *ever* meet each other!"

Wake was still laughing when Williams came up to them and blurted out, "Oh my God, I forgot until I was leaving, Captain, and I do apologize. I've got newly arrived mail for the ship that I left in the boat alongside. Do you think the crew would like it now?"

Gardiner bellowed out, "By God, man, *yes!*" and within minutes the large bag was being swayed up and out of the boat. The captain's clerk called out the addressees and the joyous day had a happy ending with sailors reading the news from home to their mates.

Wake was given a large dark blue envelope. He knew the type. It came from the Bureau of Navigation at the Navy Department in Washington—the bureau that made the assignments for naval officers. He stood by the light at the binnacle and opened it, reading slowly, his face tightening.

"Orders, Mr. Wake?" asked Gardiner. "You're not due orders

for several months yet, at least."

"They're not letting me go home in June," Wake muttered, still staring at the paper. "These are orders to join the European Squadron, effective immediately. I'm to secure transport to Genoa aboard a British packet named *Trinidad,* from Barbados. I can't even go home first." He looked up at Gardiner, shock clearly showing. "They're sending me to be on the staff of the admiral commanding the squadron over there, sir. A two-year staff job—not even a ship's complement billet—until eighteen-seventy-five. Flag lieutenant to the admiral. Flag lieutenant, of all things. Why me?"

Wake gazed off at the lights of St. John's. "God help me. Linda was expecting me home in June for a two-month leave."

"Damn it all. I'm sorry, Peter. Here, let me see that," said Gardiner, concerned for the subordinate who had become a friend, knowing there was nothing he could do. Quickly perusing the orders, he handed it back to Wake. "You know that flag lieutenant on foreign station is a routine assignment in an officer's career, Peter. There's nothing negative in that. You'll be the personal assistant to the admiral in the most prestigious squadron in the navy. It'll help your career, give you connections, get you noticed."

Gardiner shook his head. "But I sure as hell didn't see this coming. I thought you'd stay around this part of the world for a while."

"I guess old Nelson got his revenge on *me,*" Wake said as he trudged to the hatchway and his cabin below, still stunned, wondering how he would tell Linda.

6

Pensacola and Martinique

Wake thought it sadly ironic that *Omaha* was making very good time southbound, now that he was heading away from home for two years. Under almost all sail she surged along at twelve knots on a broad reach, past butterfly-shaped French Guadeloupe and then British Dominica, both of which had huge mountains dominating the horizon. While under the lee of the islands they slowed a bit, but in the open passages between the islands twenty-knot transatlantic trade winds built their speed into exhilarating rides, making everyone from captain to steward revel with the excitement of the voyage. On the morning of the second day outbound from Antigua, they saw Montagne Pelée, highest point on the legendary French island of Martinique.

Gardiner had explained to Wake at Antigua that he was not going to head directly to Barbados to drop him off, but instead would complete their patrol of the Leeward Islands down to Martinique, then start their patrol of the Windward Islands at Barbados. He did not tell Wake that he wanted to delay his executive officer's departure as long as possible, hoping that someone or something would intervene.

By mid-afternoon they were passing the quaint town of St. Pierre, which was situated below the volcanic mountain. Wake had seen many coastal towns in the islands, but St. Pierre captured his soul like no other. The pastel coral-stone buildings strung out along the beach were set against hills carpeted in four or five shades of green, all of which faced the aqua-blue Caribbean water. Flowers provided splashes of purples and pinks and yellows everywhere. And over the whole scene loomed Pelée, a 4800-foot-high giant whose head was wreathed in clouds, like an omnipotent god overseeing its brood. For some reason he didn't understand, St. Pierre enchanted him, and he stood at the port rail gazing at it for a long time as *Omaha* transited down the coast.

At the end of the day they headed into the open harbor at Fort de France on the central west coast, passing the black-walled Fortress St. Louis sprawling over a point of land to port. The small city spread out before them around the large bay. Ascending the hillsides, it presented a different image than St. Pierre, however. It was more haughty and cynical-looking, arrogant almost, with none of St. Pierre's visually pleasing imagery of nature in harmony with man. As they went through the formalities of entering the port, Wake wondered if it would be as unfriendly as it looked. After what had happened at Antigua and the shock of his new orders, he hoped for an easy time and amicable visit.

The guns of the fortress saluted *Omaha's* Stars and Stripes, the blasts echoing around the bay and alerting all the merchants that a foreign warship, and potential customer, was in port. They anchored just aft of the French gunboat *Bouvet*, which three years earlier, during the Franco-Prussian War, had fought the only ocean naval battle of the conflict against the German gunboat *Meteor*. Wake knew that the action, between Havana and Key West, was indecisive, but had heard both sides pompously claim victory ever since.

Shortly after the hook was buried, the American consul came aboard, accompanied by the aide-de-camp of the French admiral commanding the West Indies Squadron. The American consul was a nonchalant former New Orleans ship chandler named Paul Mas, who fled to Martinique after the Civil War, proclaimed himself a Republican, and was appointed to the post of consul because no one else wanted it. Wake had dealt with the type all over the West Indies and didn't like, and certainly didn't trust, most of them.

Leaving the French naval officer waiting up on the main deck, Mas got straight to the point as he sat down at the table in Gardiner's cabin with the captain and Wake.

"Captain Gardiner, the French here want to make a good impression on y'all by entertaining you and your officers ashore. Things are rough for 'em back home politically and it looks to me like they have orders to cement the relationship with America so they don't have to worry about any potential problems here. Their navy doesn't have much of a presence these days and I think they'd appreciate the support of our navy."

Mas waved a hand. "Just wanted to say that, 'cause I do believe y'all are gonna get to see some French hospitality."

"Oh God, I suppose we'll have to act appreciative and some-body'll have to attend some damned French social event. I'm get-ting too old for this," moaned Gardiner. "Mr. Wake has the duty on the social front, Mr. Mas."

"Consider yourselves lucky, gentlemen," Mas said. "Believe me, it doesn't happen often."

After a few administrative details they invited the Frenchman inside. He was Lieutenant Claude Martin, aide-de-camp to Rear Admiral Jacques Normand, commander of all French naval forces in the Americas. Martin was every inch the young professional, trying to impress the Americans with the power and responsibility of the French Navy in the New World.

With a disarming smile and smooth flourish, Martin invited Gardiner in very good English to a soirée that evening at the admiral's quarters next to the fortress, and asked him to bring along two other officers, explaining there would, of course, be young ladies who would need dinner and dance partners.

"I accept the admiral's very gracious invitation, so magnificently presented by you, Lieutenant, and we will have the officers attend." Gardiner pleasantly smiled back at Martin and gestured to Wake. "Led by Lieutenant Peter Wake, my *executive*," he greatly exaggerated the word, "officer, whom I have designed the *official* soirée officer of this command. I will, unfortunately, be indisposed aboard. Thank you so much for allowing us the honor of attending."

Martin bowed and acknowledged the acceptance and compliment, as Mas's eyes revealed his admiration for Gardiner's deft handling of the French.

After the visitors departed, Gardiner turned to Wake. "Peter, this morning I have just used up the few diplomatic words I can muster. Please do not incite an international incident at *this* island. I fear I just wouldn't be able to handle it."

"Yes, sir."

He knew the captain meant it. Wake stood to leave. "I guess I'll take Lieutenant Laporte and Engineer Grimsrud with me, sir."

"Oh, and Peter . . ."

"Sir?"

"Relax a bit. I know that aboard you're the executive officer, but ashore at a party you're allowed to have fun. Enjoy the French girls' company."

Wake laughed and said he would, then went to his cabin where the ship's clerk had dropped off a letter that had come aboard with the consul. It was from Linda. He tore it open, sat on his berth and read it, his heart clenching.

Pensacola, Florida *December 3rd, 1873*
Dear Peter,

I hope this letter finds you well on your voyage around the West Indies. Frequently I lie in bed at night and try to imagine the sights and sounds you experience, the people you meet, and the challenges you overcome. I'm glad you have a good ship and captain at last. I so look forward to your letters about all you do, but wish you were here next to me to tell the stories in person, late at night, when it's just the two of us. In June that will happen and I can wait until then, but barely.

The children are fine, as active and playful as ever. They miss their Daddy and Sean asks if every ship he sees in the bay has Daddy aboard. I have news about Useppa. I took her to a doctor in Mobile who specializes in children's maladies. After examining her, his diagnosis was that she had a bone growth problem and that it might resolve itself with age. He recommended against any strong pain relievers such as opiates or laudanum—explaining that as difficult as that is for us to agree with as parents of a suffering child, it's because of the addictive qualities of those drugs.

Wake understood that very well, he had seen it in a captain of his only a few years earlier—a captain he had relieved of command by force to save the ship and men. His heart lightened when he read on.

He said that special exercises would be beneficial and prescribed some stretching and lifting. He then gave her the same powder medicine given to elderly arthritics, thinking that might help with the pain. I feel so much better after the consultation and I am having Useppa do the exercises every day, but know that it might take a while to see the results. Oh Peter, now I have some hope she'll lead a normal life.

Then he read her next paragraph and almost cried.

Peter, as happy as I am for the good news about Useppa, I have to tell you that I am also very tired. Tired of running a household alone, tired of sleeping alone, tired of another Christmas without my husband, tired of trying to get by on navy pay, and tired of living in cold Pensacola. I want you to know this but I haven't told anyone else. You are the only person I confide in.

I am trying to be patient and will wait until your arrival in June. Then we'll have two months together to figure out what to do, because something has to change, Peter—I cannot go on like this. I'm sorry, but I'm just not strong enough.

With all the love in my heart,
Linda

Wake vaguely heard the change of watch on the deck above him as he sat there, knowing she was right in so many ways and angry for it. For reasons he could never fully explain, even to himself, Wake loved the navy and his life at sea. And it appeared that Linda was about to give him the spousal ultimatum he had heard about from so many other officers.

He pulled two sheets of paper out of his desk drawer and began to write a letter. He explained his transfer and newest assignment, knowing what effect it would have on Linda and fearing her reply. But it didn't come out as he wanted—it came out plainly, matter-of-fact, cold. Crumpling the paper, Wake started over, his mind blank, struggling for the right words. He felt tears forming from frustration and he buried his head in his hands on the desk, desperate to tell his wife what was in his heart and embarrassed that he couldn't.

A moment later the steward knocked on his cabin door, announcing the boat for shore was being swayed out and readied for him. When Wake acknowledged the message he kept emotion from his voice. Returning the paper to the drawer, he went to his trunk and pulled out his seldom-used formal uniform accoutrements. Mechanically going through the procedure of dressing, his mind kept seeing Linda's reaction when she would read his letter. His depression deepened as he fastened each button. By the time he adjusted the heavy dress uniform coat and gold epaulets, ridiculous to wear in the tropics, it was all he could do muster the strength to leave his cabin.

Exhaling loudly, Wake checked himself in the small mirror on the back of his door, set his jaw, and went up to the main deck, where he met the other officers. They were standing at the accommodation ladder, waiting for him to lead them into the diplomatic maze ashore that naval officers of all ranks were expected to navigate. They were excited, chattering about the evening to come. Wake didn't hear a word they said.

"Good evening, Lieutenant, how very kind you are to join us tonight. We love to have Americans visit us here in our humble little island," welcomed a beautiful girl. Wake handed her a glass of champagne from a passing steward's tray. She was draped in a pale blue gown of soft-looking material and he guessed her age at around eighteen, though he found women very difficult to gauge on that matter. Her name was unpronounceable for him and so he bowed and said, "*Merci,* mademoiselle, it is our honor to be invited and our pleasure to attend."

"Oh, Lieutenant!" she softly replied. "You Americans are so very *gallant.* So much kinder than those brutes, the British."

The governor's ballroom was hot but the partiers, men in formal evening attire and women in low-cut gowns displaying mounded bosoms, didn't seem to notice. The glances and whispered asides regarding the social gossip of who was doing what to, or with, whom appeared to Wake to be the main occupation of the attendees.

A string quartet began an annoying tune he didn't know—someone said it was Tchaikovsky—but which made the locals gasp in appreciation and spontaneous applause. The evening was like that for him, a swirl of unfamiliar conversational topics and social customs that reminded him of what it was like to steer a ship among uncharted reefs. Carrying on the role of representative of his nation's navy was a tiring endeavor for him, but Wake saw Consul Mas sliding among the elite, speaking and laughing effortlessly. Mas made it look easy and gay, but Wake knew it was a very serious business. He cleared his mind of Linda and concentrated on his professional responsibilities.

It reminded him of what a Venezuelan diplomat friend, Pablo Monteblanco, had told him back in '69—that naval officers were their nation's warriors armed with cannons facing adversaries in battles, and diplomats were their nation's warriors armed with words facing their adversaries at cocktail parties. A naval officer might certainly kill hundreds with cannon in a battle, Pablo had explained sadly, but a diplomat could arrange the death of millions over an aperitif.

Wake had been at the gathering for two hours when he decided it was time to round up Lieutenant Laporte and Engineer Grimsrud and head back to the ship. American prestige had been dutifully upheld and Wake was exhausted. He found his officers in a corner of the room surrounded by giggling young French ladies and nodded toward the door. Grimsrud, a second-generation Norwegian-American who normally was the quiet type, frowned. Laporte, who spoke a little French and was using every word he knew, did his best to ignore *Omaha*'s executive officer. Finally Wake walked over. "Gentlemen, it's time we say good night to these charming ladies and get under way."

Laporte's eyes locked onto Wake's and he glanced toward a very comely girl. "Lieutenant, can't we stay just for a minute longer? I was just telling darling Yvette about how we went into Mobile Bay back in sixty-four."

"Yeah," said Grimsrud, suppressing a grin, "he told her about how Farragut asked *him* what to do next when that torpedo blew up *Tecumseh*. He was just explaining how he told the confused admiral to 'just damn those torpedoes and steam at full speed ahead.' You might want to hear this, sir. Turns out that our John was quite the hero at Mobile."

Laporte was known aboard ship for stories of his suave ability with women. Now Wake knew how. "Really? Was it *John* who made that famous saying? And to think that Admiral Farragut got credit for it," he asked, going along with the charade. Looking at Laporte's pained expression, Wake smiled for the first time that night.

"Well, sir . . . ah, it may have come out a bit wrong in the translation. Actually I was about to tell her . . ." protested Laporte, as one of the girls asked if he had ever been wounded and another begged Wake not to take *their* officers away from them.

The governor and admiral appeared beside the group, and Admiral Normand put a hand on Wake's arm. "Ladies, ladies, I could not help overhearing. Our handsome American guests have had a very long day and must return to their ship." He held up a finger. "Let us allow them to do so and return tomorrow with even more energy for the New Year's Eve gala at St. Pierre. Lieutenant Wake, would you be so kind as to grant our request? You will enjoy the ride across the island and will be absolutely enchanted by St. Pierre. It is known as the Paris of the West Indies, as you may have heard, and its New Year's Eve gala is famous throughout the French world."

Before Wake could reply, His Excellency, Simon Graisse, governor of the French West Indies, made his own plea. "Lieutenant, I ask you in the name of the French Republic and in the name of our ancestor who forged the bond between our two nations so long ago, the Marquis de Lafayette—please attend the gala in St. Pierre. And bring two of your magnificent officers also."

Seven people now leaned forward, waiting for his reply, the most eager of whom were Laporte and Grimsrud. Wake saw others around the room were also watching. He thought of all the routine work that needed to be attended to aboard *Omaha,* but then the vision of St. Pierre along the coast came to mind. Taking a deep breath he turned to the governor. "Your Excellency, how can I say anything other than a very humble 'yes.' I must confess something, sir. We have been absolutely captivated by the charms of your hospitality and, most especially, by the beauty of your ladies."

7

Enchanté à St. Pierre

They stayed at the Hotel République, welcomed in grand fashion by the entire staff, who lined up in front. The hotel was the town's finest and overlooked the Caribbean on Rue Petite Versailles in the heart of St. Pierre. The first reception of the evening would be held in two hours, and anticipation was in the air as workers put together the last-minute touches.

Aboard the ship early that morning, Wake picked Second Engineer Les Partington and Ensign Ed Davies to accompany him to St. Pierre, the explanation being that he wanted as many of the *Omaha*'s officers as possible to sample French hospitality while the ships were visiting Martinique. Besides, he admitted to himself, he was more than a little apprehensive about bringing Laporte and Grimsrud along on an *overnight* excursion after their obvious social success with the ladies of Fort de France.

Wake was tired but content after an amazing all-day ride through the mountains of the interior. Sights unlike any he had seen before were indelibly imprinted in his mind. Martinique was a tropical paradise and the American naval officers spent most of the ride wide-eyed, commenting on the exotic beauty of the scenery. Fortunately, their transport was a newly imported carriage with good suspension, unlike the old one used at Antigua, so the trip was not nearly as physically stressful. Though it took all day, it seemed as if it had only lasted a few hours.

Each curve of the road through the interior of the island had provided a vista that outdid its predecessor. Silvery waterfalls, verdant jungle, quaint pink villages, ragged three-thousand-foot peaks, and colorfully clothed people of every shade of skin, from pasty white to the darkest blue-black, were seen along the way. Wake's senses were overwhelmed. Music heard while passing through villages ranged from ominous African to elegant French, the pastries they had for lunch at a plantation house were delicately exquisite, and the language was a wonderful jumble of patois from three continents. Even the air was a mixture of powerful scents, from flowers to bakeries to fetid earth.

As they passed through the villages of Balata, Absalon, and Fond St. Denis, the Americans heard stories from the driver of bravery and treachery among the island's various inhabitants over the centuries, and marveled at how those hearty souls managed not only to survive, but to keep their French culture alive and thriving. They also heard tales of the most dreaded animal threat of the island, a blackish-brown snake called the fer de lance, that lived in the humid tropical forest, could kill with a single bite, and claimed several unwary human victims each year. Wake had a terror of snakes and his imagination started seeing them at every turn.

When the carriage had rounded the top of Morne des Cadets in the mid-afternoon after a steep two-thousand-foot climb, the travelers were treated to the breathtaking sight of Montagne Pelée, its base covering the entire northern horizon and its ridges reaching up beyond the clouds. Descending through cool mists to the valley of the Riviére Roxelane, they followed the south bank to the coast, emerging at St. Pierre as the sun lowered over the sparkling Caribbean, turning the sea from dark blue to shimmering gold.

"Sir, it is my honor to introduce to you my daughter, Audrey," announced the Hotel République's proprietor, Raoul Jason, with pride when Wake arrived in the bar after dark to meet the others before heading to the first reception. Partington and Davies looked decidedly uncomfortable in their full-dress uniforms— young Davies had to borrow half of his from other officers—and they stayed in the background as Wake took the social lead and spoke with Jason's daughter as the guests moved into the salon.

In modest light blue dress, twenty-year-old Audrey was one of the most beautiful girls Wake had ever seen—the blood of her French father and Creole mother combining to create a lithe young woman with creamy milk-chocolate skin, long shiny black hair, and perfectly alluring brown eyes. She was scented with a delicately flowered perfume he couldn't place. But Wake thought her physical appearance was only half her attraction.

Audrey was also a very gentle and charming person, as he found out in the ensuing conversation, for she was fluent in English and had a delicious laugh and fresh, natural smile. He found her quiet self-confidence quite attractive as she told him about the history of the hotel, the town of St. Pierre, and the island of Martinique. She told him how her father had raised her alone, since her mother had died of smallpox years earlier. It was fascinating, and before Wake realized it, almost an hour had gone by. Everything was so completely and pleasantly alien to him—a world away from the life of men aboard a warship. And a respite from depression over his marriage. Realizing he had been with only the hotelier's daughter the whole time, his face flushed with embarrassment. He knew he had to circulate the room and talk with other guests.

"Audrey, thank you so much. You have been a wonderful guide to St. Pierre for me and we haven't even left the room!" he said, looking into her lovely smile.

"It is my pleasure, Lieutenant. We on Martinique are great admirers of Americans and enjoy spending time with them. You are so open, without pretenses."

Audrey's face suddenly stiffened and her voice lost its gaiety. "Hmm. . . . Here come the Fabers. Including Catherine, I see. I will go and find my father to introduce you to them. Please excuse me, Lieutenant."

Wake glanced around to see who she was talking about. A distinguished older couple were entering the room, accompanied by a petite woman in her mid-twenties expensively gowned in forest green. Her long brown hair was swept up in the latest Paris coif and the glittering diamonds in her earrings and necklace accentuated a sad-eyed face, as if she held some dark grief. Wake wondered if a loved one had died recently and, if so, why she wasn't wearing black according to custom. She was the precise opposite of Audrey, more fragile and unsure but stunningly beautiful also, and every man in the room watched her glide across the floor behind the older couple.

"Ah, yes," called out Raoul Jason as he emerged from the crowd. "Monsieur *et* Madame Faber, *et* Madame Catherine. How very lovely you ladies look this evening. Thank you for gracing our humble reception." The older man mumbled something in French, then abruptly departed the room as his wife went to a woman friend in the corner, leaving the young lady alone in the middle of the room. Jason deftly guided her toward Wake, who couldn't retreat and wondered what to say.

As Jason introduced Catherine Faber de Champlain to Wake the young lady's face slowly creased into a smile, more of duty than enjoyment. Wake learned that she was the wife of Monsieur Faber's younger brother and had been visiting for the last month from France before returning to Europe to join her husband in Genoa, where he was newly posted as the French consul general. Jason further explained that Catherine spoke English, Spanish, and Italian in addition to her native tongue and therefore he hoped they could take pleasure in a conversation. Having fulfilled his social responsibility, Jason moved on around the room.

"*Enchanté*, Madame Faber," Wake said, trying to look and sound more elegant than he felt. He felt the urge to make her smile, a real smile, so he tried to make a joke.

"I am headed to the European Squadron of our navy, so perhaps you can teach me some things to say in those languages that will *not* get me in trouble."

Another forced smile fleetingly crossed her face. "Just never say the following, Lieutenant, unless you truly mean it—*Je t'aime.*"

Her tone was sadly serious and Wake realized his joke had fallen flat. "I'm afraid you already have me at a disadvantage, Madame Faber, for I don't know that particular phrase."

"It is French for 'I love you,' Lieutenant. It is cruelly overused as a *ruse de guerre* between men and women and too often believed by the intended victim."

He instantly knew she was speaking for herself, explaining her apparent melancholy. He replied gently, "Then I promise to stay with the words I know, madame. They all start with *bon*. Like '*bonjour, bon appetit,* and *bon voyage.*' I don't think they could hurt. Would that be safe for both people in the conversation?"

He was rewarded with a genuine giggle as her face softened. "Yes, Lieutenant. I think that you will be quite safe with those words, and depending on where and when you say them, you may very well inject a little good humor into the conversation. You Americans are so wonderfully *naïfs*. So different from Europeans."

"Naïve, madame? Sometimes it is better to be that way. At least it's more comfortable to not know what's impossible before you attempt it."

Her eyes held his as her hand touched his arm. "You Americans are becoming famous for accomplishing the impossible. But I must warn you about being *naïf*, Lieutenant . . ."

He felt himself being drawn into her dark blue, almost indigo, eyes. "Yes, madame?"

"When you go to the Continent the women will love you for being *naïf*, but the men will despise you for it. They will think you weak and vulnerable. They try to take advantage of the weak and vulnerable, Lieutenant. Be very careful."

Wake nodded his acknowledgment, so surprised by the change in her tone and sincerity of her warning that he couldn't form a reply.

"And, Lieutenant," she said as her smile returned, this one gentle, "it would please me greatly if you called me by my given Christian name of Catherine."

"All right, Catherine," Wake answered, still mesmerized by her eyes. His words seemed to come from someone else. "Please call me Peter."

He dimly heard dinner being announced by a man in the doorway, then felt Catherine's arm entwine around his. Without a further word they walked amid the guests to the banquet room, oblivious to the observations being made about the Yankee naval officer and the diplomat's wife.

At dinner, Wake was seated at the table with the governor and admiral, with Catherine beside him. Her brother- and sister-in-law were to her other side, Monsieur Faber occasionally studying the American next to his brother's wife. Wake became engaged in conversations with every man present, mainly about political situations in the United States and in Europe, but he couldn't help now and then stealing a glance at Catherine next to him.

The French naval officers wanted to know about his wartime blockade assignments, and an artillery colonel was eager to hear how Yankee ships had defeated the Confederate forts. They asked his assessment of the Spanish navy, which he politely dodged, changing the subject instead to steam machinery. When Wake was able to speak with her, he saw that Catherine had the disconcerting habit of looking directly into his eyes. Her smile melted him inside.

He also saw that Audrey, seated at another table, was watching him with a look of concern. Wake knew he was on the verge of trouble, but he couldn't stop glancing at Catherine. Worse, he did not *want* to stop.

After dinner, the third locale of the all-night gala was the theater—a block's stroll down the street in the moonlight. The mass of gaily tipsy people arrived at the theater and noisily filed inside for a performance by the local symphony. Catherine and Wake were still together, arm in arm, an hour later while Paul Mas introduced Wake to various dignitaries and artists during the intermission, lastly bringing him to a large-framed man with darting eyes named François Lessere. He was patron of the theater and owner of the most well-known plantation and rum distillery on the island.

"*Bienvenue á Martinique,* Lieutenant. I trust that you are having a good time?" said Lessere perfunctorily while staring Catherine's bosom with undisguised lust.

"Yes. I have found most of the people of Martinique to be as enchanting as the scenery," said Wake, angry at the man's indecent leering.

"Yes, our scenery is very beautiful." Lessere's gaze shifted to Wake. "But only *most* of the people, Lieutenant? We pride ourselves on the beauty of our women and on the strength and honor of our men. You evidently have met some who did not measure up? They were probably not from here. Probably foreigners."

"I've met only *one* man who acted less than honorably, Lessere. And yes, he is from here," Wake replied evenly, deliberately omitting *Monsieur.*

Lessere leveled his gaze and cocked his head. "I hope then that you do not underestimate that man as an enemy, Lieutenant. You Americans are unfortunately known for that."

Wake smiled. "Yes, well, so were the Mexicans until eighteen-sixty-two—on *Cinco de Mayo* if my memory serves well, when they proved themselves superior to some Europeans who had occupied their country. You know, Lessere, we Americans greatly admired their ability in that particular war." He turned to Catherine as Lessere's face darkened. "Would you like to get some fresh air, Madame Faber? It's a bit musty in here suddenly. Smells badly."

As they walked out to the balcony she squeezed his arm. "Perhaps you are not as *naïf* as I first thought, Peter Wake. Lessere is a pig whose only protection is his money. You understood that immediately, did you not?"

"Catherine, Americans may be naïve but we aren't stupid. A pig acts the same in any culture, my dear."

"Just remember, Peter, that some pigs have tusks. Lessere is one of them."

During the fourth reception Wake danced with her three times, when the local dandies weren't trying to get her attention and cutting in on him. They finally sat at a table, where their talk centered on his wife and children. He spoke of how he and Linda had met and eventually married during the war years, but he avoided the current crisis in his marriage. Catherine listened closely, expressing empathy for a woman whose husband was gone from her so much. She added that someday she would like to meet the lady who had captured his heart so many years earlier.

She did not speak of her husband, his work, or her new home in Genoa, explaining that those were boring subjects and she wanted to know more about *him*. She seemed to be genuinely interested—not in the war stories most women asked him to tell, but about his personal opinions and hopes and regrets. Wake knew he was talking more than usual, having never drunk that much wine and cognac before. He also knew he should stop drinking as well as stop talking, but just couldn't bring himself to end the euphoria. It was such a wonderful feeling to have a beautiful woman to look at, to care about what he had to say, to softly touch his arm. He missed feminine company far more than he had realized during the incessant work aboard ship.

The designated clock for the countdown to midnight was the governor's pocket watch, and while he loudly led the guests in calling out the descending time, stewards snuffed out the candles. At the moment of midnight the last of the candles was extinguished and the hall became completely dark. Everyone embraced the nearest person of the opposite gender as they shouted, "*Bonne année* and *bonne santé.*"

In the cloaking darkness Wake held Catherine initially at a polite distance, until she pressed nearer, placing her hip against his. Then he surrendered to the effect of the wine and the moment and his loneliness—pulling her close and savoring the caress of her soft warm body, her head against his shoulder.

"Thank you for being so kind and gentle tonight, Peter. I had forgotten how wonderful it feels when a man can be that way," she whispered in his ear as her fingers went around his waist. "I can feel sadness in you, Peter. Sadness that you have not spoken of but is hurting you inside. I hope it goes away."

The room was being reilluminated by the stewards as he tried to reply, his words jumbling together in his lightheadedness. "Catherine, I don't know what to say or do right now, except that I don't want to let you go."

She made no reply, but she gently pushed herself away. As the revelers returned to their tables she said, loud enough for others to hear, "Lieutenant, you have acquitted the United States Navy as a gallant gentleman very well tonight. It is obvious how your navy has the reputation it enjoys. I thank you so much for taking time to dine and converse with me this evening. It has been very enjoyable and I wish you good fortune."

Wake was taken aback at the change of manner, then noticed that Catherine's in-laws, and Lessere, were watching them intently from the corner.

"It was delightful for me as well, Madame Faber," he answered with a slight bow.

"Perhaps we shall meet again, Lieutenant. I shall hope to introduce you to my husband if you ever get to Genoa. And now I must leave and go home with my brother-in-law and his wife." She gave him a parting neutral smile, but added a quiet aside before she turned away. "*Au revoir,* Peter." Then she walked toward her in-laws as calmly as if they were all in church.

Wake stood watching them leave as he pondered what he was sure had been a fleeting personal message in her eyes when she uttered her last words.

Audrey appeared at his side, startling him as she nodded toward the Fabers. "You have no experience with French women, do you, Lieutenant?"

"Experience? Well, no, of course not. I don't have . . . *experience* . . . with any, ah. . . You see, Audrey . . ." he stammered without finding the right words.

"Madame Faber did not say goodbye to you, Lieutenant. She said *until we meet again.*"

Wake felt a flush of warmth on his cheeks. He worried that he had made a fool of himself and that Audrey, and probably everyone else, had seen him. "Yes, well, of course that is totally impossible, Audrey. I leave tomorrow and she is going to Italy soon. Besides, she is a charming lady but married. And I am *very* married. I can't imagine she meant it that way and am absolutely sure she didn't mean anything improper at all."

Audrey's expression indicated that she wasn't impressed by his remonstrations.

"St. Pierre has a way of enchanting people. The Creole people say it is the aura of Montagne Pelée that makes us do things we normally would not do, especially on a night such as tonight, with the moon and the wine and the music. It gives you thoughts that make you nervous. You appear nervous, Lieutenant," she said ruefully. "I think you have come under that *enchantment.*"

"Audrey, that's ridiculous. Really now. . . ."

She looked at him and shook her head slowly. "I don't think it matters at this point who is married, Lieutenant Wake. At this point it only matters what Catherine Faber wants. And, as they say in France, we have only to wait, for time will tell what life will bring."

Audrey waved to her father, then turned to Wake before walking away.

"*Bonne chance,* Lieutenant."

He was standing there, attempting to understand what had happened when young Ensign Davies came up to him and draped an arm around one shoulder, breath reeking as he displayed a lopsided grin and slurred, "Helllloo there, shur . . . Looie-tenant friggin' Wake! One hellova party, shur. Thansh sho mush for ashing me to come. These frog-eatin' Frenchies may be panshies in a war, but by God the bashtards *do* know how to throw a great friggin' party, don't they, shur?"

Wake took Davies' arm off his shoulder and leaned close to the ensign's ear, growling, "Mr. Davies, you have five seconds to get yourself together before I determine punishment for conduct unbecoming an officer, insubordination, and public drunkenness."

Terror instantly filled Davies' eyes as he realized what he had just done and said. He quickly stood at attention. "Very shorry, shur! I'll get Mr. Partington ready to get under way for the hotel, shur."

"Do that right now, Mr. Davies, and get out of my sight."

The ensign's conduct angered Wake, but what really scared him was his own behavior with Catherine. It was as if something had taken over his mind and body. He had come close—very close—to crossing the line with her. He realized that perhaps Audrey was right about falling under the spell of the island. Suddenly the enchantment Wake had known ever since arriving at St. Pierre was replaced by a wary dread of meeting Catherine Faber again.

And he had the dismaying feeling that he would—and the even more dismaying feeling that he fervently hoped so.

8

To Windward

January 1874

Breakfast at the hotel dining room on the first morning of 1874 started out as a subdued affair of stifled groans and silent munching of toast. The Americans were the first to arrive, the local guests taking the morning slowly. Davies was in very bad shape and Partington nearly so, each worried about appearing weak in front of his superior and struggling not to show his hangover. Even Wake was feeling worse for wear until he ate the first croissant of his life, allowing the delicate taste to improve his outlook.

Audrey and her father arrived to keep them company, explaining with hilarity the political and social backgrounds of the more notable guests the night before. Both studiously avoided speaking about the Fabers, and Wake wondered why but didn't ask. After worrying about it all night he'd decided that the previous evening with Catherine Faber was a minor moment in his life. He had only been a little lonely, no one was hurt, and he didn't violate his marital vows, he told himself. Wake vowed that

that kind of episode would never be repeated, even in the unlikely event the two did meet again.

When the Americans stood to leave, Wake felt something ominous that was another first for him. The ground trembled, like a warship's deck when a broadside went off, but it went on for almost a full minute, shaking the wine glasses into an insane cacophony and bringing forth strange oaths from the Creole chef in the kitchen. Raoul left the table to check for damage.

"Montagne Pelée," explained Audrey with a shrug. "Getting our attention. She does that frequently. This is a small one."

Wake had never been in an earthquake. The sheer latent power of it was disconcerting to him. "It does this often?"

"Yes, but the officials say it is nothing. Just a shifting of weight far below the surface."

"Aren't they afraid it will erupt, like Vesuvius at Pompeii?"

"No. They say it is no problem. Personally, I think they do not want people to worry. Or perhaps investors to leave. But what do I know?"

Wake looked out the window at the mountain. It appeared close but he knew it was five miles away. He was sure it was distant enough not to cause a problem to St. Pierre, but the rumbling started up again and made him want to get back to the ship. Like most veteran sailors, he felt vaguely unsafe on land.

When Raoul returned, he and Wake shook hands. Then Audrey hugged him and said goodbye. He thanked her for the previous night's hospitality and wished her good fortune. Both said they hoped to see the other again and both knew they wouldn't. Then he climbed into the carriage's front seat with the driver and they were off with a clatter of hooves on the stone pavement, the two recovering younger officers sprawled against the back seat. Wake sat back and took in the sights.

The ride back was by a different route, along the western coast of the island. The road was along the cliffs, at times a dizzying plunge of hundreds of feet, and they traveled through villages hidden within the coves formed by mountain rivers that emptied into the sea. It was even more winding than the interior road and several times Wake thought they would not get through, but the driver knew of detours and took paths off to the side that led them around washouts and downed trees.

They passed the dilapidated fishing village of Le Carbet, famous among the islanders for Colombus' first landing site on Martinique, and then Belle Fontaine, which Catherine had said was owned by a distant cousin in France who had never even seen his possessions in the West Indies. Finally, they topped the last" coastal mountain and saw Fort de France spread out along the shores of its great bay.

By dinner the three officers were back aboard *Omaha* and Wake was reporting to Gardiner his observations of the politics and economy of the island. He described Audrey and her father to the captain but omitted any reference to Catherine Faber. He wasn't sure how to describe her and worried that Gardiner would sense some sort of guilt over his behavior with her.

Gardiner listened to the report and thanked Wake for handling the social duties of the ship, saying that it was all far more than he cared to do. With one of his infectious grins he added that he would rely on Wake to do it one last time in Barbados.

The trades were blowing a reefed topsail breeze after they rounded Ilet Cabri at the southern end of Martinique, sailing close-hauled to the southeast for Bridgetown at the British crown colony of Barbados. The wild salt air felt clean and pure to Wake—devoid of the complicated scents in the air on land. The symbolism wasn't lost on him and he stayed on deck long past the end of his watch, gazing at Martinique receding.

In addition to being wrong, his attraction to Catherine was illogical, Wake told himself, after he had unsuccessfully tried to put her out of his memory. In so many ways Audrey was more similar to him, and to Linda. Catherine was from a world completely different from Wake's—the alien world of the leisurely cultured elite. Maybe, he pondered as the last black smudge of the island sank below the horizon, that's why I am intrigued.

But even that benign verb bothered him. Was he allowed to be intrigued by a woman? Wake shook his head at the horizon and gripped the stern rail. Martinique had profoundly disturbed him, probing into the weak spots of his soul and finding the wounds. It was a dangerous place for a man with doubts and he didn't want to go back. But no, that wasn't true. He did want to go back. He just knew that he shouldn't.

And where exactly was he headed? With each mile eastward toward Europe, life as he had always known it was fading away too. For the first time since his court-martial almost five years earlier, his professional future was uncertain and his personal one was looking more grim with each day.

They let go the hook at Bridgetown two days later, after having to short tack to windward the last fifteen miles against wind and tide. It was a frustrating effort not only because their destination was in sight, but because they had the means to get there directly but were not allowed to use the engine unless an emergency arose. It was one of the stupid things about the navy that upset Wake; however, there was nothing he could do, so he swallowed his irritation and concentrated on the neverending administrative paperwork of the ship.

When the American consul came aboard with mail, including one from Linda, Wake inquired about the *Trinidad's* schedule. He was told the passenger steamer would arrive the next day, load for two days, and be on her way on the third. Wake also found out that there would be the usual round of professional and social contacts and functions ashore that would start the next day.

In the privacy of his cabin he ripped the envelope open and read Linda's letter. Apparently she hadn't received his letter from Antigua yet, a short one that he finally got written and hoped wasn't callous. It wasn't unusual for her not to get his letter—mail normally took almost three weeks to get to Pensacola from the West Indies, and return messages between correspondents took a month and a half. Now he knew that he would not hear from her for quite a while, since transAtlantic private mail to the Mediterranean often took months.

Pensacola, Florida   *December 18th, 1873*

Dear Peter,
Here is a short note to say hello which I'll put on the steamer south-bound. The children are well and Useppa's pain is appearing to diminish, but it's too early to tell if it is permanent. The latest gossip from Pensacola is a rumor that the navy is going to shut down the yard here due to budgetary constraints, but there's nothing official from the yard commandant. That's caused some panic among the store owners. By the way, the new navy yard commandant is Alexander Semmes, an old wartime colleague of yours, I think. He told me he knew you when you had Rosalie *back in sixty-three—that seems like ages ago. He is a cousin to that famous Confederate commander of the* Alabama, *Raphael Semmes, who works in Mobile as a lawyer. Both are in good health and see each other. Alexander asks about you.*

Peter, I can't wait until you come home. We need to talk about our marriage and your work. I understand your love of the sea and have come to admire that in you. You can still have that on a merchant ship, dear—without the negativity of the navy.

I love and miss you more than you'll ever know and count the days until we can hold each other and be a real family again.
Linda

His hands were shaking when he finished reading. Folding the letter carefully back into the envelope he put it into the desk drawer devoted to her letters. They were his sole treasure—a chronologically arranged connection to his family. He took in a deep breath and tried unsuccessfully to slow his pounding heart and calm down.

A knock on his door disturbed his swirling thoughts.

"Officer of the deck present his respects, sir! He reports that the chandler's barge is alongside and they need your signature on the provision manifest."

Wake sighed—there was no real privacy aboard a warship. No place to hide, especially for the executive officer. "Pass along my compliments to the officer of the deck. I'll be there directly."

The reception was held at Farley Hill Plantation on the other side of the island. It wasn't specifically in honor of the U.S. Navy's visit, but the Americans were invited to send two officers to an annual ball given each January by the plantation owner, a titled Englishman who for some obscure reason found himself in one of the more remote stretches of the empire. Attendance necessitated an overnight stay, so when Wake picked Laporte to be the other officer he gave him a short lecture on deportment, all the while thinking about his own behavior in Martinique.

"Remember, John, you represent the navy and your country. Do not drink too much and do not let your tales go beyond your good sense. I picked you because in a few days you'll be the executive officer and I want to be confident you can handle the social duties of the ship since the captain doesn't want that chore."

"Yes, sir. Don't worry a bit about me, sir."

Wake and Laporte reported to the Royal Navy's small pier a quarter mile up the river that ran through the heart of Bridgetown. The British navy had no regular station at

Bridgetown, maintaining a supply depot only. The petty officer explained that Commander Laylock, the officer-in-charge, was already at the plantation along with the governor and awaiting their arrival. He then showed them to a government carriage reminiscent of the one at Antigua, making Wake wonder if rickety wagons were characteristic of the English islands in the Caribbean.

The ride to Farley Hill showed an island that was completely unlike Martinique. A recent drought had combined with a depression in sugar prices in '73 to devastate the economy of Barbados, and the villages along the west coast showed it. The black islanders were in a subsistence mode, fishing or farming small tracts, and the white islanders they passed were disheveled and sullen-looking. Black Rock, Holetown, and Sandy Lane had no modern equipment in sight and Laporte said the sights reminded him of parts of Georgia after the war.

At noon they ascended the last hill and arrived at their destination, which the driver reported the height of as precisely seven hundred forty-three feet, and the location to be exactly in the center of the northern part of the island, between the east and west coasts. Wake disembarked in front of the great mansion and stood for a moment taking in the sight. Incongruously, it was a giant manor house in the English Georgian style, set in a forest of pines with a magnificent view of the Atlantic ocean smashing ashore on the distant east coast, far below them. Not a palm was in view—they could've been in England.

Laporte broke Wake's reverie. "Sir, they're coming out."

Wake turned to see porters and an older Royal Navy officer with the epaulets of a commander approaching. He straightened up to attention and said, "Good afternoon, sir. We are Lieutenant Peter Wake and Lieutenant John Laporte, of the United States Navy, here for the gala. Thank you for the very kind invitation."

"I am Commander Clive Laylock, RN, station officer-in-charge. Welcome to Barbados, Lieutenants. Sorry I wasn't there to greet you when you came ashore, but I trust that Petty Officer

Edmonds did that duty well. Please, gentlemen, come this way. The porters will get your things." Laylock started toward the massive doors but stopped and gave Wake a curious look.

"Did you say your name is *Wake,* Lieutenant?"

"Ah, yes, sir. Peter Wake."

"Oh my . . . Were you the Yankee chap who was caught taking the stroll at English Harbour Naval Yard up at Antigua a few weeks ago?"

Wake was astounded. How did he know that? "I was attending a dinner there, Commander. A Marine on guard duty thought I was trespassing, but he was wrong. A minor misunderstanding, that's all."

Laylock kept up his stare. "Yes, well, Lieutenant, I'm afraid your reputation precedes you. Of course, we have nothing around here for you to trespass upon so I'm sure they'll be no misunderstandings at all."

Wake didn't like the tone. "Thank you, sir. By the way, the misunderstanding at Antigua was rectified by my captain and the governor."

Laylock raised his eyebrows. "Oh yes, I heard about that too. Quite the story. Come on in and relax gentlemen."

As they entered the main hall Wake saw Laporte grinning at him. "Yes, Mr. Laporte? Something funny?"

"Oh no, sir," Laporte replied, losing the grin. "Just trying to concentrate on being on my very best behavior, sir. Representing my navy and country, and all that, sir."

Wake caught the humor but was in no mood for it.

9

Her Majesty's Royal Marine Light Infantry

The dinner was in a grandly paneled banquet room, larger than even the largest in Martinique. It was done in a massive Tudor style, dark wood illuminated by giant chandeliers containing hundreds of candles suspended from a ceiling thirty feet high. The heavy timbers framing the hall reminded Wake of a ship and the various coats of arms were something out of a fairytale book. Unlike all the other islands in the West Indies he had visited in his career, the stewards were second-generation white servants at the plantation and silently padded around serving the food and drinks with stoic faces.

The governor and his wife were seated in the center of the longest table Wake had ever seen, and the guests were arranged in appropriate descending rank away from them. The naval officers were near one end, which Wake was thankful for, since he was tired of the posturing expected when around the political and military elite at a social function. Commander Laylock sat across from him and next to Laporte, who had immediately taken the chair beside a charming French lady named Martineve. She was there alone and explained that her husband, the consul, was away in St. Martin. Laporte was using his basic French and making her laugh with phrases Wake couldn't understand but hoped were polite.

The waiters were starting on the first course when a tall man in a scarlet red uniform, with the white cross-belt and insignia of a Marine, pulled out the chair to Wake's right.

"Lieutenant Peter Sharpe Allen, Her Majesty's Royal Marine Light Infantry, gentlemen. I presume this seat is not taken?" said Allen, using the *left*-tenant pronunciation that had always bewildered Wake.

"Not taken at all. Please sit down, Lieutenant," said Laylock as he introduced the American officers.

Wake saw a glimmer of reaction when Allen heard his name, but nothing more.

"Lieutenant Allen, you are headed back aboard the *Trinidad*, correct?" asked Laylock.

"Yes, sir. *Trinidad* should be here tomorrow," answered Allen with an easy smile. "And within a month or so I'll be back with The Andrew in the Med. Admiral Drummond's staff, I believe. Haven't the foggiest what I'll do for them."

Wake knew that "The Andrew" was slang for the Royal Navy.

"Just what I thought," said Laylock. "Say, I believe that you and Lieutenant Wake here will be shipmates on that voyage."

Allen looked at Wake, his gray eyes showing no emotion as he nodded his acknowledgment. "That will make it far more tolerable then, sir. I'm disembarking at Genoa, I believe. What about you?"

"And me as well," added Wake, wondering if it was coincidence or planned that a Royal Marine officer would be on the same ship, headed for the same area. He wanted to ask him if he had been stationed at Antigua, but thought better of it.

"Is this a routine change of duty, Lieutenant Allen?" he asked.

"Well, my West Indies duty was nearing its end, so it was not totally unexpected, Lieutenant Wake. Of course, when we Marines take the Queen's shilling, then we must do the Queen's bidding. I go wherever they send me."

"Yes, we have a similar saying about Uncle Sam's pennies."

"I'm sure you do, Lieutenant," observed Laylock as the French lady giggled at another Laporte attempt at her language.

The affair, which was not nearly as gay as the French one at Martinique, ended early, around nine o'clock. The local attendees filed out the door on their way home as the plantation's overnight guests began to retire to their rooms. Wake and Laporte shared a bedroom on the third floor and as they ascended the stairs Wake saw the governor and Laylock ask several men, including Allen, into the study for cognac.

"Guess we're not invited, sir?" said Laporte as they reached the first landing.

"No, only the Brits, evidently."

"A big powpow, then. Just doesn't seem like there's much to powpow about on this island, sir."

Wake thought about that. Laporte was right—there wasn't much going on there. It was even more of a backwater than Antigua.

"I would imagine that they're not talking solely about Barbados, Mr. Laporte. They've got a global empire that could keep them in conversation for the next hundred years."

"Then I hope it's going better for them out there than it is around here, sir."

Laporte had to make do with a cot, but the feather mattress of the bed was decadently restful and Wake slept longer and sounder than he had for some time. Laylock and Allen joined them for a pleasing English breakfast of eggs and ham and toast, and soon the conversation evolved into sea stories from around the world.

Laylock told of his service starting as a midshipman on a frigate bound for the East Indies forty years earlier and his adventures during the Opium Wars. He was now in a semi-retirement assignment and would head home for good to Yorkshire in six months.

Allen told of duty as an instructor to the locals in Egypt and of fighting pirates and slavers in Africa's Bight of Benin. Wake told of the pirates he had chased in Central America and Laporte told of the battle of Mobile, this time without the embellishment. By the time breakfast was over, each man knew the other's measure and they had formed that curious camaraderie unique among those who go to sea.

When Wake and Laporte boarded the carriage for the ride back to Bridgetown they were pleasantly surprised to see Allen hurrying out of the mansion house, sea bag slung over a shoulder.

"Thought I'd better ship out on this ride while it's here. Don't want to take a chance on missing our steamer!" he said and off they went, this time by the east coast road, the driver explaining the west coast road they had taken the day before would "today be full of them black-bellied beasts." Allen laughed and said, "He means the famous black-bellied sheep of Barbados. They're called sheep but they look like goats to me. The farmers are taking them to the market today, so that road will be jammed. The east road is rougher but has some nice scenery."

Allen pointed out the sights as they descended from the central highlands to the wild east coast. The coast road went right along the cliffs and they clearly saw wreck after wreck in the breaking surf. The waves were huge rollers that had swept unimpeded from Africa to smash on Barbados' rocky shore, producing fantastic shapes and colors among the boulders. It was a sobering sight for sailors, a graveyard where a moment's mistake meant death—Wake couldn't see how anyone would survive a wreck on that coast.

They rode through villages with quaint names like Chalky Mount, where the inhabitants made pottery from the local clay, and Bathsheba, where the African descendents were surf fishermen. All of the officers commented on the bravery and skill needed to get in and out through those incredible breaking waves, many exceeding fifteen feet. Allen pointed out the semaphore signal station at Gun Hill, explaining that a hundred years earlier the army had built them around the island to warn of a French attack. Nearby they saw the imposing White Lion, a statue erected on a hilltop a few years before, in '68, commemorating British rule and the emancipation of the slaves. Allen thought it an odd location for an imperial monument—it was in the middle of nowhere.

From Martin's Bay on the coast they ascended very steep hills up into the interior again, stopping a half mile from the sea at St. John's Church, perched atop Hackletons Cliff. The driver advised they would be there for at least one hour to change horses and that since it was noon on Sunday, they could probably attend the church picnic that was about to start. It sounded like a good idea to the weary travelers and Allen led the way into the Anglican church, a seventeenth-century crenellated structure of cut coral stone overlooking the deep blue of the Atlantic, white trace of sandy beach, and green slopes of the hills—one of the most magnificent views Wake had ever seen. Standing by a low retaining wall just outside the front doors, he could see for miles along the rugged coastline six hundred feet below them.

The old rector was delighted to have them visit and gave a tour of his church, pointing out in his gentle tone the pet finches that flitted about the rafters, their chirps echoing around the naves like a natural miniature choir. He invited them to join the congregation that was about to enjoy a picnic lunch under the giant mahogany trees. They were treated as honored guests, with parishioners competing for their attention as they ate flying fish, crane chubb, and plantains—a tasty local combination of food from English and African origin. The young ladies of the parish eyed their every move. The stopover ended too quickly when the driver announced it was time to get under way again.

Just as they were boarding the carriage to the heartfelt good wishes of the crowd, the rector came up to Allen. "I couldn't place it at first, but now I remember you! I was filling in for the sick rector up at Antigua last month, Lieutenant, and clearly recall that you had an excellent voice during the hymns. I'm sorry you are leaving us."

Wake noticed Allen glance at him when the rector said Antigua. Then the Marine answered, "Thank you, sir. I fear my voice is far more loud than excellent."

"God be with all of you gentlemen!" cried out the rector as they drove away.

"Well, now *that* was very enjoyable meal," said Allen, as if to change the subject as he wistfully looked back at the crowd.

"Yes, it was," agreed Wake, doubts about his fellow passenger ended. It was beyond mere coincidence that Lieutenant Peter Sharpe Allen, RMLI, was going to be with Wake for the next four thousand miles.

10

A Different Kind of Voyage

The *Trinidad* was owned by the British North American Steamship Company—founded by the legendary Samuel Cunard thirty years earlier. She was a ten-year-old medium-sized steamer that had been employed on the West Indies–Mediterranean route since 1871 and was commanded by a grizzled old veteran named Fletcher who, like most captains in the merchant fleet, disliked naval officers and thought most of them pompous fools tied to obsolete traditions.

The passengers, who had been arriving during the week in Bridgetown from all around the West Indies, thronged the pier shouting in several languages, soon creating a madhouse scene. Wake and Allen arrived together at the pier and slowly made their way through the mob to the gangway where they met the first officer, a middle-aged Scot named Newton who obviously had little time for them.

Wake knew he would be sharing a cabin and asked the officer who his companion was to be. Newton scrutinized a passenger list, looked up at him incredulously, and pointed to Allen. "Why, *he's* your mate for this voyage, Lieutenant. You're going to bunk in with the Royal friggin' Marines. Lobster and squid in the same cage!"

Newton's joke about the slang terms for a Royal Marine and a sailor fell flat on the two officers. Wake thought Allen's surprise at the news a bit contrived, but decided it made no real difference. Whatever the Royal Navy imagined Wake to be, they would be sadly disappointed by putting a spy in his cabin. And anyway, Wake actually liked the red coat lieutenant and by this time they were first-name friends.

They made their way through the passageways toward their assigned cabin and finally found it in the second-class accommodations, one deck down from the main weather deck. It was larger than many Wake had in his career, but smaller than he had hoped. Ten minutes later their gear was stowed and both officers were on the main deck aft, looking across the water at *Omaha* anchored two hundred yards away.

"Fine-looking ship, Peter," Allen offered.

"Aye, that she is, Pete," said Wake, using his friend's nickname—one he had never encouraged for himself. "Good captain and crew. I'll miss them."

"Seems like men in our profession are always saying hello or goodbye, doesn't it?"

"Hello there, gentlemen!" boomed a voice from behind. A giant man, well over six feet tall and square-built, wearing grease-stained coveralls, loomed up and captured their hands in his paw, almost crushing them while shaking hands. "I'm the engineer, Monroe, from Fishguard in the wild land of Wales. Since you're both in the business of going to sea, I'll show you my two great beauties below in the belly of the beast tomorrow when we're steaming, if you'd like."

Wake answered for both of them when he said, "That would be very interesting, sir. We'd like to see your engines."

Monroe beamed. "Aye, you will then. At three bells in the forenoon watch come below and I'll show you. They'll be working away the whole trip across. The more you work 'em the more they like it, you know. Not like you Yanks! I hear you're not allowed to use your engines. Afraid they'll break!"

Wake cringed in embarrassment. "Yes, you're right, sir. But it's budgetary constraints that stop us from using them on transits. Only use engines in harbors and battle."

"Sounds silly to me, mate!" said Monroe as he walked off forward, the crowd on deck parting when they saw his approach.

"You'll hear a fair amount of that in the Med, Peter," added Allen. "The first-rate navies don't understand why your government let yours go after your war. You had the second largest navy in the world. Scared the hell out of the bloody Frogs in Mexico to have your navy astride their supply lines. But now the Yanks don't have much to work with and the Continental powers know it. The Austrians are the most arrogant about it, especially after what they did to the Italian navy at Lissa in sixty-six."

"Well, I can't argue with them, because we don't understand it either, Pete. But I won't denigrate my government, of course, so I guess I'll just have to stand and take it."

Two hours later the whistle blew five long blasts and the deck began to vibrate heavily as the engines were engaged in reverse gear. The pier slid forward beside them as the ship backed out and the captain, up on the midship cross-bridge, stalked back and forth while giving orders via the speaking trumpet. *Trinidad* eased astern into the bay, then stopped and turned to starboard slightly before the captain ordered her rudder amidship and rang up revolutions for six knots. Wake and Allen walked over to the starboard rail of the quarterdeck just aft of the bridge—they were allowed where civilian passengers weren't—and stood watching the crew go about their work.

Wake was studying the rigging when Allen brought his attention over to starboard.

"Well, look at that, Peter Wake!"

·Tears welled up in Wake's eyes when he looked—the officers and men of the *Omaha* had lined the rails and yards, something normally done only for senior officers and government officials. *Trinidad* was passing within one hundred feet of *Omaha* and Wake could clearly hear Fawcett, the warship's bosun, call all hands to give Lieutenant Wake three cheers.

He came to attention himself and saluted as the passenger steamer slid by his old ship, holding the salute for a long time as the cheers echoed around the harbor. Then Captain Gardiner, not using a trumpet, bellowed out across the water, "*God bless you, Mister Wake! Give 'em hell in the Med!*" and afterward also stood at attention with a salute.

It was all that Wake could do not to succumb to his emotion when he dropped his hand and stood easy. The other passengers had grown silent during the scene, knowing instinctively the bond that was being demonstrated. Now they started talking about the Yankee officer on their deck that had been the recipient of such an honor. Standing there watching *Omaha* getting smaller in the distance as the *Trinidad* picked up speed, both men were silent for a while. Wake's thoughts were with his old crew.

"Never saw that done for a mere lieutenant, Peter. The Andrew would never do that," Allen said, quietly breaking the spell.

"You're right, Pete. It was against regulations. But sometimes we throw away the rule books."

"Yes, I've heard about that. That's what my father said about you Americans. He found out firsthand on HMS *Macedonia* back in eighteen-fourteen." Allen laughed. "Said the bloody Yank sailors wouldn't play fair by the rules!"

Wake shrugged as he watched the island fade away. "Yes, but really, war itself is the ultimate sign that the rules have failed, isn't it?"

They were at sixteen degrees north and forty degrees east, the wind was calm and the sea glassy flat. The two engines had been thumping in rhythm for days, never missing a beat and consuming forty-seven tons of fuel a day, which amazed Wake. The ship had bunkers for over eight hundred tons, far more than *Omaha*. The masts and sails were seldom used and the majority of the one hundred seven men in her crew were devoted to feeding and maintaining the mechanical heart of the ship.

Monroe showed them the engine spaces, where the massive beam engines, fed by five boilers, propelled the ship at twelve knots on average, sometimes more in calm waters. Monroe was like a proud father as he introduced them to his black gang—the seagoing slang term for the men who served the engines and became covered in grease and soot in the process—as they went about their duties in the incredibly hot and dimly lit spaces.

One of the side benefits of a steam engine was the fresh water it could distill from the seawater cooling intakes. Wake learned that *Trinidad* made the drinking water for all of the crew and passengers, a thousand gallons every day. He also learned that *Trinidad* had four auxiliary engines to handle the anchors, cargo lifts, circulating pump, and air ventilators. *Omaha* had only two extra engines and no ventilators. Monroe bragged that if they somehow got a hole the size of a cotton bale in the hull, his pumps could move so much water that they'd never sink. After seeing the machinery, Wake believed him and wished the U.S. Navy was as well equipped.

Wake had never spent time aboard an oceangoing passenger liner and was impressed by the logistics of caring for the passengers so they could continue their civilian comforts. Three meals a day were served to the two hundred fifty passengers, along with a high tea for ladies every day at four o'clock in the afternoon. The service was excellent and passengers were encouraged to relax. He felt absolutely lazy and debauched when Allen suggested they sit in deck chairs and watch the sea go by. In his entire life, Wake had never sat in a chair on a weather deck, and found it luxurious.

They ate with the ship's officers, a privilege accorded by their profession and rank, and both found the food quite superior to naval fare. The conversations centered around maritime subjects. Many of the British officers had served in the navy and were interested in the latest developments.

One evening after dinner in the officers' mess the talk shifted to torpedoes and the newest designs. Wake offered no opinion beyond stating that his navy was working on them at Newport in Rhode Island, but that he had no details. As he was speaking he saw that Allen was listening closely to all that was said, particularly by Wake. He wondered if he should bring up the incident at English Harbour and decided no—if Pete Allen was aboard to watch him and gain information from him, the man wouldn't admit it, and if not, it would just confuse him.

Ten days after leaving Barbados, the Canary Islands appeared on the horizon. At sunset that evening the steamer eased into the open anchorage of the town of Santa Cruz de Tenerife and let go her anchor. Wake was impressed—*Trinidad* had averaged about twelve knots of sustained speed under engines alone for 2,640 miles. When he mentioned it to the others at dinner, the officers said it was not an unusual journey, that the crossing had been in good weather with no mechanical problems and they did it all the time.

The stop at Tenerife was for fuel, for they had consumed over three quarters of their coal on the crossing. In addition to the loss of fuel, the ship was now lighter, with a higher center of gravity and more susceptible to capsizing, so the following morning she was moved closer to the coal depot and the work began. Coaling the steamer was as messy an event as Wake had known with a warship. Colliers came alongside and loaded pallets that were swung down to them, then hauled up by blocks and tackle. Passengers were asked to remain out of the way as the crew turned to and lugged the bags, each weighing one hundred pounds, from the cargo pallets down into the coal bunkers. Soon, fine black dust was everywhere and several ladies were making a fuss about what it had done to their dresses and their hair.

It took all day to load the coal, then stow and tamp it down. The crew that had been on the loading detail was given that night off. They looked exhausted to Wake. At sunrise, however, the ship came to life again, powered up her hook and steamed northeastward, toward the Iberian Peninsula and Europe.

"Three days till Cadiz, Peter. Planning on going ashore?" asked Allen that night as they watched the sunset astern from the quarterdeck.

"I might. Don't know yet." Wake was thinking of Linda and the children.

"Might do you a spot of good, my friend." Allen and Wake had become close, and he knew about Linda's letters and Useppa's ailments. "Cadiz is an old navy liberty port and I know my way around a bit. I'll buy the first drinks!"

Wake didn't feel like going ashore but felt his resolve failing. "You know what? I just might let you, Pete."

"Said and done, then. The cousins from opposite sides of the pond will have a holiday in Spain! It'll be our very last chance before we fall under the God-forsaken discipline of our fleets over in the Med, Peter. I really must insist that we enjoy it while we have it."

Wake smiled at his friend's enthusiasm. Other than diplomatic affairs, he hadn't had a run ashore with a friend in years. Key West came to mind.

"*Carpe diem*, Pete. Let's do it. *Spain* . . . here we come."

11

Spain

Allen's tone was reverential, as if in a cathedral. "Well there it is, Peter. A few miles off that cape the greatest sailor in our navy won his greatest victory and lost his life doing it. And the Royal Navy's never been the same since."

"Quite a sight. The wind that day was from the west, if I remember the history lesson correctly," said Wake.

He had heard of Cape Trafalgar all his life and now he was staring at the flat-topped mountain that ran right down to the edge of the sea, its black bulk looking like a huge ironclad putting out from the coast. Wake knew that the combined French and Spanish fleets had gone into a standard battle line on that afternoon of October 21, 1805, full of confidence that the British fleet was outgunned and outmanned. Horatio Nelson proved them wrong. He didn't go into a battle line but instead told his ship captains to charge ahead and close to within pistol shot. They decimated the enemy.

The rail was lined with passengers, mostly British, gazing at Trafalgar, their first landfall in Europe. Armchair admirals were pointing out where various ships had been, impressing the ladies and making Wake and Allen laugh.

"It really must have been something that day, Pete. Well over a hundred ships in all," Wake said in wonder.

"Yes, I think so too. Never been in a large fleet action myself. Just small stuff out in the empire. Still deadly, though."

"I haven't either. I spent the war in Florida and the Caribbean. The fleet actions were out on the rivers and up at Mobile and Norfolk."

Allen nodded. "I don't regret it. Do you?"

"No, and let's hope neither of us ever has to see a fleet action in the future."

"Well said. Say, it looks like we may arrive in time for dinner ashore."

The city of Cadiz was beginning to show on the starboard bow, low among the coastal mountains. Other ships were all about them, dozens of them—the shipping lanes between the Mediterranean and northern Europe went right past Trafalgar.

Wake's heart was beating faster as he took it all in. He was now in the Old World. He found it both fascinating and intimidating.

Trinidad got a pierside berth right away without having to spend a week using lighters out in the anchorage. They were lucky, Monroe told them with a wink. But then he went on to tell them that the real reason was that the steamship line found it cheaper to bribe the port officials and get the ship offloaded and reloaded relatively quickly rather than wasting time and money and incurring the wrath of the passengers while they waited at anchor.

As a result of this "luck," passengers could conveniently disembark directly to the dock after the steamer was tied up. The steamer would be there for several days, and Wake and Allen discussed the pros and cons of ranging inland beyond the port.

Wake didn't want to spend the money, since he had a family who depended on his pay. Allen, who was single, tried to overcome Wake's hesitance by explaining that it wouldn't cost that much, especially since Wake spoke a little Spanish and would therefore get better prices. He also pointed out that though they could get drunk at the port, they also could seize the opportunity and experience the real Spain if they went inland.

In the end Wake gave in and agreed to go with his friend on a two-day rail trip to Sevilla, home of the fabled Alcázar. They each quickly packed a small bag, shed their uniforms and were dressed in plain clothes by the time *Trinidad* was docked. Neither had that much civilian attire to wear and two days would stretch it, but both wanted to be free of the restrictions of a uniform. By this time his reservations were gone and Wake was excited to be seeing a land he had studied in school and whose naval officers he had known in the Caribbean.

They wormed their way through the crowd of passengers on the salon deck beseeching the ship's staff for information about going ashore, finally getting down the gangway and onto the large stone dock. Immediately they were mobbed by cab drivers, pimps, beggars, and tourist guides—all of whom looked shady to Wake. Allen led them through the noisy confusion to a taverna nearby. Inside he found that the owner spoke English and arranged for a quick meal and subsequent transport to the train station. When they finally got on the train, a rickety affair that appeared barely capable but was at least bound for Sevilla, both collapsed on a bench seat laughing. They had been in Spain for only an hour and already were overwhelmed by the chaotic sounds, sights, and smells.

The train was scheduled to arrive in Sevilla in four hours, clanking along through the rolling hill country of southern Spain. Due to frequent inspections of documents by authorities at the various stops, a water leak in the boiler, and a small blockage on the tracks, it got there ten hours later, just before dawn.

As the car swayed precariously from side to side with the

screeching wheels and creaking wood frame creating a nearly deafening noise, they met Father Juan Muñosa. He was an English-speaking Jesuit headed for the cathedral at Sevilla after having completed a three-year assignment in Texas. Intrigued by the notion of American and British naval officers visiting Sevilla as tourists, he briefed them by the dim light of a gyrating lantern about the Spanish civil war that was periodically reigniting.

He explained that there were generally two sides—Radical-Liberals who were anti-throne and somewhat anti-Church, and the Carlists, who were conservatives and pro-monarchy and pro-Church. The Liberals, who had kicked out Queen Isabella in '68 with the help of the conservatives, had become too overbearing, attacking the Church and making life miserable for many of their supporters. The Radicals had even declared October tenth, the birthday of Isabella, formerly celebrated every year, to be a day of reflection, not a national holiday. Taxes, conscription, and a radical oppression of devout Catholics had sparked a guerilla war that never really ended.

This left the conservatives, known as the Carlists for their support of Isabella's uncle Carlos, as the opposition. The Carlists wanted to put Carlos on the throne and restore autocratic control; the Radicals and Liberals wanted to have a dictatorship in the style called for by the Internationale, a group formed in the revolutions of the late 1840s. Neither group could control the Spanish Parliament, known as the Cortes, neither group could win a decisive victory, and periodically the army would declare for one side or the other, skewing the political landscape all out of kilter.

Currently, Father Muñosa said, Spain was officially a republic with an elected parliament, but no one thought the democracy would last long. A dictatorship, either by the Radicals or by the Carlist monarchists, seemed to be in the future, which he said made him sad. He warned Allen and Wake not to take sides—that already the butchery of the war was infamous and in the heat of emotion no one would care if they were foreign tourists.

"And remember this, my son," Muñosa said, looking at Wake. "The monarchists are no friends of democracy, especially American democracy. They hate you for your perceived intervention in favor of the revolutionaries in Cuba. They hate you for threatening them with your navy back there in November—and, of course, more recently here in Spain at Barcelona and Málaga, when you sent warships to protect your citizens. They hate you most of all for making them look weak in front of their own people and the powers of Europe. Do not give them a chance to express that hate, Lieutenant."

It was a sobering lesson and Wake began to regret leaving to go inland, away from the protection of the *Trinidad.* Allen, though, had no such qualms.

"Oh well, my friend. Remember? *Carpe diem. Carpe diem* and see the glory of Spain."

The train station was deserted, except for the bodies. At first Wake thought they were dead, but then saw them stirring off the floor as the disembarking passengers moved off the train cars. Soon they stood, waiting for the crowd to move through them to get to the station gates. The filthy drunks and beggars, reeking of urine and wine, started touching the passengers, hands going into their pockets, while moaning and muttering unintelligible words. Many of the vacant-eyed men wore remnants of different types of uniforms, the military detritus from years of internal war. Some appeared to be semi-lunatics.

When Wake felt fingers in his coat pocket he instantly reacted with an elbow to the throat—the man gasped for air and moved away toward another potential victim without retaliation to Wake, almost as if he expected to be hurt. Shouts of rage toward the men didn't deter them, only painful action could stop them. Even after the war in America, which dwarfed the one in

Spain by size and scope, Wake had never seen such depravity. Allen and Wake quickly walked out of the station and into fresh air, neither saying a word but both shaken. Then they looked up.

The skyline of the city was starting to silhouette against the dawn and it was an awe-inspiring sight. Across the Guadalquivir River were the palaces and cathedrals of old Spain. Seventy miles up the broad river, Sevilla was the designated royal port of deposit for the riches of the New World during the first two hundred years of the Spanish global empire, and the wealth of that time was reflected in the domes and spires and towers that gracefully filled the sky. In the middle was a tall slender tower, which Allen said must be La Giralda, the ancient minaret of the Moors.

"And look over there!" exclaimed Allen. "That's where Father Muñosa was headed, the Catedral de Sevilla, largest one of Gothic design in the entire world. Oh, there's the Casa de Pilatos from the Moors. And that over there must be the Alcázar. Just look at that, Peter, the fabled Alcázar . . ."

Wake was astonished by the vision before him, his mind going back to his school days in New England. "A history lesson in stone."

"Incredible, simply incredible . . ." said Allen.

"And I always thought Havana was impressive. Now I know where the real money went," chuckled Wake.

They walked along the river, past the Spanish Navy docks and over a long stone bridge, crossing into the central part of the city. Wake saw that the banks of the river were sandy and wondered what the depths were. It must have been difficult to sail up to Sevilla all those years, he guessed, but they had to since the city was the most secure location for the riches against the pirates of the coast.

The center of the city gave the opposite impression from the train station. Wake noticed that the city had wide tree-lined boulevards and massive buildings, and that it was clean and the people well clothed. He saw no beggars and few policemen, only people starting their day and going about their lives. Many people gave them morning greetings, women smiled, and music—even at that time in the morning—could be heard everywhere. It was a normal working city like any other, but within a living museum of some of the most famous historical buildings in the world.

Father Muñosa's warning came to his mind. Here there was death and treachery? Amidst this splendor, this celebration of what Spain once was and could be again? Perhaps the priest was just overly cautious, he thought.

Three blocks into their walk they came upon a Hotel Lancaster and entered inside. It was owned by an elderly but tough-looking Englishman, George King, and his Spanish wife Carlota. King smiled when Allen reacted to his name.

"Yes, my father had a sense of humor when he named me. But The Andrew had none when they took me fifty-five long years ago. My sarcastic name did me no good then!"

They got a room on the third story with two cots for the night. Intending to get some rest before setting out to see the sights, they ended up talking for a long time about what they had experienced so far. Finally, the two exhausted travelers closed their eyes, snoring within minutes.

Wake heard a thud on the door and King's thundering voice—the old topman in him coming out.

"You said to get you up at noon. Well, noon it is, gentlemen!"

They got up and performed their toiletries, then went down to a lunch of gazpacho. King loaned them his tattered map of the old city, oriented them on it, and wished them well. As they walked out the front door he called to them.

"Gentlemen, you are young men in a very old city. Beware of what you do. Stay in the main areas and do not, under any circumstances, initiate any involvement with any policemen or soldiers. Just ignore them and stay as far away from them as possible. But, of course, have a good time."

The day was bright and cool, a perfect day for walking. Wake translated various signs the best he could for Allen. The British Marine, who had served as an assistant attaché in Egypt, explained how the Muslim architecture they saw, built when the Moors ruled the peninsula, incorporated complex curves and mosaics. After walking for an hour they stopped at a café, sat at a street-side table, drinking cool invigorating sangria served by a pretty girl who spoke English.

"I think I know why George King never left Sevilla," said Allen, watching the girl gracefully walk away to the kitchen and return with their food.

Wake remembered the Latin beauties of the Caribbean. "Oh yeah, Pete, to be sure. Many a sailor has left the sea for the ladies of Spain. It's their eyes, I think. Same thing in the Spanish West Indies."

"Lieutenant Wake, my dear chap," Allen said with a roguish grin, "I do believe that attraction has to do with far *more* than merely their eyes. . . ."

Just then an ornate carriage came down the street and passed by the café. In the front passenger seat were two matrons in black and in the rear were two beautiful teen-aged girls in brightly colored dresses, holding multicolored fans and smiling toward them. The girls spoke to each other and glanced back at Wake and Allen, suddenly spreading their fans wide and then placing them horizontally along their right cheeks, then giggled and put their fans in front of their mouth and nose. Wake didn't understand the humor but thought it quaintly cute.

"It is a festival day, señores," explained the serving girl. "That is why they are dressed in such a fashion and parading through the streets in their family's carriage. By custom they are forbidden to talk with men who are not a brother or father, but they are speaking to you through Sevilla's language of the fans."

Allen looked around. "The what? What in the world did they say to us?"

"When the fan is placed by the cheek it means 'I like you.' When it then goes in front of the mouth it means 'please kiss me.' They liked you both. Very much."

"Good Lord. I never saw such a thing. How wonderful. But what about those older motherly types in the front?"

"Those are the chaperones—old women with no humor, who are there to make certain the language is only with fans. They have but to say a word to the driver and he would strike into your face with his horse whip."

"Whoa, now *that* sounds serious!" laughed Wake as Allen grimaced.

The serving girl's face tightened as she watched the carriage clatter away. "They are rich Carlistos and the driver is one of their trained dogs. Whipping a man in the face is nothing compared to what else they have done to the people of Spain."

Her hostile tone brought the priest's warning to Wake's mind. "Hmm . . . an expensive lesson learned cheaply, eh Lieutenant Allen?" he said.

"Very cheap, my friend." Allen's hand touched his face. "Very cheap, indeed. What a strange place we've found ourselves in."

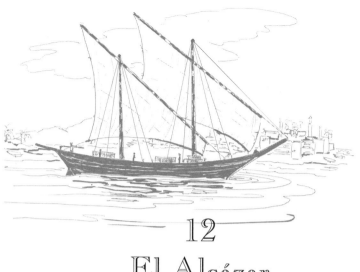

12

El Alcázar

Wake and his friend wandered into the very oldest part of the city, where the streets became snaking alleyways with frustrating dead ends, and they soon lost all sense of direction. They were in the heart of Sevilla, a city created by the Muslim Moors of Africa who had ruled Spain for almost six hundred years. Looking up as they walked under the shadows of arches and towers and domes, the antecedents of which had been in Damascus and Baghdad a thousand years earlier, the two officers were enthralled by the ambiance of the city.

The pastel colors and sensual curves and intricate mosaics of the buildings were complimented by guitar music with a staccato beat and smells of cooking fish and chicken coming from the many tiny tavernas. Roses and gardenias added their own scent everywhere, and the hourly bells of the cathedral were echoed by dozens of smaller churches across the city.

It was a world where the mysterious twelfth-century East met the modern nineteenth-century West—and Wake found himself intrigued by the Islamic culture that had produced such beauty so long ago. He, like so many other Westerners, had thought Muslims backward and primitive. Walking through Sevilla replaced that image and made him want to learn more about a people who, as Allen explained, had brought knowledge in science and the arts to half the known world during the Dark Ages—a time when much of Europe had reverted to wearing animal skins.

"I saw things somewhat similar in Egypt, but nothing as splendid as this. Just beautiful, really." Allen looked up. "How does one take it all in?"

"You know, I admit I was wondering for a while why I made the trip. But this is more than worth the problems of getting here," added Wake.

After admiring the Spanish Naval Academy, they turned a corner and found an open plaza facing a giant arched portal in a fortress wall thirty feet high. Over the entrance was a fierce-looking lion grimacing in the intricate façade, with the shield of the Christian kingdoms of Spain below him. Incongruously, Arabic script went across the base of the façade, with mosaics decorating the borders.

"I do believe we have arrived at the fabled Lion's Gate of the Alcázar, my friend," Allen beamed with pleasure. "It was built by Moorish workmen for King Pedro the Cruel of Castile six hundred years ago. Always wanted to see it after studying about it for years, and now here we are."

Allen examined the Arabic inscription. "Well, now. Look at that. It's a Qu'ranic verse. I've seen that written before—'the one true God is Allah.' "

"You can read Arabic?" asked Wake.

"No. Wish I could, but I've seen that verse all over Egypt and recognized it. The inside of the Alcázar is said to be absolutely beautiful." He sighed. "I can't get this close after all these years and not see it. Come on, I'm going inside. "

Wake wasn't so sure. "Those soldiers over there look pretty serious, Pete. I don't think we can go in there."

A soldier in dress uniform was at parade rest in front of the entrance, watching the crowd of pedestrians. Against the massive wooden doors, two more soldiers stood. All three had fixed bayonets on their rifles, which, Allen observed with surprise, were the newest type of German Mausers.

A large group of about forty men, apparently city and church leaders by their dress and manner, came down a side street, crossed the plaza and headed for the archway without slowing. The soldiers opened the doors and stood at attention, eyes straight forward.

"Ah, ha! Just the thing. Thank you, Allah," Allen jovially commented as he joined the back of the group, some of whom were conversing in somber tones.

Wake followed, trying to stop his friend with a hushed voice. "Pete! No. We can't do this. . . ."

The soldiers presented arms with a synchronized crash of rifles as the group approached the portal. Wake struggled to understand what the men in the group were saying in the unusual lisping Andalusian dialect. He caught a couple of the words and hoped that he misunderstood them.

"Can't stop now, Wake. Good God, man, this is my chance to see the inside of the fabled *Alcázar!* Besides, Peter, in for a penny—in for a pound," Allen insisted as they all walked through the archway and entered a small patio.

Heading across the patio toward another archway, the group continued without slowing as the heavy doors thundered shut behind them. When the lone soldier inside the gate looked the other way, Wake grabbed Allen and pulled him into a side room.

"Pete!" Wake whispered into Allen's ear. "I just got part of what these people were saying. They're saying something about executing insurrectionists, and it sounds like they're getting ready to do it right now. Right here! I think these are the Carlists we've heard about. These fellas aren't playing around, Pete. Let's get out of here. Now."

The Marine's face lost its humor. "Oh, well, I guess that does put a bit of a different flavor on it, doesn't it?" Allen gazed at the ornate patterns in the gingerbreading on the walls and columns around him. "Damn it all, though, I really wanted to see the Alcázar. But yes, I know, of course you're right."

He peeked around the wall. "Hmm . . . that soldier chap is standing on the inside of the gateway, so we'll have to get out through another door. Let's go this way. . . ."

They went through interior doorways from room to room, the latticed windows to their left allowing sunlight to filter in from the various patios and give a kind of half-light effect, enhanced by the shadows from the delicate patterns. Wake was just about to comment about how deserted the palace seemed to be when a female voice in the lilt of Andalusian Spanish softly called out to them from a dark corner.

"*Perdidos, señores?*"

Wake couldn't see well, but guessed her to be behind a latticed wall he could barely discern. She had asked them if they were lost.

"*Sí, señora. Estamos perdidos. ¿Dónde esta la puerta?*"

She answered in very good English, vaguely amused. "Oh, not only are you lost, but you are Americans who are lost. And in the Alcázar, of all places. Why are you in here?"

Wake looked at Allen and said, "Very good question, señora, and one that I was about to ask my friend here. We are tourists, passengers from a British steamship at Cadiz. We always wanted to see your famous city, took the train, and here we are, apparently lost."

"But how did you get in?" the voice asked, growing wary.

"Well, we simply walked in with a group when they opened the doors, madam," interjected Allen, attempting to sound innocent. "Are tourists not allowed to visit?"

"An American and a *Britisher!* This is getting much more interesting. Of all the foreigners that could be inside the Alcázar, you are certainly the least welcome. I think your story has, as I have heard said in English, *holes* in it. Very big holes."

Wake tried a change of tack. "Ma'am. Your English is excellent and we thank you for your kindness. But it appears we have entered the wrong area. Can you help us to find our way out?

"You mean escape?"

"Oh no, we are not prisoners, ma'am. We just want to leave."

The voice came closer in the darkness. "*Everyone* is a prisoner of one kind or another at the Alcázar, gentlemen."

She emerged from the shadows into the dim light, a woman of perhaps thirty dressed in expensive yet simple taste, the classic beauty of her face and her deportment indicating that she was from the upper classes. Wake noticed a heavy gold ring on her left hand and wondered who her husband was.

"Pardon my manners. I am Peter Wake, ma'am. And this is my friend and fellow passenger, Peter Sharpe Allen. I'm sorry for the unusual circumstances of our introduction."

She stood there for a moment, examining them. "I am Doña Carmena Garza Rodriguez del San Anton, wife of Colonel-General Oswaldo Garza, commander of the royal guard regiment for the prince regent, who will be the next king of Spain. And make no mistake about it, gentlemen—you are both now prisoners within the walls of the Alcázar, the fortress of the kings of Spain for the last eighteen generations."

Wake glanced at Allen and seethed, "I can't believe I let you lead me into this."

Allen held up his hands and shrugged. "I'm sorry. I know it's a bit of a bloody cock-up, Peter, but really, I'm sure cool heads will prevail here." He turned his attention to Carmena Garza. "Madam, this is a misunderstanding—"

A single deep-throated scream, in piercing agony, knifed through the room from somewhere in the palace. It echoed several times in the nearby courtyards, then faded.

"This particular room is known as the Ambassador's Chamber," the woman began in a strange monotone, as if in a trance, ignoring the scream. "It was built to impress foreign ambassadors by having them come through the many elaborate rooms from the entrance and then wait here for the king to summon them. They were to be impressed by the grandeur of Spain. Are you impressed yet, Mr. Wake and Mr. Allen?"

Another scream, this time muffled at the end, came from outside the room. This is a nightmare, Wake told himself.

"I said—*are you impressed yet,* gentlemen?"

Allen answered. "By the building yes, but what's going on here, madam? This is no longer amusing."

She sighed. "Why, we are reestablishing the monarchy, gentlemen. One person at a time."

Allen gave Wake a concerned look just as the sound of several soldiers' boots reverberated through the hall nearby, getting closer. Before either man could say a word, the woman quietly said, "Be *very* quiet and follow me," then disappeared back into the shadow again.

The long passageway grew narrower as they went further. It let in just enough ambient light to allow them to see their way along the twists and turns. The woman was far ahead of them, her footsteps barely audible. By the sounds behind them, the soldiers seemed to be heading somewhere else. Suddenly it got lighter in the passageway and Wake and Allen started up a narrow rough-stoned circular stairway, emerging bent over through a short door into a room filled with light from open windows.

Wake looked around. They had emerged from an entrance covered by a panel of the wall. A hidden entrance. The woman was standing by one of the windows and pointed outside. "Ah, yes. There are some our patriots now, doing the future king's work."

Wake and Allen looked out the window and down into another courtyard three floors below. Half a dozen hooded men with hands bound behind them were standing in a row. A man dressed in black came up behind one of the prisoners, gripped his shoulder forcefully, and raised an object that Wake couldn't discern. In an instant, he slashed a large shining, curved knife across the man's throat, the victim screaming for a mere second before collapsing in spasms. In an unseen corner of the courtyard a voice made some kind of pronouncement and a group of people applauded. Wake could hear his heart pounding as the woman spoke in her eerie tone again.

"You see, gentlemen. The Alcázar is not just a useless historical relict. Spain is not simply a quaint land of past romance. Oh no, we are a modern nation in the nineteenth century, a global empire. An enlightened people led by a benevolent Church. But it appears that we still need a king and his noblemen to lead us— and of course, to make those difficult decisions," she nodded toward the execution ground, "of life and death in these trying times."

Wake and Allen turned from the window to the woman, faces registering their shock. "Madam, I really think that . . ." Allen started, stopping when she held up her hand.

"Call me Carmena, please. I think we are going to be close friends very soon. In fact, I think that all three of us will be dead, by the hand of those men in the patio, within minutes if we are not close friends."

She went to the paneled wall across from where they had emerged and knocked four times, then two more. A short section of the pale green paneling on the wall was pushed open by a man inside a tiny hidden cubicle, who quickly stood and stretched to full height, eyeing Wake and Allen closely. He embraced the woman, speaking to her in Spanish. "English? These men are English, Carmena? Why are they here? Will they help?"

She answered in English. "One is an American who speaks Spanish, the other is English. They *say* they are tourists, but with the actions of the American and British navies lately I think the timing is very suspicious. And they have no choice about helping us—if they want to live. I will explain it to them after the tunnel."

The man tightened his face, speaking English to Wake. "Do what she says."

Wake stood there, trying to fathom what he was involved with and how to get out of it—and trying to control the anger at himself for stupidly going along with his friend, like some youngster on a dare. He and Allen were in a very dangerous spot, one for which their governments would correctly deny any responsibility. After her comment, he didn't dare tell Carmena their profession.

Another scream rent the air from below, followed by hands clapping. Allen, visibly shaken, moved toward the main doorway until Carmena said, "No! They will see you that way. We will all escape this way."

She gathered her skirts, ducked down, and reentered the passageway they had come through, quickly moving down the steps. Wake and Allen stayed close behind her with the mysterious man in the rear, shutting the panel behind him. Instead of returning to their original place on the first floor, she made a right turn at the second level into a passage Wake hadn't noticed before. A moment later they entered an even dimmer room, looking through thickly latticed windows down onto yet another small patio on the floor under them.

"We will stay here for a moment to listen. Few come here anymore. These were the harem's quarters for the caliph when the Muslims ruled. We can see out but they cannot see in."

Wake ran out of patience, grabbing her arm. "All right, Carmena, we'll wait here for a moment. Now, what *exactly* is going on?"

"I will tell you later. Shh . . ." She shook free of his grip and cocked her ear, listening. Wake heard it too. Boots again, this time in the patio below. Angry shouts echoed. Wake understood a man to say in an apologetic tone that he had searched something, but the rest was unintelligible. Another shout, a command perhaps.

Carmena smiled, looked at her companion and whispered in Spanish. "They know."

13

Disturbing the Bishop of Sevilla

The four of them crawled back into the tunnel and waited there three hours by Wake's watch, which he saw by the light of a match from Allen. Crouching in the dark with his ear to the wood panel, Wake listened to Carmena explain what they had gotten themselves into when they entered the ancient fortress.

The man beside Carmena was Manuel Salmerón, son of Nicolás Salmerón, one of the leaders of the Republicans in the Spanish Cortes, or parliament. The Republicans were trying to build a coalition of all the parties to unify the country, and Salmerón senior was widely regarded as most probably the next prime minister. But only a few days earlier General Pavia, the captain-general of Madrid who was allied with the Radicals and Democrats, had declared against the federalist Republican government and called on the other national parties, except for the Carlists, to form a new government.

She explained that the men in the Alcázar were Carlists who were executing local Republicans first, before embarking on a campaign against Pavia and the Radicals. The royal guard regiment her husband commanded was not a real regiment in the army, but a unit of German mercenaries hired by the Carlists to form a cadre around which the people would be expected to rally.

Carmena's husband and a few Carlists had been living at the Alcázar for five months as part of the coalition government. They, and others in positions of power within the city, had been waiting for an opportune moment to begin another attempt at restoring the reign of the monarchy and the Church. Her husband had been promised a title of nobility, a grant of lands in the Phillipines and Cuba, and the proceeds from the tenants on them. General Pavia's declaration had given them the anarchy they needed, and the Carlists had moved their mercenaries into positions around the city the previous day. The small regular army guard detail at the Alcázar left when the mercenaries arrived, and the regular Spanish Army garrison at the main fortress outside the city had not decided which side to take as of early that afternoon.

Wake didn't understand. "But why are you with Manuel?"

"Because he is my lover and my leader. I am a Republican."

"A Republican? Then why are you married to your husband, the Carlist?" Wake insisted.

"I can assure you it was not my idea or choice, Mr. Wake. It was arranged in the old manner, years ago, when I was sixteen. I have been a prisoner in my marriage and a prisoner in the Alcázar. Tonight, his men have found me missing and their suspicions of my affair will finally be confirmed." She took an audible breath. "When my husband finds out, he will give orders for me to be killed. His honor demands it."

"It's eighteen-seventy-four for God's sake, not the Middle Ages. This is insane," muttered Allen.

"Yes, Mr. Allen, my life has been insane for many years— until Manuel, two years ago. And tonight the insanity will stop. One way or another."

"What do you want *us* to do?"

"I know a way out of the Alcázar. Once we escape, you will get us aboard that British ship at Cadiz and we will leave Spain.

You are an unforeseen gift of good luck—our way out of the country. They won't publicly search a British ship, especially after what happened at Santiago in Cuba last year. They are still afraid of the British."

Wake remembered the *Virginius* incident where the local Spanish general in Santiago went into a rage and began shooting American and British citizens who had been traveling on a British ship suspected of supporting rebels. The Royal Navy had arrived and the executions stopped. That was when Porter had mustered the American fleet at Key West.

"And if we don't?" he asked. "We could just walk up to these men and say the truth—that we are foreign citizens who are lost. America and Great Britain are not part of this civil war. We might get killed, but we also might get out of here. Staying with you increases the likelihood of getting ourselves killed."

Carmena's tone chilled Wake. "I have absolutely nothing to lose. If you walk out there and surrender, then I will too, and tell them that you have been hiding with us. You know what will happen then. You just saw an example. And I do not think you are mere *citizens*. I am not sure what you are, but you both walk and talk differently from mere citizens. The Carlists will find out exactly what you are—as you die slowly."

"That's blackmail, madam," said Allen.

She hissed her reply. "Precisely . . ."

Wake forced himself to be calm and think the situation through. Once they got out of the Alcázar using the woman's escape route, they could attempt to get away from them and make their way back to the ship.

Then, as if reading his mind, she shook her head. "And should you try to abandon us outside the walls we will commit suicide by calling for a policeman and letting him know about you two. The police are controlled by the Carlists. Since we would die anyway without a way out of Spain, I will make sure you do too."

"That would be your word against ours, madam, and you are

the perceived traitor," Wake countered, trying to control his rage. He hated her attitude.

"The perceived *leader* of the traitors, Mr. Wake. My last confession will be about how you hid in the Alcázar after observing the executions. At that point they will not care who or what you are. They eliminate unfriendly witnesses. You will never see daylight once they seize you."

Manuel broke his silence and said, "Stop this sparring of words. Either come with us or do not. We are prepared to die. Are you?"

Allen lit another match, its flare making a ghoulish sight in the tunnel. All their faces reflected strain, but the woman's was the most determined.

As the light dimmed Wake looked from Carmen to his watch. It would be dark outside by now. He glanced at Allen. "Well, old *chap*. I think it was you who said 'in for a penny, in for a pound.'"

"Yes. One of my weaker moments in life . . ." came back out of the darkness.

"Carmena, when do you want to try this?"

"Now. It is time."

A sliver of moon shown through the window as they climbed out of it one by one onto a ledge along the inside of the walls facing the large plaza known as the French Gardens. Filing along the ivy-covered ledge with Carmena in the lead, they made their way to a trellis of flowering bougainvillea. They climbed carefully around the bush's needlelike thorns, then lowered themselves to the ground, Allen stifling an expletive when he lost his footing. Soldiers were everywhere along the tops of the walls and Wake couldn't see how they could possibly escape, but followed directly behind Carmena, keeping one hand on her shoulder.

She led them along the bottom of the wall to another building. Climbing an orange tree, she leveraged her way up and over an ornate balcony on the second floor, whispering for the others to hurry as an officer walked by sixty feet away by a large entrance.

Once they had all climbed the tree and reached the balcony, Manuel shook his head at her. "Your room? You led us *here*?"

"Safest place in the Alcázar right now," she said. She went thru the interior door to her bedroom without hesitation and out into a hall. They waited while she walked down the dark hall into another doorway, then waved for them to follow. It was a lady's attendant's quarters and the side wall had a door that led to another balcony. Manuel smiled, for he knew it well. It was the private place at which they had met for over a year.

She leaned over the railing and looked up, then over at each side. "The guards are not overhead right now, but they follow a schedule and will walk this way soon. We go now."

Carmena put a leg over the rail. Wake heard a grunt as she hit the ground, twenty feet below. He looked over and saw her crawling across the grass of a lawn. She made it to a tree by a side street, hidden behind the trunk.

"*¿Que fue éso?*" Wake heard a guard above him ask what that noise was. A tall peaked cap appeared over the ramparts.

"*Nada, 'migo. Un gato, probablamente,*" came another voice from farther along the top of the wall, speculating that it was a cat.

"*Entonces un gato gordo!*" replied the first guard, joking that it was a fat cat.

Wake and the other men on the balcony held their breath as they flattened themselves against the wall under the overhang. The first guard was still above them, looking around. Then Manuel let out a howling animal wail, screeching louder, then letting it fade away.

"*Ay!*" said the first guard to his comrade as he started to walk away. "*Sí, es un gato gordo, con amor en su mente! Pobre gato.*"

The men let out their collective breaths and Wake grinned at Manuel, who shrugged. Then the Spaniard tipped himself over the edge of the railing and landed in the grass, followed by Allen. Wake was last off the balcony, hitting the ground just as the guard reappeared. A pain shot up his right leg, but he knew it wasn't broken, just strained.

"*Alto! Alto, ahora!*"

Carmena and the others were waiting by the bushy tree along the street. When the guard issued the challenge for Wake to stop, she and Manuel started running across the street and down an alley. Allen said, "Run, Peter!" which Wake did at full speed, pain ignored as he imagined the rifle coming around and the sights centering on his back.

Wake made it to the tree and dashed across the street with Allen next to him, searching for their Spanish companions, but he couldn't see them. As they pounded over the cobblestone pavement, each step jolting his leg, he saw a hand beckon them into another alleyway and turned obliquely toward it, still running as fast as he could.

Behind them the alert was being raised by the guard and more shouts could be heard. Dogs started barking in the streets and alleyways and inhabitants leaned out of windows, asking what was happening, some threatening harm, thinking Wake and Allen were thieves.

Wake caught sight of Carmena turning a corner ahead of him and followed, almost colliding with her and Manuel. All four of them stood there a moment, chests heaving with the exertion and terror.

Manuel spoke first. "We go to the river, swim across to the other side and get to the train to Cadiz."

The others nodded and started behind him at a fast walk, spurred on by the sounds of soldiers running toward them. Manuel darted to the left and led them past a street, down an alleyway and into a plaza, in front of the Giralda Tower, the ancient Moorish minaret that was now part of the gigantic

Cathedral of Sevilla. He stopped abruptly and held up his hand for silence. Horses were coming from the riverside. Shouts of foot soldiers from the Alcázar in the other direction. They were trapped.

"Into the church!" Allen said as he ran to a heavy iron-studded door. It was locked. Wake ran to another, but it too was locked. There was a crumbling ancient wall further along. A portal in the wall was also locked. Wake ran to a gnarled olive tree next to the wall and launched himself up, flailing through the branches until he could grab the top of the stone wall and pull himself over to it. The Briton was next up in the tree and pulled Carmena aloft into the leaves, followed by Manuel.

Perched atop the wall, Wake heard the clatter of hooves close by and immediately dropped down through the dark into yet another large open space. As the horsemen arrived in the plaza, the others in the tree stopped in mid-motion while the cavalry circled within feet of them before splitting up to search the side streets. The last cavalryman rode off, and the fugitives dropped inside the patio, just as the soldiers on foot flooded into the plaza from two streets, fanning out and checking the doors of every building, including those of the church.

The four of them were gasping for air, leaning against the inside of the wall next to the huge closed portal. Above them stood the towering Giralda minaret, next to it the twin steeples of the cathedral. Wake peered through the dim moonlight and recognized orange trees dotting the vast stone-floored plaza. On one side, a hundred fifty yards away, was the gigantic cathedral and on the other two sides were four three-story buildings—the rectories and dormitories, he surmised. He wondered if the cathedral's doors facing the patio were locked.

"This is the old mosque's patio. The Patio de Los Naranjos, a thousand years old," Carmena explained between breaths. "It is part of the cathedral now."

"Then we should be safe," offered Allen, hopefully.

She shook her head. "No, *no!* Remember? The Carlists have

great supporters among the church leaders. Many in the Church want the monarchy back."

Wake recalled seeing men in clerical robes in the group that had entered the Alcázar. He hoped they hadn't taken part in the execution but remembered that one voice saying something that sounded religious.

"Oh bloody hell . . ." groaned Allen as he gave vent to his frustration. "This bloody, God-forsaken, maniacal, damnably convoluted, museum of a city is really making me friggin' angry now."

"Maybe we can wait here for a while and catch our breaths," Wake suggested. "Let things calm down a bit . . ."

Just then the door thudded loudly. Voices shouted for it to open in the name of the crown. Wake quickly surveyed his surroundings. Could they make the main doors of the cathedral before someone came out of the dormitory buildings and opened the door? Would they be seen by someone as they ran across the patio past the orange trees? The door thudded again, the commands more insistent. His mind was calculating the distance he'd have to cover, about to will his legs to run again, when he heard a vaguely familiar voice call out quietly in accented English.

"Hmm . . . I see you didn't heed my lesson on Spanish political affairs, gentlemen."

Wake almost fell down from the sight. It was the priest from the train. Carmena and Manuel looked like cornered dogs, their eyes wide and darting around, looking for escape. Wake felt his strength ebb as the priest stood there with a rueful look, gently shaking his head. Another thud boomed from the door beside them.

Allen looked at the priest and groaned again. "Well, if this doesn't just cap the friggin' night! I bloody well give up if God's against us. I can't run from Him."

"You should never run *from* Him, my son," said the priest with a smile. He calmly walked to the massive doors and opened the speaking port at eye level. His raised his voice, tone turned to dismissive, using the classical form of Spanish in addressing the soldiers outside.

"Yes, Captain? Is there something important for you to be waking us all up at this time of night. The bishop gets very angry when awakened for no good reason, and even angrier when it's a soldier *disrespecting* the house of the Lord. What is your precise name?"

"I am only a sergeant, sir. Sergeant Alonzo Padillo. Padre, I am very sorry—"

The priest nearly shouted. "A mere *sergeant*—not even a commissioned officer—dares to do this to the Cathedral of Sevilla?"

"Oh, I am so very sorry, Padre," said the soldier, whose dialect was of the lower class in the north of Spain. "But there are fugitives on the loose and we wanted to know if they had entered the patio or cathedral."

"No, they have not entered the cathedral! I have been on my nightly stroll and would have seen such a thing. Now, may the bishop and the rest of our religious community get back to sleep without any further disrespect or disturbance from *you?*"

"Yes, Padre. We are very sorry for disturbing you. My apologies. Please, sir, tell the—" but the sergeant never finished, for the priest slammed the port shut in his face.

The priest then held a finger up to his mouth and beckoned with his hand for Wake and the others to follow him as he strode rapidly across the patio. Several minutes later they were in a tiny room on the sixth floor of the cathedral, just off the Giralda Tower and near the belfry, again gasping for air from the steep climb. The priest produced a match and lit three candle sconces on the stone wall, their flickering illumination making an eerie scene. Then he sat on a small leather stool.

Amazingly to Wake, the priest was not out of breath and serenely motioned for them to sit on the bench against the wall as he intoned as if to a class on ethics. "Let the record of my life at the gate of Saint Peter accurately reflect that I did not *lie* to that unfortunate sergeant. I told him the truth when I said that I did not see anyone enter the cathedral at *that* particular point in time." He wagged a finger. "And I never said that I would not take someone into the cathedral later."

"Oh, I'm sure that Saint Peter knows that, sir," said Wake, his leg throbbing. "Thank you so much for giving us some respite, Padre. It's *extremely* good to see you again. May I introduce you to my companions? You remember Peter Allen, of course. This is Doña Carmena Garza and Manuel Salmerón. I believe you recognize those two last names."

The priest's smile disappeared as he nodded. Wake turned to the two stunned Spaniards. "And this is Father Juan Muñosa, a Jesuit who has just returned to Sevilla after many years absence. Pete and I met him on the train here. He warned us against getting involved in the political turmoil here. Unfortunately," he paused and glared at Allen, "we have."

"My dear Lieutenant Wake," said Muñosa. "I sense that there is an absolutely delicious story here and I would love to hear it." He spread his hands. "It's only two o'clock in the morning and I have nothing but time until first vespers at dawn."

Manuel was visibly confused. Carmena's eyes flared. "*Lieutenant* Wake?"

Allen looked at Wake and inhaled audibly. "Oh, my dear boy. This'll be a bit of a long story, won't it?"

14

The Perils of Land

It took an hour for Wake to tell everyone everything, starting with how he and Allen had met in the West Indies. He explained to Muñosa about Carmena and Manuel and the idea for an escape. During that hour the others sat silent—Muñosa enthralled with the story and Carmena and Manuel worried by it. Wake repeatedly emphasized that he and Allen were in Sevilla as tourists and that no one in authority, from any country, knew they were there.

Muñosa spoke up first when Wake had finished his narration. "So it appears that this is a tale of friendship," he gestured to Wake and Allen, "and of love." A nod went to Carmena and Manuel. "How very wonderful. It is all as if in a novel!"

He registered the surprise on their faces. "You expected reproach from me? You think that a priest, even an old one like me, does not appreciate a little intrigue and some romance? I am a Jesuit, not an ogre, my friends."

"Thank you, Padre," said Manuel. "Carmena and I are very much in love. We know well the Church's teachings, but don't know how to handle the situation."

Muñosa shrugged. "First things first, my children. Save your lives, then worry about the rules of the Church. You can repent later. Better yet, you can arrange an annulment according to the laws of God later. But for now, let's get you out of here and on that British ship at Cadiz.

"As for the situation in Spain, you know the Church has all kinds of leaders. Some of them are supporting the Carlists, some support the other factions. I support the people." He winked at them. "And after all of these years as a priest, I know a thing or two about intrigue and getting things done outside of the regulations myself."

Muñosa then suggested they use one of the secret tunnels below the cathedral that exited at the river. Few people knew of the tunnels, which were hundreds of years old. At the river he proposed that they could "borrow" a boat and make their way down the river to Sanlúcar and take a carriage from there to Jerez. At Jerez they could join the train to Cadiz. With luck, they would be at the ship by mid-afternoon. It would be up to Wake and Allen to get the two lovers aboard, however.

Manuel was about to speak, but Muñosa held up a hand and grinned. "But let us also bait the field in the other direction. Carmena, please write out a letter to Manuel, explaining that you will meet him at the carriage station in Córdoba to the east when the sun goes down. Put in it some affection, for spice to establish authenticity, and sign it with your full name, so it is obvious who wrote it. I will arrange for it to be found in a street on the north side of the Alcázar—the opposite side of the city from your route."

As the four of them began thanking him, Muñosa held up his hand again, looking serious. "To try to save lives is the right thing to do. I only ask one thing in return."

Wake asked, "What's that, Padre?"

Muñosa leaned forward, the grin returning. "I want a letter from *you*, Peter Wake, six months from now, telling how the rest of this tale finally unfolded—in exciting detail."

They descended to the deserted main sanctuary of the cathedral. The vast space, dimly lit by a few candles and smelling of sickly sweet incense, seemed ominous to Wake. Their footsteps echoed but Muñosa seemed unconcerned, saying that no one would be about at that time of the night. They followed him into the privileged chapel of the kings of Spain, dating from the thirteenth century. As they walked, Muñosa gave Wake a brief whispered recital of the cathedral's history, from Muslim mosque in the eleventh century to the third largest Gothic designed Roman Catholic cathedral in the entire world. Only the Vatican and Notre Dame were larger. " . . . as our brother priests from France keep reminding us," he explained with a shrug.

From the royal chapel they crossed to a corner where they reached the ancient treasury chamber by the main sacristy. Muñosa stepped into the shadow behind a column and Wake heard a grunt and the sound of stone grinding on stone. A moment later the priest reappeared, gave Wake a short sconce and lit it, then gestured to follow him as he went back around behind the column again.

One by one they said an emotional goodbye to Muñosa, then followed Wake into a small square hole in the wall where a section of the surrounding stone block had been pushed away. Once inside they descended rough steps into complete darkness as the stone block thudded shut behind them.

The tunnel was completely different from the one at the fortress. It was wet and rough-hewn and very small; in many places they had to walk bent over for quite a distance. Wake went in front with the light, examining the tunnel as he went. It dated from the Inquisition and, outside of a few Jesuits, no one knew of its existence, according to Muñosa.

When they reached the end they found the small boulder the

priest said would be there. Grunting with the effort, the men moved the rock and stepped back as a landslide rained down, filling the entrance with white sand to within a foot or two of the top. Clawing their way through it, they emerged into the night, Wake extinguishing the flame and all of them listening for any alarm. There was none.

Allen spotted the boat first, fifty yards away. It was a short wherryman's skiff, probably used for taking people across the river, and large enough to carry all of them. Better yet, it was tied up to a short wobbly-looking dock on their bank of the Guadalquivir. Allen started out for it after telling Wake, "Don't worry, Royal Marines know how to get out of trouble as well as into it, Peter. Please let me arrange our transportation, old son. Really, it's the least I can do."

Wake watched as his friend ran crouched across the sand and down through the slimy mud, climbed up onto the dock and crawled out to the boat. Then he was down in it and unlashing the line. Once free, the boat drifted downriver a short way and grounded at the bank, the Marine waving for them to join him. When they got there he shook his head and said, "Now I know why the owner left his boat in the water. He took the oars."

Wake looked at the eastern sky. The Giralda Tower was beginning to be silhouetted. They needed to go, immediately.

"Forget them. We'll ride the current, paddle and steer with our hands. Get in now, it'll be light shortly."

No one hesitated and they shoved off into the fast-moving cold waters of the Guadalquivir, flowing hundreds of miles from the snows of the Sierra Morena, west to the Atlantic Ocean.

An hour after the sun rose Wake woke up from a dream, but the nightmare around him was still real. Floating past the village of Trebujuena, he thought the reality preposterous, a situation that was beyond the power of any dream to conjure up. Here he was, floating on a boat with no oars, with three other fugitives, two of whom were leaders of a treasonous group and all of whom would be shot on sight, on a river flowing through a country in a civil war, totally against his naval regulations—and all because a man he really barely knew talked him into taking a once-in-a-lifetime opportunity to see an old building.

Manuel had been steering while the others rested, paddling with his hands to turn the boat and keep it in the current of the main channel. Wake estimated they were moving at four knots and with Manuel's information about the geography of the area estimated they would reach Sanlúcar in a few hours. No one had tried to stop them or even paid any attention, which Wake didn't understand. Then he remembered what day it was—Sunday. He realized that, ironically, the fishermen and bargemen of the river would probably be in church, maybe even some of them in the great cathedral at Sevilla.

His watch said one o'clock when they paddled their way to the opposite bank, just upriver from the town of Sanlúcar. Manuel took charge after they trudged up the bank, saying that he knew the area and where to get a carriage. Carmena explained that she had some money. The two officers walked along behind them, Wake wondering how he could get the two aboard the *Trinidad*. For some reason he didn't even know himself, it no longer occurred to him to not try and help them escape the country.

Slipping him some extra money and promising more, Manuel told the driver of an enclosed carriage at a livery to hurry, that they were enroute to a wedding in Jerez, an hour and a half away, and already late. Pocketing the money in one smooth motion, the driver never said a word about the wet and disheveled appearance of his passengers, who obviously were not going to a wedding. The jarring ride that followed stopped any plans of rest, but it did get them to Jerez by midafternoon, where they started to walk across the town to the train station.

When Wake heard English accents among the crowd in the main square and asked about them, Carmena explained that there were many immigrant residents from Great Britain there, Allen adding that some of the very best sherry wine came from the region. Carmena agreed, saying the name of the wine came from the inability of the British to pronounce Jerez correctly, Anglicizing it to sherry. By the time that conversation had ended, the foursome had completed their walk to the station. Manuel arranged the tickets while the others waited, Carmena eyeing Wake but saying nothing. As the shadows began to lengthen around them, the train left the station, bound for Cadiz, two hours away.

The wharf was jammed with people, cargo, wagons, carriages, and draft horses—a cacophony of sounds and smells and swirling motion. They stood a distance away, studying the *Trinidad* while her booms swung up and inboard as her loading was finished, passengers walking aboard, deck crew starting to secure her for sea. No chance for a stowaway brought aboard in the cargo, Wake realized. He looked in the harbor. There were no bumboats alongside the ship, so no way to get Carmena and her lover aboard that way. The police were checking papers at the gangway, but they had no false papers. That left only one way to get them aboard.

"Best way is to just stroll up that gangway like you own it," Wake said, hoping he sounded confident.

"Quite right, Peter," agreed Allen. "Command presence, that's what's called for now. Just like Father Muñosa at Sevilla."

"Ah, I do not know about that, Peter," worried Manuel. "It

will be difficult to get past those police guards. They are inspecting everyone."

Carmena spoke up. "No. It will work. Wait for the last-minute rush of people. That will overwhelm the authorities. They are the same around the world. When bureaucrats become overwhelmed they are not so vigilant."

They got in line, Wake knowing that their appearance would stand out. He was first and as he got to the control point of the Guardia civil police Wake saw the captain of the *Trinidad* standing at the main deck railing, surveying the scene below. An idea formed and he seized on it. Waving wildly, he yelled out, "Good afternoon, Captain! Lieutenant Wake here. I've brought some friends back to the ship to meet you."

The captain had met Wake only a few times and was not a close friend at all, but he did acknowledge the greeting with a puzzled look and noticeable wave of his hand, which was seen by the police officer at the gate. The ship's third mate, who remembered Wake well, was also at the gate. Wake loudly introduced him to Carmena and Manuel, using false names of Useppa and Sean Rork, vintners from Jerez, and repeating with pride that they were going aboard to meet the captain. Carmena and Manuel smiled, mumbled something and kept walking as the third mate said hello and turned to someone else who was asking him something. Faced with the obvious stature of Wake and his companions, the policeman didn't even ask for identification as they blithely walked right past him.

Once on the main deck the captain came over and asked Wake what he wanted. Wake, heart pounding, introduced his two Spanish companions, using the same names and explaining that they wanted to view the ship as possible transport for an upcoming trip to the West Indies. The two imposters muttered something about it looking pretty and began looking around at the boats slung in the davits as Wake thanked the captain for his time. He then turned to his companions and pointed out the ship's funnel, launching into an explanation of the reliability of her engines. The captain, still confused, was distracted by another person who wanted to know in imperious tones when exactly dinner was starting and with whom they were seated.

Wake and Allen led Carmena and Manuel away and down into their cabin, where all of them let out a collective gasp of relief. A moment later they heard the plaintive wail of the ship's whistle and the call of the stewards in the passageways for all non-passengers to go ashore.

"Ah, yes, back at sea!" said Allen with a contented sigh as he leaned back on his berth. "And I must say, very smartly done down there on the gangway, old chap. Was going to think of something along those lines myself, but you beat me to it, fair and square."

"Yes, we thank you so much, Peter," said Carmena, clutching Manuel's hand, her eyes filling. "We owe you our lives. We will never forget this."

Allen rolled over on the berth and gave the two lovers a disappointed look, quickly replaced by a grin. "My dear, it was *my* idea to go to Sevilla in the first place—had to practically drag this Yankee ashore. And the Alcázar? Why, it was *me* that led him inside, just as nice as you please. He copied that very plan on the gangway here." Allen theatrically rolled his eyes. "Oh well, imitation is the sincerest form of flattery, they say."

Wake nodded at his friend's irrepressible humor. "Well, you've certainly got me there, Lieutenant Peter Sharpe Allen, of Her Britannic Majesty's Royal Marine Light Infantry. And you're completely correct—if you hadn't gotten us into this mess, then it wouldn't feel so good to be out of it and back to sea where we belong."

He remembered the sensation of that rifle aiming at him and it reminded him of something he had discovered many years earlier, during the war. Sailors are always safer out at sea—away from the perils of land.

15

Goodbyes and Hellos

The Straits of Gibraltar were far narrower than Wake had always imagined, though the mountains on both sides being illuminated by the sun setting out over the Atlantic Ocean made the distance tricky to estimate. Looking like a section of the moon dropped down to earth, pocked gray cliffs—the famed Pillars of Hercules—rose up thousands of feet on the African side, like a wall barring passage into Morocco. The Spanish side was lower, more gentle, with high mountains further back from the coast, appearing as if the Iberian Peninsula had bowed down and invited the Moorish invasion a thousand years earlier. He looked for the famed Rock, but couldn't see it. Allen explained that it wasn't at the narrowest part of the straits, a mere ten miles wide or so, but actually around the inside corner on the Spanish side.

For hours they steamed east, approaching, then going through, the strait. They passed ship after ship coming out of the Mediterranean, most under sail but several steaming also. As the sun disappeared in a blaze of molten copper, they steamed past Cape Marroquí on the north and Cape Malabata on the south.

Long after Allen, Carmena, and Manuel left the cold windy deck, Wake stayed, bundled up and scrutinizing everything with a ship's telescope. Like most of the passengers who were making their first transit of the strait, he stood for hours wanting to memorize the sight, knowing that years later he would be asked about it when sitting in front of a warm fire on a cold night. Finally, well after passing the narrows, as blackness was enveloping the scene, he saw Gibraltar itself well off to port, a tall black shadow against the lights of the Spanish town of San Roque.

Allen had come back on deck and pointed out the sights to Wake—the jagged peak, the gentle lights in the town of Gibraltar, the fleet resting at the anchorage, and Cape Europa jutting out. He had been there as a young subaltern and knew every tunnel and fort. Allen told Wake that of all the honors they were authorized, the Royal Marine Light Infantry only carried one battle honor streamer on their regimental flag, the one for winning the 1704 battle that secured the Rock's possession for the Royal Navy and Great Britain. Since that time several attempts had been made to wrest the fortress away. All had failed. Allen said it was the most heavily fortified piece of British territory in the entire world. A legendary place for British sailors, it was also one of the few where British tars could have liberty ashore—captains knew there was nowhere for them to run.

That depressing thought brought Wake's mind back to the mail he had received on *Trinidad* while ashore in Spain—an unperfumed envelope from Pensacola. It was given to him after the ship left the port and he had read it alone in the cabin while Allen was out.

Pensacola, Florida   *December 28th, 1873*

Dear Peter,
I received your letter and Christmas presents today. Thank you very much for the lovely dress and robe from Puerto Rico. Even if I do say so myself (there is no one else here to tell me), they look very nice on

me. Sean is enthralled with his wooden boat and he is playing with it as I write this. Useppa loved wearing her beautiful little dress to church last Sunday, especially since her Daddy wrote that it was made for a princess.

I see you aren't coming home in June, but instead are heading to the Mediterranean for two years. I think you know what I think of that. Another naval wife told me just this week that officers who have served over five years can resign their commission at any time—that they're not bound by any further commitment to the navy. So it appears that you don't have to go to the European Squadron—you have chosen to go. Your children and your wife need you. If you need them, you should resign and be a husband and a father.

You can still be a sailor and love the sea on a merchant ship, but on your terms, not some politician's in Washington. Peter, the navy has used you and never appreciated your efforts and loyalty and sacrifice. You are just another cog in their mechanical beast of burden. When they are through with you, you'll be left high and dry on the beach, like so many others.

I do not understand why you choose them over us. What is this hold they have over you? I pray you will come to your senses.

Your loving wife,
Linda

He didn't know what to do. In so many ways she was right, absolutely right. But in one way she was wrong. He was a naval officer and didn't want to be a merchant marine seaman. He didn't want to carry cargo endlessly or, God forbid, be a fisherman. As a naval officer he was part of something more important, more useful. The navy had presented him with pain and frustration, but it had also enabled him to face challenges and have victories that few men ever knew. And he relished that. To pretend to be anything else would be a fraud. Wake decided to wait before he answered the letter. He needed time to think.

Allen knew about the letter and sensed his friend's quiet depression, but in the manner of warriors neither had spoken of it. It was something that would end badly either way, Allen thought, and silently wished Wake the strength to get through it.

The bright spot of the voyage from Cadiz had been that Carmena and Manuel—alias Mr. and Mrs. Sean and Useppa Rork, Irish-Hispanic vintners from Jerez—had managed to pull off the "accidentally stranded aboard" excuse to the purser and first mate. They paid for a first-class cabin—luxurious compared to Wake and Allen's second-class cabin—and passage all the way to Genoa, and were now being treated as important guests. It appeared that their escape was proceeding well, but they still stayed in their cabin most of the day, worried that someone might recognize them. They had no plans beyond Genoa, but Wake had faith that somehow they would be able to make their way in the world and overcome what might come.

And that made him wonder about how he would solve the major dilemma of his own life.

The first port after Cadiz was Palma de Mallorca, in the Spanish Balearic Islands. Warships from several nations, including Great Britain, were anchored out as the steamer came alongside the pier to offload and pick up cargo and passengers.

"What do you think, should I pay my respects to them? You can come along," offered Allen, looking at the Royal Navy sloop.

"I suppose you should, but I'm just not in the mood to go through the naval routine right now," answered Wake, thinking of Linda.

"Yes, of course, my friend. We can do that later. Let's go ashore for a walk and a drink."

He went ashore in plainclothes with the Brit—who had been there several times—Allen promising to show the American the giant Cathedral de Mallorca on the harbor front and suggesting that they perhaps get a bite to eat at one of the many tavernas.

"No escapades here, Peter," promised Allen.

"Gonna have to be none, Lieutenant Allen," answered Wake as they walked along the seaside promenade. "I used up all my good luck back in Sevilla and Cadiz."

Inside the cathedral, in reply to their question, a priest explained to them that the war raging on the Spanish mainland had not extended to the islands out in the Mediterranean, that the inhabitants of the city were not taking sides so far. "We are different people out here. Simpler, more traditional," he said. "Less liberal and involved in politics."

Wake wondered if that meant the Church's view of the conflict, and therefore the Carlists', was dominant locally, but he decided not to press the issue. The priest, a native Mallorcan, went on to explain with pride about the cathedral—that the golden sandstone structure's construction was begun six hundred years earlier out of gratitude by a Spanish sailor-king who had just survived a near-death experience. Hearing the tale, the two officers exchanged chagrined looks.

"Well, I certainly understand that completely," said Allen as they walked out into the sunlight. "Just might start a little chapel of my own back in Teignmouth when, and if, I return."

"I wouldn't bother, it'd probably crack open and fall down. . . ." quipped Wake.

"Quite humorous, old boy. Another example of your famed Yankee humor, I suppose—" Allen stopped in mid-sentence and touched Wake's arm.

"Say, don't look now, Peter, and keep walking. Is it my imagination, or is that army officer regarding us rather seriously? When you get a chance, see if you can nonchalantly glance back," asked Allen as they passed by the Spanish army's ancient arsenal and barracks across the street from the cathedral. An officer in full dress uniform, from the corner of his eye Wake guessed him to be the officer of the guard, was standing in front of the massive doors at the gate and watching them.

"Oh, Lord, I hope not," Wake whispered. "Keep on walking

and let's go around this corner and duck into a taverna. See if we can spot if someone follows us."

They moved up the Calle Palau, turned the corner and entered the Plaza Major in the center of the city, which was filled with hundreds of people walking in various directions. Wake scanned the buildings, looking for a taverna to enter. There were none facing the plaza, only government and church offices. He crossed over to the right edge of the plaza, with Allen following a few paces behind. At Calle Santa Clara they made another right and ducked into a doorway. Wake heard the ringing echo of hob-nailed boots coming into the street from the plaza.

"*¡Señor! ¿Un pasaje, por favor?*" Wake quickly called out to the driver of an empty carriage going by toward the plaza they had just left.

The driver stopped and waved them over, then took off once they were seated. Wake had no idea of where to tell the man to drive, so he gestured toward the plaza. As the carriage clattered along the stone street Wake and Allen saw the Spanish officer striding toward them, having just turned the corner himself. He was middle-aged, a captain or major, and his eyes were looking far ahead, straining to examine the people walking away. He wasn't eyeing the carriage coming toward him.

The naval officers gazed off to their right, hiding their faces as they rode by. Wake's mind was reeling. Why was that officer after them? Had the Carlists in Sevilla discovered their prey was on the *Trinidad?* Had their description been given out to all ports on her route? But no shout came and the carriage continued past.

Moments later the driver stopped in the middle of the busy plaza, wondering where his fares wanted to go. "*¿A dónde, señores?*"

"To a pub, by God!" blurted Allen. "I don't know about you, Peter, but I could damn well use a strong drink to steady my nerves!"

"*Un pub. Sí señores,*" said the driver with a shrug. Wake decided that was a good idea—lay low for a while and get some other local knowledge of the situation in Mallorca. Besides, he admitted inwardly, a stiff tot of rum sounded good. He let out the breath he'd been holding. Then he heard the boots again.

"¡*Pare el coche!* Stop!"

Both officers spun around in the seat, hearts sinking when they saw the Spaniard running toward them. The driver pulled in his reins with a jerk, glowering at the two foreigners in his carriage who had somehow gotten him involved with the military. The army officer slowed his approached. Wake saw that he didn't pull out his sidearm, then saw the man smile.

"You are English navy man, yes?" the officer asked.

Allen bristled and sat at attention. "Navy? Most certainly not, sir! I am one of the *Royal Marines* of her Britannic Majesty, Queen Victoria. Lieutenant Peter Sharpe Allen, at your service, sir."

Wake felt like shaking his head in amazement how his friend could be offended at this particular moment. The Spanish officer didn't understand the subtlety and continued.

"*Señor* Allen, yes? I have a *mensaje* . . . a message . . . for you from your ship. They say you are to go to your ship."

"My ship? I'm not aboard a Royal Navy ship here. I'm in transit." Allen looked at Wake as the Spaniard held up his hands.

"I find you and give the message, *señor.* Go to . . . your . . . ship. There," he pointed twice at the harbor. "Thank you." With that said the officer left, shaking his head. Wake heard the man muttering in Spanish about the things he was sometimes tasked to do by the *idiotas* above him in rank. In the back of the carriage the two friends looked at each other and burst out laughing, confusing the driver.

"Good Lord, I thought it was over there for a second," Wake declared. "I think I'm getting too old for this kind of thing."

"Me too. Now I suppose I'll have to go out to the ship and see what's what," said Allen. "They've probably changed my orders and want me assigned to that ship, but right now I still want that drink. Driver, on to *el pub!*"

"Good idea, Pete. I really need a drink about now, too.

Besides, it might be our last together," added Wake as the jarring carriage accelerated over the uneven pavement.

Moments later Allen exclaimed, "My God, Peter, look at that! He found one," as they rounded a corner down by the waterfront and stopped suddenly.

The driver turned around in his seat, beaming as he held his hand out toward O'Brien's Irish Pub. *"¡Señores, el pub!"*

Wake laughed. "Oh, boy. I can tell that this is gonna be a hell of a goodbye, Peter Sharpe Allen. A hell of a goodbye."

When Wake said goodbye to Allen at the pierhead several hours later, he asked him the question that had been on his mind since Barbados. "Pete, did they assign you to spy on me because of what happened at Antigua?"

The British Marine's face tightened. "Even if they did, I wouldn't be able to tell you, Peter. But, having said that, I don't think Great Britain has anything to worry about with you. And quite inexplicably, despite my reticence about fraternizing with you colonials, you've actually become my *friend*."

Allen changed the serious mood by breaking into a grin and clasped Wake's hand. "I'll see you somewhere in the Med, Peter Wake. And by the way, Yank, unlike the last few, next drink's on you!"

The British frigate left an hour after Allen reported aboard. That evening a bumboatman delivered a note to Wake aboard the *Trinidad*, which he read prior to dinner.

Lt. Peter Wake, USN
In transit aboard RMS Trinidad

Peter,   *2ⁿᵈ February 1874*
    They did change my orders. Aboard Immortalitie now, heading
immediately for Malta and Vice Admiral Drummond's flagship,
HMS Lord Warden. I guess they can't do without me anymore! The
Flying Squadron is combining with the Med Squadron for evolutions
in western Med. Should be interesting, but pretty dull compared to
our adventure in Spain. Maybe see you in Genoa.
                                                    Your friend,
                        Peter Sharpe Allen, Lieutenant, RMLI

The next morning Wake made his official visit to the American
consulate. The consul handed Wake a dark blue envelope, the
kind that came from the Navy Department. Wake had a fleeting
hope that it was a rescindment of his orders, but that was dashed
when he read it.

It was a routine change in orders, copies of which were sent
to all ports on his route. He was not to go to Villefranche in
France to meet the squadron, since they had been recalled again
to the West Indies, due to tensions there with the Spanish.
Instead he was to disembark at Genoa and wait there for the
European Squadron to eventually return. Accommodations were
authorized and the consulate at Genoa would have funds for him
upon his reporting in. At the bottom he saw there was a post-
script ordering him not to go ashore at any Spanish port due to
the bilateral tensions and the Spanish civil war.

"Wish I'd gotten this at Cadiz," he muttered to himself.

The consul looked at him. "What was that?"

"Orders to stay at Genoa and wait for the fleet. And I'm not
to go ashore at a Spanish port. Civil war going on and tensions
over Cuba."

"Yes, the squadron is off demonstrating to the Spanish at Cuba how tough we are. The Brits are doing the same around here. Suppose you saw their frigate in the harbor?"

"Yes, had a friend report aboard her."

"Oh, you know Fisher? I met him at a reception two nights ago. Just came in from England and went aboard her. Some sort of torpedo expert. Everybody calls him Jackie. Up and comer in the Royal Navy they say. Interesting fella to talk with."

Wake turned around and faced the consul. "Who?"

"Commander John Fisher. Wasn't that your friend? I heard he went aboard the frigate just before they weighed anchor."

"No. My friend was a Royal Marine."

The consul saw the pensive look on Wake's face and didn't ask anything further. It was obvious the naval officer was bothered by something he had said.

16

The Old World

February 1874

"Not exactly the sunny Italy you read about, is it?" said the engineer as the *Trinidad* steamed up the channel toward Genoa's harbor.

"No, Mr. Monroe, it's not," agreed Wake, standing at the rail bundled up in his great coat. It was freezing cold. "And I thought it would be a bit more . . . historic. Quaint."

"Reminds me of Liverpool. Even the stink is the same. Ach, I'm going below to my domain and a better sight for my old eyes—my beautiful iron darlins!"

The city slowly came into view through the winter rain squalls. Wake took it all in, overwhelmed by the magnitude, first seeing an ancient stone lighthouse on a point of land, then the jumbled gray city surrounding the crowded harbor, finally the brown hills rising rapidly from the city. The colors were faded and tired. Ornate cathedral domes, utilitarian government buildings, and bustling commercial blocks covered his view, and smoke from a thousand chimneys melded with the rainy mist to present an unreal aspect to the scene. Rancid sewage and smoky cooking fires filled his nostrils. The shriek of steam cranes and clattering of hooves echoed around the stone buildings. Frenzied motion was everywhere.

The harbor held dozens of steamers and hundreds of smaller sailing vessels. Wake saw warships from Austria, France, Italy, Spain, and the Ottoman Empire at anchor. All of them were more powerful than any American naval vessel he had known since the war. Genoa wasn't anything like what Wake expected.

As they came alongside a dock crowded with jumbled piles of cargo, he heard shouts from the stevedores in several languages—French, Italian, and German, from what he could tell. The Italian passengers aboard were excitedly showing others the points of interest, and seeing their euphoria, Wake was plunged into sadness. They were going home, but he was on the far side of the world from his own home and family, in a place as alien as any jungle he had known in the Caribbean.

Beyond his sense of remoteness, he was worried about heading for a staff officer assignment as flag lieutenant to the admiral—a task he didn't understand, wasn't trained for, and which was far more daunting to him than facing an armed enemy.

Carmena and Manuel came to his cabin just before they disembarked. Thanking him for getting them out of Spain, Carmena lost her composure. A flood of tears burst and Manuel took over, asking Wake if they could please continue to use the aliases he had given them. He said yes and wished them luck. Then with hugs and a chorus of hopeless "*hasta luego*" the three were parted—Wake knowing that he would probably never see the two lovers again.

As he descended the gangway into the throng of people on the dock an hour later, the rain started to pour down even harder. He felt the gloomy weather fill his soul.

"Well, this isn't starting out very impressively," Wake said to no one in particular as he felt his uniform soak through.

The Marino Hotel was a cheap one by the docks. The consulate used it for naval officers and state department officials in transit, but Wake was the only American there at the time. Vermin could be heard scurrying about all night, a rancid smell permeated the place, the food was atrocious, and the servants were sullen. It reminded Wake of a naval vessel that had been at sea for several months.

A week after checking in with a harried clerk at the consulate, Wake still languished in his musty hotel room. The rain was almost constant, but in between the squalls that swept down from the surrounding mountains he took walks around the harbor, speaking Spanish, for few spoke English, and trying with difficulty to learn the northern Italian dialect. He considered stopping by the French consulate to see if Catherine Faber had returned to her husband in Genoa—she should have been there a month already—but decided that might not be a wise thing to do. He didn't want to get involved in her marital life and was afraid of what she might do to his.

Desperate for something to do, Wake read a novel he had brought with him, John Esten Cooke's *Her Majesty the Queen,* which had become a bestseller the year before. He thought Cooke's depiction of early colonial Virginia's countryside appealing and the characters' complicated inter-twinings rather absorbing. It made for a nice diversion. Wake had never met an author before and wondered how a novelist could put it all together, creating a world within a book. Perhaps I'll meet one among the cultured elite of Europe on this assignment, he pondered, then speculated about when his assignment would actually begin. He hadn't heard any word about when the squadron was due to arrive, or even where it would arrive.

His mind was constantly on Linda and the children, wondering what they were doing, where they were going, how they were feeling. He worried that they were slipping away from him, and his worry turned into melancholy. He knew it wasn't healthy to dwell on such things, but he couldn't help it. The melancholy grew into a deep depression and he lost his fortitude to do the simplest things. He stopped eating in the dining room or shaving in the morning. The following day he stayed in bed. Then, after three days of mind-numbing lethargy, when he saw the dawn light enter his room he cursed the ceiling and forced himself to get cleaned up and go for a walk.

On the afternoon of the eighth day he received an invitation from the consul general himself, whom he had never met. It was to a diplomatic reception at the British Consulate the following evening. Attire was full dress and Wake, in the absence of any senior American officers, would represent the United States Navy. The invitation was not worded as a request, or he would have ignored it. It was more of a summons, so he felt compelled to go.

He walked to the room's tiny window and peered out. He needed to take a walk, be outside, see the sky, and think. Think about his life and his career. It was raining heavily, again. He returned to his bed and sat there, staring at the novel, wishing he was anywhere but there.

"Lieutenant Peter Wake, United States Navy!" called out the major-domo above the sound of the string quartet's waltz.

No one in the crowded ballroom obviously noticed his introduction, for which Wake was grateful, and he made his way toward a bar table set up in the far corner. He felt uncomfortable in his heavy dress mess uniform and was already starting to sweat, for even though it was cold outside, the room was jammed with people and stuffy. And he was worried about meeting Catherine Faber, or her husband. A servant was handing him a fluted glass of cold champagne when a tall fair-haired young man in coat and tails approached him, held out his hand, and spoke in the clear voice of a Midwesterner.

"Lieutenant Wake? I am Daniel Davis, chargé d'affaires to Consul General Strom. Thank you for coming. I must sincerely apologize for not getting with you before this evening, I hope your stay in Genoa has been pleasant."

Wake wasn't in the mood for small talk. "No, it's been a bit boring really. Does it always rain constantly like this?"

Davis grinned disarmingly and let out a laugh. "Only in the winter, Lieutenant. And admittedly, this winter has been worse for some reason."

"Do you have any word on the squadron? When are they returning? Are they going to Villefranche, or where?"

"Yes, well that's the good news I have for you. We got a telegraph today that they will be here soon. They left Lisbon yesterday. There is some sort of problem with them staying at their normal anchorage at Villefranche—I don't know for sure what, but I've heard various rumors—so their winter station will be here at Genoa."

Wake quickly worked out the navigation in his head. Barring severe headwinds, the squadron could sail the thirteen hundred miles and be at Genoa in approximately seven days at eight knots under canvas. He sighed. Another week alone in that room.

"Thank you, Mr. Davis. I suppose I'll wait in Genoa then."

"And I understand you'll be the flag lieutenant to Admiral Case?"

"Yes, I will."

"Excellent. Then you and I will be working a lot together while the squadron is at Genoa. Oh, the consul general wants to meet you too."

"Listen, before I meet him, can you fill me in on the situation here?" Wake asked. "This is my first time in this part of the world and I don't have a clue, except that it's all completely alien to me. I need to understand what's going on and who is who."

"Well, I'll be damned, a man who admits it when he doesn't know something." Davis slapped Wake on the shoulder. "What a breath of fresh air you are! I like that. So you really want to know what goes on around here?"

"Got to, Mr. Davis—before the admiral gets here. He's got a reputation in the navy for not tolerating fools at all."

Davis smiled. "So I've heard. Of course, he's been very engaging when I've been with him, and the consul general gets along famously with the admiral. War hero, I think. Got over here last year from duty at Washington. A gunnery expert, I believe."

Wake knew that. Case was well known in the navy for being an innovator and stickler for practice in gunnery. He also was the senior officer who implemented the torpedo station at Newport, Rhode Island, for prior to taking over command of the squadron he was chief of the Bureau of Ordnance in Washington. "What about the diplomatic situation here, though? The international politics. And please, call me Peter."

"All right, and I'm Dan. Now there, ah yes, the politics. For that, we'll need at *least* one more drink." Davis paused and looked around the crowded room. "Come with me, Peter, and we'll talk outside."

Davis signaled the bar servant for more champagne, put a glass in each hand and beckoned Wake to do the same, then they headed away from the noise of the guests to one of the several balconies that ran along one wall. The rain had just stopped and the gentle breeze felt good as Wake violated regulations and opened his coat to cool off once they were outside. Davis downed one glass straight away.

"A briefing on the situation here? Very well. Start out with your mindset, Peter. You are in the Old World now. Forget honesty. Forget trust. Forget right and wrong. The situation right here, right now, started a thousand years ago. And every one of those two-faced bastards in that ballroom knows each twisted facet, each perceived slight and insult, and each moment of supposed glory, of that convoluted history for every single one of those thousand years. They think that we in the New World are children because our history is only a couple of hundred years old. We're naïve children that should be seen but not heard, and grateful for what our mother countries have given and taught us."

Wake remembered what Catherine had told him that night at St. Pierre about European attitudes toward Americans. "That's pretty cynical, Dan. How long've you been in the diplomatic business?"

Davis downed his second glass and reached for one of Wake's. His tone was completely different from the jovial one he had displayed inside the ballroom.

"I call it *realistic,* and I've been with the Department of State for four years. You know, when I started I used to think Washington was bad. Did my first two years there. For the last two years I've been here among these pompous, antiquated blowhards. That's time enough to get cynical enough to deal with them without illusions. Welcome to the Old World, Peter Wake of Uncle Sam's not so glorious navy . . ."

17

Lay of the Land

Davis drank the other glasses of champagne without a word. Then he let out a great sigh and began to describe the international scene in Europe, which he said effectively meant the rest of the world as well since Europe dominated it.

"Very good, we'll start with the ever-so-cultured French Republic. Our friends the French are really mere shadows of their former imperial glory, which was mainly self-promoted anyway, since they didn't have too much to brag about in the first place. The Franco-Prussian War three years ago, following right on the heels of their stupid Mexican disaster, has sapped their military-political strength and national self-confidence almost completely. Lots of recriminations as to whose fault it was, who tried the hardest, who ran away. That sort of thing.

"Their national government's no longer a monarchy, it's now a republic, but a republic in chaos. I don't know how much longer Patrice MacMahon will be president, he's considered part of their past problems, and who can tell what de Broglie will do once he gets in, which he will. That whole situation in Paris is a mess. Nobody understands or can explain it, not even the French."

Davis gave a Gallic shrug to emphasize his point before continuing.

"The professional French army was humiliated at the siege of Paris, and most of the real fighting was done by ad hoc militia groups, some of which have emerged as political entities. The career army officers, who didn't come out of it looking very sharp, still haven't recovered their morale yet. The army currently is barely strong enough to control their colonial possessions, though they're trying to rebuild. In a few years they'll be a factor again, but not now."

Davis paused for a breath, then warmed back into the subject.

"The French navy, which in fact actually had a brigade of sailors fight bravely on land at the Paris siege, emerged with its ships unhurt and generally unused during the war, since their leadership was afraid to attack the German coast. But their navy is in decline now because the national leadership couldn't care less about naval matters these days, they're focused on accommodating the Germans and British in Europe. Word is that in the next war they are following the Confederate global strategy of raiders to harass an enemy's trade routes, since their fleet is weak."

Davis ruefully added, "I certainly don't despise the French. Quite the opposite. The French still have the very best wine, cognac, cheese—and women—in Europe, bar none. The quiet joke—do *not* repeat this to a Frenchman—among the Germans is that they were quite appreciative back in seventy that the French didn't let their women defend the country at the border, or the German invasion never would've made it all the way to Paris. By the way, Peter, beware of French ladies. They are very intelligent and strong-willed."

No need for *that* warning, Wake said to himself, nodding for Davis to go on.

"The Brits are the top dogs in Europe, but quiet about it. Their navy, of course, is everything to them, protecting their island nation and offering protection to others who go along with their foreign policy. They affect to espouse liberal progressive ideas, but the bottom line to them will always be protecting their worldwide empire's trade so that Great Britain keeps the "Great" in their name. They'll ally themselves with anyone, anywhere, to further that goal. It looks like Gladstone will soon be out of office and that Disraeli will be in, at least from what we read in the British papers we get here."

"That's what I heard in the West Indies, too," agreed Wake.

Davis went on. "I think that won't change anything in the British foreign policy, though. They'll continue to be the deal-makers of Europe. That's how they control Europe, through deals, not through deterrence by military action on land. The British army's only for colonial expansion and control. Quite good at frightening ignorant natives really—Queen Vicky loves having an empire—but not a viable force in European affairs. It doesn't have to be since they've got the Royal Navy, which dom-inates the Mediterranean and the North Sea, much to the annoy-ance of the Frogs and Germans. The Brits secretly delight in that, you know."

Davis leaned into the ballroom and flagged down a waiter, who gave him three more glasses of champagne. He tossed one down and continued his discourse, slurring his words more fre-quently now.

"Now, where were we? Ah yes, our hosts, formerly of the Roman Empire, of which they continually remind everyone. *Ad nauseum . . .*" Davis rolled his eyes theatrically.

"The Italians are getting stronger internally as they consoli-date their unification. The defeat, humiliation is a better word, in eighteen-sixty-six at the hands of the Austrians stunned them badly, but they're coming back fast and have allied themselves with anyone who would shield them from the Austrian-Hungarian Empire, just across the Alps. Those folks are the ones the Italians really worry about the most, especially up here in the north. And by allies I mean mostly the French and British. The Italian army is led mostly by northerners from the Piedmont, as is the national government, and it's credible but mainly used for internal control. The king, Vittorio Emanuele the second, is mostly a dilettante who leaves it up to the prime minister, who this week is Marco Minghetti, a pleasant fella who has his hands full just getting the Italians to all like each other. There is a big divide culturally between the north and the south in this country. Hell, Peter, they don't even speak the same language—"

Suddenly an elegantly dressed, gray-haired, and bejeweled lady emerged from the ballroom onto the balcony, smiled at Davis, then cast an undisguised look of lust at Wake, staring at his crotch. Davis' tone changed immediately. "Ah, Countess. *Enchanté, madame.* May I present Lieutenant Peter Wake, of the United States Navy?"

She curtsied low, showing her ample bosom to Wake.

"Lieutenant, this is Countess Lucia Lovran de Rijeka, of Croatia, which so unfortunately is currently being run by the Hungarians. A pity that you cannot live there, madame."

The countess gave Davis a quick reproving glance as she stared at Wake. It was unnerving to Wake—he had never seen a woman leer before. Davis came to the rescue.

"Countess, I think I heard the Russian consul asking for you earlier. He was in the anteroom." Davis winked at her. "I believe he is taken with your beauty, madame. It is your gift from God, and a burden also, I know."

"Really? I am unhappy I must leave you, Lieutenant. I shall return later and then prevail upon your honor to escort me to a dance inside. A slow waltz, perhaps." She smiled coquettishly and swept back into the ballroom.

"Thanks, Dan. Must admit, I've never met anyone like her before."

"Yeah, well, there are a lot of them around here. Displaced nobility with nothing to live on but a charade. Come to think of it, this whole diplomatic culture is a charade."

"Then why do you do it, if you hate it so much?" asked Wake.

"I never said I hate it, Peter. Quite the opposite—I love this." He drunkenly spread his arms. "All of it. What other job do they pay you to eat and drink expensively and mingle with important people? No, no. I don't like these arrogant fakes very much—but by God I do love this job!"

"Slow down that drinking part of the job a bit, Dan. You're starting to get loud."

"Yes. You're right. It went down too easy and I've had too much. Now where was I in my lecture, before we were so lecherously interrupted by the countess?"

"The Italians . . ."

"Those Italians! I can't help it, I love 'em. Their navy has some modern ships and good leaders these days, but it's really a coastal defense force. All in all, the Italian influence in Europe is mostly financial and cultural."

"But," Davis warned as he waved a finger, "remember, the Italians are the ones who transformed diplomatic intrigue into a fine art, a long time ago. They haven't forgotten it. Do not underestimate the Italians.

"And now we come to the Germans. Bismarck and Wilhelm have them firmly under control and motivated. I should say Bismarck does, because old Wilhelm is seventy-seven now. He lets Bismarck do what he wants, as long as everyone pretends the emperor is in charge. It's an amazing story, really, how they got the kings to submit and name Wilhelm emperor at Versailles three years ago. But that's for another time, Peter.

"Back to the subject. The Germans are gaining in industrial power quicker than anyone and are the bull elephants on this continent, scaring the hell out of everyone else, including the British, though they won't dare admit it. The Germans, now united under the emperor in a federation of states that's becoming stronger every day, are expanding their influence around the world too.

"Just wait, they're determined to rival the French and British in imperial possessions and I think they'll damn well do it. And one region they're looking at is the Mediterranean, particularly Morocco, which especially vexes the French, an added feature that delights the Germans, as if crowning their emperor at Versailles wasn't insult enough to the Frogs.

"And here is a most important thing. The German army is *the* dominant force on land in Europe. Those Prussians scare the hell out of everybody. Fortunately, their navy isn't strong enough to offer a threat to anyone—yet. But I've no doubt that the Germans, who are learning from British innovations, will at some point challenge the British at sea, as farfetched as that's seems now."

"What about Spain?" asked Wake.

"The Spanish are in turmoil and pretty much the sad joke of Europe. No one's afraid of them and no one needs them. Oh, they give good parties and are pleasant people, I really like their music, but they aren't a threat to anyone—except each other. The current civil war is applauded by revolutionaries and republicans, *and* by conservatives and monarchists, and mostly ignored by everyone else in the world, Peter."

Wake could hear the sarcasm dripping as Davis explained it all to him. Good Lord, if he's this way in only four years, ruminated Wake, what will he be like in ten?

Another champagne glass was emptied. "Now the British, French, and sometimes our warships, periodically have visited Spanish ports to protect their nationals living there, but it's all for show. No one in Europe really cares and most think that Madrid will sell Cuba to the Americans to keep the imperial treasury restocked. And the war scare over Cuba a few months ago? Most diplomats here think it was all bravado on the part of the Spanish. Yep, the only thing the Spanish have going for them is geography—the Straits of Gibraltar. And the Brits won't let that into the hands of a hostile power. What did you see when you were there last month?"

"Hatred. Chaos," said Wake, watching for a reaction from Davis but seeing none. He had been wondering if anyone in

Sevilla had ever identified Allen or him as the ones in the Alcázar, but hadn't seen any indication of it so far. Thank God.

"Yes, proves my point. Now we come to the Austrian-Hungarians. They're strong, with a professional army and a navy worth reckoning with, but they're currently busy opposing the Ottoman Empire over its frontier in Europe. Alleged religious atrocities—you hear these things about both sides—have fueled the dispute and fanned the hatred among the peasants for centuries, but the politicians are really sparring over economic control and deterrence of Russia's influence and expansion in the Balkans. Vienna and Istanbul have been to the verge of war several times recently, but they've backed down at the last moment each time. It appears, to me at least, they're content with fighting their war in small scale along the Balkan borders, like they've done for the last five hundred years. The Italians, though, watch them like a sparrow watches a hawk. Most of the Italian army is up on the northeastern plains of the country, ready to defend against an invasion."

"And Russia? We hear a lot about them these days back home."

"Russia is the odd man out, who desperately wants to be invited to the party. The Russians want to be considered as Europeans, with culture and power, but are considered by most real Europeans to be a backward feudal state lost in the Middle Ages, and generally a nuisance. Except by the Ottomans, who are deathly afraid of the Russia's influence with the Christian peoples of the Caucasus and the Balkans."

Wake had heard of "the Caucasus and the Balkans" but had no definitive knowledge of where they were. He was going to ask, but didn't have time, since Davis was moving forward in his recital.

"The Russians have a huge army, it's true, but the professional military men here in Europe aren't impressed. Worst conscripts they've seen, one of 'em told me. They discount it as obsolete, ill-led, and fit only as target practice for the German army's

Prussian artillery. Likewise for the navy, which Tsar Alexander had built for his own viewing pleasure, actually thinking that it might impress someone else, as incredible as *that* seems."

Davis chortled as he said, "It's not even allowed through the Bosporus by the Turks. And talk about embarrassment, Peter, the Russian Baltic Fleet can't even send ships around to the Med without them breaking down enroute and asking for help from the Brits, who've given it out of some treaty obligation they never thought would be used."

Davis took in a deep breath. "Let's see, that leaves us with the cradle of democracy, doesn't it? The Greeks are pretty much like the Spanish—in chaos and civil war internally. Externally they're consumed by their hatred of the Turks. The Greek peoples within the Ottoman area of Europe are fighting their incessant war of liberation, while the Greeks in the homeland fight each other. The rest of Europe prefers to focus on Greece's culture, and *that* peaked three thousand years ago. No one expects the Greeks to really unify or expel the Turks from Macedonia."

"What about the Scandinavians or the Dutch?" asked Wake.

"No influence down here in the Med. Little influence elsewhere in Europe. King Oscar's new up there in Sweden and King Christian's too busy making money. Doesn't have time or interest in playing Continental politics with the big boys."

"So it appears that the Brits are the most powerful and therefore influential, followed by the Germans and then the Austrians."

"Yes, that's pretty much it. The problem though, is that the French and the Italians *want* to be more powerful. And the French are starting to *think* they're more powerful." Davis shook his head. "That leads to posturing or double-dealing. These folks are absolute masters of that." He raised an eyebrow. "You'll see."

18

Diplomats, Mohammed, and Missionaries

Davis exhaled slowly, then breathed the night air in. "Come on, let's go in. I need to introduce you to the consul general. He's definitely not your average diplomat. And I can show you who's who in there."

Wake just wanted to go back to his room and rest—his mind was awash with names and events and histories of the countries in the region. More than ever, he felt inadequate for the job ahead. But instead, he buttoned his coat and followed Davis, marveling at the man's ease at handling the strong champagne, recitation of all that information, and ability to energize again and put on a chameleon-like change in demeanor upon reentering the swirling chaos of the ballroom.

Wake was three steps behind Davis when the younger man stopped and pointed to the corner. "Ah, there he is, by the bar, as one would expect. Come along and meet my boss." The crush of people pushed Wake toward a middle-aged, salt-and-pepper-haired man whose massive frame undulated as he laughed loudly at a joke told by a pretty girl.

Davis smiled ingratiatingly as he touched the man's shoulder.

"Sir, this is Lieutenant Peter Wake, who's been at the hotel for about a week waiting for the squadron to return. Lieutenant, this is Mr. Beauregard Strom, Consul General for the United States at Genoa."

Strom turned and slapped a huge hand into Wake's, booming out a Southern-tinged greeting that could be heard across the room. "Why, hello there, Lieutenant. Good to finally meet you. Sorry we didn't have a chance to meet before this. Hope you're as comfortable as can be expected over there at that hotel. I know it isn't much. Funding constraints, you see."

Wake was nonplussed. He was six feet tall himself, but Strom was taller and bigger by fifty pounds, an imposing figure. And the man was completely different from every other diplomat Wake had met in his career. He wasn't soft-spoken or suave. He had what sounded to Wake to be a Louisiana accent and a voice that was without elitist affect, sincerely jovial and direct to the point. Unlike most of the diplomats he had met, who usually made his skin crawl with suspicion, Strom was someone Wake instantly liked.

"Thank you, sir. An honor to meet you. The hotel room is adequate for my needs, sir."

"Adequate! It's a dump, Lieutenant. But it's all we can do. Has young Dan here given you a briefing on the situation with your squadron, and Europe in general?"

"Yes, sir. A good one."

Strom leaned forward and lowered his tone, his bass voice still audible above the tinkling of glasses and the string music. "Europe is a stew, Lieutenant. A stew of poisons that's been brewing for centuries. I've been here since Grant sent me in seventy. It was really a mess then, what with the Germans making monkeys out of the French and everybody wondering what would come next. Getting slightly better now, though. Things are calming down a bit. Still, the trick is to sit at the table and compliment the stew, just don't eat it. If you catch my drift. The navy will have to be careful to not alienate the people in charge of Europe.

Especially around here, in Italy. They get mighty touchy about some things."

"Aye, aye, sir," replied Wake reflexively to what he considered an order.

"By God, a sailor's answer! Did you hear that, Dan? I do believe we'll be seeing a lot of Lieutenant Wake in the future, since Case's squadron will be stationed here until May and probably beyond."

Strom put a hand on Davis' shoulder. "Dan, let him know about northern Africa and the Ottomans too. That's the area where things will be changing. We want to be *extremely* careful down there." Then the consul general engaged an elderly man in conversation, switching into what sounded to Wake like fluent French.

"I'll do that now, sir," acknowledged Davis to Strom's back, picking up two more champagnes, before gesturing Wake back to the balcony.

"Interesting man," offered Wake when they arrived back at their perch overlooking the city. With the rain clouds lifted, the ancient *lanterna* lighthouse winking over on the western side of the harbor, and the night cloaking the city filth, Wake thought Genoa looked its best. Or it could be the champagne, he realized, as Davis replied.

"*Very* interesting. I'll tell you about his background later. But first I'd better cover the lands of Mohammed. Completely alien culture."

Wake laughed as he gestured around them. "Dan, I thought all *this* was pretty bizarre."

"It is, but the Ottoman world makes this place look like home."

"All right, what about this infamous Muslim world? I hear we have to rescue missionaries there frequently," asked Wake after unbuttoning his coat again in the cool air.

Davis nodded. "Yes, and sometimes it's the same ones over and over. Blustering fools. Worse than the politicians who curry their favor back home and bully us into supporting their crusades against non-Christians—that means Muslims, by the way. The missionaries don't care about Jews."

"Why do the politicians back home curry the favor of a few missionaries on the other side of the world?"

"Because those few missionaries are supported financially by tens of thousands of people back home through special societies. *Un-Godly*—pardon the pun—amounts of money get raised. You've seen the pamphlets, haven't you?"

Wake had indeed, but had never donated or even given it much thought. His rather meager weekly offerings to the Methodist church in Pensacola had been for that congregation's benefit. There was so much need for help in the recovering South that he never contemplated foreign aid and dismissed the appeals he'd seen. "The politicians don't want to alienate voters, so they make it look like they care."

"Yes," Davis grumbled. "And when the missionaries scream for help to the local U.S. consulate after they've gotten into some dicey situation or other, the consulate passes the call onto you—the American navy. You get to go and rescue them."

"How often?"

"Couple of times a year. Usually it happens over in the Levant, where we've got a lot of missionaries. They love living in the Holy Land, trying to convert people who have been doing just fine with Mohammed for the last thousand years. Once they've insulted and aggravated the locals enough to get the attention and retribution of the regional Ottoman authorities, in comes a request for a warship to intimidate the natives. Missionaries have extra-legal status. Generally, they are considered by the Ottoman Empire not to be under the authority of the local courts and laws. So the local leaders try their best to ignore them. And remember, the Turks control everything, to varying degrees, from Persia to Algiers. Morocco is one of the few Arab places that's independent of the Ottoman Empire.

"However, if the authorities get frustrated and actually end up doing anything against a missionary, then the request is for a bombardment. If a missionary is imprisoned, then a landing party is called to go ashore. Bombardments and shore parties are rare, maybe once a year. Boy, the Ottomans do not like that. Not at all."

"It's a request, though. A consul has no command over a ship captain."

"No, but they try. We've got a fool of a consul at Beirut who cannot get along with anyone. The Consul General at Constantinople, George Boker, tries to keep him from doing a lot of harm, but the idiot manages to make himself infamous anyway, constantly asking for his country to back him up with gunfire. Tried once to make a local pasha eat dirt for insulting him. And no, I'm not jesting."

"Hmm. What about the Europeans? What do they do?"

"Same thing with their gunboats. They've got missionaries everywhere too. Hell, their diplos are even more bloodthirsty than our consuls. My impression is their navies use it as good opportunities for gun practice. You'll hear 'em brag about it. Of course they want to expand their empires. We don't have an empire."

"Which of the European powers are where in northern Africa?" inquired Wake. Northern Africa was in the squadron's area of responsibility.

"Spanish have enclaves in Morocco on the Med. The French have a large presence in Morocco and Algiers, and a bit in Egypt. The Italians are big in Tunis and Tripoli. The Brits are big in Egypt. Of course, the French built the Suez Canal, but the Brits are edging them out pretty fast. That's their main route to India now. Crucial for them."

Wake heard a bell ring. Davis pulled out his watch and said, "Damn, it's that late already? This soirée is over, Peter. Sorry, I got to talking and forgot the time—didn't even introduce you around to the other legations. Well, at least you've got the general lay of the land now."

"Thanks for that, Dan. You've given me a lot to think about. I appreciate the help."

"Well, you still need to know about the diplomatic personalities here. Guess I'll have to do that at lunch before the next bash, which is only a few nights from now."

Seeing Wake's reaction, Davis laughed. "Don't worry. Usually they're only once a week. This week is unusual. The French are throwing this next party for the feast of Saint Peter Damian. That's to gain favor with the Italians—you see Peter Damian is an Italian saint. Very big around here."

"The French consul does that reception?" asked Wake, his mind swimming with an image of Catherine.

"Oh, yes. And let me tell you, they *do* know how to give a good party. I'll give 'em that."

Davis and Wake joined the throng exiting the main doors to the street. Wake was trying to memorize all that he'd just learned when Davis pointed to a man entering a closed carriage where a gowned woman waited in inside, her face hidden in shadow.

"Hey, there they are now. Consul General Henri Faber de Champlain. A real live hero of the Third French Republic, and his wife. I'll tell you about him later, but I've got to see to my own consul general now. Good night, Peter."

Wake vaguely answered, but his eyes were on the man glowering out of the carriage's window at the crowd as it trotted off down the darkened street. Wake felt a chill go through him as he looked at those cold eyes.

19

The Empires' Men

Wake met with Davis over lunch two days later, getting further background on the situation around the Mediterranean. At Café Cavour, on the shady side of the Piazza Portello, Davis explained Strom was out of town and he had plenty of time that day to fill in Wake on who exactly was who, in the diplomatic corps at Genoa. Between bites of pasta, he proudly described it as one of the plum diplomatic assignments of Europe because of its economic importance and central geographic location. Then he flashed his boyish grin and added that its proximity to the casinos and ladies of the Cote d'Azur didn't hurt either.

"And, of course, how can you help it? Everybody loves Italy, Peter. Especially these fellas coming from northern Europe. You think it's cold and wet here—try Hamburg or Copenhagen or Saint Petersburg."

Devouring a mound of toasted ravioli, a Genovese specialty, Davis proceeded to tell the particulars of the various consuls, offering that the most interesting of them were Brown, the British representative; Burgos, the Spaniard; Strom, the American; and Faber, the Frenchman. Each of these had a special story of his own, and after a tumbler of Barolo red wine, Davis began.

"Let's take the Brit first. Montegue Yeats Brown lives at a romantic little hilltop castle overlooking the sea thirty miles down the coast from here at a quaint fishing village called Porto Fino. He relies upon his staff to run the office in Genoa, while he attends to the weightier matters of state, especially entertainment of the European elite at his castle. Brown's owned the place for seven years, having bought it as a rundown ruin from the state of Liguria for seven thousand lire—that's about five hundred dollars—after he fell in love with it from the deck of his yacht, the *Black Tulip*. Our boy Strom has some money, but ol' Monty has oodles of it, Peter. And he likes to use it for pleasure, God bless him."

"Well-to-do nobility back in England?"

"No, surprisingly he's not. I think he was a donor to one of the liberal causes favored by Gladstone years ago—probably a reelection campaign—and that's how he got the job. But money around here can overcome a lack of blue-blood or title and make you the hit of the social climbers. Titles are a dime a dozen over here. *Money* is the thing. You should see the lady sharks go after men with money. Fascinating to see how they do it. Had one try it with me, till she figured my true worth."

Cynda Denaud Williams—now Saunders—flashed into Wake's mind and he smiled. He knew the type.

"Brown married a local Englishwoman, Agnes Bellingham, four years ago, but most folks think it was actually for love," Davis said with cocked eyebrow. "Which shocked more than a few at the time. Either way, he's therefore off the eligible bachelor list, but still throwing those fancy soirées. His gatherings are famous for including those who are at the very top of the list. Because of the remoteness of Castello Brown, guests usually stay the night—the most valued within the walls, the others at inns close by. Big honor to get invited."

"What're the circumstances of Strom?"

"Circumstances? How very genteel, Peter . . ."

Wake laughed. "I'm trying, Dan."

"You're doing pretty well! About Strom, he's the most genuine person I've ever met. Can be a best friend or worst enemy—and there'll be no doubt which he is to you. He made his money the old-fashioned way—he *inherited* it when his father died before the war. Then our Beau did something really smart. He put it all in New York banks under a corporation's name in April of sixty-one. Hid it during the war. He fought, with the rest of his family, in the Tenth Louisiana, an infantry regiment that served under Lee in Virginia. Took horrible casualties—out of six hundred men that started out in the fall of sixty-one, only thirteen enlisted men and four officers made it to the surrender four years later. Strom was one of those. He's told me that everything in life is easy after living through that hell. Gave him a sense of perspective about trials and travails, he says.

"After the war he got his money back, made a few investments in land and hooked up with Longstreet in Louisiana. Became a Republican and helped Grant out. Grant gave him this job as a thank-you. Happens all the time, but we were lucky in getting him. Unlike many political appointees, he's got spine and he's got brains. Oh, Strom plays the *bon vivant* all right, but he can cut through the dung in a second and tell it like it is. He likes *you*, by the way. Says you have 'old eyes' and that means you've seen a lot in life."

"And the Spanish diplomat? What of him?"

"The Spanish consul general is quite a work of art, too—in the opposite direction. Colonel Ramon Burgos, de something or other, has been here about a year. He recently declared himself to be one of the Carlists who are trying to reestablish the throne, but only with their guy on it, though everyone suspected he was for a long time. He fought for the crown in sixty-eight and is a friend of that Spanish general who butchered the Americans and Brits in Santiago. Keeps defending him."

"He's a Carlist? But he represented the Republican government here."

"They're all inter-mixed. And they change sides with the wind."

"Must make it difficult to keep track of who's on what side," suggested Wake.

"It does. But we always knew Burgos was anti-American. No confusion there. Burgos never lets an occasion go by without indelicately suggesting that Spain needs to bloody the *yanquis'* nose over Cuba once and for all so the U.S. will stop supporting the revolutionaries. Said our navy was a joke and the Spanish were tired of hearing about it. One night Strom suggested that Burgos should just go there to Cuba so he could be first on the front lines if it did come to blows. Burgos answered that he'd already been in Cuba and killed a bunch of 'the revolutionary swine,' which he considered nothing more than American puppets, and he would go wherever needed once the shooting started.

"Peter, just wait till you meet *that* fella wearing your nice blue *yanqui* navy uniform. That'll be fun to watch. Oh, and just so you know, your admiral hates his guts."

Wake wanted to ask about his new commander, Rear Admiral Augustus Ludlow Case, but knew that would be inappropriate. Davis wasn't in the navy and Wake couldn't give the impression of gossiping about naval officers. Instead he inquired about the man in the carriage.

"What about the French consul?"

"Ah yes, Monsieur Henri Faber de Champlain. Hero of the Siege of Paris, adventurer and entrepeneur, and defender of the new French Republic. One of the most interesting and least likable in our little cast of characters. He made his fortune through old family money too. Sugar money from a brother who's still in the West Indies, textiles in India, printing in Paris, and more recently, rubber in Cochin China."

"How's he a hero of the siege at Paris? They lost that one."

"The country lost, but a few men did prove themselves. Faber was one of them. He was always interested in ballooning, and when he got caught in Paris during the war he was one of a small band of balloon enthusiasts who assembled their aerial crafts and flew out people, pigeons, and important documents."

"Pigeons?"

"Yeah, believe it or not, they were transporting homing pigeons out of the city so the birds would carry messages back into the city from French-held territory. The Germans tried but couldn't stop the aerial flights, neither the balloons nor the birds. Sounds ridiculous now, but it was deadly serious then and it worked. One of the few things the French have to brag about from that siege—birds and bags of air. You should hear Faber's tales. He made one of those flights himself. Crashed down with the bag deflated and a bunch of bullet holes in the fabric. Damned near died."

"How is he the least likable?"

"His attitude. No skill at talking with people. Strom's a natural—you instinctively trust what he's saying. I can at least fake it in the company of these people. But Faber, he talks with a mean edge, like he's got a grudge against life itself. Manages to put off just about everyone who listens to him for longer than thirty seconds. Gotta voice like the sound of doom. Never seen the man laugh or even smile."

Wake remembered the eyes and could well imagine the voice. "Then why did they send him here as a *diplomat?*"

"Good question. Nobody knows, but everyone assumes it's a *quid pro quo* for his sacrifice during the war. He lost a lot of money and almost his life. That's how senior diplomatic posts get filled by most countries. Payback."

"Is Faber anti-American, like the Spaniard?"

"I don't really know. He acts like he's anti-everyone."

"I wonder what his relationship with the leaders in Paris is now?"

Davis tilted his head. "Tenuous, I should think. The leadership will be changing soon."

Lunch was done and Davis appeared ready to leave, but Wake had one more question. "All these politicos, what's their opinion of the U.S. Navy?"

Davis sighed and looked down at his plate. "You really want

to know? You won't like it."

Wake nodded.

"They think it's a joke. Just like our Monroe Doctrine of protecting the Western Hemisphere from their incursions. They treat us, and our navy, as they would a young nephew, with condescending charity, but no professional respect. Our navy is neither powerful nor numerous, and so its image—and our national prestige—are on a par with countries like Argentina."

Wake thought as much. He remembered Catherine's warning about appearing weak to Europeans.

"And you know what really galls the hell out of me about all that, Peter?"

Wake shook his head, the myriad of information circulating in his mind while Davis' face tightened with anger.

"The sons of bitches are right. . . ."

The day following that lunch brought a letter from Linda. Wake opened it fast, hoping for positive news.

January 15th, 1874
Dear Peter,

First things first. The children are fine. Sean is playing at climbing trees now, pretending they are masts on a ship and you are the captain. Useppa's limp is the same but she says she is in less pain, but I wonder if she's just trying to make me feel better. She can tell that Mommy is sad. I never say anything in front of them about us, but Useppa can tell, I think.

I found out from Mrs. Leary that the Navy department has a rule they started back in 1869 saying an officer will do 3 years sea duty, followed by 3 years of shore duty—alternating every 3 years. I couldn't believe it! She got me that order number from her husband. It's General Order 112 from the 17th of March 1869. Her husband came ashore three months ago after only two years. And I've talked with other wives whose husbands haven't as much sea time as you.

Peter, since your court-martial in '69 you've been on continuous sea duty, and now they say you're staying on it until 1875? That's six years of straight sea duty and it's absolutely outrageous!

I'm very angry at how they've treated you and how you put up with it, like some whipped dog. It's time for you to tell them either they give you another shore duty assignment or you'll leave. You have every right and your family needs you at home.

Forgive me for being blunt, but I love you and want the best for us, and our children. I don't even know where you are right now, which really just adds to the worry. It's a new year and time for you to have a new outlook on your life and your responsibilities to your family. Now, Peter. This is making me more bitter by the day.

With love,
Linda

Wake sat for a long time staring at the ultimatum. Looking at the curls and swirls of her handwriting, the slant of her script, the black ink's shades, trying to divine more from the letter, to understand the depth of her anger. Since the court-martial she had been increasingly angry with his naval career, but Linda knew that he was a naval officer when she married him. Now the guilt he had felt for some time over her unhappiness was turning to anger. An *ultimatum?* Heat rose through his body, flooding into his mind. His jaw tensed as he thought about the tone of her letter.

Wake stood and looked out the window at the ships moving around the harbor, taking in a deep breath and letting it out slowly, trying to calm himself. He knew of that regulation, but it was a guide, not an ironclad rule, and most officers knew that. Most of their wives knew it too. And understood. He exhaled slowly again, willing himself to calm down. Then he looked down at the letter in his left hand and noticed his right hand. It was clenched in a fist.

20

The French First Lady of Genoa

Wake already wasn't feeling well when he arrived—an hour late—the stress of his deteriorating family situation upsetting his stomach and making him edgy. Then he entered the French embassy's ballroom and instantly felt worse. The gaslights at the consulate's soirée were the brightest Wake had ever seen. Piercingly bright—bringing slices of pain through his eyes directly into the recesses of his brain. The headache was instantaneous and brutal. Wake cringed. Even the string quartet's music was conspiring to hurt his head.

"What the hell kind of music is that?" Wake grumbled to Davis, who met him at the door of the ballroom and was regarding him dubiously. The naval officer was late, but at least he was there, though Davis thought he looked in pretty bad shape.

"That music would be from Giuseppi Verdi, the famous Italian composer. And please don't make any negative comments, Peter, since the great man himself is standing over there in the corner. Next to his mistress, Teresa Stolz, the acclaimed soprano."

Wake just wanted the infernal racket to stop hurting his head. "What's this Verdi fellow famous for, anyway?"

"Well, that particular music, for one," said Davis, trying to be patient. "It's from *Aida,* the opera he composed for the Khedive of Egypt to celebrate the opening of their canal. A canal our French hosts built, by the way."

A giant hand slapped Wake's shoulder from behind, almost knocking him down. Strom suddenly filled Wake's vision. "Why, if it isn't our gallant Lieutenant Wake. Glad you could make it, Lieutenant."

"Ah, thank you, sir. Sorry I'm late."

Strom let out a belly laugh and slapped Wake's shoulder again. "Not to worry, Wake. I'm just happy you're here," the joviality left his voice and his eyes, "to do your job. You are *it* around here for the U.S. Navy, Lieutenant. No one else to help you for a while."

"Yes, sir. The job will get done, sir."

"I know that, Lieutenant. No doubts there. Introduce him around, Dan. I want the lieutenant up to date and immediately ready to fulfill his duties as naval representative," said Strom as he moved away to mingle with the other guests.

Wake looked at Davis. "You had to tell him I was late?"

"I don't work for you, Peter. I work for him. Come on, I'll introduce you around."

Davis started with Verdi, an older, flamboyantly bearded man with imperious eyes that glanced dismissively at Wake. The composer didn't bother to introduce Stolz, standing next to him, who appeared to be not enjoying the evening at all. After a round of courteous preliminaries, Davis steered Wake away and toward a tall, hatched-nosed man in a Royal Navy formal dress coat, the shoulders of which supported enormous gold epaulets, dwarfing every other officer's in the room. The man was surrounded by lesser-ranked naval officers chuckling over some joke.

"Vice Admiral Drummond, it's good to see you again, sir," began Davis. "May I introduce Lieutenant Peter Wake, of the United States Navy, sir? He will be our naval representative here for a bit, while the squadron's away."

"You certainly may, Mr. Davis. Good to meet you, Lieutenant Wake." Drummond waved a hand at the others. "Gentlemen, kindly introduce yourselves to Lieutenant Wake."

The British officers went around the circle, introducing themselves and their assigned ships. Peter Allen wasn't among them, and Wake asked about the Royal Marine. They said he had the watch aboard that evening and would pass along Wake's good wishes. Each officer made small talk as they introduced themselves, mundane words with forgettable monotony—until the last one. He had prematurely graying hair above serious gray-blue eyes that were mismatched with a smiling mouth. Wake thought him in his early thirties, about his own age, but the man's demeanor was of someone far older, a man used to commanding men. As the other Royal Navy entourage departed to follow their admiral toward the bar table, this officer shook Wake's hand with a firm grip, holding it for an instant longer than usual.

"Commander John Fisher, Lieutenant Wake. Commanding officer, HMS *Vernon.*"

Wake almost fell down. He instantly envisioned that night at the dockyard on Antigua, remembering well the crate that had stenciled on it *Vernon,* and the name Fisher. "The torpedo school at Portsmouth, sir?"

"The very same, Lieutenant. It's still a bit new. Do you know of it?"

Wake was aware Fisher was scrutinizing him, but whether from his worn-out appearance or his West Indies escapade he knew not. "Only by reputation, sir. It has an excellent one, as do you."

"And you as well, Lieutenant," Fisher replied as Wake's heart stopped. Fisher knew of him? That meant he also knew about his escapade in Antigua. He struggled not to look anxious while Fisher continued. "I heard of your work in the Caribbean back in sixty-nine, by accounts, against quite a maniacal foe, under rather difficult circumstances. Commander Russell of HMS *Plover* told me of it a few months ago when he reported aboard *Vernon.* Said he assisted you a bit. He's a great admirer of yours."

Wake hoped his sigh of relief wasn't audible. "Commander Russell is an outstanding naval officer and a considerable credit to the Royal Navy, sir. I am honored that he spoke kindly of me."

Fisher allowed a chuckle to emerge. "Rodney Russell didn't speak *kindly* of you, Lieutenant Wake. Nothing that benign. No, he said you were the most bloody dangerous pirate in the Caribbean and he thanked God he was on your side in that affair! He thinks you are a *warrior,* which is high praise indeed coming from him."

Davis stood there amused, and Wake didn't know what to say. Russell had been part of the search for a pirate, a mission that ended in Wake's court-martial in Washington, at which Russell testified for the defense. "I am appreciative of that, sir and hope Commander Russell is doing well."

"That he is, Lieutenant. He is attached to me at *Vernon*. A torpedo specialist and instructor."

Davis cleared his throat. "The automotive torpedo. That's the new weapon of the future, isn't it, Commander?"

"I believe so, Mr. Davis. Though some of our more senior officers think it a silly contraption, bound for failure."

Wake was intrigued now. He had the feeling Fisher was toying with him, baiting him, but he couldn't resist. "You've done some innovative work in that area, haven't you, sir? I think I've read about it. And there are some scientists over here working on it as well."

The smile returned, but the eyes were as serious as ever. "I think you haven't *read* about the Royal Navy's efforts, Lieutenant. Such matters are confidential, of course. But yes, we have been working on improving our weaponry and much has been done in the field. By Europe's navies, and by your navy also, at Newport I believe."

There it is, Wake told himself. They know that I know. The confrontation between Captain Gardiner and the British authorities in Antigua must be known by Fisher too. Probably a copy of the report must have been sent back to the Admiralty, he surmised.

"I wish you good luck in your endeavors, sir. It's amazing how fast the science is advancing. I hear the torpedoes are moving at ten knots now and up to a thousand yards."

"Really?" replied Fisher, "Where would you hear something like that?"

"Wardroom gossip, sir. Nothing definitive."

"Ah, yes, the ever-elusive wardroom gossip—a fount of knowledge for naval officers over the centuries. Well, I must go and say hello to others here. Have an interesting tour here in the Med, Lieutenant. Your first time here?"

"Yes, sir."

"Then it will be *very* interesting for you, I'm sure." Fisher started away.

"I'll see you around then, sir," called out Wake. "Our squadrons frequently interact, I understand."

Fisher stopped, turned and smiled. "I think not, Lieutenant. I'm not here with the squadron and won't be in Genoa very long. Off on holiday to see English friends on the other side of Italy."

Before Wake could ask where, Fisher was gone, merged into the crowd. But by that point Wake could guess Fisher's destination—Whitehead's torpedo factory in Fiume, along the Austrian-Hungarian side of the Adriatic Sea. On the other side of Italy.

The evening was excruciating for Wake, his head pounding, mouth dry, and eyes blurred. He drifted from person to person as Davis introduced him to a bewildering array of self-impressed people, whose positions in life he gave up trying remember, except for one very eccentric character, Craven Walker.

The disheveled Walker was a Singapore-born English vulcanologist studying the volcanic formations of the Mediterranean.

He had a personal research project on the use of thermal energy to illuminate lamps and power engines. Walker launched forth with a monologue on lava that almost drove Wake to scream, but he endured until Davis came over and introduced him to a matron of the Milan opera, who then waxed on about Verdi's latest efforts, which she pronounced as *magnifico.*

Wake didn't come into to contact with the one person he both feared and was curious to meet. Then, as he drank his sixth glass of water *sans gaz*—he couldn't bear even the mere thought of alcohol—Wake heard Davis' tone rise in volume and cheerfulness beside him.

"Ah, Consul General Faber, what a wonderful evening you have arranged! The feast of St. Peter Damian is well complimented by your efforts this evening. You may remember me, I'm Dan Davis of the American consulate, sir."

Faber, a tall square-shouldered man in his late forties with unruly black wavy hair, stopped in mid-sentence in a conversation with a woman beside him and regarded Davis neutrally for an instant. Faber's eyes, devoid of emotion, scanned Davis up and down, after which he replied, "*Merci, monsieur,*" and returned to his conversation in French. Wake looked around, but Catherine was nowhere in sight. His heart started to pound, knowing she must be close.

Davis shrugged at Wake and tried again. "*Excusez-moi, Votre Excellence.* But I have been asked by Consul General Strom to introduce our naval representative to you, sir. May I have the honor to formally introduce Lieutenant Peter Wake, temporary representative in this region of the United States Navy."

Without waiting for Faber to respond, Davis continued with great flair, "And, Lieutenant Wake, it is my great honor to introduce His Excellency, Henri Faber de Champlain, *hero* of Paris, scientist, adventurer, and Consul General for Genoa and northern Italy for the Republic of France."

Wake thought Davis' fawning a bit obvious, but saw Faber straighten when the word hero came out. The Frenchman eyed Wake, then droned rapidly.

"*Bonsoir et bienvenue á la Mer Méditerranée, Lieutenant. Bonne chance avec votre mission.*"

Wake got the gist of it—he was welcomed to the Mediterranean and wished good luck—and was about to try a reply in French when Faber abruptly turned around again and spoke to an older man in Italian. Davis raised an eyebrow and slightly shook his head, so Wake said nothing and began to move away, worrying if Faber's rudeness had anything to do with his attention to Catherine in Martinique.

But he didn't have much time to ponder the question before Genoa's British diplomat arrived, with Strom beside him. The Louisianan boomed out an introduction.

"Well, here's Wake! Consul General Brown, this is Lieutenant Peter Wake, our head navy man in these parts while the squadron's off sailing someplace. Lieutenant, this is Consul General Montague Yeats Brown, of Her Britannic Majesty's government."

Brown shook hands politely. "It is an honor to meet you, Lieutenant. And a pleasure for me as well. I served in our navy for a few years and have an affinity for ships and the sea. If we can ever assist, please let us know."

Despite his throbbing head, Wake decided to try his hand at diplomacy. "Thank you, sir. I understand you have a beautiful yacht. The *Black Tulip,* I believe."

Brown's face lit up. "Very good, Lieutenant! By Jove, I think you've got a good one here, Beauregard. He's actually done some inquiry about the diplomatic corps upon arrival. Very commendable."

"Thank you, sir," said Wake. "Just some preliminary information that Mr. Davis here was kind enough to share with me. I found it interesting that you're a sailor. What exact type of ship is *Black Tulip,* sir? Someday I'd like to see her."

Brown exploded with mirth. "Lieutenant, you shall! I'm having a simple little weekend affair at my castle at Porto Fino and you can see her in all her glory there. Can you come for overnight on a weekend?" With a mock serious scowl Brown lowered his voice, sounding like a vicar preaching. "This is where you say *yes,* young man."

Brown seemed sincerely friendly and Wake had never seen, much less been in, a real castle. "Ah, well, yes, sir. It would be a tremendous honor to visit your castle. Thank you very much for the invitation."

"Excellent decision, Lieutenant. It will be in a week." He gestured toward Strom. "My friend Beauregard and his lovely lady will be there, along with some other diplomats, a couple of our own naval staff officers and a few other charmers that always seem to appear. An interesting and diverse assembly, I think."

Brown's face beamed. "And now, Beauregard, I must pay my respects to his eminence the cardinal over there—after all, it is a saint's day!"

As Brown conversed with the red-capped Catholic cardinal of Genoa, Wake asked, "Sir, did I say something wrong about the *Black Tulip* to Consul General Brown?"

Strom shook his head while grinning at Wake's discomfort. "No, Wake. Nothing's wrong. Just that there's a bit of good humor in what you said and you'll find out why when you arrive at the castle. Davis here will assist on your travel arrangements." Strom looked over Wake's shoulder. "Oh, I see we have the good fortune to have the first lady of the consulate among us tonight."

Wake turned and felt his legs weaken. Not four feet away was Catherine, stunningly beautiful in that same green gown from St. Pierre, and looking directly into his eyes.

21

Soldier of Fortune

Even while his heart melted at the vision of her gentle smile, soft hair, and sad eyes—as if the intervening months had not happened and they were both still at Martinique—Wake realized that his appearance must be anything but attractive. He felt worn out, while she looked young and fresh and feminine.

"Madame Faber," offered Strom. "May I present Lieutenant Peter Wake of the United States Navy? Lieutenant Wake represents our navy here in the Mediterranean at the moment. Lieutenant, this charming lady is Madame Catherine Faber de Champlain, wife of the consul general of the Republic of France, a man whom you've already had the honor of meeting."

Wake stood spellbound she stepped forward with her hand extended. He took it in both of his and kissed it, fighting the desperate urge to pull her into his arms.

"*Enchanté*, Madame Faber," he said, ignoring the shocked faces of Strom and Davis, who immediately deduced their shy naval officer already knew the lady.

"*Merci*, Lieutenant—" Catherine's eyes darted suddenly and Wake belatedly registered that her husband had rejoined the group and was watching him. Feeling his cheeks heat up, he tried to think of something to say, but his mind went blank.

Faber slid an arm around his wife and gestured toward the dance floor. *"Voulez-vous danser, ma chérie?"* Without waiting for her, he headed to the center of the room where couples swirled to a Chopin waltz.

"Excusez-moi," she said with a little curtsy to them all, before following Faber.

There was a moment of silence among the three Americans, broken by Strom. "It appears you have met the lady, Lieutenant. But I thought you said you've never been to the Med prior to this?"

"I *haven't* been across the Atlantic before this, sir. I met the lady at Martinique in December. She is a delightful person."

Strom was worried by Wake's reaction when he saw the Frenchman's wife. "I know she is delightful, Lieutenant. I also know she is *married*—to a high-ranking French diplomat. Kindly remember that. Your behavior will reflect upon our national character."

When he heard Strom's words, Wake's headache hammered his temples and before he knew it he retorted, "Consul General— I am married also, and you, sir, are on the edge of insulting my honor and that of the lady in question . . ."

"You dare to chastise *me?*" Strom seethed, his bulk leaning forward so others couldn't hear. "Let's get something straight here, Wake. I don't give one iota of a damn about your *honor*. It doesn't impress anybody around here. You're just another underling here, another minion who does servants' work for a joke of a navy. So don't you ever *dare* to get high and mighty with me, you little pipsqueak. I've *killed* bigger, badder, and brighter men than you in war, boy."

Wake got ready for the blow he was sure would come as Davis stepped between them, laughing loudly as if one of them had told a joke, then whispering, "Gentlemen, please. Nothing untoward has happened, so let us not make a scene. I think some cool champagne would do us all some good. Please, gentlemen."

Strom glared at Davis, then relaxed and laughed as he punched Wake hard on the arm. "Say, that was a good one, Lieutenant," he bellowed. "You had me going there for a moment!"

The hit looked playful but Wake's bone ached. He felt Davis step on his shoe, took the hint and swallowed his pride, muttering loudly, "Yes, sir. My humor is sometimes misunderstood. Dry, I've been told. I'm glad you appreciated it." Then, quieter, "I apologize for any misunderstanding, sir. The lady and I are brief acquaintances. I didn't mean for it to appear like anything more."

Strom paused, then said, "Perhaps I jumped the gun a bit myself, Lieutenant. Got nervous. Lesson learned for us both. This is a dangerous continent in more ways than one. Just beware of the women here, Lieutenant. Be *very* wary of them. They start wars more often than you know."

"Very good, gentlemen," whispered Davis, his relief evident. "I think the particular lady's beauty excites emotions beyond the norm. I'm sure we can put this in perspective and that no one meant any offense. I'll go fetch us some refreshments."

When Davis brought the drinks over Strom lifted his in a toast. "To beautiful ladies, and lessons we've learned about them."

"There are three ways to get to Porto Fino, all of which present challenges," explained Davis as he ate his trout during lunch in the sporting club overlooking the harbor. It was the prettiest day Wake had yet seen in Italy, for the new week had brought with it sun. The *Lanterna* lighthouse stood above the harbor a mile across the crowded anchorage, the bright day reflecting in an almost reddish glow from its 380-foot tower of squared stonework. Faded pastels of the homes in the hills surrounding the city came to life and Wake was seeing colors in Genoa for the first time.

"Are you going with me?" asked Wake, concerned about heading out across a country whose language he didn't understand or speak.

"Wasn't invited, Peter. You're the lucky one."

"Hmm, don't know about *that* yet. Is the consulate paying for my transport?" asked Wake.

"No, it was a personal invitation, so we can't fund it, Peter."

"Then tell me about the cheapest way to get there. Lieutenants don't make much money, Dan, and almost all of mine goes to my family."

"Ah, then it's the donkey carts for you, my friend. Italy traveled like an Italian—a poor Italian. It'll take about three days to go the fifty miles, at least."

"Three days for only fifty miles! I could walk it faster."

"No, you couldn't. There are mountains that go all the way down into the sea between here and there. The crow may only fly, or a ship steam fifty miles, but you'll do at least a hundred, what with all the curves and switchbacks and such."

Wake sighed. "Very well, what about the train?"

"Expensive, only six to seven hours."

"Six to seven hours? And a steamer?"

"The most expensive. Five hours, give or take a few."

"Train it is, then." Wake sighed. "I wonder. Do I really have to go? Can I get out of this?"

"Up to you. But everyone is expecting you to go now. It's an invitation many wait a long time for. You would be insulting Brown. National pride, Peter."

"Damn. Wish a little national money went with it to pay the way. All right. I'll go."

The train station at Genoa was in total confusion. Wake's experience in Latin America was nothing like what he was seeing here—a combination of technological achievement and cultural chaos. He said goodbye to Davis, who had translated the purchase of round trip tickets for Wake, then edged his way onto the train and found his seat by a window. The private compartment could hold four, but the only others there were an elderly couple heading back to Rome from Milan. The occupants nodded politely to each other but could not converse beyond pantomime.

Wake was settling in, about to read the foreign issue of the *London Times*, when he noticed a commotion on the platform, forty feet from the window. A tall, barrel-chested passenger in an oversized plain tan coat and carrying a valise had grabbed a local panhandler—Wake had seen him plying his trade aggressively earlier and thought him a pickpocket—by the collar and was kicking him in the rear. The street scoundrel produced a knife and flourished it in the face of the tall man, screaming something in Italian. The man in the coat immediately let go of the thief, but did not retreat. Instead his lip curled up on one side—not quite a smile but close—as if he regarded his adversary with curiosity.

The man in the coat was different from the small crowd who stopped to watch the confrontation unfold. He stood straight, with short-cropped black hair, large expressionless eyes, and a Vandyke goatee worn like an insignia of rank. His appearance added up to obvious command bearing and Wake marked him as a military or naval officer, nationality as yet unknown.

Without warning, the officer's right hand swept up, grasped the knife hand of his assailant, swung the blade through an arc and in one fluid move plunged it into the thief's eye. The military man then executed a right oblique and marched up the steps and into the train.

A collective gasp rose from the crowd as the target, which is how Wake thought of the thief, crumpled to the deck of the platform. Wake was amazed that during the whole time the valise never dropped from the officer's left hand. The entire event took seconds.

The older couple watched the drama as well, exchanging words in fearful undertones. The lady's clucking became a stifled scream when the compartment door opened seconds later. There stood the man in the overcoat.

"This compartment five?" he said in an aggravated tone with an American accent. Wake and the couple were astonished. The man tried again, louder, more frustrated. "*Camera cinque?*"

Wake came to his senses. "Yes. Yes, this is compartment five."

"Good, this is where my seat is then. You sound American."

"Ah, yes. Peter Wake. Massachusetts." Wake gestured to the frightened people sitting opposite him. "These folks are from Rome, I think. They don't speak English. I don't really speak Italian."

"Michael Woodgerd. Ohio." He nodded to Wake and then to the wide-eyed couple, who bobbed their heads quickly in return. Outside on the platform the police were arriving on the scene, listening to a dozen accounts of the incident while they examined the body. Two people pointed to the train.

"Did that man try to steal your money?" asked Wake, still incredulous at what he had witnessed.

"No. He was kicking that little dog over there. For fun," said Woodgerd, shaking his head and pointing to a mangy brown emaciated dog cringing in the corner of the waiting area. "I think he broke her ribs, the slimy sonovabitch. She was only begging for food and he kicked her hard half a dozen times. Could hear her cry out on the street and none of these damn scum," Woodgerd waved at the crowd, "were stopping him."

"Oh, I didn't see that part. I just saw you kicking him."

"Yep, a little equalizer for what he did to the dog. That bastard didn't seem to like it when he had it done to him."

"Then he pulled a knife on you. I saw that."

Woodgerd swiveled his head toward Wake, eyes locking on

him as a deathly grin spread across his face. "Yeah . . ."

"I suppose that's self-defense on your part, then."

Woodgerd nodded slowly, never removing his eyes from Wake's. "Ya shouldn't kick little dogs. Or pull a knife on a man unless ya know how to use it. He didn't."

"Yes, well, I see your point." Wake sat uncomfortably close to Woodgerd, their forearms touching on the seat's armrest. The man was at least four inches taller than Wake and twenty to thirty pounds heavier, all of it muscle, he suspected, though the coat hid Woodgerd's frame. The moment was interrupted when the train's whistle screamed and steam blew by the window.

"Been a very long friggin' day," sighed Woodgerd. "Don't know about you, but I'm gonna catch some sleep." He exhaled loudly again, tilted his head back and closed his eyes.

The train jolted a few feet, then rumbled slowly forward, picking up speed. Wake glanced outside and saw one policeman scanning the windows of the train. He wondered if they had come aboard. Then the station was behind them and they chugged slowly east through the city.

An hour later, after stopping many times for street traffic, they emerged from the old city and crossed the Bisagno River into the outlying hill country. Without warning Woodgerd startled Wake, who had begun to doze.

"So why are you in Italy, Wake?"

After what he had seen earlier, Wake was unsure of how much to tell the man. "Just traveling down to see friends at Porto Fino."

"Hmm. Army or navy? You got a hellova tan, so I'm guessing navy."

Stunned, Wake worried where this was heading. "And how exactly did you know?"

Woodgerd smiled his death-grin again. "I can spot a believer every time. Got real good at it during 'The Recent Unpleasantness,' as those Rebel fools call it. Saw believers die by the thousands. Oh yeah—you're a believer, Wake. No doubt on that."

Wake struggled to control his anger, "Want to explain that?"

"Not a very hard thing to deduce, Wake. You've got an honest, open, strong face. You don't have the jowls of a glutton, the nose of a drunk, the breath of a smoker, the hands of a clerk, the clothes of a banker or a farmer—or a tourist, for that matter. You spoke well and gently, smiled at the old folks to calm them, and are polite to me, even though you don't like what I'm saying. You sit straight up, look me in the eye, keep your voice controlled, and haven't fled the compartment—a sign of discipline. It's obvious you're an American officer. And thus, a gentleman. Ah yes, a believer in doing the right things for the right reasons. God, flag, and family. I'm not any of that, which is obvious, of course, and you don't very much like or trust me."

Wake replied with a level tone, "You're absolutely right on all accounts." He was aware that the elderly couple was watching the exchange like frightened animals. "But, as you say, it wasn't very hard to deduce all that. So what are *you* doing in Italy, Mr. Woodgerd?"

"Just passing through, from Budapest. Unlike you, Wake. You're not on leave. Nope, I can tell you're working. Stationed with the European Squadron probably, but they're not here, so you're on independent assignment, I'd wager."

Woodgerd's arrogance was overwhelming, but Wake maintained a cool countenance, extremely curious as to who this man really was, and what he was about. "And how is it that you know so much about naval affairs, Mr. Woodgerd?"

Woodgerd's laugh came out as a cynical hiss. "Naval affairs? I don't know jack about what you squids do, and I don't care to know. I just know one when I see 'im. You're useless on land, and that's where I ply *my* trade."

"Which would be?"

"I kill people." Woodgerd made the statement flatly, without shame or pride or threat.

"I just saw an example of that. Very efficient."

The hiss again from Woodgerd. "Oh, that fool? No, not that. I kill *soldiers*."

"So you're a mercenary?"

"We prefer 'soldier of fortune.' Sounds so much more pleasant. And the fortune part is important. Very important."

"Former U.S. Army?"

The death grin returned, followed by a gleeful, "Yep. That's where I learned the basics of killing soldiers. Four long years with that Godforsaken Army of the Potomac chasing ol' Marse Bobby. Learned that true believers are valuable to have around as cannon fodder privates, but disasters as commanding officers. Too damned weak. Good thing Grant came finally came along though. Now *that* whiskey-soaked sonovabitch knew what to do—kill. As fast and as many as you can."

Having seen combat ashore and afloat himself during the war, Wake was unimpressed by Woodgerd's comments. "Four years? Volunteer or regular?"

"West Point. Class of fifty-nine."

"A regular. So you must have been made at least a brevet lieutenant colonel by the end of the war."

"Colonel . . . before they cashiered me in sixty-five."

Dishonorably discharging a colonel was highly unusual. Especially a West Point colonel. Wake had to ask. "For what? After what I saw I can't imagine it was for cowardice."

"Conduct unbecoming an officer of the United States Army, and theft of regimental funds."

Wake wanted to ask more but Woodgerd's tone negated that. Still, Wake's curiosity was whetted. "Very interesting, Mr. Woodgerd. Sounds like an eventful life. So who do you kill soldiers for now?"

"Fella named Hassan. He's the brand new sultan of Morocco. Heading there now for a three-year contract. Advisor to the sultan and colonel of the royal guard. Pays better than my last job with the Khedive in Egypt, guarding French canal engineers." Woodgerd looked pensive for a moment, then wagged his head sarcastically. "You know, I don't think Sultan Hassan likes the French very much. Neither do I, really. Hmm, I wonder if he'll want me to kill *them*. Can you imagine that, Peter Wake?"

The only thing Wake could imagine at that point was getting away from the madman. Woodgerd was more than merely another cynical veteran—he looked dangerously unstable. He reminded Wake of the man he had been ordered to track down—and kill—in the Caribbean five years earlier. That man had been an American officer also. And a maniacal killer, turned pirate, in addition.

Glancing at the couple across from him and smiling at them for reassurance, Wake nodded a vague reply to Woodgerd and gazed out the window at the hills that were becoming mountains with each mile.

When he turned back Woodgerd was asleep again, a tranquil smile spread on his relaxed face, as if dreaming of something pleasant. The notion of what that might be made Wake particularly uneasy.

22

The Castle

March 1874

Woodgerd stayed aboard when Wake disembarked the train at the Santa Margherita station. As Wake got up from his seat, he and the soldier never said a word, just quickly glanced at each other, Woodgerd's eyes steady, gauging him.

Following Davis' instructions, Wake made his way down the hill from the station along a maze of streets that canyoned through three- and four-story buildings toward the waterfront. Once at the piazza on the waterfront, he found a crowd waiting at a small steamer alongside a stone wharf and joined the line, confirming with pantomime and a few Italian words that it was the one to Porto Fino. Davis had suggested that he not walk the winding cart path out to the remote village on a peninsula jutting west from the coast—the ferry steamer would be far easier and faster, even if it did further deplete Wake's dwindling supply of money.

The steamer rattled and rumbled along the coast as an elderly gentleman aboard explained in broken English the sights to the American: Antico Castle, built four hundred years earlier to guard against Saracen pirates, the ancient convent at Punta della Cervara, Monte Pollone rising high above everything, and in the distance the jagged cape of Porto Fino. Occasionally the cart path could be seen, a treacherous ribbon winding back and forth, sometimes edging precariously over the sea. The rockslides he could see on the path, where it looked like the whole thing had suddenly dropped into the Mediterranean, made Wake congratulate himself for not trying to save coins on this part of his journey.

Then, with a gentle sigh, the man pointed to an opening in the rocky cliffs along the coast to starboard. A beautiful little cove came into sight with vessels nested together at anchor, a village clustered against the hills on one side.

"Porto Fino," the man said proudly. *"Molto magnifico!"*

Wake went to the bow to watch their approach as the vessel turned into the opening and slowed, weaving its way among the anchored small craft. He looked for a yacht named the *Black Tulip* but saw nothing but fishing smacks. Soon they were tied up along a seawall and a throng of passengers overflowed off the steamer and into the waterside street of taverns and shops, greeting friends with shouts of glee. Behind the tan buildings spread along the water and painted with realistic-looking faux cornices and columns, small houses of faded pink and blue clung to the hillsides. Mandolin music and laughter filled the air from one of the tavernas, gaily colored flowers in window boxes everywhere. Smells of sizzling food and scented cigar smoke floated among the café diners busy in animated discussions.

The whole place appeared magical to Wake as he was swept along by the crowd. His head swiveled around as he stared up at the walls of green foliage that covered the cliffs surrounding the village and he almost tripped and fell into the water. Finding a man in a uniform that he presumed to be a policeman, Wake spread his hands in the universal gesture of one who is lost. "Castle Brown?"

"Il Castello Brown?" The man raised an eyebrow, pointed among the trees atop a cliff on the opposite side of the cove and spoke rapidly. *"Sopra la scogliera piccola."* Then he sauntered away, calling back, *"Buona fortuna!"*

Wake stood, totally confused, not understanding a word but disliking the sound of it. Looking up at the indicated trees he saw the outlines of a stone wall, but no castle. Down by the water, there was a narrow paved walk fronting small businesses around the cove's seawall, but he couldn't see any way from the waterfront up the cliff to the stone wall.

He walked around the cove, noting a massive pile of discarded wood in the village's small piazza of Martiri della Olivetta, built up into an as-yet-untorched pyre. Fishermen were adding a battered old dinghy to the base while women were stringing garlands of flowers around the whole, all of them singing a jaunty tune.

Around the other side he found steps carved deeply into the rock face and disappearing in a curve thirty feet up. It was steep but looked like it might lead to the top. Shifting his sea bag and valise, Wake took a breath and began to climb the uneven steps, up and around the first curve, then another curve as the rough-hewn stairs got closer and vines of ivy and wisteria crowded the passageway, creating a tunnel effect. He was feeling the strain in his legs and arms by the time he got to a little landing area that gave a view of the cove a hundred feet below.

"Mi scusi! Mi scusi!" echoed from above just before two young men carrying large burlap bags on their shoulders raced down past Wake, taking the steps two or three at a time and laughing all the way. Leaning on the rocky ledge, Wake caught his breath, then started up again, trudging slower this time.

It seemed to be an endless succession of steps, curving back and forth so that no long view could be seen of where he was going. He just knew his course was rising and that there were no more places where he could see out and get his bearings. Following another curve to the left his feet registered that the slope was easing and he heard voices. Dragging his baggage now, Wake struggled to hear above the pounding of blood in his ears to determine what they were saying, for it seemed as if it was English. British English. It was at that point that he rounded a final corner and emerged from the stairs of the cliff, almost falling onto a cobblestone street. The man who had been speaking was right there and stopped as if a ghost had appeared.

"What the bloody hell!" exclaimed Lieutenant Peter Sharpe Allen of Her Britannic Majesty's Royal Marines. To a man in naval blue beside him he muttered, "Well, I'll be a vicar in hell if it ain't my old friend, the Yank."

Wake dropped his things and stood there, gasping for air as Allen continued. "What are you doing here, Peter? And why the deuce did you take that blasted suicidal cliff walk? Why not take the road?"

"What," asked Wake after another breath, " . . . road?"

"The one you're standing on, old boy. The one with the easy slope that comes up from the village. Could've ridden on a cart, actually. Much easier route to the castle instead of having your heart burst by carrying your baggage two hundred and fifty feet damn near straight up. You Yanks always have to do things a bit differently, don't you. Silly, really, if you ask me."

Allen held out a hand and Wake shook it while the Marine introduced the other man as a temporary messenger for the British admiral. Wake nodded hello and asked Allen, "Are you staying at the castle this weekend too?"

"Yes. As an aide to the admiral. But I have to stay at a house nearby though. Not allowed to rest my head within the storied walls. I heard that you got a personal invitation to stay *inside*. Must be that boyish American charm. Brown's pretty close with who he invites."

The other officer said goodbye, leaving the two friends. Allen picked up the heavier bag and they started toward the castle towering above them just ahead.

"I can't believe I didn't see this road down at the village. That climb almost killed me," Wake admitted.

"Well, I will restrain myself from commenting any further about your navigational skills, Lieutenant Peter Wake, of the United States Navy. I suppose a Marine can't expect much from a sailor ashore, and the most important thing is that you've arrived." Allen stopped at the portal of a rock-faced wall that surrounded the castle. A guard standing nonchalantly against the door said, *"Buon giorno, signores,"* and waved them inside.

Crossing a fruit orchard they entered a garden splotched with red and yellow roses among the greenery. Allen led Wake through a heavy double door and up into the thick walls of the castle itself, where they climbed circular stone stairs. Finally, they entered a cool foyer, floored with white marble and walled with striped yellow silk. A tall long-jawed and ancient dark face topped by a white turban stood before them. His slow deliberate words sounded like they came from a deep cave.

"Good afternoon, Lieutenant Allen. I have not had the pleasure of meeting your friend." The turban bobbed in Wake's direction. "Good afternoon, sir. I am Variam, major-domo of Castle Brown. Are you one of our guests this weekend?"

Wake stood there mute for a moment. The man was like someone out of a novel from the exotic East. He recovered his wits. "Yes, I'm a guest. Lieutenant Peter Wake. United States Navy. I'm here for the party. Consul General Brown invited me."

"Ah yes, Lieutenant Wake. The Consul General is very pleased that you could come. He is a great admirer of your country and people. I am at your service, sir."

Allen interjected. "Peter, Variam is a Sikh warrior from Lahore, in the Punjab." Wake nodded politely at Variam, who was waiting at parade rest, but Allen could see his American friend didn't understand and continued. "The Punjab is part of India, the crown jewel of the British Empire. Variam was a sergeant major, serving for thirty years in the Khalsa Army under the famous Runjeet Singh, until Singh died unfortunately back in the forties. Sikh warriors are very well respected in the British

Empire. Variam's name means 'The Brave One' and he can be an ally or an enemy." Allen glanced at Variam playfully. "I hope he'll be the former for us."

Wake was impressed. Not by the recitation of historical facts, for he comprehended none of what Allen told him, but by the stalwart appearance of Variam. The man looked about sixty, but Wake's quick math showed that he must be at least eighty years old.

"Lieutenant Allen is too kind, but I thank him for his explanation of my background. It will be a pleasure to be your servant, gentlemen. You are both warriors. We understand each other. It is the way of warriors."

He reached over and effortlessly picked up both pieces of baggage, beckoning them to follow with a nod of his head. "Please come this way, gentlemen, and I will show you to your room, Lieutenant Wake."

Wake faintly registered the Spanish Gothic motif of the first-floor hall, out from which spanned several small parlors and a paneled grand dining room. Ascending the stairs, he noticed they were thickly carpeted—unlike his cliff climb—and had the silly urge to go barefoot as he used to when a boy seaman years earlier. On the second level he was shown a small bedroom, furnished simply but comfortably. Variam announced that should Wake need anything, he had but to pull the bell-rope in the corner and it would be attended to. Dinner, he added with an air of pleasant anticipation, would be at six and the guests would meet on the patio at that time.

After Variam departed, Wake went to the window. Leaning out he saw clear aqua-jade water 250 feet straight down, the walls of the castle blending into the cliff face, the whole covered with tangles of vines and bushes. He realized that the passenger steamer had passed within a thousand feet of the castle upon entering Porto Fino but the foliage had obscured it. Beyond the cliff his panorama spread out for miles, from the mountains of the distant Italian mainland across the Golfo de Tigullio, around to the vast shimmering

Mediterranean. He took in the smell of flowers, the gentle sound of distant stringed music, the whispering of the waves and wind through the trees, and the view. That view. The stuff of tales. It was breathtaking.

Allen broke the silence. "Quite the billet, eh? I dare say that no other lieutenant in your navy has been a guest here. Maybe not the admiral himself. I've been here only once so far, and only during the day."

"Pete, this is unbelievable. Beautiful."

"Just wait, my friend. You haven't seen the best yet."

Allen had left hours before and Wake lay on his bed, the hall door closed for privacy, letting the sea breeze coming through the window wash over him. In his peculiar fashion, he analyzed events of the previous three months, calculating the problems he faced, the decisions he had made, and the consequences that would come.

The March air was cool but not nearly as frigid as when he had arrived in Italy six weeks earlier. Six weeks, he thought. Six weeks in a hotel room waiting for . . . what? A squadron that kept getting delayed? A nebulous job he wasn't prepared for? His marriage to completely fall apart? In his letters back to Linda, the products of many drafts, Wake had tried to be understanding and hopeful of the future. Positive and loving, but firm on one point—he was not leaving the navy. And what would be the result of that decision?

Now, in the most luxurious and tranquil place he had ever visited, he was scared down to his gut, sure that his life would soon descend into the desolate existence he had seen in other officers when their marriages ended. Why didn't she understand? She always had before. But her letters were clear. Forbearance of his career had taken its toll and her empathy was at an end. Over. Am I prepared to lose her?—he asked himself grimly, with the sad thought that maybe he already had, years before.

Sounds of people again drifted into the room from along the passageway. Wake made out Variam explaining something, then a British reply and someone speaking in a guttural tone—he guessed it was German. Guests had been arriving all day and at one point he had heard French, making him wonder if the Fabers were invited. And that, against his best judgment and willpower, had set his heart to racing. Would he see those mesmerizing eyes, hear that lilting voice, feel the gentle caress of her hand as they melded together and swayed to a romantic song in the night air?

His nerves, keyed up by a hectic day of exertion and uncertainty, finally gave out and Wake closed his eyes, shutting out the world. To his semiconscious embarrassment, Catherine glided into view in his mind, standing there, beautiful, her eyes saying without words what he wanted to hear, beckoning to come closer. Wake felt the tension slowly leave him, and then he abandoned himself into the realm of his dream—discipline and judgment gone. And unlamented.

23

A Vision in Green

Wake's ears filled with the sounds of the party the moment he opened the door to his room and stepped into the passageway. Mandolins with a lively beat pleasantly set the mood. Laughter and clinking glasses provided a background as French, Italian, German, and English floated up from the first floor, gaining intensity as he descended the stairs to the main foyer. There Variam stood, booming out the announcement of each guest, his words echoing along the high vaulted ceiling, the pause afterward heightening its profundity.

"Lieutenant Peter . . . Wake, . . . of the United . . . States . . . Navy. . . ."

Rigged out once again in his formal dress uniform, Wake felt awkward among the elite mingling around him, but followed the almost imperceptible nod of the major-domo and marched along the main hall toward the double doors at the end that opened onto the patio. As he passed through the massive oak doors something about them struck a chord with him, a familiarity that surprised him, but that he couldn't place. At any rate, he had no time to evaluate for immediately he was in front of Consul Brown, who was greeting each guest as they emerged onto the graveled patio surrounded by a waist-high parapet and decorated with cedar and pine trees growing up out of the pebbles.

"My dear Lieutenant Wake! How positively wonderful that you've come to share this weekend with us here. I hope your stay at the castle will be an oasis of calm in this turbulent world." Brown theatrically cocked an eyebrow. "Enjoy yourself this evening. All work and no play make for a very grumpy gentleman in anyone's navy."

"Thank you, sir. The invitation was very kind of you. And your home here is . . . well, sir, it is magnificent. Something out of a fairy tale."

"Yes, it is. It is indeed. Originally, in Roman times, this was a small outpost, a lookout, but the castle as you see it now was built in the middle fifteen-hundreds by the Genovese republic to protect their coastal trade. Took twenty-three years to complete. By the late seventeen-hundreds the French, English, Austrians, Sardinians, and Venetians had all fought over it and owned it at one point or another. In fact, Porto Fino was renamed by that rascal Napoleon in 1798 as Port Napoleon, which I think is a bit much, even for him. Fell into disrepair fifty years ago. I've been here since sixty-seven, restoring it."

"Fascinating history, sir," said Wake, confused by Brown's dissertation, wondering why Napoleon even cared.

"Well, I could go on, of course, but here's Agnes, my wife and the lovely lady of the castle."

Brown made the introductions as Agnes Brown surveyed Wake with interested eyes that were at least fifteen years younger than her husband's. Brown explained that he was just telling the American about the castle's history. She pointed to two pine trees near the west wall, overlooking the cove far below. "Montague and I planted those on our wedding day four years ago. We're hoping they'll last for eternity and that someday people will remember this place for love as well as war."

Wake bowed. "I am sure they will, ma'am." He swept a hand

around the patio. "This is a garden of peacefulness now. And of romance."

"I'm so glad you noticed, Lieutenant."

He turned back to Brown. "By the way, sir, I looked for *Black Tulip* upon arrival but didn't see her. Is she out at sea now?"

As his wife looked surprised, Brown grinned at Wake. "No, Lieutenant. She's not in the water at all. She's all around you. Right here. In fact, you walked right through her to come out onto the patio!"

Wake glanced around the patio but saw nothing. "Sir?"

"The doors, the windows, the ceiling beams, the end tables, the flooring, and much more. It's all from *Black Tulip!* You see, Lieutenant, she wrecked on the point while we were renovating the castle in sixty-nine, so we salvaged her to build up the wooden components here. *Black Tulip* is all around you, so the castle is part ship. At least in her soul. Rather brilliant, even if I do say so myself."

Then it dawned on Wake, those doors were former hatch covers and an end table he had passed in the hall was a binnacle box. He and Brown walked over and examined the window frames and Wake could see the elbow beams of a ship in them. The overhead beams in the great hall were ship's rib timbers. The interior doors were deck planking—the flooring of the foyer as well. It made him smile with appreciation of a job well done.

"Consul General, I am in awe."

"I thought you would be, Lieutenant," said Brown, his pride showing. "And I knew that you, more than most, would understand what it took to accomplish this."

Brown took him for a tour of the ramparts and the tower. The castle was not large, but Wake inwardly admitted that it did have a very formidable defense, even against a modern army of the late nineteenth century. The consul showed his guest the Browns' private apartments and his personal study, located on the fourth floor, up in the tower. They returned by way of a perimeter walk along the ramparts, according to Brown nicknamed the

"Lovers' Walk" for its seclusion and romantic flowers and vinery.

Upon reentering the patio Brown caught the glance of Strom, who had just appeared on the patio. "Beauregard, I'll let you introduce young Mr. Wake here around to our collection of intrigues and scoundrels, if you would be so kind, my friend. For I see that I have to now attend to the German Federation's diplomat, who seems to be getting a bit vociferous with the bishop over there—you know how much care Prussians always seem to require."

Strom introduced Wake to his wife Christine, a pretty blond with a Midwestern accent and a shy manner—the very opposite of her husband. Then they toured the patio, speaking with various guests. He recognized some of them, including Vice Admiral Drummond and the bishop of Genoa. At the corner of the patio, near a niche in the rampart, Wake heard the guttural voice again and saw Strom tense.

"Ach, Herr Strom! How good it is to see you. And your handsome wife."

The severe-looking, middle-aged man addressing the Stroms clicked his heels and bowed violently to Christine. Wake had heard of such a gesture, but never actually seen it done. It appeared ridiculous.

"Thank you, Mr. Moltke. And it is always interesting to see you. May I present Lieutenant Peter Wake, of our navy. He is our naval representative at the moment while the squadron is away. Lieutenant, Mr. Karl von Moltke is the German Federation's consul general for northern Italy."

Wake felt like a bug being examined by a naturalist as Moltke surveyed him, then said perfunctorily, "Lieutenant Wake, a pleasure, of course, to meet you."

"And an honor for me to meet you, sir." The name was familiar to Wake, so he added, "Von Moltke? Any relation to the famous field marshal who won the war against France recently?"

Wake saw that it did the trick. Moltke stiffened his spine even more and almost clicked his heels again. He ventured a slight, very slight, smile. "Yes, of course. I am honored to be a *first* cousin of the world-famous Helmuth Karl Bernhard von Moltke, Field Marshal of all German Forces and Chief of the General Staff. Our fathers were brothers and our family is from Mecklenburg-Schwerin, the ancestral home of the greatest of the warriors of our nation. Naturally, I am a warrior as well. In artillery—the king of battle, as Carl von Clausewitz, another Prussian warrior, has presented forth. Perhaps you know of him?"

What a pompous windbag, thought Wake, who decided to show Moltke that Americans were not *that* ignorant. "Yes, sir, I am aware of him. Clausewitz certainly did have experience in war. He was involved in several losing battles and got captured by the French in eighteen-o-six. I think that losing frequently teaches more than winning, especially if it's the *French* you lose to. And, of course, Consul General, it was *Napoleon* who named infantry as the queen of battle and artillery as the king of battle. Napoleon really was pretty good at using artillery. Carl von Clausewitz expounded further on that in his famous text. But who am I to tell you, a Prussian warrior, these things?"

Moltke said nothing for a moment, his hooded eyes boring into Wake. "How very American your views are, Lieutenant. But I expect too much that you would understand our history in Europe. Now, exactly where are *you* from in North America? And what is your family's history?"

Wake thought it all absurd, a stage parody, except that Moltke was very real and had real power. He was closely related to the man who controlled the most powerful military machine in Europe. In the world. "Well, sir, I am from a fishing village in the state of Massachusetts. My family is not famous and they are not warriors. They sail schooners on the coastal trade. I am the first warrior in the family. I sincerely hope I'm the last."

Moltke huffed, "Ach, and so you had to have training in the art of war at the academy, since you had no family tradition and upbringing in it?"

Christine had already made a quick departure, but Strom

leaned against the parapet and watched with amused interest as Wake replied, "No, sir. I did not go to the academy."

Moltke's tone lowered as he clucked, "Then how are you trained in war!"

Wake tried to submerge his anger and gave the Prussian his best smile. "By doing, not talking."

Then he turned to Strom. "I think I hear my name being called, sir. I must bid both of you *au revoir* for now." As he walked away he heard Moltke mutter something about an American speaking French, badly.

His blood pounding, Wake made his way to the champagne table, where a steward presented him with a glass. Wake found his hand was shaking, but downed the drink and signaled for two more. Taking his glasses to the area by the two pine trees, he gazed out at the sea across the tiny peninsula below. The glitter of the sunset on the distant waves was calming, a sight he had known all his life. He exhaled and stretched his neck, then his arms, willing himself to relax—wishing he was out there and away from pompous bastards like Moltke. It was clean *out there*. He stared at the reddening sun, letting it dazzle his eyes like a kaleidoscope and take him far away.

"I liked your answer to that strutting Prussian pig, Peter. Men like him have a mind for domination, a body for war, and a heart for hate. They know about everything masculine—except how to love a woman. . . ."

Suddenly next to him, Catherine reached over and touched his hand. His eyes slowly focused on her face, her beautiful face, and Wake felt all his strength leaving. She was a vision in green, wearing the same forest-green gown, trimmed with golden threads, now almost luminescent in the sunset. Her brown hair was swept up with a single gold and green comb, and Wake had to fight an urge to take it out and let Catherine's soft tresses fall down around her shoulders. Emeralds draped across her chest brought his eyes to her bosom, and he saw her take in a breath. Her hand squeezed his, and just then all he wanted in the world was to hold her and let her caress him.

"I hoped you'd be here," he murmured, oblivious to the dozens of people around them.

Her eyes never left his, making him shiver inside as he realized she was looking at him the same way she had in his dream that afternoon. Her eyes were calling him to her, gently, sadly. He moved closer.

"I heard you would be here, Peter. I wore the dress that I could tell you liked in St. Pierre. And Genoa."

Wake held her hand, staring at her, drinking her in. Behind her, in the dimming sun, he saw the lights of Porto Fino coming on. A final shaft of golden sunlight glowed on her face, bringing out the flecks of green in her eyes as she looked up at him. "It's lovely, especially because you're wearing it, Catherine."

"I wanted to remind you of gentle moments in faraway places, Peter. I am happy that you are here. You are the only happiness I have here." She glanced back at the crowd of guests that were starting to line up for the dining room. "They are, at best, boring and false. Some, like Moltke, are worse, and frighten me. I felt so alone here before I saw you."

"I was melancholy too, Catherine. But not now. Now I'm feeling much better. Have you been here before?"

"Yes. We get invited each month. It is a lovely place, is it not? I just wish I was here alone with you."

Wake quickly looked around the patio. "Is your husband—"

A commotion erupted at the guest line, an angry threat in French returned by an equally malevolent-sounding phrase in German. Wake saw Henri Faber facing Moltke, who was grimacing with anger, his words hissing out in English. "You cowardly French *swine*. You dare to call the Germanic people uncivilized! Look at your pathetic selves, little Frenchman. Your country's never risen above its sick past except under that despotic Corsican's illusions of grandeur, and in the effeminate playtimes of life. Wine and women are the only successes you are known for—and good for. There are no *men* in France, Faber, as we easily showed the world only three years ago."

Faber's hand was fast. Moltke fell backward a step, his cheek crimson from the slap. Faber moved closer, his gray eyes lifeless. "You may have beaten us then, Moltke, but *never* again. French honor will someday soon see the German barbarians bow down in apology and beg for mercy. And as for *you*, I will stand ready at dawn to defend my personal honor outside the walls of this castle. Any weapon you choose, German."

Moltke glared at Faber, sputtered something in German and stalked off. Wake was astounded. He was witnessing a challenge to duel—something he had previously only heard of, like so much else he was now experiencing in Europe. Catherine immediately went to her husband as the buzzing crowd parted for Brown, who stepped up on a flower planter. "That war is over and I'll not have any of this behavior here, in my home. You two gentlemen will separate for the evening. What you do tomorrow after you leave these walls I cannot control. But I will not have this kind of activity within this castle. Really, gentlemen, how very unseemly, especially for *diplomats.* . . ."

Wake followed Catherine into the crowd and watched as Faber gruffly ordered her to go to their room, adding that he would be there shortly, then brushed aside a protesting Brown and strode over to the bar table. Catherine was on the verge of tears as she glanced at Wake before disappearing from view.

He almost followed her, but held back, for Brown abruptly spoke up again, asking everyone to ignore the incident and not let it spoil the evening that he had planned for them. "Our martial entertainment is over, ladies and gentlemen. Now we'll move on to some culinary entertainment, for which my chef is justly famous."

The guests, chattering excitedly, reformed their line and filed past a taciturn Variam, who shepherded them into the two dining rooms. Strom appeared and spoke quietly. "Nice demonstration of European manners, wasn't it? They do get their feathers ruffled here. Especially the French and the Prussians."

"Are those two really going to duel at dawn, sir?"

Strom grinned. "Looks that way, doesn't it. No great loss, no matter who loses. They're both obnoxious."

"Mr. Consul General, perhaps I'm naïve, but I didn't think people still did that."

Strom regarded Wake for a second. "They may look pretty polished around here, Peter Wake, but just under the glitter they get as tribal as any African. Fortunately, they don't think we Americans are worth getting upset over."

24

Sotto la Luna

Wake was in a trance for the rest of the evening. He couldn't keep his mind off that vision of Catherine in the sunset. At dinner he sat between Christine Strom and the Greek consul's wife, who kept telling him that English food was dull and she could do so much better. Across from him was the vulcanologist he had met at the French soirée in Genoa, still boring people with rantings about how volcanic lava could energize lights in lamps. Catherine never returned and Wake worried about her. Faber didn't appear too stable when he went inside after filling himself at the bar. It was an excruciating evening and he wanted to lash out at someone in frustration.

After dinner, the Royal Navy contingent—minus Drummond, who was with the senior diplomats in Brown's private study—clustered in a corner of the dining room, the ladies having adjourned to a parlor somewhere in the castle. Allen came over and passed along an invitation to join the British naval officers, Wake almost leaping at the chance to get away from the society people and be with his own kind. When he arrived at the smoky gathering—Wake didn't mind pipe smoke but had never abided cigars very much—he was offered some British West Indian rum, which he accepted with grateful enthusiasm. Sea stories and war stories ensued, with Allen asking Wake to tell of his experiences during the American Civil War. Wake did, prefacing that they weren't of real tale-telling quality but could show the character of blockade duty.

As the evening grew late he noticed Drummond return to the dining room, which was now raucous with laughter and shouting. The admiral was in deep conversation with none other than Commander John Fisher, who stopped midsentence when he saw Wake.

"Hello, Wake. Didn't think you'd be here," Fisher said with a smile as Drummond poured himself some rum over at the side table. "Got on the diplo party list, eh? Dreary stuff, most of the time, but old Brown's got quite the hideout here, doesn't he?"

"Yes, sir. I'm very impressed with the castle and appreciate his invitation. But I think it's because the senior American naval officers are gone, sir."

Fisher shook his head. "No, Lieutenant. It's because Brown likes your mettle. Heard of your reputation and was keen on having you around."

"Well, that's flattering, sir. I hope I haven't disappointed him." Wake remembered his earlier suspicion on where Fisher had been headed and decided to be bold. "Is your holiday with friends over now, sir? On your way back to England?"

Fisher tilted his jaw back, then allowed the smile to return. "Yes."

Wake decided to press, his eyes on Fisher's, willing his voice to sound nonchalant. "And where did you say you were visiting, sir? Croatia, I think?"

"I don't believe that I did, Lieutenant. Have a pleasant evening. I must be going now."

Fisher rejoined Drummond, and Wake saw by his watch that it was almost midnight, the realization making him suddenly tired. He said his thank-yous and bid good night, then climbed the stairs to the second floor. The hallway was lit by two small lamps, creating a gloomy cast that brought Craven Walker's dream of lava lights to mind. Wake was ruminating on the feasibility of using lava for energy when Variam quietly came up from the shadows at the end of the hall and stood at attention, handing over an envelope.

"A message for you, sir. No reply desired."

Wake thought perhaps it was Fisher or Allen, or maybe Strom or Brown, who wanted to meet him for breakfast the next morning and discuss something privately. Then he saw the script on the outside of the envelope and instantly knew. Variam bowed and made his way silently down the hall, leaving Wake to study his name written in feminine cursive. A moment later Wake was holding the note under the dim light, trying to read the words. All it said was: *Lovers' Walk—midnight.*

He pulled out his watch again. Both tiny brass hands were pointing up.

Wake slipped into his room and, in a shaft of light through the window from a full moon, exchanged his heavy formal coat for his lighter one. Heart fluttering, he checked the hall, then ascended the stairs. Faint sounds of final revelry drifted up, heavy tones punctuated by laughter, but the upper floors were quiet.

When he reached the third floor he paused, trying to remember how to get to the secluded balcony walk Brown had shown him. The door to the right of the tower room was slightly open and he opened it and stepped out into the moonlit walk. It abruptly hit him that this could be a trap, the walk was a perfect ambush site. His mind raced with the possibilities of who and why. It might be an irate Faber, or a humiliated Moltke—or even cold, calculating Fisher, intent on stopping him from intruding further on British torpedo innovations. Halting, Wake peered around the shadows that filled the corners and background areas, wishing he had a weapon and chastising himself for even getting into this position.

Tensed for an attack, Wake crept forward and around the curve of the tower wall. He decided that if he saw no one in another ten feet he would return to his room and stop this foolishness. Then footsteps clicked on the flag stones of the walkway behind him—his only route of escape blocked. He spun around in a crouch, prepared to lunge to the wall side of the narrow space and throw his attacker over the waist-high rampart.

Catherine, still in the green gown, let out a little laugh, continuing into a stifled giggle as Wake clutched his chest in shock and caught his breath. "Oh Peter! You don't have to be afraid. I won't hurt you."

He let out a sigh and collapsed against the wall, "Good God above, Catherine. I damned near killed you out of fright! I got to thinking when I walked out here that maybe this was all a trap."

"It *is*. . . ." came the sultry whisper in his ear while her body molded against him.

Wake's heart was still hammering. He wrapped his arms around her, stroking her long soft hair as she laid her head against his chest.

"Your heart is beating very fast," said Catherine. "Are you all right? It really is safe here, Peter. No one will attack you. We are alone." She looked up at him, her sad eyes dissolving his tension. "It is our moment, Peter—no one else's. *Our* special moment in time, *sotto la luna*." She touched his cheek and smiled. "It means 'under the moon.' I think that right now in our lives, each of us needs to have someone hold us gently."

They embraced each other for a long time, neither talking nor moving from their spot, just caressing each other, as the moon slowly soared high across the night sky. Wake realized Catherine was not wearing a corset and held her waist tightly, inadvertently making her squirm away.

"*Ooh, ça chatouille!*" she laughed.

He thought he'd hurt her. "What?"

"I am, how is it that you say? . . . ticklish . . . there." She returned to his arms and put his hands back where they were. "It is a good feeling, Peter. *S'il vous plaît, mon cheri,* do not stop what you are doing—you do it *very* well. And I need you to keep doing it."

"Catherine . . ." he said, terrified of where this was heading, but incapable of stopping. "Where is your husband?"

"Passed out drunk and dead to the world. As usual."

"Catherine, I want to hold you, to do more than hold you, but this is—"

She put a finger against his lips. "I know what you are going to say, Peter. Please do not say it. Let us just hold on to each other and dream, shutting out this sick world. Just you and me, making a memory here, under the moon, we will remember forever." Her hands glided over his back and then downward, around his hips, making him moan. Wake held her face, so very soft in his hands, and bent down to kiss her, something he'd wanted to do at Martinique, and at Genoa, and earlier that very evening.

"You know, by all reason, we shouldn't be doing this, Catherine," he murmured, inches from her lips. He knew he was crumbling inside, losing any semblance of restraint. "But I can't help it. You have this incredible effect on me, this overwhelming power. I don't know exactly how you do it, but I—"

Out of the darkness came Variam's deep voice.

"*Ah hmm!* . . . Sir, may I respectfully suggest that you and the lady return to your rooms. There could be some unpleasantness in a moment, as Consul General Faber is heading this way. And he appears to be rather considerably agitated."

Variam stepped forward into a shaft of moonlight, his white turban almost glowing above his blood-red tunic. The three of them made a momentary tableau, eerie in the moonlight, Wake and Catherine stunned by fear.

"This way, sir." The Sikh pointed back toward the door to the inside. His tone then changed from request to command. "*Immediately,* sir."

25

In bocca al lupo!

They followed Variam through a hidden paneled door that was recessed in the wall next to the main circular stairway. Catherine's dress swished in and Variam closed the door just as the heavy clump of footsteps came up around the last curve of the main stairs. The major-domo lit a match and reached for a lamp on a shelf, then led the way down a narrow and steep set of stone steps.

Wake waited for a shout from the other side of the wall, but none came, and as he descended he tried to unravel the confusion that was fogging his mind. How did Variam know where they were? The envelope was sealed. How did he know that Faber was coming? What did Faber know? What did Brown and Strom know? How was he going to get out of this?

Variam stopped and opened a door. "Here, sir. Your room is on this floor. I will lead Madame Faber to the main floor where she can stroll along the patio, then come inside and up to her room nonchalantly, as if nothing was the matter."

Her voice calm, almost distant, Catherine said, "*Merci,* Variam. I will never forget your assistance, and your discretion."

She turned to Wake. "Thank you for the wonderful conversation, Peter. It is a memory that will last my lifetime."

Wake started to reply, but she had already begun to go down the steps again, calling back, "Come Variam, and bring that light so I do not fall. I need to take that stroll on the patio. Right now."

Variam glanced at Wake, nodded at the door, and said, "Yes, Madame Faber. As you wish."

The small light flickered as they moved downward in silence. Soon Catherine was lost to Wake's view as they rounded a corner in the steps. He quietly walked down the hall of his floor, went into his room, and sat on the bed. Lifting a hand, he saw it shaking uncontrollably and tried to will it to stop, but it wouldn't. He went to the window and looked around at the cliffs and the sea, previously magnificent in their beauty but now ghostly and ominous in the pale light.

His instincts returned and he secured the room's lock, then reclined on the bed, trying to reason out what he was doing, but a swirl of emotions negated the workings of his usually analytical mind. Shame, fear, anger, and confusion took over. Deep breaths and slow exhales were of no use. His heart was beating as it had in the moments before past battles. He lay there, eyes staring at the ornately plastered ceiling, his mind dreading the inevitable pounding on his door, wondering what had happened with Catherine and her husband, worrying about the consequences of his weakness. Dozens of horrific scenarios flashed before him of what was to come in the morning, and for hours he lay there, senses acute, depressed over what he had done and had been about to do. His predominate emotion was anger—at himself.

"You're an idiot, Wake," he growled to the ceiling. "A frigging bilge-to-topmast, incredibly stupid, number-one *idiot. . . .*"

Wake's eyes were open but heavy when he realized it was getting light outside. He saw by his watch it was six A.M. and remembered Brown saying that breakfast would start to be served at seven, "for those naval early birds who can't break their rustic habits."

Shaving with his hand still shaking proved to be difficult and he cut himself on the jaw, inches below the old wound on his right temple. After changing his underclothes and shirt, he tied his cravat, put on his coat and unlocked the door. Then Wake made his way to the castle's main patio, scene of the previous night's revelry, where a long table covered with fruit and breakfast dishes awaited.

Variam was there, as starched and inscrutable as ever. "Good morning, sir. Unfortunately you've missed the British naval officers. They just left. However, sir, there is still plenty of breakfast left. We have an English country breakfast, along with fruits. And some French pastries."

Wake winced at the last and checked Variam's eyes, but they revealed nothing. Wake moved closer. "I didn't get a chance to say thank you last night, Variam. I am now."

"It is the duty of a major-domo to make his master's house tranquil, sir. I was merely fulfilling my duty."

"And that duty includes briefing your master on last night's events?"

"Of course, sir. But last night the order was reversed. The consul general briefed me on the situation and directed that I assist you and the lady."

Variam saw Wake's face blush and anticipated the next questions. "The lady and her husband have not come downstairs yet this morning. And there was no confrontation between them last night. I believe the gentleman's intoxication led him to pass out after walking up all those steps, sir. I helped him to his room, where the lady was already ensconced and evinced surprise upon our arrival."

Wake abruptly remembered Faber's challenge to Moltke. "Oh, what about the German? There was to be a duel at sunrise."

"Last night Consul General Brown spoke with Bishop Ferro, who counseled the gentlemen involved in that dispute. They were dissuaded from continuing with it, but I'm afraid there is still much ill will, sir. I believe that was the initial reason for Monsieur Faber's alcohol intake last evening. Then, as such things tend to do, one thing led to another and he began to search for his wife."

"Where's the German now?"

"He departed last night, sir. Quite upset with the Frenchman."

Variam bowed deeply to the bishop of Genoa passing by, then continued his aside to Wake. "Consul General Brown will be down momentarily to greet his guests and enjoy his breakfast." He swiveled his head as if on parade, small black eyes locking on Wake's. "And no, sir, I cannot answer if anyone else has knowledge of last night's events on the parapet."

The major-domo's demeanor was daunting to Wake, who managed to croak out, "Yes, well, again Variam, thank you for your considerable help. You've been very candid this morning. May I ask why?"

"You are entirely welcome for the assistance, sir. These things sometimes happen here. As for my candor . . ." A flicker of a smile crossed his face. "I was ordered to assist you all that I can, sir. It's seems you have friends you don't know about."

Before Wake could ask the obvious, the Sikh executed a right-face as Bishop Ferro approached, trailed by an aide holding a plate mounded with food. Wake couldn't get away as the bishop enthusiastically queried him, "Ah, you are the American naval man here, yes?"

"Yes, Your Excellency," responded Wake, concerned about what Ferro had heard about him. "I am Lieutenant Peter Wake, of the American Navy."

"Well come join us, Lieutenant Wake," offered the bishop in good English. "These large British morning feasts require an equally large amount of time to vanquish them. I'd like some company and the opportunity to practice your language."

Movement at the double doors in the castle wall caught Wake's attention and he saw Catherine and her husband, escorted by Brown, enter the patio. Faber looked unsteady, Brown bemused, and Catherine serene, all of which unsettled Wake. He remembered his manners and turned to the waiting bishop. "It is my great honor to accompany you, Your Excellency. Thank you for your very kind invitation."

Bishop Ferro spoke rapidly in Italian to the aide, then regarded Wake. "And are you a blessed Catholic, my son?"

"No, Your Excellency, but I was raised as an Episcopalian, which we were told is about as close as one can be to the Catholic teachings. Now I am a Methodist."

"Oh, my! A Methodist. Getting even further away from us, I should think. Hmm, you know, I met a Methodist once."

They sat down at the table, facing a beautiful peach-colored sunrise over mountains shadowed in lavender as the aide delivered a plate to Wake. He waited until they said their prayers and asked, "And did you like him, Your Excellency?"

"I did! Knew his version of the Bible very well and the original—that would be *ours,* my son—relatively well. Tremendous sense of humor, he had. One joke after another. Made me laugh from here," he pointed to his ample belly.

Belatedly, Wake comprehended that the only chairs left open at the table were the two directly opposite him. But it was too late to move before Catherine and her husband took them. Faber merely grunted after sitting and morosely picked at his food. His wife smiled at the clergyman and said, "*Bonjour, bonjour.* Good morning to everyone. Your Excellency. And to you, Lieutenant Wake. I trust everyone slept well?"

The bishop replied with both hands held wide. "Wonderful sleep after an enchanting evening. And now we have a delicious start to a beautiful day. God is shining upon our new day. You look as if you had a night of wonderful slumber too, my dear. This coastal sea air will do a person good."

"So do gentle dreams, Your Excellency," she answered, as her husband belched. "You didn't respond, Lieutenant. Did you sleep well?"

Wake thought her apparent ease in the awkward situation odd. "No, Madame Faber, actually I did not. My mind was filled with problems that precluded any rest."

She shook her head, full of concern. "That is a shame, Lieutenant. It must have been that moon last night. They say that a beautiful moon can alter a man's mood. That sometimes it can make them positively *mad*. I have heard stories of what they do under that influence."

"Yes, Madame Faber. I think it might have done just *that* last night."

Wake heard Brown announce that more food was being brought out and not to be sparse with their appetite. "*Buon giorno, La Vostra Eccellenza. Bonjour, Madame.* Good morning, Lieutenant Wake. What do you think of our little place here now that you've had an overnight stay, Lieutenant?"

Wake could see no sign of disapproval in Brown's eyes. "Very nice home, sir. As the bishop has said, it was an enchanting evening."

Faber grunted again, looking as if he would vomit. He stood, then fled the table, heading indoors. "I must apologize for my husband," said Catherine with a shrug. "He is ill this morning. A minor ailment."

Brown sat at Faber's chair. "Yes, well he had quite a lot of excitement last night. Challenging a Prussian to a duel is a sub-stantial demonstration of emotion. Fortunately, it was not con-summated."

Catherine was not amused at Brown's dry wit. "Thank God—and you, Your Excellency—that more mature heads have prevailed in that matter. Dueling. In this day and age. How very silly for grown men. Who are they trying to impress?"

Brown cocked his head slightly at her. "Grown men are known to do many silly things, Madame Faber. Usually in regard to the fairer sex."

"I am not sure what you mean by that in this context, Consul General," Catherine replied frostily. "Perhaps my English is not adequate to understand your intent."

"Merely a general observation about men, my dear. I agree with you about duels, by the way. Far too much violence in the world already, even here in Europe, among us supposedly civilized people. Don't you agree, Your Excellency? You've just come from Spain, where sadness prevails."

"Yes, there is too much of this senseless violence going on. Spain used to be a civilized nation devoted to the word and rule of God, but just look at her now."

Catherine interjected. "It is like that all over Europe. We are no better than the savages in Africa. Hah, and we tell *them* how to behave."

Wake tore his gaze away from Catherine and looked at the bishop beside him. "You were in Spain, sir? May I ask where?"

Brown and Catherine became involved in a conversation with the Greek assistant consul next to them, who suggested that religion might be the cause of wars. The bishop ignored the obvious slight and answered Wake. "I was at the cathedral in Sevilla, Lieutenant."

"Really? I was there too, sir. Back in January. I met a Jesuit priest. Father Muñosa. Do you know of him?"

Bishop Ferro grinned. "Yes I do, my son." He then leaned over and whispered. "He liked you. Described you as typical American. Unaware and unafraid. Closest man to Don Quixote he had ever met. And he said that if I ever met you to tell you he is still waiting for a letter from you. A letter that will tell a great tale. He told me you were being transferred to Genoa."

Wake shook his head, now understanding the bishop's friendliness. But he also wondered how much the bishop knew of the events in Sevilla. He whispered back, "When the time is right, it will be sent to him, Your Excellency. It's a bit early yet. Things need to settle down there first."

"Yes, I understand that. Perhaps your friends will be able to return someday, God willing."

Surprised at how much the man knew, Wake got the feeling that the bishop's concern was genuine. Then it struck him—was Bishop Ferro the mystery friend Variam was speaking of? He and Brown were the best of friends. Could Ferro have intervened and asked Brown to look after him? How bizarre, he thought. No, he decided, it was preposterous.

Bishop Ferro stood. "And now I regret that I must go. I have business to attend to at Rapallo, then must take that infernal train back to Genoa. Goodbye to you all. Montague, as always, it was a magnificent—and I must say, *exciting*—affair, and I thank you for including this old priest in the fun. Madame Faber, you are entirely correct about this continent and the violence we perpetuate. Perhaps between the two of us we can do a little to mitigate that."

He shook Wake's hand. "And to you, my adventurous young American friend, I will say the traditional farewell greeting of good luck to a man such as yourself." He paused for a dramatic moment and began to walk away, shouting over his shoulder with a flourish of his hand, "*In bocca al lupo!*"

Brown laughed while he watched the bishop depart. "Do you know what that means, Lieutenant? It's pretty appropriate for *you*."

"No, sir. Not a clue," said Wake, worried.

"It means 'into the mouth of the wolf' and it's an Italian way of showing disdain for danger. It is said to the brave. The response is to shout *'crepi!'* which means 'die!' Let's hope that neither is prophetic, eh, Lieutenant?"

Catherine gave Wake a playful caress of her toe, which did nothing to dispel his apprehension. Overwhelmed by the thought of all he'd been through in his first three months in Europe, he sighed.

"I understand that saying *entirely*, sir. . . ."

26

Showing the flag

The rest of the morning was painful. Wake rose from the breakfast table just as Beauregard and Christine Strom made their appearance on the patio.

Catherine said, "*Au revoir, Lieutenant.*" Her manner was assured, her smile confident, her eyes strong in the morning sun.

Wake inwardly winced as he thought of events spiraling out of control the night before. Ashamed at his behavior, he was fearful of the consequences, both personal and professional. The first one wasn't long in coming.

"Good morning, Lieutenant. Pleasant evening?" asked Strom levelly.

"Good morning, sir. Yes, sir. Pleasant evening."

"Yes, that was my impression, Lieutenant. I would hope last night's excitement was educational for you."

Wake chilled. "Sir? What excitement?"

"Why, the incident of the French diplomat threatening the German diplomat, Lieutenant. An instructive example of how things can go wrong in a heartbeat. Moltke is on the telegraph to Berlin and Otto Bismarck as we speak, I'd wager. By noon, the wires between Paris, Berlin, Rome, and London will be humming. *Wars* have started over such theatrics, Mr. Wake, and there'll be repercussions within several countries. Remember, this incident has become common knowledge—embarrassing to the French and insulting to the Germans." Strom scrutinized Wake. "But whatever did you think I meant? Was there any *other* excitement last night, Lieutenant?"

"Ah, no, sir. No excitement comparable to the threats between the diplomats, sir."

Strom showed no reaction. An image flashed through Wake's mind of Strom as a riverboat gambler.

"Yes, so I've heard. We are certainly lucky there was no *other* excitement last night, aren't we, Lieutenant?"

Wake felt his face flush. "Yes, sir."

"You are leaving for Genoa this morning, I believe?"

"Yes, sir."

"Very good, Lieutenant. When you get back there you'll find some useful naval work to do. I got word by telegram last night that all the ships of your squadron are due to arrive soon. Evidently the Spanish are sufficiently awed that they won't hurt American citizens during their little bloodbath and the squadron is returning to the central Med. The *Franklin* will be here tomorrow, with Rear Admiral Case aboard. You will no longer work out of the consulate, but instead will work your billet on his staff. By Tuesday you will be out of the hotel and on the ship."

"Aye, aye, sir."

"That is all, Lieutenant. I hope you've learned something while you've been with us."

The diplomat had already turned when Wake said, "Yes, sir. I have. Thank you." There was no reply as Strom walked away.

When he got to his room he found one of the castle's Italian stewards lifting his bags and walking out. "Variam say to me to pack things for you, *signore.* I carry them for you down to boat at harbor. We go now, *signore.* Boat to leave in one hour."

The steward strode out of the room without waiting for a

reply, Wake behind him marveling at the fact that he was being very politely thrown out of a castle. At the main gate Variam stood at parade rest.

"Have a good journey, Lieutenant Wake." The massive turban dipped briefly as the hooded eyes watched Wake. Then the major-domo turned away to give orders in Italian to a guard.

When they reached the waterfront, via the easy slope of the road, Wake looked back up at the castle perched atop the cliff. He could see the rampart of the "lovers' walk," above the surrounding terrain and trees. The steward hustled him over to the ferry steamer and dumped his baggage aboard in the large pile of passengers' belongings. Disappearing in the crowd ashore, he left Wake standing on the deck, surrounded by excited locals, staring up at the castle and trying to ignore a disheveled Craven Walker standing next to him chattering on about Italian lava flows.

"Good God, what have I gotten into here?" he muttered to himself, not liking the answer.

"Oh yes, my friend, I heard it was a hellova show," exclaimed Davis at lunch two days later. "Word is that Faber's being removed and sent to represent the Republic of France someplace way out in the sticks."

"It's *that* serious?" asked Wake.

"Nobody threatens the Germans. Even the Brits are respectful of them. Remember that the Germans, led by Field Marshal Moltke and Otto Bismarck, have kicked everybody's rear end who managed to get in their way. So nobody gets in their way."

"I wonder where he'll be sent? Maybe Martinique? His brother lives there."

Davis noticed the far-off look on Wake. "Yeah, I heard that's where you first met Madame Faber. Oh, don't look shocked, Peter. It's common knowledge that you've paid a lot of attention to her. Strom isn't thrilled, by the way. Faber has a short fuse, as you saw, and the Strom's afraid you'll light it with a little amorous friction. He actually likes you, but he's worried about Faber's possible reaction. Or overreaction."

"Madame Faber and I are merely friends, Dan. Friends, that is it. Damn it all, I don't need those kinds of rumors. I'm married."

"Thou doth protest too much, Lieutenant. And the rumors are already out there, whether you need them or not. But, hey, don't worry too much, *amico*. By the end of the week your beautiful friend and her husband will be out of Genoa and on a ship bound for the French consulate at God knows where. Then the rumor mill will start grinding on about someone else—with a much juicier story, no doubt—and in a month at the most nobody will remember your pitiful gossip."

Wake saw sixty-two-year-old, ramrod-straight, squinty-eyed Rear Admiral Augustus Ludlow Case as every inch the image of a veteran naval officer. He also knew the man's reputation in the navy as an intellectual and a warrior. Case, a naval officer for forty-six years, had been on several scientific expeditions before the war and after the war had headed the Bureau of Ordnance. It was Case who was pushing for torpedo development and oversaw the establishment of the navy's fledgling torpedo station at Newport in 1871. Shortly afterward, he was made a rear admiral and sent to command American ships in Europe.

During the war Case had fought on the treacherous coast of North Carolina, where the weather was a much worse enemy than the Confederates, and was instrumental in the capture of two forts. Wake had heard that the man could be brutally hard in his insistence on keeping his blockade station no matter what the weather.

Just the year before, of all the navy's senior officers, it was

Case whom Admiral Porter had selected to lead the combined squadrons in the naval demonstrations off Key West that were designed to intimidate the Spanish in Cuba. Porter came down in person later, to the snickers of the fleet's officers, once Case had gotten everything together. Though Case was not large in stature, Wake knew he was not a man to be underestimated or trifled with.

Unfortunately, his flagship did not befit the man. The 5,000-ton United States Ship *Franklin* was an obsolete steam screw frigate, having been laid down in 1854, twenty years earlier. Built partially of old materials from her namesake forerunner that had been built forty years before that, she was considered by most in the navy to be the product of bad contractors, bad material, and bad luck. Ten long years after she was started, she was launched but only used as a barracks ship. Later, after the war, she served in the Med, but her boilers and engines were in constant need of repair, her guns were outmoded, and her upper spars cracked. She returned home, was assessed as not worth repairing and decommissioned from seventy-one to seventy-three. *Franklin* had been dragged back out and put in commission for this cruise. No one trusted the ship and everyone, including her captain, referred to her as "the bitch."

Wake was depressed the moment he stepped aboard.

The officer of the deck, a slack-jawed self-important lieutenant, disbelieved Wake's assignment as the new flag lieutenant until Wake dug out his papers and showed them to him. The decks were under repair everywhere. It appeared that most of the crew was foreign as he heard several languages being spoken, but it was the look on the crew's faces that bothered him most. The sullen glances he saw were indicative of other problems.

When he was shown to the squadron's chief of staff, Fleet Captain Cadwell Luther Staunton, that man dismissed Wake with barely a word of introduction and told him to return to the staff office the next day when they could find something useful for him to do.

The corpulent squadron chief surgeon, Wally Cutter, advised Wake later at dinner in the wardroom that Staunton was trying to make it to his retirement in four months without any making decisions that could cause his career to end prematurely. Hansen, the staff chief engineer, commented that Staunton was safe in that regard—he hadn't made a decision for years. That led to a round of laughs at the table, which made Wake very uneasy. He knew of Case's reputation but not that of the other staff officers. Their behavior was insubordinate and contrary to good discipline, in his opinion, but he also learned upon arrival that they had all been together for almost a year, so he kept his mouth shut.

To his consternation Wake found out his cabin mate was the surgeon. Within hours Wake was trying to figure out how to switch with someone else, since the man reeked of medical alcohol—other hard spirits being illegal—and of intense body odor. Wake thought of the days during the war when he had commanded the *Rosalie,* a tiny sailing gunboat, and had slept out on an open deck in the weather, both foul and fair. His first night aboard the *Franklin* was an exercise in self-discipline, as Cutter snored and passed wind and generally filled the miniscule cabin with a stench that reminded Wake of rotting death.

The next morning he was summoned to the admiral's quarters in the great cabin aft, presenting himself to Case while wondering if the surgeon's stink had permeated his uniform.

Case's desk was covered with paperwork. He didn't appear to have noticed any foul odor, but instead looked and sounded busy. "Yes, Lieutenant Wake, come in and stand easy. You are my new flag lieutenant, I understand."

"Yes, sir."

"I see by your report file that you are not an academy man. You started out a volunteer officer during the war. And you got a regular commission? How very unusual."

"Yes, sir. I was commissioned in early sixty-five. East Gulf Blockading Squadron."

"Yes. Then shore duty at Pensacola. Then . . ." Case looked up from the file on his desk. Wake felt the man's eyes boring into him. The admiral continued, "The *Canton* affair down in Panama. Some legal confusion on that, I believe."

Wake had had to explain that situation so many times to so many people. But admirals were different. "The court ruled that there was insufficient cause for a prosecution of violations of regulations, sir."

"So no censure, no acquittal."

"No *trial*, sir. The court-martial decided that it would be a court of inquiry, then ruled there was insufficient cause to do anything further. In effect, that no rules were violated, sir."

"And yet, Lieutenant, you have been under a cloud for the five years since then, haven't you?"

Wake didn't like the direction this was taking, but controlled his anger. "Admiral, I have been at sea and in the jungles of Panama on the canal survey expedition in the five years since then. I have done my duty and none of my commanding officers have given me the slightest indication of anything other than satisfaction with my performance. I know nothing of any cloud over my career, sir."

Case slapped his hand down on the desk and allowed the beginning of a smile. "By God, that's the attitude I like! Good for you, Mr. Wake. I didn't graduate from that damned school of arrogance either. I learned seamanship and leadership on the deck of a *ship*, from the age of sixteen onward."

Wake let his breath out. "Thank you, sir. I will do my very best for you, Admiral."

"I do believe that you will, Lieutenant. I heard in Brooklyn from my friend Frankie Munroe that you were a man of decision and action. That's good, Lieutenant, 'cause there're damn few of 'em around anymore, especially in this scow, and I need one right about now to take care of a problem so I can concentrate in more important things."

Rear Admiral Monroe was the president of the court that had ruled on Wake's actions in relieving his captain aboard *Canton* on the coast of Panama. Wake wondered exactly what Monroe had told Case and if it was his influence that was behind this assignment.

He snapped his attention back to the admiral. "Yes, sir."

"We have some sort of potential problem on the African Med coast at some Gawdforsaken place called Chetaibi. No idea where the hell it is, except it's some fishing village between Tunis and Algiers. Usual kind of thing—missionaries reporting that they are being harassed and are in fear of their lives. Report arrived back in January—it was sent in December—so it's already five months since they asked for help. Hell and tarnation, they could be dead by now. That'll make the papermen howl with indignation at Uncle Sam's Navy. At any rate, now that the squadron's back we've got to look into it. You will join the first available ship as my representative, go to this Chetaibi place, and ascertain the situation. Then, without angering whoever is the national authority in that area, or the ship's captain either, you will *solve it*. It's called showing the flag, Lieutenant. Understood?"

"Yes, sir. Very well."

"Good. Now, what is the next ship due to arrive here?"

Wake didn't know. Hadn't a clue since no one had briefed him what ships were where. He stood there trying to conjure up an answer.

"You don't know?" asked Case. "At your reporting-in briefing no one informed you?"

Wake knew he was stepping on dangerous ground. There had been no briefing since no one had cared enough to fill Wake in on the squadron's business, but to let Case know that would be fatal to establishing a rapport with the staff.

"Sir, I reported aboard late yesterday and was just about to be briefed. I can find out immediately, sir, if I can have a moment."

"Hmm. Go ahead and find out from the staff yeoman. Those petty officers know everything anyway."

Wake was back in seconds with the answer, one that pleased him greatly, since his best friend in the navy was aboard.

"Sir, it's the *Alaska!* She departed Cadiz three days ago and will be here tomorrow. I can be aboard and under way the moment she arrives, sir."

"Very well, Mr. Wake. Get orders cut for *Alaska* to proceed to wherever the hell I said to go to. After that mission is completed she will return here for further assignment. Make it so." Case returned to scrutinizing the purser's report in his hand, then looked up.

"Oh, and one more thing, Lieutenant Wake."

"Sir?"

"Kindly take that ridiculous grin off your face before exiting my cabin. I realize you are overjoyed at the prospect of escaping the confines of the flagship, but I do have a certain reputation to uphold. Can't have junior officers grinning like monkeys when they're seen walking out of here, can I?"

"No, sir," replied Wake, face flushing red again, this time from embarrassment.

"Very well. You are dismissed now, Lieutenant Wake. Good luck."

Wake managed to get out "Aye, aye, sir" before he fled the cabin. Once in the passageway and beyond the sight of the Marine sentry, he glanced overhead and whispered, "Thank you."

He was free at last. Free of the rancid surgeon, the dungeon of a ship, the sick social mess of Genoa, and of Europe with all its pretensions. And it would be wonderful to sail with Sean Rork again.

27

Fishing for Apostates

A *laska* was new, clean, strong. She was surging ahead at ten knots to the south along the western coast of Corsica, a northeasterly filling her canvas on the perfect point of sailing. Along the decks the warrant officers and their men were toiling in their sections—the carpenters in the waist caulking the launches, sailmakers on the foredeck stitching the heavy storm sails, gunners cleaning their "iron daughters." High aloft, Wake could see Sean Rork near the truck of the fore-topmast securing a new upper lee shroud, he and his men easily swaying with the motion of the spars as they dangled one hundred and fifty feet over the sea. Wake had always envied Rork's lack of fear aloft.

Earlier he and Rork had had a subdued reunion. Officers and enlisted men, even senior enlisted men such as Rork, did not fraternize aboard ship and very seldom ashore. Naval discipline demanded that, and the two friends understood it. A heartfelt greeting, a strong handshake, and brief summary of how Wake's family was doing, was all that could be done at the time.

They both agreed that ashore would be another matter, and that rum would definitely be in order at that time. Decent rum.

Wake added that it was his turn to buy the first. Rork replied with a grin that that was just fine, but it would have to wait for their return to Europe, since they were headed into Muslim lands, where possession of hard spirits could get your head lopped off.

Wake gazed around the horizon and took in a deep breath of salt air. It was good to be back at sea on a real naval vessel and breathe clean air. And good to have a real mission to accomplish. Especially with Sean Rork close by.

Lieutenant William Standing, the officer of the watch, who had served in the Med twice before, pointed out a headland to Wake. "There's the fabled isle of Napoleon Bonaparte. And around that cape there is Ajaccio, where the little devil grew up."

Wake was still getting used to being a passenger on a warship. He had offered his services as a watchstander, but Captain Donald Bunt declined. Bunt understood why Wake was aboard and offered no resentment, but wanted to retain his command's "integrity of operations," as he put it. Wake thought Bunt was entirely within his rights, and probably would have done the same. He surveyed the distant craggy landscape and wondered what Bonaparte would do in Bunt's place.

"Napoleon's name still gets people's attention around this part of the world, doesn't it, William?"

"Aye, that it does, Peter. That it does. And it keeps on in others, too. His namesake's only been dead a year, you know."

Standing was referring to Louis Napoleon III, emperor of France, who had lost to the Germans in the Franco-Prussian War three years earlier. And what would your uncle, the first and only real Napoleon, think of *that* particular humiliation, Wake speculated.

"I think they're better off without him, William. All he got 'em was trouble," observed Wake.

"Aye on that—a ton of trouble and misery. Speaking of that, I heard that you're the man who'll go ashore when we find this place. What're you going do if they've taken the friggin' kittle cargo of sin bosuns off to their kasbah, or wherever?"

Wake laughed at Standing's use of the old sailor term for a preacher. Sailors didn't trust clergymen and thought them very bad luck on a ship—"kittle" meant dangerous.

"Not sure, William. Guess I'm going to have to talk some sense into them."

Standing guffawed at that notion. "An eleven-inch shell fused to properly explode at twenty feet above 'em would be a hellova lot more effective, Peter."

"Yes. You're probably right on that." Wake gestured toward the town of Ajaccio, just becoming visible on the coast. "And I think old Boney would agree completely with you. Heavy artillery has the most wonderful ability to make a potential enemy focus on what you're trying to say. Just might come to that, but I hope not."

"Kill just a couple of the bastards and the rest will get real friendly, real fast."

Wake smiled, for Standing had just paraphrased a famous quip of Napoleon Bonaparte pretty well. It was a tactic that usually worked—with most cultures. But would the Mohammedan fanatics of North Africa be cowed by a threat of force, or even the use of it? Wake had heard stories about their fearlessness. He sighed, realizing the outcome rested on *his* decisions and that he didn't have much time before he would have to make them. Not far ahead of them was the western hook of Sardinia.

And beyond that was the mysterious continent of Africa.

Wake looked at his watch in the eerie light of the gyrating lamp overhead in the wardroom, where he, as a supernumerary, was stretched out to sleep on the deck. It read six A.M., which should have been dawn, but there was no light through the deadlight in the deck above. The motion of the ship had increased through the night, the wind coming from forward and the deck heeling over as the canvas strained. Wake hadn't given it another thought when he shut his eyes five hours earlier—just one more rough night at sea in a lifetime of them. But where was the dawn? Was a storm covering the sky? The evening had been crystal clear.

Emerging carefully from the after hatch onto the main deck Wake was greeted with a sight he had never seen. The duty watch was huddled under the lee of any item on the deck, and those that couldn't hide were leaning forward into the wind with heads swathed in rags, hands shielding their eyes. The sky was as black as a storm in the tropics and visibility wasn't even to the bow of the ship. The wind howled and shrieked up and down the scale in the rigging, the hull plunging and rising thirty feet at a time. All this looked like a storm, except for one thing.

There wasn't any rain. Instead, there was something in the hot wind, something tiny and hard, stinging Wake's exposed flesh to the point of pain, intense pain. He reflexively ducked back down below the hatch and caught his breath—a man could barely breathe up there—and saw that sand covered the lower deck, piled in drifts against stanchions and bulwarks. It was raining sand.

He returned topside in his foul weather oilskins with a galley rag over his face and made his way to the afterdeck, where the captain stood huddled over the binnacle. Bunt looked up, then screamed in Wake's ear.

"*Ever been in a sirocco, Lieutenant Wake?*"

Wake shook his head. It was difficult to hear and speak. He could actually hear the sand hitting the ship.

"*It's the hot wind from the Sahara desert, blown up across the Mediterranean. A bitch to navigate in! That damned shore is up there ahead, somewhere.*"

"*How long do they last?*" Wake yelled.

"*Sometimes one day. Sometimes more. We'll heave to if it don't stop soon. To hell with the damned missionary fools. We'll wait it out at sea!*"

It lasted six excruciating days.

When the sky finally cleared they had no idea where they were. The dead reckoning of Captain Bunt put them somewhere to the north and west of Sicily, almost three hundred miles downwind and to the east of their destination.

Lookouts scanned the distance but saw nothing, as if all the ships at sea had been sunk—an apocalyptic sight that left the men aboard nervous. It was an eerie day, the wind light out of the east, the leftover swells from the south rolling *Alaska* and making the yards creak and the canvas slat as if the ship was groaning in pain at what she had gone through.

They didn't dare fire up the boilers, they had to clean everything mechanical first, for the sand had penetrated and piled everywhere, fouling everything. The deepest bilges and most secure ammunition magazines were filmed with the stuff. The food and drink tasted gritty, guns were useless, paint was blasted off, clothing was ripped, sails were torn. The crew was exhausted by the exertions in the storm—just hanging on and breathing was an effort—before they started the huge task of cleaning the entire ship. All hands, including the indefatigable Rork, went about their work dazed and silent.

Bunt got a noon sight that first clear day, then a forty-five degree additional sight later on. That was enough to tell him his dead reckoning wasn't off by much, which impressed Wake. They were east of Sardinia at latitude forty—a lot closer to Rome than Africa—and very very lucky they hadn't fetched up on the rocky capes of Sardinia's southern end. With bloodshot eyes, Bunt estimated to Wake that with the current wind they would take another five days to reach Chetaibi.

"They've been waiting for us for five months already. What's another five days?"

Chetaibi was totally unlike Wake had pictured beforehand. It was not a tropical coast—they were at the same latitude as Norfolk— and there was no jungle, not even any foliage to speak of among the mud-walled huts lining the shore and stretching away up the slopes. Only a few date palms were scattered around on the hills behind the town. There were no large buildings, and the only breaks in the roof lines were about a dozen tall narrow mud block towers of maybe thirty feet. A lone unintimidating fortress of crumbling walls perched on a low hill. The universal color was brown. It was as alien a place as he had ever seen, and his first thought was to question why in the world a Christian missionary group would send anyone to it.

They anchored amidst a crawling mass of native craft, with no other European vessels in sight. Lieutenant Thomas Fyock, *Alaska*'s dark-eyed executive officer, had been to North Africa on an earlier cruise in the Med aboard *Constellation*. Something of an amateur linguist who picked up foreign tongues easily, he wasted no time in giving some unusual orders.

"Rig the boarding nets and have the duty watch armed and set to repel boarders, Mr. Standing! I want no bumboats along-side. Give one warning, then pike their hulls and sink 'em. They can swim to shore."

The executive officer glanced aft at Bunt, who nodded approvingly, then Fyock strode over to the starboard quarterdeck and yelled *"Seer fhalek!"* at a harbor bumboat filled with men in rags that was already alongside. His goatee and dark complexion, combined with those deadly eyes, gave off a fiery appearance. Then he picked up a boarding pike and pointed it at the boat, pretending to lunge it at them. Instantly the boat sheered off, the occupants loudly grumbling.

"Set the rules straight away," Fyock said to Wake as he passed him headed forward.

"Thievery?" asked Wake.

"Hell, Lieutenant. That'd be easy to thwart. No, I'm not worried about their thieves. I'm worried about their typhoid and pox! No one from shore comes about. And only a picked few will go ashore. That would be you."

The blood drained from Wake's face. He hadn't thought of that. No one had told him, warned him. Typhoid or smallpox was as bad or worse than the yellow jack he had seen during the war and known personally in Panama.

"Typhoid? Smallpox? Are you sure?"

"Never sure. That's the point. They have it on this coast. All over this coast. I saw it in Tripoli, in Algiers, in Tunis. They say that after a *sirocco*—around here they call it a *chergui*—typhoid increases. The heat and wind bring it out and spread it around, where it finds weakened people and infects them. The pox is here all the time. You never know, so you assume the worst. You be damned careful ashore. When you come back, you'll be in quarantine in a ship's boat for two days at least."

Seeing Wake's reaction, Fyock shrugged. "Welcome to Africa, Lieutenant Wake. You've just gone back in time."

The boat coxswain had orders to touch the jetty long enough for Wake to jump off, then back away and loiter off in the harbor, taking care to keep all other craft away from it. Wake and two other men had jumped off the bow as a crowd ashore watched with sullen curiosity.

In Bunt's cabin an hour earlier, the captain had asked if Wake had anyone he wanted to go ashore with him. The captain would allow Wake two men to accompany him—but they had to be volunteers who understood the physical and medical dangers.

Wake knew who one of them would be—Sean Rork. He had no doubt the bosun would volunteer, would in fact be angry if not allowed to go. But the other one surprised him. It was Fyock. The executive officer explained nonchalantly that his life would actually be easier if he went ashore with Wake, since he might be able to prevent a problem from happening due to his knowledge of the lingo and culture.

Fyock looked at Captain Bunt apologetically. "Sir, if I don't go and one of 'em gets killed, can you imagine the paperwork we'll have? It's just simpler for me to go and get it over with."

Bunt wasn't impressed. "I'm not thrilled at the prospect of losing my number- one officer. This is a ridiculous political show anyway. Why waste good men for a bunch of Bible-thumpers who go to places they're not wanted? Just stupidity."

A moment later he relented. "Oh hell, go ahead and get it done. I'll give you until sundown. I want you all three back aboard by sundown." Bunt looked at his watch. "That gives you seven hours. Understood? Back by the time the sun is down."

"Aye, aye, sir," came back the chorus from the two lieutenants, Wake not confident at all at that point that he would ever see the *Alaska* again.

Two minutes later Wake was on the foredeck, explaining the mission ashore to Rork. The bosun didn't wait for the details. "Very good, sir. Then I'll be venturin' ashore wi' ya. I'm thinkin' you'll be needin' a wee bit o' Celtic luck, an' maybe a few decent curses, wi' that bad lot o' scum I see o'er there."

"Thank you, my friend. I knew I could count on you."

Wake studied everyone around them for signs of sickness, but beyond the normal state of dishevelment he saw none. Fyock said, "*S-salaama 'lekum*" to every man they passed on the way, explaining to Wake and Rork that it meant peace upon you and was the standard greeting. Most of the locals muttered a reply, some ignored them, and a few replied vividly with smoldering eyes. No officials met them, though Wake was certain the local authorities knew of their arrival.

The three of them walked for five "blocks" through the huts toward the fortress before they saw their first European, dressed in a faded and torn suit, coming toward them in an agitated manner. The European approached hesitantly, glancing over his shoulder toward the fortress.

"You are Yankee, yes?" he asked with a French accent. His eyes, dark slits, darted around and made Wake nervous.

"Yes, we are," said Wake. "U.S. Navy. Who are you, sir?"

"Me? I am the commercial facilitator for this area. Claude Coffre, at your service, *monsieur*. How can I help you?"

As he spoke the little man walked backwards toward an alley off the main street. Wake was curious about his profession. "Commercial facilitator?"

Fyock wasn't amused. "Pimp, thief, and fence for stolen property."

"Oh *monsieur*, you hurt my soul with that description," protested Coffre. He turned his attention back to Wake. "I am a conveyor of all things, sir. Anything you need, I can procure. What is it you need, sir?"

Wake stood still. "I want to know where the American Christian Holy Mission is located. I need to talk to the leader there. An American man named Sharlton."

Coffre's eyes slid from one side to the other without moving his head. He shook his head sadly. "Ah, so regretfully, they are not here. They left months ago. *Monsieur* Sharlton left too. A fine man of faith. But now there are no Americans here. And I am the only European."

Rork stepped around behind Coffre and watched the crowd that was beginning to form. Wake leaned forward. "What happened to them?"

Coffre's voice went up an octave. "Who, *monsieur?*"

"The Americans!"

"Please, sir. As I said to you, they have all left this place. They had no more work to do. They all left. *Monsieur* Sharlton, his wife, and the four teacher ladies. They are gone for three months now."

Wake put his hand on Coffre's shoulder and felt him wince. "Where did they go?"

"I do not know, sir. They did not like me and would not converse with me. I was not of their . . . their station in life. I only know they all left this place. There are no Americans here. There was no reason to stay here for them."

Wake's blood chilled. The information he had received back in Genoa was that Sharlton had been at Chetaibi for years. And now he had suddenly left? Something overwhelming must have happened.

"Why did they leave?"

"The local people did not want to be converted to be followers of Jesus. They wanted to be followers of Mohammed and stay with Allah. It is also the law. The sheik enforced the law."

Fyock nodded in understanding. *"Irtidàd?"*

The crowd heard that word and pressed in, their inquisitiveness hardening. Coffre looked terrified. *"Oui, monsieur.* Apostasy. The law prescribes punishment of those that reject the one true faith. It is the law of the *hadith*—the teachings of Mohammed. According to that, there is only one punishment for a man, and one for a woman. You know of it?"

Fyock sighed. "Yes. How many?"

"Eleven men and three women. The three women are in slavery now and gone into the desert."

"What's he talking about, Thomas?" asked Wake.

"The Christians came here thinking they were going to fish for souls. Saint Peter and all that. I've seen it before, in Palestine. The problem is that only a few people in these parts want to switch sides, and those that do take the chance of running afoul of the law and the local leadership. This sheik couldn't care less about what religion claims the souls of the people around here, but if he thinks for one minute that the foreigners are getting into a position of power rivaling him, then he'll invoke the *hadith* of *itridàd*—the teachings of Mohammed about apostasy. Apostasy is where a person rejects their faith. In Islamic law, the punishment is death for men and life imprisonment for women. That's what's happened here."

"So the sheik eliminated his potential rivals by eliminating potential converts. He killed eleven men and sold off three women to slavery. And now no one will want to be converts, or even be seen with foreigners. Like us."

Fyock raised an eyebrow, his eyes on the fortress on the hill. "Exactly. And the other locals probably blame Sharlton for starting it all in the first place."

Wake returned his gaze to the shaking Coffre. "It's now early April. When and how did Sharlton and the Americans leave? By ship?"

"No, *monsieur.* There were no ships. There seldom are. They left months ago along the coast road toward Tunis. The Bey of Tunis has good relations with Christians. They are safe there."

"How long does it take to get there by this coastal road?"

Coffre gave a Gallic shrug. "Many weeks, *monsieur.* Maybe two months."

"Two months! It's only a few hundred miles east along the coast."

Fyock intervened. "The road only goes along the coast for fifty miles or so, then it winds inland across the mountains. This little weasel just might be right on the time. Camels don't go fast in a caravan."

Now it was Wake's turn to sigh. It appeared there was nothing more to do here—they were too late. But he thought he'd better check in with the authorities. "Why hasn't the sheik sent an official to meet with us?"

"He has, *monsieur.* Me. I am his interpreter for foreigners. I greet the ships that come here, few as they are. I deal with the foreigners for the sheik."

"Including missionaries."

"Yes, *monsieur*."

"So you are the one who told them of the sheik's orders to kill their people, their newly converted Christians?"

"Yes. Then they left. It is as your officer here says. The missionaries told people here they were like fishermen looking to gather conversions to Jesus. Fishing for apostates."

"And they just gave up?"

Another shrug. "The fish were scared away, *monsieur*. No fish means no mission for the missionaries."

"I need to speak with the sheik."

"He will not see you. He has nothing to say, other than if you are not buying any supplies, then you are to leave immediately. Since the missionaries left, foreigners are only allowed ashore if they will buy something."

"Incredible."

"*Oui, monsieur. Incrédible. C'est l'Afrique.*"

28
Staff duty

April 1874

So let me get this straight. All the Americans got out of
Chetaibi alive and fled the area? I don't have to worry about
them anymore, right?"

"Yes, sir," answered Wake, standing in front of Admiral Case
at his desk aboard the *Franklin*. "I checked and found out they
did make it to Tunis. Worse for wear, but they made it. They left
there on April thirteenth, sir. Packet steamer to Málaga and then
on to London."

"Good. One less damn problem to worry about. I've got to
get *Alaska* over to the Levant anyway. The Turks are in a lather
about American merchant ships failing to pay some fee or something, probably a bribe."

Wake had been back aboard the *Franklin* for a day. The surgeon stank worse than ever, the wardroom was still full of
depressing talk, and the ship hadn't moved from her anchorage in
a month. He already missed *Alaska's* freedom from the world of
staff duty.

224

Case had been in a bad mood all morning. The Genovese merchants were clamoring for payments due on supplies for the squadron, the Spanish were reluctant to allow an American warship at Barcelona to evacuate U.S. citizens from the conflict, and then there was the American ambassador in Turkey pleading to Washington for a demonstration of force at the Dardanelles because the Turks threatened shipping that didn't pay the newly raised "fees" there.

"All right. Decision time!" Case exhaled loudly.

"*Alaska* looks the most impressive, so she goes to Turkey and deals with that mess. *Juniata* has boiler problems—again—so she stays at Malta for a friggin' month to get that damned thing fixed. *Congress* gets to go to Spain and play referee and rescue our brethren who are idiot enough to live there. The consulate at Venice wants a flag visit but they lose—that will have to wait until this summer. *Franklin* isn't in shape for a cruise and we're tapped out of ships."

Wake didn't see why the admiral was telling him this. This was for the chief of staff to consult about and the staff yeomen to record. He said, "Yes, sir," and stood mute.

Case looked up from the three stacks of papers and studied Wake. "Hmm. I've got something else that came in while you were gone. Another missionary malady someplace down that way you just came from. Requires some show at investigation." His hands went through the piles, scattering them across the desk. "Now where the hell did I put that? Ah, here it is. Through the miracle of modern communications it comes from the ambassador in Morocco to the powers that be in Washington to me—by telegraph in only a week. Amazing. Hmm, can you believe we even have an *ambassador* in Morocco?"

"Yes, sir," offered Wake, trying to sound professional. He went on echoing what Fyock had told him about the Arab world of northern Africa on the voyage back from Chetaibi. "Morocco is the only independent nation left in Africa, besides Ethiopia on the other side. Never been conquered, though the French have big interests and influence there. I've heard the sultan there is directly descended from Mohammed. Sultan Hassan, I believe, sir."

Case smiled. "Really? Sounds like you are just the man to solve this little problem, Lieutenant Wake, and keep me from bothering myself with it. I've got bigger fish to fry around here. I have a mission for you, which I'm afraid will take you away from the flagship yet again. I know how you hate *that*."

"Aye, aye, sir," Wake acknowledged neutrally, though his insides were leaping at the chance to escape *Franklin* again. "I'll do my best, sir."

"More missionaries are missing. Seems that a group of French Catholic missionaries, fifteen or so, are gone from a place outside the coastal imperial city in Morocco. Rabat, it's called. Disappeared without a trace a few weeks ago. The group was partially funded by an American Catholic charity and evidently some of the women were American, which is why we are involved. Various Congressmen—who fund the navy, by the way—passed along constituent complaints to the secretary of state, who passed them along to the secretary of the navy, who passed them along to me. Now you have it. Understood so far?"

"Yes, sir."

"Very good. You will go there and investigate this, sending word back to me what the situation is and your recommendation to solve it. Our ambassador there will give you more details. The locals are searching and French diplomatic people are involved, but no joy yet. Also no ransom yet, which is odd."

Case looked up from the desk. "I imagine there's nothing we can do, but we have to appear like we care and will offer help—which is *you*. I want the French and the locals and Congress to get the impression the United States Navy takes this sort of thing seriously." Case wagged a finger. "But not too seriously, of course. We don't have anything to really threaten with, so I do not want a recommendation for us to use force, Lieutenant. We don't have any to spare and posturing without credibility is worse than admitting weakness up front.

"No, I want you to be *creative*, Mr. Wake. Without embarrassing us. And remember, this is about our navy's image in Congress as much as anything else."

Wake wasn't clear on exactly what he could or would do, but he said the only thing expected. "Aye, aye, sir."

"You won't get there on one of our ships, so commercial transport is authorized. You can take one man. I know you'll ask for him but no, you can't have Fyock—he'll be needed with *Alaska* at Turkey. Do you want that bosun that went ashore with you at Chetaibi?"

"Yes, sir. And I'll need somebody who speaks Magreb, sir."

"What the hell is that?"

"The Arabic of northwestern Africa, sir. Fyock's the only American I know who speaks it."

"Fyock is out. Forget him. Hire an interpreter when you get there. You'll get some funding for that. Here is a copy of the message from the ambassador—that's all I know at this point. Now go ahead and cut the appropriate orders and get them here for me to sign. I want you under way at dawn. Dismissed."

Case waved a hand. "Stop standing there and go! And tell Captain Staunton and Paymaster Howell to get in here. I want to go over these damned squadron bills with them. Something is sure-fire cooked up *someplace* in these things . . ."

"We're headin' where exactly, sir?" asked Rork when Wake explained the mission to him.

"Place called Rabat. On the Atlantic coast. It's where the foreigners have their embassies. We find the U.S. ambassador and start there."

"How do we get from here to there, sir?"

"Not easily, I fear. After the bad delay in us getting to the last missionary complaint, the admiral wants us on this one fast. And the fastest way is an Italian steamer that gets under way from here tomorrow bound for the Spanish enclave at Melilla on the Barbary coast—that's the Mediterranean coast. Then we hop a French sailing vessel, go through the Straits of Gibraltar and around to Rabat. Probably take a couple of weeks."

"Sounds like a bit o' exotic adventure an' fun, sir. Just the thing for the likes o' us!"

Wake laughed at Rork's irrepressible Irish humor that celebrated adversity. The man never seemed to flinch from the idea of a dicey scene ahead.

"I'll remind you of that when we get there, Sean Rork—just in case you forget in the heat of the moment."

"Aye, an' I'll wager a bishop's crown that we'll be havin' plenty o' that heat, sir. That's certain as rain in Derry, o' I'm not a son o' the sea."

The steamer was a haphazard affair that made six knots with the wind astern and every stitch of canvas showing. Wake and Rork, wearing plainclothes for the journey, bunked together in a cabin jammed with a half dozen men of various tongues, none of whom gave the appearance of gentility. After meeting their neighbors, one of the two Americans always stayed with their sea bags, knife ready in a pocket.

Melilla was one of the traditional haunts of the Barbary corsairs, who had plundered the Mediterranean and Atlantic coasts of Europe and Africa since the fifteenth century, when a Greek named Red Beard led them. Now it was officially Spanish territory, but in actuality a no-man's land of renegades, predators, ne'er-do-wells, and slaves. They landed at the wharf after dark and cautiously shuffled along the streets, sounding out their locale and not liking what they saw and heard.

Wake found them a room for the night at a barnlike bordello, where they anxiously stayed up listening to the sounds of creaking beds on the floor above them and the screams of a riot in the street below, which subsided after two hours and several mortalities. The next morning the bodies were still there, stripped of valuables and even clothing.

The French packet vessel was a figment of someone's imagination in Genoa. There were no French vessels in port and no one knew when there would be. The Italian steamer had departed, no other foreign ship was among the clusters of Arab dhows, and Wake admitted to Rork that it was beginning to look like they were temporarily stranded. There were no Europeans in sight, a local pointing to a small fortified building a half-mile away when Wake asked for the Spanish authorities.

When they arrived there they found a native militia company, with no one that spoke English. The officer in charge spoke a type of guttural Spanish unlike anything Wake had heard. Frustratingly, Wake couldn't understand the man's patois or even be understood with his own basic Spanish. Finally the two of them gave up and walked back to the shoreline, weighing the possibilities for engaging a local dhow just to get them out of Melilla bound for someplace, anyplace.

The final argument for taking passage in a native boat bound for Tangier occurred as they stood along the harbor, gazing at the oily water that reeked of sewage. Visions of typhoid and smallpox and yellow fever floated in Wake's mind. He rubbed his face, massaging his temples to ease the tension that was building inside his head. A shout suddenly came from only feet away.

"Barak, barak!"

A form in filthy robes hurtled by them, followed by another brandishing a large curved knife. The prey tripped and fell with a terrified look right in front of Wake, who was thrown backward by Rork just as the pursuer plunged the knife into the throat of the first man. He ripped it viciously across with a growl and then impaled the victim repeatedly, each time ripping the blade out sideways—disemboweling him in front of the astonished sailors. In seconds a huge puddle of blood spread around the body.

Both heaving with fear, Wake and Rork fell back a few steps and caught their breath, standing back to back, ready for an onslaught against them next. But to their confusion, they saw that the one-sided butchery incited no observers from the crowd going to and fro around them.

"Good God, Rork. We're getting out of here, native boat or whatever," decided Wake, his heart still pounding as the victor robbed the corpse of a pocketful of beads and coins, then strode off with a slope-jawed grin, holding his loot in the air and singing something incongruously lighthearted in Arabic.

"Them scows're lookin' better all the time, sir," muttered Rork.

"Let's go over there and ask about passage," said Wake, pointing to some men wearing slightly cleaner robes by a dhow on the wharf. "We need to get out of here. Now."

Rork's face tightened into a grim smile. "We're a bit o' a far cry from staff duty on the flagship now, eh, sir?"

29

Barbary Corsairs

The heavily laden dhow heeled over in the breeze away from the shore.

"So these bugger's is the Barbary pirates? By God, a rum-lookin' piratical lot, ain't they, sir?" asked Rork, leaning while the dhow heeled over in the breeze.

"Oh yes, I do believe we're right in among them, Rork."

Through gestures, and the flash of five gold coins, the Americans had managed to get aboard a vessel said to be leaving that afternoon for Gibraltar. Once aboard they sat atop a pile of cargo crates, waiting for hours and trying to blend in as much as they could in their Western clothes. It turned out that the head man's interpretation of "afternoon" included the whole time up until sunset, which is when they shoved away from the dock.

The leader of the crew, Wake couldn't think of him as a captain, was a nasty-faced old man with fierce eyes and a shaggy face that emerged from his cloaked head. Rork determined with a laugh that the man's name was Dam Khanjar, and after several hours of listening Wake finally figured out that the name meant "bloody dagger" in Arabic—which, in fact, was what the man displayed prominently stuck inside a sash on the front of his robes, complete with dried stains crusted on the unsheathed blade.

"For pirates they sail this relic pretty fancy, sir. Looks like five or maybe six knots at least, in spite o' being loaded down," opined Rork, watching the crew setting up a backstay and hauling the sheet in. The coastal mountains faded into a purple haze behind them after they rounded Cap des Trois-Fourches and headed due west into the pink afterglow of the sunken sun. The wind was from the northeast and the lanteen-rigged single-master was on her best point of sail.

"Ancient skills. They're the ones who taught the Europeans about the lanteen and the gaff a thousand years ago," said Wake, marveling at the simple yet effective rig. He glanced around and changed tone. "Listen, I don't like the looks of this. One of us should be on watch at all times. You sleep. I'll get you up in two hours."

"Aye, aye, sir. How long till Gib, d'ya think?"

"Not sure, Rork. If the wind holds fair, then tomorrow evening."

A scar-faced crewman moving forward elbowed his way past Rork, who glanced at Wake. "That'll be none too soon for the tastes o' me, sir. I don't trust these shifty boyos as far as I can throw 'em. Remind me o' some o' the skullduggerers in them dark alleys o' Dublin, they do."

Wake remembered Fyock's words. "They think we're infidels and primitive in *our* morals, Rork. Even the poorest Arab has a sense of dignity and a sense of strength they get from their faith. So I guess we're all even. Get some sleep."

Rork laughed. "Sleep, sir? Like a poxy trollop in a new church, me thinks. But I'll give it one hellova try anyway."

In the dark Wake's ribs were jammed hard by Rork's elbow. The bosun's breath was warm against Wake's ear as he whispered. "Somethin's happenin', sir. 'Nother vessel comin' alongside from windward."

Wake heard Arabs shouting apparent curses and blinked his eyes awake. Rork spoke louder this time. "Sweet Jesus, it's an attack!"

Straightening his back from the corner of the crate he had been leaning against, Wake saw a sail loom above them against the night sky on the starboard beam, then flinched as a light-caliber cannon, like an old brass four-pounder, cracked close by and shredded the cargo around him. Musket shots popped from all around, and suddenly the dhow heeled over with a splintering crash, knocking Wake and Rork backwards, as the other vessel rammed her broadside.

The deck was swarmed with figures in the dark starlight, all of them looking alike, fighting with their khanjars and screaming in rage. Rork yelled, "This way," and led Wake forward, away from the mass of clanging metal and pistol flashes.

On the foredeck Rork parried a pike thrust toward them and growled a Gaelic oath, smashing the rod away and pushing its owner overboard. Wake grabbed his friend's arm, pulling him forward. With their backs against the very bow, they looked at the scene swirling aft. The pike now clenched in Rork's hands, the bosun glared fiercely at the mortal combat fifteen feet away.

"Pirates," gasped Wake as a pistol flashed near them and the cannon banged again. It was on the other dhow, which was now lashed to their own vessel.

"We may have to swim—our boys're losing!"

Wake caught a glimpse of Dam Khanjar roaring an Arabic curse and slashing around in the circle at the robed men around him. More gunfire cracked and Rork pointed to a fire licking up fast from some of the piled cargo. Oil had been ignited, flaring up into the sail. Seconds later, it whooshed into a huge flame, engulfing the after half of the boat, and lighting a nightmare scene.

The melee stopped for a moment as the stunned mob looked above them. Then one of the pirates saw the two Americans huddled on the bow and pointed toward them, screaming something as he leveled an ancient blunderbuss and clicked an empty trigger. Throwing it down, he pulled out a cutlass, his eyes blazing with hate.

"Get ready to jump, Sean!" Wake screamed.

He crouched, ready to dive overboard before the pirate could reach them, but stopped abruptly, cocking his head. A weird shriek, strange and yet familiar, ripped through the night sky, ending in an explosion and geyser a hundred yards off the starboard side. Another one even closer drenched them seconds later.

The pirate heading for them stopped, glared at Rork, then leaped back aboard his dhow alongside. Wake knelt down on the deck. "What the hell is *that!*"

"A shell from a warship, by God!" Rork yelled. "Well, I'll be a sonovabitch. Look at that."

A steamer was surging up on their port quarter, belching cinders into the sky and throwing a huge bow wave. Rifle shots from her crew were already peppering the other dhow and Wake heard shouts in English. The Arabs on the deck aft—Wake couldn't tell who was pirate and who was not—all put up their hands and stared at the ship towering next to them.

"Stop that! Gets your hands up, now!" came an eerie muffled voice through a speaking trumpet. "We are Her Britannic Majesty's Ship *Inconstant* and we order you to stop, right now."

"It's the friggin' Royal Navy, sir!" muttered Rork. "I never thought I'd fancy those arrogant bastards, but right now, by Jesus' name, I *love* the sight o' them Limey bluejackets."

The flames suddenly diminished as sheets of canvas ash floated down. The steamer's bow wave arrived and rocked the dhows, dropping charred rigging and felling some of the combatants. Wake couldn't see anyone aboard the warship in the dim light, just the hull and spars, black and ominous. The ship's inhuman trumpet spoke again. "You there, down on the bow, who are you?"

Wake realized the thumping he felt was his heart. Rork nudged him. "That's us, sir. You'd better answer. Hell, they probably think we're Froggies."

Wake shook himself back to reality and called up to the black mass above them, "Lieutenant Peter Wake and Bosun Sean Rork of the United States Navy. In transit to Morocco."

Another voice on the trumpet. "Well, I'll be damned. Peter bloody Wake on a native scow. I don't believe it."

Wake didn't either. The voice he was hearing was Lieutenant Peter Sharpe Allen, Royal Marine Light Infantry. Another, older, man on the ship shouted an order. "Get them up here straight away!"

Wake and Rork rose unsteadily to their feet and stumbled their way aft to where British seamen and Marines were boarding the dhow. They found their seabags, covered with a slime of ash and blood, and were helped up the boarding ladder to the waist of *Inconstant* by a hulking Marine sergeant. "Up ye go, sir. Home to old England."

"Am I glad to see you!" Wake cried out to Allen, almost hugging him in relief. Rork was immediately bundled forward by some petty officers, bound for the gunroom and some of that famous issue rum.

The Marine lieutenant grinned ear to ear. "Wake, you never fail to amaze me. Yachting with the natives, are we?"

Wake felt the strength go out of him, "Voyage of the damned, more like it—"

"Lieutenant Wake? Is that really you" asked the older man, stepping forward into the battle lantern light. Wake was completely nonplussed. It was Commander John Fisher, the torpedo expert. The sight of him reminded Wake of why *Inconstant* was a ship that he felt familiar with—it was the ship the Royal Navy had used for torpedo trials at Antigua. Now he remembered hearing she was back in the Med.

Befuddled as his mind was, his curiosity was overwhelming. Why was *Inconstant* in these waters? Why was a staff officer like

Peter Sharpe Allen aboard? Why was Fisher, the torpedo expert, aboard? How did they come across the fight with the pirates? Why did they stop?

"Commander Fisher, I am in your debt, sir."

"No, no. You're not in my debt, Lieutenant. I'm but a passenger aboard. Captain Fraser is the man of your salvation." Fisher turned to a broad-shouldered man who emerged from the darkness. "Captain . . . may I present Lieutenant Peter Wake, of the American Navy. Lieutenant Wake is attached to their squadron here and seems to turn up in the strangest circumstances. Lieutenant, this is the man who saved you. Commander George MacDonald Fraser."

"Honored and *very* thankful to meet you, sir."

"Glad we decided to investigate, Lieutenant. Rather obvious it was a pirate attack, so I thought we might as well get some target practice in while eliminating a menace to merchant sailors at the same time." Fraser winked at Fisher. "Two birds with one stone, so to say. Their Lordships of the Admiralty would be impressed by our efficiency, eh, Jackie?"

"Quite so, George," added Fisher.

"I just can't believe my luck, sir. That you would be right here. We were about done for when your shells arrived overhead."

"Fate, Lieutenant. We're cruising through the Straits to home," said Fraser.

Fisher held up a hand. "Now you know why we are here, Lieutenant Wake, but we don't know why *you* are here, incognito aboard an Arab dhow. Would it be rude to ask? You seem to lead a very . . . unique . . . life. I must confess, I am most intrigued as to what you are about here and now."

Wake laughed. It would sound ridiculous. It was ridiculous. "Bound for Rabat, sir. Special mission to look into missing American and French missionaries. We had no ships available to transport, so I took commercial craft to Melilla. Then this dhow was headed for Gibraltar where I hoped to get passage south. The attack caught us unprepared. I didn't think they were still doing this in the Straits."

"They are, and it's damned embarrassing to the Royal Navy, which is why George here decided to show the flag a bit. Might deter the rascals from going after a merchie. So you were at Melilla, eh? Quite the pest-hole, that. Missing missionaries? Ah yes, I see you chaps are pestered by that too."

"Are you headed for Gibraltar, Captain Fraser?" asked Wake.

The captain glanced at his passenger and Wake thought he saw a slight shake of Fisher's head. Fraser smiled at the American. "No, not heading into Gib this go 'round. Already re-coaled at Malta."

Fisher slightly bobbed his head to Fraser, who continued. "But I think we might be able to divert and give you a lift to Rabat, Lieutenant. A goodwill gift from the Royal Navy."

Wake was surprised *Inconstant* wasn't stopping at the huge naval station at Gibraltar but had time to make the side trip to Rabat in Morocco, but he didn't ask why. "Thank you, sir. I am much obliged again, sir."

The officer in charge of the boarding party came up and saluted the captain. "Sir, we tied up the pirates, and the innocent Arabs are taking them back to Tangier for the authorities there. On the pirates' own boat. Shoulda' seen the look on the nasty buggers' faces when they found out where they're bound for— pure fright. Those Muslim courts ain't got no mercy."

"Very well," ordered Fraser. "Write up the boarding report and get it to me as soon as possible. Now make revolutions for eight knots and set the topsails. Hold the course due west until Cape Spartel bears south, then steer so'west. I want to stay off the coast a bit. Destination is Rabat."

"So'west to Rabat? Aye, aye, sir."

"And show Mr. Wake to the wardroom for something to eat. He can use Mr. Devon's cabin."

The lieutenant slid a glance at Wake, then said, "Aye, aye, sir." It was clear he was surprised at their sudden deviation too, but at that point Wake was too exhausted to care. The sky was lightening into gray in the east as he trudged down the ladder steps to breakfast in the wardroom, already imagining what a real bed would feel like.

As he sank into the mattress an hour later Wake sighed, remembering the look in the eye of the pirate who was coming after him on the bow of the boat.

"Damn near killed by Barbary corsairs," he said to the beams overhead. "Nobody will ever believe it back home. . . ."

30

Descendant of Mohammed

It took them another day and a half to steam to Rabat. During that time Wake was given a tour of *Inconstant,* one of the newer, and most impressive, ships in the Royal Navy. A state-of-the-art, 5780-ton, iron-hulled, wooden-sheathed frigate, she boasted several innovations of naval science. Her engineers were very proud of her machinery, which was a horizontal single expansion engine of huge size—7360 indicated horse power—that had pushed her at an unprecedented fifteen and a half knots for twenty-four consecutive hours on her trials. Her documented top speed was over sixteen and a half knots. That was striking to Wake, but what really got his attention was her armament.

It included ten nine-inch guns in broadside, another six seven-inch guns, and of special interest to Wake, ten machine guns. He had never seen a machine gun. These fired forty-five-caliber rounds from a hand-cranked gun mechanism. The gunner's mates took glee in demonstrating to Wake and Rork how they could cover an area of the ocean with lead at a thousand yards. Rork was astonished, saying, "I wish we'd had these darlin's ten years ago. The war woulda' been done right then an' there, sir."

"Yes, Rork, you're right," a British voice said from behind. "They are very effective close-in weapons. But we have others that can keep an enemy at a distance. Weapons of terror that can *deter* an enemy as well as destroy them."

Wake faced Fisher, who continued, "Would you like to see it, Lieutenant Wake? I know you're curious, since you've already demonstrated *that* at Antigua and again in Italy." Seeing Wake's reaction, he said, "And yes, of course we knew what you were trying to do. Understandable, I suppose—trying find out what we had come up with. Though I wish you'd been a little less . . . indelicate . . . about it."

One of Fisher's eyebrows went roguishly high. Wake shook his head and admitted, "Yes, sir, I did get curious about the torpedo at Antigua. *Inconstant* was there, but it wasn't for speed trials, was it?"

"No, it wasn't. We could've done that anywhere," said Fisher, his smile replaced by a thoughtful pose. "You see, Peter, the torpedo work needed to be done in an out-of-the-way spot. The damned Germans and French had informants all over the Portsmouth area, so the torpedo development station there was impractical. I thought Nelson's Yard was a bit brilliant, myself. Three thousand miles from England, in a backwater of the empire. No one would find out—that is until your ship showed up and you started asking questions."

"Sorry, Commander. I thought it would be valuable if we knew how you were getting a ship to go so fast—I literally stumbled upon the torpedo in the shed and just wanted to know more."

"Yes, well, your curiosity got London and Washington in quite the twit, Peter Wake. Some people on our side have the sadly suspicious idea that the Yanks are still a potential enemy and shouldn't be allowed to know what we had paid dearly in effort and treasure to find out. You were almost considered a spy, don't you know? In fact, the only reason there weren't more severe consequences was the rather delicate condition of internal British politics. The whole thing was bloody embarrassing for us. Her Majesty's government was not amused."

"And now, Commander? Why are you showing it to me now?"

"Because you aren't a threat to us. You know, and will know, nothing of the secret technical details. But you'll understand that with this new weapon the Royal Navy is not to be trifled with by anyone. It is useful for us that the American navy, and others in the world, comprehend this. Plus, you're really not a very proficient anti-British spy, are you? That has been determined beyond a doubt."

"By a certain Royal Marine lieutenant?"

"Among others," Fisher said with mock mystery. "Come, let's see the objects of your desire, shall we?"

They descended the forehatch to the gun deck, then down another deck. In a dark compartment near the bows Fisher showed Wake the stacked torpedoes and their two launching mechanisms, a contraption that slid them down a retractable ramp through a door in the hull on each side of the stem. The first thing that hit Wake was their size. Like the one at Antigua, they were twenty feet at least.

"These must be very difficult to handle safely up here forward with the pitching of the bow?"

"Very good observation," said Fisher. "They *are* difficult to handle and set the fusing in any kind of sea. But once we can launch them, they will do the job better than any previous torpedo."

"Before I saw yours in Antigua I thought only our navy had torpedoes this big, sir. Is some of this innovation from our developments?"

"Yes. We know some of the basics of what Howell is doing at Newport. And no, to your unasked question—we have not spied upon your work. No need—it was published in *Scientific American* magazine. But most of the capability in this model comes from Whitehead's work in his factory on the Adriatic. This is the newest torpedo in the world, Peter. It outperforms all others."

"How? If I may ask, sir?"

"We can sink a stationary ship at two thousand yards, a moving one at one thousand yards. We can fill an area several thousand yards square with a few of these and deny that area to the enemy. It's not the hits that count, Peter. It's the fear of the unseen weapon that might be there. Terror—a very effective deterrent. Especially toward Continental Europeans."

Wake didn't understand that. "Sir?"

"Unlike us, they are land animals and overanalyze everything having to do with the sea, so they end up not doing anything. Probably wouldn't work toward Americans, though. You Yanks have the *very* disconcerting habit of not caring about the odds."

"Of course," Fisher's voice relaxed. "We in the Royal Navy like to flatter ourselves that you got that trait from us."

Wake chuckled. "I do believe we did, sir!"

He grew serious. "Thank you for showing me this. It's very impressive, sir. Is Peter Allen part of your work?"

"Oh no, he's Marine—they're useless for this kind of thing, you know. He was coincidentally convenient for us a few months back when you crossed paths. He's a courier to England on this trip; he'll be back in the Med in a month. Admiral Drummond uses him for special assignments."

"I *thought* he was keeping an eye on me. We've become good friends, sir. He's a good man." Wake paused. "Commander, the Royal Navy is the forerunner of the American Navy. We learned our profession from you. We're not your enemy. I have a feeling that one of these days we'll be fighting together against a common foe."

"Peter, you're right. And I have a feeling that foe's name will have a Teutonic sound to it. Maybe not in the next ten years, but definitely in our lifetime."

Fisher sighed, gestured aft and said, "I think that lunch is probably laid on in the wardroom by now, Peter. Shall we join the respected Lieutenant Allen? Marines generally make poor dinner companions—all that growling and drooling—but they do tell a good tale."

"Aye, aye, sir!"

Rabat had no harbor. The open roadstead off the mouth of the Oued Bou Regreg river undulated with rollers coming down the Atlantic coast and *Inconstant* swayed her masts in the swells when she stopped a half mile off the beach. Rork and Wake, back in their blues, said their farewells.

Rork slapped the backs of his new British petty officer pals, pronouncing them the "best o' the best—almost Irish!" then leaped with a grin down into the cutter waiting alongside to take the Americans ashore. Wake's departure was considerably more subdued but no less heartfelt.

"Goodbye, Captain. Thank you for making that decision to get some target practice. You saved our lives."

He turned to his friend Peter Allen. "After the Alcázar and the Barbary corsairs, I think we're even now, Pete. Good luck and have fun with those pretty English girls. I know we'll see each other again someplace."

Allen shook his head. "I can't believe you, Yank. Just when I think it's smooth sailing and life might even get a bit dull, you show up. So of course I know we'll meet again—when I least expect it. Good luck to you and your man Rork. And beware ashore, my friend. There're pirates there too."

Fisher stepped forward and offered his hand. "Best of luck, Peter. Do keep in touch. I think it's time your lads and our lads worked together. And as our Marine here has said, beware ashore in these parts. The only true friend you'll have is Rork."

As naval custom dictated, Rork and Wake sat in opposite ends of the boat on the way in. Rork in the bow faced aft and studied the work of the crew. In the sternsheets, Wake looked forward and surveyed Rabat. He wasn't impressed.

It reminded him of a larger version of Melilla.

Remembering the Franco influence in Morocco and not knowing Arabic, Wake tried out his bad French, asking a man on the wharf, *"Où se trouve le ambassade de Etats Unis?"* The man waved a hand angrily and said something unintelligible.

"De France?" Wake asked again.

That got a nonchalant wave toward a huddle of buildings beside the fort that squatted on a low hilltop overlooking the mouth of the river. On that side of the river, near the fort, there were some substantial structures, but on the other side of the river, which Wake later learned was Salè, a mass of hovels squatted along the sand dunes.

As they started walking toward the indicated buildings, Rork said, "I didn't know you could speak Frog, sir."

"Picked up a little in the West Indies and a little in Italy. Know just enough to get me into trouble. That's why I've got you here, Rork. To get me out of trouble!"

"Aye, aye, sir. Jes' don't make it too difficult, if you please, sir. I'm gettin' a bit old now."

Just down from the walls of the fortress they found the French embassy, which was anything but impressive. A mud hut of two stories with no windows in the front, it had a solid mahogany door emblazoned with a faded seal of the Second Empire. Wake guessed that the new seal of the Third Republic hadn't quite made it out to the lesser diplomatic posts.

As he was about to open the door and was wondering what the American embassy looked like, he saw a battered sign for it next door and walked over. It was one story, even more ramshackle in appearance with the mud crumbling in the corners and cracked everywhere, a torn banner hung limply on a four-foot pole over its doorway. As he got closer Wake realized with a flash of anger that it was an American flag.

He and Rork entered a sparse anteroom with a few chairs scattered about and a print of Lincoln on the wall.

"Oh, hello!" A thin grandfatherly man in shirtsleeves peeked around the doorway leading to a back room. "Did you just come ashore from the British warship that just arrived? The British legation is a block down to the right—"

"Yes, we did," answered Wake. "Lieutenant Peter Wake and Bosun's Mate Sean Rork, United States Navy, here on special assignment to see the ambassador, sir. When can we see him? It's a matter of the utmost seriousness."

"A serious matter?" the man said pleasantly. "My goodness, I would suppose so. Sent the Navy, did they? Well, I can only imagine then how serious this must be."

"Yes, sir. Could you please notify the ambassador of my arrival?"

"I think we already have, young man. I'm the ambassador. John Pickering, at your service, sir. I surmise that you're here regarding the missing missionaries?"

Wake heard a whispered snicker from Rork as he replied to Pickering. "Sir, I apologize. I thought—"

"Ah, don't fret it, son. This is a one-man shop. I do it all. Now, let's get you both comfortable and talk this mess over."

Pickering brought out orange juice. Around a low, beautifully inlaid table he explained the situation. Two months earlier, in early March, a new group of Catholic missionaries had begun a hospital in the hill country northeast of Rabat, on the road to the ancient imperial city of Meknes, in the central highlands of Morocco. They were the only Christians in the area and were not there to convert the locals, merely fulfill their Christian duty and serve the people with modern medicine. The missionaries were mostly French, but there were a few from Louisiana also, which was how the U.S. got involved. One of the missing was the

French ambassador's wife, who was an interested patron of the mission and had been visiting when everything happened.

The missionaries had disappeared overnight—all twenty-one of them. There was no warning, no impending crisis, no conflict with local people or authorities. The local sheik proclaimed innocence and outrage and put out a reward for information. The sultan of Morocco, Hassan, ordered the army to search for them and all of his subjects to assist to the effort. The efforts were to no avail. No sign of the missing ten men and eleven women of the Charity of Kindness Mission had ever been found and no clue uncovered.

The Vatican, the French government, and the American government protested to Sultan Hassan, the French threatening economic sanctions and possible military force if the missionaries were not returned.

Pickering said he believed Hassan was not in cahoots with the abductors. It would have been against his best interest, for it was a perfect excuse for the French to do to Morocco what they had done to Algeria forty years earlier—occupy it totally and install a puppet sultan. No, said Pickering, whatever happened, it was not authorized by the sultan or even the sheik.

"What can *we* do, sir?" asked Wake.

"Well, Lieutenant, I thought there would be at least one ship and a lot of men. No offense, but just the two of you can't do very much, can you? Still, the sultan is mounting another search, led by the commander of his personal guards. The French ambassador is going along. Perhaps you could go too, to demonstrate our concern?"

"Bosun Rork and I would be happy to assist him, sir. My admiral has directed me to assess the situation, advise him via telegraph or letter, then do what we can, as a show of solidarity with the French and support for our own people, sir. I am authorized to hire an interpreter, also."

Pickering looked somewhat relieved. "Good, then I don't have to go out there. I'm too old for that sort of thing anymore.

You won't need to hire an interpreter, they'll already have several. And I can introduce you to the ambassador at the audience with the sultan this evening at the palace. Be back here at six and we'll head for the palace. In the meantime you and the bosun can get a room at the hotel across the street. Tomorrow you can send a telegraph on the French commercial line to your admiral."

Wake thought the building across the street was a stable. He tried not to cringe.

"Thank you, sir, for your time and explanation of the situation. Bosun Rork and I will be pleased to accompany you this evening and will stand ready to assist in all ways we can."

They didn't ride to the palace, they walked. Through a slum of huts and hovels, past the walls of the fort, which Pickering said was called the Kasbah des Oudaias. He also explained the city as they went. Salè was the slum across the river and the traditional home of pirates, thieves, and the poor. It was a lawless area even to the Sultan's troops, and the Kasbah was there not so much to protect against foreigners as against the riffraff of Salè from crossing the river. It was also the reason there was no bridge.

The Kasbah—Wake felt like he was in some novelist's fairy-tale—had been built eight hundred years earlier and was the home of not only the fortress, but also the main royal palace in Rabat. There were two others of lesser import in the town, but the sultan, whom Pickering said he got along with quite well, preferred the Kasbah. Pickering thought was it because there he was far more secure from his own people.

The three of them walked around the Kasbah with the river wall on their right side, to the Andalusian Gardens, a beautifully tended park of scented trees with red and yellow flowers everywhere, like an oasis in a city of gray and brown. From there they continued around to the Bab Oudaia—the main gate, built in

1195. On their left was the Medina, the old walled city consisting of a maze of alleyways.

Wake had marveled at Islamic architecture four months earlier in Spain, but it was new to Rork and he gasped at the grandeur of the gate's mosaic patterns and curves, intricately tricked out in greens and blues. "I'll be son o' a Orangeman if it ain't a sight more beautiful than any cathedral, sir."

"And older. Wait until you see inside," added Pickering.

Slit-eyed guards splendidly dressed in robes of white and green, with long curved cutlasses and pikes watched them approach. Evidently recognizing Pickering as the United States ambassador, they presented arms in the Western fashion and opened the massive paneled doors. The three Americans never even broke stride as they entered the forbidden world of Sultan Hassan. It reminded Wake uncomfortably of his entrance into the Alcázar, and he silently asked God to let this time be different—without unpleasant surprises.

Rork was told by a servant that he was to stay back near the gate with the other diplomats' underlings, his rank not being sufficient for admittance to the inner sanctum. Wake told him to watch and listen for any intelligence of value, but Rork still worried about Wake heading further into the Kasbah without him.

Pickering and Wake were led through winding passages to a chamber deep in the palace, latticed windows casting a pattern of shadows as the setting sun filtered its way into the room and created a golden ambient light. The alabaster walls had torches and lamps flickering in between richly woven blue and green carpets. The marble floor was polished to the sheen of glass and the carved cedar benches gave off an intoxicating aroma that mixed with intoxicating incense wafting in clouds from smoke pots in the corners. A quartet in the shadows played haunting melodies on exotic long-stringed lutes, giving a funereal sound to the scene.

Servants and courtiers padded around silently, their brows furrowed in some unknown heavy responsibility, and here and there ominous Senegalese giants guarded doorways. Designed to overawe a visitor, Wake decided it was even more successful than the Alcázar. The contrast between the abject poverty outside and the Oriental opulence within was stark, disconcerting.

As usual, according to Pickering, his highness the sultan was late, keeping everyone waiting to enter the royal chamber. Pickering explained who was in the room, from the angry-looking Belgian ambassador to the elderly Spanish ambassador to the raven-eyed Jewish Rabbi of Morocco.

"What about the French? I thought they had quite a presence here?"

Pickering frowned. "Yes, they do have a presence here, but at his first audience a couple of months ago, the new French ambassador managed to insult the sultan with his candidness about the Morocco's relationship to France. The sultan doesn't like him, but is polite to the ambassador because his wife is one of the missing. The Frenchman'll be along shortly—he's showing disdain by coming late."

A commotion started at the entryway. "Well, speak of the devil and he shall appear," he harrumphed. "Here's your French ambassador now. The man seems incapable of entering a room quietly . . ."

Henri Faber marched in and Wake felt his bowels turn to jelly.

A huge golden-robed courtier arrived, intoned something imperious in Arabic, and sounded a tiny bell three times. Without a word, everyone stood and formed a line by protocol rank of diplomatic seniority, the Americans near the front, then filed through doors that were flung open by the guards, who slashed their curved swords up and out, forming an arch for the procession to walk under. Wake saw that Faber had not recognized him, joining the line behind the Americans.

As they entered the *mechouar*, the royal chamber, Pickering, his forehead sweating, whispered another piece of advice to Wake. "One more thing, Lieutenant. Whatever the sultan says, if he speaks to us at all—agree and thank him. His Majesty Sultan Hassan of Morocco, Lion of the Atlas, Protector of the Faith and Defender of the People of Islam, is a direct descendant of the Prophet Mohammed and is considered *absolutely* infallible. He can, and he will, have you killed instantly if you incur his displeasure. . . ."

Seconds later Wake was standing before the man himself.

31

Let no man or beast fail

"You are here to assist the search for these poor missing souls?" Hassan, seated amid overstuffed silken pillows on a green dais several feet off the floor, had abruptly stopped talking with the Belgian, pointed to Wake and asked the question in French. Pickering translated between the two.

"Yes, Your Majesty. I will assist your government in any way that I am able to."

"And you are here because your admiral is responding to the request of the ambassador?" Wake could hear a touch of disbelief in the tone of the Arabic, though he noticed Pickering didn't echo it.

"Yes, Your Majesty. The admiral is very concerned and wants to help you in this matter."

Hassan was a large man, muscular and not fat. Pickering said during the long walk that the sultan was rumored to have killed ten men in battle and others in the palace intrigues of his dynasty, the Alawites. Pickering explained he could not prove Hassan had killed his predecessor, Moulay Sulimane, but there were persistent rumors to that effect. Some said that poison had hastened Sulimane's death along.

Wake could believe it. Framed by a dark-haired head that never turned, Hassan's black eyes betrayed no emotion, moving back and forth over the assembled audience. Only his mouth occasionally showed expression, his severe smile emerging as more cruel than relaxed. Gowned in a silk robe of pale green, outlined in emeralds along the front seam, Hassan waved his right hand, his tone almost bored.

"That is good. Then it will please me that you will go on the search being organized by the colonel of my Royal Guards regiment. The French ambassador will be going also, for he has the strongest reasons of us all." Catherine flooded into Wake's mind as Hassan continued with a sigh, "I want all these people found and returned safely. Then I want them out of the land of Morocco. It is too dangerous here for infidel pacifists. You will leave then also."

Wake remembered Pickering's admonition. "Yes, Your Majesty."

"And in addition to my colonel and my guard, I will send the Royal Scholar, Mu'al-lim Sohkoor." Hassan stroked his goatee. "Yes, he will be valuable for the expedition."

Wake wasn't sure he should respond, but he got out, "Thank you, sir . . ." before Hassan leaned forward and with a fierce glare, boomed out in a loud bass that seemed like doom itself, Pickering shaking as he translated.

"I *command* that these missing People of the Book be brought before me, by the laws and customs of Islam and of the Great Prophet Mohammed, my ancestor and teacher. Let no man or beast fail in this command, and they that would try to stop my appointed—will be smitten from the face of the Earth! As I have said, *it will be done!*"

Everyone recoiled and even the fan-boys stopped, dead silence filling the room. Wake waited, but no one moved. He heard breathing again but everyone was riveted on the sultan out of the corners of their eyes, since all were looking downward. Pickering had explained earlier that royal audiences frequently went on for hours, until all the applicants for favors were heard, or royal business completed.

Wake, seeing the line form when they entered the royal chamber, assumed the sultan would speak with each, so he was taken aback when Hassan abruptly stood and snarled an order, prompting the guards to snap to attention and an elderly member of the royal retinue to proclaim something. Then a purple curtain suddenly came down, turbaned ushers cleared everyone out. Wake made his exit—walking backward with head bowed like the others, wondering how and why Catherine was in his life again—and wishing her husband wasn't.

Pickering and Wake flowed out of the palace with the court entourage into the central plaza within the Kasbah. Wake looked around the torch-lit evening for Faber but couldn't find him. As Rork joined up with them, Pickering touched Wake's shoulder. "The courtier just advised me that the colonel of the royal guards has requested Ambassador Faber, you, and me immediately. Wants to talk about the search expedition. He's over at the main gate."

Faber was there already, grimacing when he saw Wake coming. Faber wasn't subtle as he spoke to a man in the shadows, jerking his head toward the American naval officer. "Him! No—I will *not* have him on the search."

Then Wake saw who Faber was speaking to and his heart stopped—things were getting worse. It was the man on the train months earlier who had said he was going to Morocco as a mercenary. He was decked out in a tan uniform with some sort of shoulder insignia, looking even more dangerous than when he killed the street tough in Genoa.

"Good evening, Colonel . . . *Woodgerd*, isn't it?" said Wake, seeing surprise flicker on the other's face. Turning to Faber he added, "Mr. Ambassador, I'm here to assist in the search for your wife. Lieutenant Peter Wake, U.S. Navy. We've met in Genoa, sir."

Faber's face tightened. "You, of all people. No ship, no Marines, just *you?*"

"I'm not particularly thrilled to be with you either, sir, but I think the main thing here is to find Catherine and the others, and I will assist in any way possible."

With an amused expression, Woodgerd watched the exchange, then said, "Well I'll be damned. The train in Italy. You're that sailor who was heading to Porto Fino. Hell and damnation. Now I've got a friggin' fish out of water coming along. Just what I need."

Rork's face showed his surprise as he glanced at his friend, then glared at Woodgerd. Pickering asked, "Lieutenant, how in the world do you know these gentlemen?"

"I know Mr. Faber only briefly." Wake bowed to the Frenchman. "He was the consul general in Genoa and his wife Catherine was an *acquaintance* of mine. Colonel Woodgerd and I met briefly on a train back in Italy." Wake sighed. "It seems, gentlemen, that though we all three don't like it, we're going to have to live with it to accomplish this mission."

They sat in Woodgerd's small office as the colonel put his finger on a wall map of Morocco and began a brief on the expedition that would leave the next morning. There were no clues to follow, the plan being to talk to various tribes and leaders along the way and generate some intelligence, then follow up on it. The yellow cast of a large army lantern showed Wake his companions' emotions—Woodgerd was grim, Faber angry, Pickering confused, and Rork stoically watching them all.

Wake wondered exactly what Faber knew, deciding that it

was probably supposition only, or the volatile Frenchman's reaction would've been far more violent. Then he reminded himself that, although it could've gone farther with Catherine, it didn't, and that he had to keep his wits or things would get worse.

Woodgerd turned his attention to Wake and Faber. "I don't know or care why you don't like each other, gentlemen. But I will not have either of you jeopardize this mission. So bury your differences. I am in command. *Total* command. Clear?"

"*Oui* . . ." muttered Faber.

"We speak English among ourselves during this operation, Mr. Faber," Woodgerd said quickly.

"Then, yes, I understand you, Colonel. I simply want my wife back."

"Yes, sir. I understand also." Wake held out a hand to Faber. "Everyone wants your wife to safely return to you, sir."

Faber stared at the hand for a moment without taking it.

Woodgerd cleared his throat. "Very good. Now that it seems we're working together, I'll continue. Mr. Faber, Mr. Wake, Rork, be here at the Bab Oudaia gate at five in the morning. The expedition will depart half an hour later. By sunrise we will be out of the city and moving on the road to the highlands. Limit your personal gear to one bag. Provisions are provided. We will be moving light and moving fast. You all heard the sultan. We're not coming back, gentlemen, until we solve this—one way or another. Any further questions?"

No one had any, so Woodgerd dismissed them. As they left the office Wake saw Rork studying him. On the way back to their room neither said a word about the exchange between Faber and Wake, instead listening to Pickering prattle on about the sultan's relationship with the Berber tribes of the highlands, who didn't get along with the Arabs of the lowlands. Wake's last words with Pickering were to request he send a three-line telegraph message to Admiral Case: "No word about missing people. Only one option—I am on government search party. Will report afterward."

That night Wake couldn't sleep. His mind kept visualizing Faber, Catherine on the lover's rampart, Hassan's sinister glare, and Linda laughing with their children. He wondered where his life had gone astray; at exactly what moment had it descended into the cruel swirl of shame and fear that was consuming him?

He rolled over and tried to shut it all out, knowing he desperately needed to rest. From the darkness he heard Rork.

"Doan' worry on it too much, sir. We've seen a bit o' this sort o' thing afore. Got through that, an' by God, we'll get through this 'un too . . ."

Wake smiled, glad that his friend was there. They *had* been in some mortal scrapes before, and always, somehow, had come through. But it had never been like this.

He thought of Hassan's words, *". . . let no man or beast fail."*

32

Mu'al-lim Sohkoor

The courtyard of the Kasbah was jammed with donkeys, horses, camels, and carts. The mass of motion and sound and stench, lit by flaming torches and dim lanterns, was accented by the occasional shouted command or curse. Wake couldn't tell how many men were there, but it looked to be a good number, and he saw that they were uniformed and armed in the Western style. New French Gras bolt-actions were the issued rifle, and British-influenced khaki shirts and trousers were the dress. Each man also carried an ammunition pouch belt filled with thirty innovative eleven-millimeter metallic Gras cartridges.

The only concession to the East was the caps. Green fezzes topped the troops, giving them a deadly comical appearance. Humorous hats or not, Wake studied the troops' faces with professional interest.

Impressed, he instantly knew these men were veterans of combat. There was no fear, no bravado, just meticulous preparation.

Rork sat astride a horse in the predawn dark. He, like many sailors—Wake included—was distinctly uncomfortable in a saddle. "Oh Lord, I'd rather be ridin' the end o' a upper yard in a gale o' wind in the Southern Ocean than this here beast o' burden. The bugger looks like he wants ta capsize me bones a' the first chance. 'Tisn't natural, I tell ya, to be aloft on a critter such as this."

Wake was on an older nag—he asked specifically for that—and he laughed at the sight of big bad Bosun Rork afraid of a horse. "Don't the Irish love horses, Sean?"

"Aye, we all love 'em, but only a few ride 'em. Ya know, it's mostly the rich English landowners what have 'em back home in Ireland, sir. The peasants, now they ride the draft an' work horses, not this kind o' high-strung crazies."

"Rork, your horse hasn't even moved since you boarded him. He looks pretty calm to me."

Rork wagged a finger. "Aye, an' that's what the big bastards want ya ta think, sir. Then they kill ya when ya least expect it."

Wake laughed, a good belly laugh that freed the tension from his body. Rork could be so damn funny sometimes—usually when he was trying to be serious.

Faber was mounted just ahead of them in the column, looking every inch the gentleman, having said little beyond "good morning" to Woodgerd and Wake.

Woodgerd rode up. "Hope you're both ready, Wake, 'cause we're moving out now. Do *not* fall behind." With that he was off, spurring his horse toward the front of the column fifty feet forward of them. Wake took out his watch—Woodgerd was right on time.

"*Yamshee!*" rang out, repeated several times back along the line. Unbidden, the horses all began to walk, the slow clatter sounding thunderous as it echoed around the walls of the Kasbah. As they passed through the massive gate Wake saw several of the men glance up at a solitary window cut into a wall of the fortress. A deep voice from the window chanted above the noise of the horses.

"*Hadh hasan . . . wa 'alaikum as-salaam wa're hhmat ulaahi wa barakaatuh . . .*"

Horsemen around them exchanged glances and began whispering, as Rork said, "Oh Lord, I didn't like the sound o' that, sir."

Wake didn't either. "It did sound pretty ominous, didn't it? I wonder what it meant?"

Both were startled by a cultivated reply in the dark. "In English a rough translation is 'Well done, and peace is upon you, as well as God's mercy and His blessings.' It is not *ominous* gentlemen—it is beneficent, and the guardsmen around you appreciate that His Majesty took the time to say it to them."

Wake and Rork turned around in their saddles to look at the horseman who had ridden up behind them. He was a short nondescript man dressed in dark trousers and shirt, with a check-patterned cloth around his head. Riding a gray with an ease that showed he was at home on a horse, the man came closer. His beard and moustache were neatly trimmed, complementing a pleasant face. Unlike many people Wake had met in Morocco, the man looked him straight in the eyes.

"Lieutenant Peter Wake and Bosun Sean Rork, sir, of the United States Navy. Thank you for translating that, or I should say *shukran*, I believe. I hope I pronounced that correctly. Your English is perfect, by the way."

The man trotted up to ride beside them. "How very quick you are to learn our language, Lieutenant. Yes, you said 'thank you' very well. Of course, I need no introduction to you two gentlemen, for everyone around here knows that America has sent two of her gallant sailors to assist in this sad, and somewhat dangerous, endeavor."

He swept his hand with a flourish from his chest out in a circle, then toward Wake and Rork. In anyone else Wake would have thought it a silly gesture. With this man it came across as a normal adjunct to the conversation. He went on.

"However, I have been remiss in not introducing myself to you earlier and must sincerely apologize. Please do not think me crass. I am Mu'al-lim Sohkoor, the Royal Scholar of the Court of

Hassan, Sultan of Morocco, Lion of the Atlas, Protector of the Faith, and Defender of the People of Islam."

Another flourish, followed by a disarming smile. "*As-salaamu aliakum. Sabaa al-khair.* Peace be upon you and good morning."

Wake glanced at Rork, bouncing along staring at their companion, dumbfounded. Wake felt pretty dumb himself. "Sir, it is an honor to meet you. I'm afraid you have us at a disadvantage with your extensive knowledge of our two languages, for we only speak English and a little Spanish, and just a few words in French."

Again the paternal smile. "It is one of the reasons I am along, Lieutenant. To translate and facilitate. These are my people and I understand them better than most." Sohkoor shrugged. "Sometimes even the mightiest swordsman needs the songbird to beguile the wily foe he cannot come to grips with."

"Now *that* sounds Irish," offered Rork.

Sohkoor chuckled. "Ah yes, my new friend. The Gaels have many sayings that are worthy of all peoples, Mr. Rork. But that one is Berber. Perhaps they learned it from the Irish."

"Aye, mayhaps they did, sir—we Irish do travel a bit."

"I must go bid my respects to the French ambassador, gentlemen. His is a particularly sad journey," Sohkoor eyed Wake, "which we must all do our best do assist. *Ma'a s-salaama.*"

He leaned over, whispering a word in his horse's ear, then galloped forward to trot alongside Faber in front of them. Wake heard Sohkoor speaking in French without hesitation.

Rork nodded toward Sohkoor. "Watch that one, sir. He knows more than he lets on."

Wake recalled Sohkoor's face moments earlier when referring to Faber. Sohkoor wasn't there just to assist, Wake decided. No, the man radiated confidence and command. He wasn't just a scholar.

"I think we'd better watch them all, Rork. We've no friends here."

The sun was blazing, chokingly hot in the dust of the road, less than an hour after it rose. In the light Wake was able to see the composition of the force. It was considerable—a reinforced company of mounted troops and a battery of horse artillery. But they weren't dragging light cannon. Instead, they had two wicked-looking American Gatling guns.

After winding their way through the Jewish Quarter, or Mellah, they emerged from the congestion of the city and followed the south bank of the river. A mile further they joined the main coast road to cross the river at a ford to the Salè side, scouts reporting in to Woodgerd that the road was clear of bandits. More scouts came from the seacoast village of Casablanca, forty-five miles to the south, reporting no sign of trouble in that direction. The evident relief of the scouts made Wake wonder how much control the sultan exerted outside the walls of his palaces in the cities of Morocco.

In the afternoon the column turned easterly and began to climb the eucalyptus-scented hills that ranged parallel to the coast. Faber still rode alone twenty feet ahead of Wake, his back ramrod straight and face stoic as it swept the dismal brown hills. Stretched out for a quarter-mile, the entire procession seemed far too ponderous and leisurely to Wake, who had envisioned galloping around after renegades in a desert and rescuing Catherine and the missionaries from an Arab tent. He said so to Woodgerd when the colonel rode back along the line.

"This is all a bit slow, isn't it, Colonel?"

"That's exactly what I want the enemy to think, Wake. That we're bloated and fat, just like the sultan's armies have been for a hundred years. The Berbers are anything but bloated and fat. I want them to see us moving slow today. And be assured, they *are* watching us. Right now."

"Ah yes, deception in war can save a hundred men or kill a thousand," added Sohkoor as he trotted up, bowing in the saddle without effort. "Our dear colonel is a master of that art."

"Sounds like a quote from Napoleon or Jomini," offered Wake, hurting all over, especially his crotch and thighs, from the strain of merely staying in his saddle. He hoped he'd be able to walk normally again but doubted it.

Woodgerd answered before Sohkoor. "It's from one of the greatest of warriors—Saladin the Magnificent."

"Don't know of him. Sounds famous though with a name like that," Wake said.

"Oh, he's famous all right," said Woodgerd. "Probably the most famous Arab warrior in modern history. Every Muslim knows of him. He's the one who defeated the Crusaders under Richard the Lion-Hearted."

"And protected the Christian prisoners," added Sohkoor. "He is known for his terror in battle and his compassion afterward. He sent fruit and snow ice to the sick Richard, whom he honored as a true warrior."

"Let's hope we don't run into any Saladins on this little jaunt," muttered Wake.

Sohkoor laughed and wheeled his horse around, bound for the van of the column as Woodgerd continued back along the line of troops. The road ahead inclined steeply and Wake couldn't see far ahead. The hills were getting higher.

Rork twisted around and pointed west. "Say goodbye to the sea, sir. Won't see it anymore after this here hill. An' I don't feel good about *that,* sir."

Wake tried to calm the gnawing in his gut as he watched the sea disappear behind them. "I agree with you there, Rork."

Even in the gray dusk Wake could see the chieftain didn't look impressed. Sohkoor had asked the man if he had any knowledge of captured foreigners in the area, to which the leathery ancient, head of the mountain Berber clan who lived in the tiny cluster of skin-walled huts, simply shrugged, then smiled idiotically. Told that he was now a hostage, the man didn't even flinch. He knew he would be taken the moment he saw the sultan's banner.

Sohkoor explained to Wake as they resumed the march. "He knows we consider him an enemy, until he proves himself a friend. He further knows that one should hold their enemies closely, until the issue is resolved."

"Another of Saladin's sayings, sir?"

The scholar grinned. "No, my friend. That one comes from Caesar. *Tene tuum inimicum etiam iuxtior quam tuum amicum.* He had very good reason to know that rule."

Wake was astonished. "You speak Latin too?"

"And Greek and Hebrew and French and Spanish. I am but a scholar and I study knowledge already gained by others. It is not much, admittedly, but it is what I do."

"You are a very interesting man, sir," said Wake. "I think I'll be learning quite a lot from you in the next few days."

"The ability to learn is a salient, but rare, characteristic in men, Lieutenant Wake. Done humbly, it is what separates the few from the many. I shall look forward to learning from you, too, as we travel together on this journey."

Two hours later they stopped for the night on the crest of a hill, the blue and silver stars above them crisp in the gradually chilling air. Tired as they must have been, Wake registered that the camp was set up in minutes, the soldiers going about their business without direction. First the perimeter pickets were posted and interior works erected, next the horses fed and watered and groomed, and only then did the cooks prepare a mush of vegetables and grains as others put up tents for the officers. His watch said ten in the evening when Wake lay down next to Rork under a goatskin lean-to.

Sohkoor appeared out of the gloom and walked by. *"Bonne nuit, mes amis."*

263

"I'm sorry, sir. I didn't understand that. What did you say, sir?" asked Wake.

Sohkoor stopped. "Oh, it is for me to be sorry, Lieutenant. I was under the impression that you had recently learned conversational French." He paused in thought for a second. "Please pardon me. I said to you, 'good night, my friends.' I fear our departure will be early and I hope you gain a good rest. Good night."

"Yes, sir. Good night to you, too, sir."

"Oh, *sir* really is far too pretentious a word for a humble scholar such as myself. I am no soldier and need no rank. And Mu'al-lim Sohkoor is a bit long for your western tongue. Please just call me Sohkoor and I would be honored to have the privilege of calling you Peter and Sean."

"Yes, sir . . . er, I mean . . . Sohkoor."

The scholar slipped away in the dark, calling back, "Pleasant dreams, Peter."

Lying there on the rocky ground, assailed by a hundred images of doom, Wake had the distinct feeling that Sohkoor didn't mean a word of it. But he wasn't fearful anymore. Now he was just plain angry at being stuck in the middle of nowhere with a vague plan at rescuing vanished people, one of whom had nearly ruined his life.

33

Wind of the Atlas

They didn't leave at dawn. They left at three in the morning—
without the column. Woodgerd woke them up and told them
"the interesting part is about to begin." Then he rounded up
Sohkoor, Faber, and half a dozen of the troopers and they silently
slipped out of the camp, moving off the road and across the shale
rock hills toward three stars on the eastern horizon barely seen in
the loom of the bright half moon. Woodgerd forbade them to
make any noise and told them he would brief them more after the
sun rose, but that now they had to be stealthy and get another
twenty miles across the hills toward a place he called Volubilis—
and that their lives would depend on it.

When the sun rose a few degrees above the horizon
Woodgerd led them into a grove of poplar trees along a shallow
creek and let them rest. Groaning and limping, they unloaded
their horses of gear and saddles, then collapsed. The troopers first
pulled *jellabas*, the flowing robes of the Berber and Arab, over
their uniforms, then flopped down prone and formed a loose
perimeter. Woodgerd put on a *jellaba* and leaned against a tree,
taking a deep breath, briefing the others as they donned their
robes.

"The reason we left the column is so we can move fast. The column is going to continue to the northeast toward the Rif Mountains, where the northern Berbers are. Many people think the Berbers are behind the disappearance of the missionaries. They are wrong. But we want everyone to believe that we suspect them and are headed that way."

Faber, who'd been staring off in the distance, swung around. "I was told the most likely perpetrators of this crime were the Berber bandits of the Rif. And now you say no? Was that a deception? Against me! Do you have proof of something else, Colonel?"

"Yes, it was a deception and I hope like hell it worked. I want everyone from here to the Rif to think that you and I are still with the column and headed that way. Meanwhile we are going to Volubilis, the ancient Roman city, where we'll be obtaining some information on where to go next."

Wake asked, "How far off is this Roman place, Colonel?"

"Another thirty miles, up into the lower mountains on the western side of the Middle Atlas. We lay low here during today and we leave at sunset. We should be there a few hours after midnight."

Faber stood, angrily kicking up a dust cloud with a boot. "Why not keep going *now?* We must spare no effort, no time, to find Catherine and the others! There is no time to lose and too much has been lost already!"

Woodgerd wasn't cowed. "Because we need to find them *alive,* Mr. Faber. And that means getting them by surprise. And that means sneaking into the area."

"What is 'sneaking?' I do not know this word!"

"It means to use stealth, Mr. Ambassador," answered Wake. "I think it's the best way."

Faber glared at him. "Yes, of course. *You* would."

Wake tried to defuse the man. "We're all trying to save them, sir."

"Stop the whining," Woodgerd growled. "From now on we

all wear *jellabas.* Guard watches will be set for all day. Everyone takes a turn. No one leaves the trees. Anybody approaches, Sohkoor or the troopers will talk to them. We are a group of clansmen heading for a wedding feast."

Woodgerd waited but no one had questions. "All right, get some sleep—you'll need it later. Wake and Sohkoor are first on watch, then in two hours, Faber and Rork."

The watches passed excruciatingly slowly. Faber didn't speak with anyone and Sohkoor was in a quiet, almost mystical mood. The five daily prayers of the Muslims were done silently and quickly, and everyone waited and watched the shadows tell the time as the sun slid toward the distant hills behind them.

The little line of men were mounted and ready as the last of the molten sun fell into the hills and Woodgerd uttered, "*Yamshee*" in a hoarse voice, starting them away from the dusk toward a ridge in the distance.

Following no road they crossed a dry creek, which Woodgerd called a *wadi,* and in the growing starlight began to climb the steepening slopes, their gear muffled against noise, the only sounds the labored breathing of man and horse, with an occasional oath when a horse stumbled.

Climbing and climbing, never finding level ground but always pushing higher into the Middle Atlas, they went on. The pace was slow but steady, Wake estimating they were moving at about three knots and wondering how they would cover the thirty miles in the time predicted.

He found out how just after eleven P.M. Skirting an open copper mine, they circled to the north and then east again to the top of a ridge, then gazed across a broad valley. By this time the moon illuminated the gray rocky surface pretty well, and Wake could make out a village in the distance, darkened huts looking like black dots.

Now moving faster on level ground, Woodgerd and Sohkoor led them north along the ridge, taking care to keep below the crest and not be silhouetted. Two more ridgelines and three hours later they stopped for the last rest before their destination, which they saw spread out in the plain a mile away. As they sat their horses, stretching their backs and legs, Sohkoor reined up between Wake and Faber. He waved a hand across the ruins and whispered.

"That is the ghost city of Volubilis. First founded by Carthage four thousand years ago, it was expanded into a major city of twenty thousand persons by the Romans at the time of Jesus, blessed be his name. It was abandoned by the Romans two hundred years later, a generation before Constantine became a Christian and changed that empire forever, when the Berber people rose up in revolt. For the next four hundred years the people of this city still spoke Latin, until the word of Islam came to this land."

"Who lives there now?" asked Wake.

"Only the ghosts of the dead, who come from a dozen cultures over four millennia. After the earthquake of seventeen fifty-five, in your calendar, it was abandoned by all people, the marble being plundered for the royal palaces of our sultans. Many people think it haunted. All people believe it is a mystical place. Most are afraid of it, especially at night."

"And we go there now, in the middle of the night?" said Faber.

"Yes. We must go there now."

"And please tell me why, again?" persisted Faber, sounding tired.

"To pray and think, Monsieur Faber. And wait for information that should be forthcoming."

Woodgerd called back to them, "Move out. Stay quiet. We'll hide in the ruins for the rest of the night and the day. Tomorrow at sunset we'll start off again."

Faber shook his head. "I do *not* understand this waste of time. . . ."

Sohkoor held up a hand. "You will, my friend. You will."

The night was incredibly still and the moonlit landscape unnerving. Having entered the ruins along the *Decumanus Maximus,* as Sohkoor explained the main street, the group turned left onto another major thoroughfare and followed the scholar through the leveled remnants of the city to a structure he described as the forum and capitol, whose walls and columns were still relatively intact. There they settled into the shadows, hidden below the surrounding terrain within the crumbled foundation of a building next door. The troopers—in their *jellabas* Wake now thought of them as Arab warriors—were scattered among the other ruins, leaving Faber, the Americans and Sohkoor resting near an intricate mosaic on the floor of the capitol.

"Hmm. I'm wonderin' jus' what *that* might be?" whispered Rork, pointing at figures formed in the mosaic.

"A Roman myth, I suppose, but I don't know which," replied Wake, trying to remember his lessons on the classics from twenty years earlier. He had always considered them a waste of time. Oh, if only that headmaster could see me now, he thought.

"The trilogy of Jupiter, Juno, and Minerva," said Faber with a sigh as he lay out on the rocks. "One of the Romans' major mythologies."

Sohkoor looked bemused. "Quite correct, Mr. Ambassador. And quite possibly *apropos* of our current situation. But we must wait to find that out. And unfortunately, waiting is not a trait well practiced in European and American cultures."

Faber rolled over, facing the royal scholar. "I am not impressed by you and this *charade* of a search, Sohkoor, and I am *sick* of this heartless hell of a place and its backward ways. By God, you need a civilized country to come in here and teach you how to live in the modern world!" Faber was snarling by then.

"And *you* think you know everything, playing the scholar and spouting other people's languages. You know absolutely nothing!"

Sohkoor, unfazed, tilted his head to study the Frenchman. In the silvered light, Wake could see the dark eyes hood over into slits and hear the tone descend into a slow graveled bass.

"Mr. Ambassador . . . you may be right . . . but I think not. And I do know some things, more exactly, what is going to happen to *you* . . . to your soul . . . on the evening of this coming Tuesday. You will become a better man."

Rork and Wake exchanged glances as Faber rolled away from Sohkoor and grumbled, "Oh, go to hell, you pagan savage. . . ."

"*Laa, ensha'llaah,*" Sohkoor hissed, then with a smile translated for Wake and Rork, "No, God willing. . . ."

The cool air rustled up some dust for a moment, then a gentle wind sprang up, bringing a whiff of juniper. Within minutes it grew to a real breeze with no clouds in the sky, no storm on the horizon. It was a wind from nowhere.

Sohkoor stood up from the rubble, faced east, and spread his hands upward, raising a lilting chant to the sky, "*Irifi! Bekheer, bekheer, lhamdoo llaah! Shukran bezzef 'llaah. A'llaah akbar! Aqmaar 'adHeem!*"

He let out a huge sigh and sat again with a smile, nodding at Woodgerd, who cocked an eyebrow at Wake and shrugged. Wake couldn't stand it and asked the scholar, "Sir, what was it you said just then?"

"That the dry wind has come and it is fine, praise God. Thank you so much, oh God. For God is great and the moon, it is marvelous."

"I'm sorry, but I can't quite follow you, Sohkoor."

The Arab reached out and touched Wake's shoulder. In the cool air his fingers felt amazingly hot through the cloth. "We have been blessed tonight with two omens of success—the *irifi* wind of the Atlas that flows down from the mountains to the desert, and the moon that shines bright though it is only half full-grown. I thanked God for giving us these signs. We are on the right path."

"Oh, I see," said Wake, looking into those eyes that seemed so old yet so fierce.

"No, I think you cannot yet, my friend, but you will. You will see clearly soon."

34
Fés

Just before dawn Wake shook Rork and spoke close to his ear. "Company arriving, Sean. Something's happening."

They watched as a bent figure in a dark woolen *burnous* met with Sohkoor and Woodgerd on the main street, the conversation animated with gestures. It went on for at least ten minutes, then each said farewell, the stranger hobbling down the old Roman road out of the ruined city.

"Everybody up. We leave now," Woodgerd ordered. He pointed to the ridge a few miles to the east. "By sunrise I want us over there."

Sohkoor looked pleased. "Good information."

"Who was that man?" asked Wake.

"A mystical friend of mine. Known as a *marabout*—a holy man. He is one hundred and two years in age in your calendar, and very wise. He just told us where to go and what to look for. Tonight we shall be near Meknes and when the moon shines again, we shall see, then we shall hear, then we will know."

It sounded like hokum to Wake, who was beginning to question if they were intentionally being led astray. "Ah, know exactly *what*, Sohkoor?"

"Where the missing people are located. Oh, I see the doubt in your eyes, Peter Wake. Just as in the holy book of your people there was a man named Thomas. Have faith, my friend."

Wake wasn't impressed. "Yes, well I'm not Muslim, Sohkoor. I'm a Protestant Christian, a Methodist, and I'd like something a little more solid."

"True, but you and I, and everyone of us here on Earth, share the strongest bond—for we are *all* the sons of Ibramin, or Abraham as you pronounce it. We must all share peace and work together."

Sohkoor held up a hand. "You should know that the faith of Islam has Judaism and Christianity as its foundation, and is considered to be a refinement of the respected teachings of Moses and Jesus, whom we revere as blessed prophets. And it was your very own Augustine, the saint, who said that true faith is believing what you do not see—the reward is to see what you believe. Something you Christians have done for almost two thousand years."

"Yes, well, I guess you've got me there, Sohkoor," Wake said, admitting inwardly that the man had an infectious way about him. "When you start quoting the saints I give up."

Meknes, the great former imperial capital of the Berbers, was to their south, but their route went east and then southerly into the mountains around a small town. Wake noticed the Arab soldiers kept glancing at it in the distance and murmuring reverently. He finally asked Sohkoor, "What is in that town? The troops keep watching it. Is there danger there?"

"That is Moulay-Idriss, named after the man who built it. He came to us from Mecca, taught us the peace of Islam and united us as one people. Our sultan, the great Hassan, is a direct descendant of Moulay-Idriss, who himself was the great-grandson of the Prophet Mohammed. It is a very holy place, respected beyond others and reserved for only the truest of believers— Muslims only, as your Vatican's *sanctum sanctorum* is for your believers. Non-Muslims cannot go through there, which is why we are taking this detour."

"Yes, but we're all wrapped up in these *jallabas* and *burnouses*— nobody will really know and this is taking us out of our way to Meknes."

"Ah, but *we* will know, Peter. So we go around."

Wake glanced at Faber, riding behind him. "Well, don't tell our French friend there or he will throw a French fit."

After passing Moulay-Idriss, the trek continued along a ridge for hours, the main road visible in the valley a hundred feet below. Finally Meknes appeared and they descended closer to the city in midafternoon.

Sohkoor took the lead through steep narrow valley outside the walls of the city and through the congestion of a *souk,* the market a mass of energy and noise. At the Bab Al-Mansour, a massive ceremonial gate exquisitely decorated in mosaics and carved cedar wood, they came up to a formation of mounted men in tan cavalry uniforms, each one menacing with huge *scimitars* and lances. To the shout of their leader, the formation pranced their horses back and forth on a parade ground, charging and yelling in unison, the mock combat a terrifying medieval sight.

Wake thought Woodgerd would stop to receive professional courtesy and assistance. But instead he and Sohkoor nodded to each other and kept going around the city walls, the rest of them trailing along. At Bab Merima, near the Jewish Mella with its exterior windows and balconies that the Muslim dwellings didn't have, they entered the maze of curving alleys in the Arab Medina of Meknes. Wake was instantly lost. The dark alleys were like canyons, the main streets about ten feet wide and the side streets maybe six. The din and stench assaulted Wake's senses.

A thousand feet into the Medina, Sohkoor stopped at a small paneled door set into a large double door in the forty-foot-high mud wall of an alley. No sign or description was on the wall of the seven-foot-wide alley, jammed with people and beasts of burden, and Wake couldn't see how Sohkoor had known where to stop—they had already passed at least a dozen similar doors. Sohkoor motioned Wake and Rork to dismount and come over, where he showed them a small carving on the door. "The hand of Fatima, revered daughter of The Prophet, placed here to ward off the Evil Eye of the Devil himself, just as you, the People of the Book, believe also. The Devil is very real, Peter."

In Arabic he snapped out something to the guardsmen and stepped inside the little doorway, beckoning the others to follow. Inside, Wake was shocked to see a large dirt-floored courtyard, roofed with straw matting and surrounded by three stories of balconied buildings.

"A *caravanserai,* where the caravans put their beasts and cargo for the night," explained Sohkoor. "The *maalik,* the owner, of a *caravanserai,* sees and hears many things from many people. Especially in Meknes, for caravans from Marakesh to the south, and across the High Atlas to the east, come through here."

Stalls for horses and camels rimmed the sides of the ground floor. An outside stair led to the second level, where two men stood on the balcony, staring at the newcomers. They didn't appear friendly, but Sohkoor and Woodgerd ascended the steps with no words or hesitation, leaving the others waiting below.

Faber was still in a foul mood, fuming at what he described as childish delays and subterfuges. Rork, as usual, stood quietly behind and to the right of Wake, who was astounded by this country scene deep within a filthy sprawling ancient city. It reminded him of some biblical story from his youth.

A heated discussion took place on the balcony, ending when Woodgerd violently pushed the larger man's shoulder. Woodgerd's oath was unintelligible to Wake, but the look on the other's face was unmistakable. The man went from arrogant to terrified.

"Be ready to get under way, Rork. Trouble's coming, dead ahead."

"Aye, aye, sir. I'll keep the door open." Rork stood in the doorway, watching the pedestrian-filled alleyway for signs of attack.

"Trouble up there?" Wake asked Woodgerd as the colonel and Sohkoor joined them below.

"Nah, just a little object lesson on hospitality. Hell, I didn't even have to touch him . . . much. Don't worry, we got what we came for. We're leaving anyway."

Sohkoor looked pensive and disappointed. "It is regrettable that sometimes common courtesy is not a common behavior. You know, Peter, they say in England that courtesy is the lubricant of an advanced society. I tend to agree with that, but unfortunately it is a mannerism that the man up there never learned. So sad. Now he has to live in fear of dire consequences." Sohkoor shrugged. "The sultan does not suffer impolite people."

Faber huffed. "That is interesting, but why is it we are we in this particular slum in the first place?"

A patient softness came over Sohkoor's face, as if a child had acted up. "To get the information we came here for, Monsieur. I now know that three days ago your wife and the others were in Fés, thirty English miles to the east from here. Renegade Blue Men on the run from their chief had taken them for ransom. They did not get what they wanted in price and returned south when they heard the sultan was sending a search party from Rabat. These renegades are not afraid of mortal men, but all men are afraid of Hassan, Lion of the Atlas."

"Blue Men?" asked Wake.

"Men of the Tuareg, the tribes of the desert. Named for their indigo-dyed robes. Very independent, but most recognize the sovereignty of the sultan. These particular men are renegades from their clan. One must be very careful with Tuareg."

Faber seized Sohkoor's *burnous*, shaking him in rage. "To hell with being careful—let us go *now!* Get after them!"

Woodgerd stepped up and locked Faber's wrists in an iron grip, prying them away from the scholar. "We all understand your anger, Mr. Faber, but we don't even know where they are now to chase them. We have to go to another place tonight to find out more information, but we are finally on the right trail. And Sohkoor is crucial to our finding your wife and the others. He's doing his best."

Faber suddenly swung around and slammed his fist down onto a cart, swearing in French and startling everyone but Sohkoor, who took Faber's fist and held it in his hands. "We will find her, Monsieur Faber. As Allah is my witness, I am saying that we *will* find her for you. . . ."

The scholar glanced at Woodgerd, who spoke quietly. "Very good, gentlemen, Now we go, and we go fast. We need to be at the spice *souk* at Fés in the morning."

Faber, deflated, looked up at the man still standing on the balcony. "What about him?"

Woodgerd shook his head. "We know what he knows now. He will stay here and inquire for more intelligence. Mr. Faber, that man is definitely on our side now."

"How can you let him go? Trust him?"

Woodgerd transformed into the man Wake had seen on the train platform—the face of death. "Because he knows he will die slowly, inch by inch, in front of thousands of people, if he does not do exactly what he has been told to do."

None of them said a further word as they wound their way back out of the maze of alleyways, emerging from the walls of Meknes as the sun was turning golden in the west. Once outside the inner city, they stopped to water and feed the horses for a few minutes. Then, following Sohkoor, they rode east, this time on a main road.

Sohkoor turned around and watched the sunset for a few minutes, then leaned over and spoke to Woodgerd. The colonel called back, "We're picking up the pace. We don't have much time."

They stopped at midnight and camped without a fire on a mountain top just outside the city of Fés. Sohkoor sat apart from the others, gazing at the moon and stars, continually singing a low chant.

When Wake and Rork were roused before dawn Sohkoor was still there, still chanting. The Arab cavalrymen ignored him as they went about the business of saying their morning prayers, eating their *couscous,* and saddling up. When the line was formed Sohkoor stood and walked over, fresh and relaxed, as if he had just woken.

He swept his arm over the valley where Fés lay sprawled. "And now we go to the capital, a city of ancient moral certainty. And of artistic creativity, which you will see. The great Idriss himself decided that Volubilis was too small for a capital so he began Fés in the Christian year seven eighty-nine. It has been the center of our life and empire since then."

"Rabat's not the capital?" said Wake.

"The sultan maintains the foreign embassies there and visits often, but this is the traditional capital. This is where it began and where it continues. It will offend the sultan greatly that the renegades came *here,* in this beautiful place, to further their horrific crime."

"I thought that the palace we visited in Rabat was the royal palace and the center of his government."

Sohkoor's face crinkled into a smile. "Peter, the great Hassan has twenty-six royal palaces across his land. The one in Rabat is small compared to some. You have only seen a tiny fraction of our land and people. We are spread far and wide, for thousands of your English miles, from the Sahara to the ocean, from the Mediterranean to Senegal. Hassan, may Allah bless and protect him, is the leader of it all and travels constantly to see and hear all."

"Sohkoor, if I may ask, what were you chanting all night? You don't even look tired."

Sohkoor touched Wake's shoulder but didn't answer. Without a further word, he mounted his horse, Woodgerd nodded and everyone trotted off, joining the main road and descending to the city.

Fés was even bigger and busier than Meknes. To Wake's surprise, they did not enter the Fés el-Jdid, the old Kasbah, Mella, and palace area, instead walking their horses around the city wall to the other side. Sohkoor explained that the sultan wasn't currently in residence—he was in the north of the country—and that they were traveling incognito, so there was no reason to check in at the palace. Wake wanted to ask Sohkoor how he knew where the sultan was, but didn't. Sohkoor's demeanor had changed since approaching the city. The scholar was tense, and that worried Wake.

The sun had risen when Sohkoor led the way through the gate of Bab Bou Jeloud into the Medina of Fés el-Bali. Inside, jostled by the crowd in the narrow streets, they walked their horses for a few hundred yards, then left them at a stall, all the disguised troopers except one staying with them. Sohkoor, the trooper, a nervous corporal named Ahmed, and the others plunged into Medina, bound for the *souk* of the spice traders.

The sights and smells and sounds assailed Wake as they passed through *souks* of iron workers, dye makers, carpet weavers, dagger forgers, copper and silver smiths, silk and cotton spinners, pot makers, leather tanners, and gun makers. Not a modern convenience was in sight, everything being done as it had been for centuries.

Rork's eyes were wide with wonder as he saw silk being woven with gold thread, leather being carved with razor sharp *khanjars,* red-hot wrought iron being bent by hammers, and six-foot-long rifles being fashioned into works of silver inlaid art. The heavy aroma of acrid smelting and sweet cooking fires was accented by whiffs of spices and incense. Throughout there was singing, from guttural working beats to religious chants to lilting melodies.

They passed a silk spinner, the thread stretching for twenty feet as he wove delicate strands of gold through it. "Incredible, sir," said Rork. "Like going back in time, it is."

"A thousand years back in time," agreed Wake.

Cutting through the dyers' *souk,* they followed Sohkoor around huge mud-walled vats of bright-colored dyes created from indigenous plants: indigo blue, mascara black, mint green, poppy red, henna orange, and the most expensive—guarded by armed men—saffron yellow. Inside the vats were men dyed the same color, pressing the dyes into cloths of agave and cotton and silk.

He watched a green-skinned man plod his way around the vat, eyes downcast with a hopeless look. Sohkoor explained that the same families had worked in these *souks* for generations upon generations. It was what they had always done in life, and what their descendants would always do in the future, which Wake found depressing.

After the dyers' *souk* they walked fast down a main street, across a tiny plaza and joined a crowd squeezing into another alley. After making lefts and rights at unmarked passageways, Sohkoor led them down a final side passage only three feet wide—the thirty-foot-high walls towering above them, giving Wake the terrifying vision of what it must be like to be buried alive. Sohkoor glanced back, gestured for them to follow, then darted into an open doorway on the right and a vast open space lined with vendor stalls. This was the rear entrance to the spice market and Wake's nostrils were immediately overwhelmed by flower perfumes from rose and jasmine, seed pressings from sandalwood and cedar and curry, and crushed mélange of amber and musk.

Sohkoor motioned for Woodgerd and Wake to enter a stall through a short door and for Faber, Rork, and the soldier to stay outside. Faber's protest was lost to the crowd as Wake bent down and entered a dark room lit by lamps. Strange incense overpowered all his senses, making him feel light-headed, while haunting melodies echoed from a hidden flute player. The half-light gave off disquieting shadows and he struggled to keep his equilibrium while keeping up with Woodgerd and Sohkoor. They stopped at a larger room, dim like the rest, where a man dressed in ornate robes of red and purple stripes reclined on a pillowed couch. The man immediately rose and embraced Sohkoor, greeting him warmly.

Sohkoor pointed to pillows set against a wall for the two Americans, then sat with the host, smiling and making small talk in Berber as servants brought tea and round bread for everyone. The two were still conversing rapidly in their language when a servant brought a tray of spices out for Wake and Woodgerd to peruse, gesturing that they should sample them. The rose oil was beautifully delicate, the jasmine very strong. Then the servant started rubbing a cloth bag of anise seeds, suddenly thrusting the bag tight against Wake's nose. He couldn't believe the result—the heated seeds created a smell that blasted open his sinuses, intruded into his brain, and made his head fly backward.

The usually taciturn Woodgerd laughed. "They did that to me too when I first got here. It is supposed to help clear your mind, in addition, of course, to blowing your nose wide open. They think they just gave you a great gift—most people have to pay for that, Wake. Say thank you."

Wake tried to focus on the grinning servant and gasped out, *"Shukran,"* to which he got the enthusiastic reply, *"la shukran 'la wezhb!"* repeatedly.

Sohkoor concluded his talk, standing and bowing to the other man, who was never introduced to the foreigners. Woodgerd and Wake followed suit and stood, a little unsteadily on Wake's part, then followed the scholar out they way they had come. Sohkoor didn't speak until they got close to the doorway, still in the gloom of the lamps.

"I do not want our French companion to hear this, but it is what I thought, Colonel. The Berbers of *Tilaal Mumeet,* three hours' journey from here to the south, were approached by the renegades only two days ago and offered sale of the captives. They declined, knowing it to be a crime and, most importantly, hearing that the sultan was angry. We must go to them tonight. And, of course, we have another task tonight as well."

"Yes, I remember," acknowledged Woodgerd. "We can do both. *Tilaal Mumeet,* did you say?"

"Yes, Colonel. I see your knowledge of our language is improving. You know what that means, do you not?"

Woodgerd grimly nodded and Sohkoor turned to walk outside the low doorway to where the others waited. Wake tugged at Woodgerd's sleeve before they emerged.

"So what does that mean? Why's it so bad?"

"Means the 'hill of death.' These aren't your friendliest of natives, Wake. This is going be a long damn night."

35

Ibn Aqnaar

Tilaal Mumeet was a small village that clung to the side of a steep hill by the same name. The leader of the clan in that area was a hulk of a man, apparently middle-aged, who towered over everyone else and had a voice incongruously mild and soft. The rest of the party waited outside while Sohkoor and Woodgerd entered a wattled hut in the center of the village. A frigid wind had sprung up that day from the High Atlas in the distance, now blowing across the hillside and reaching inside their burnouses to freeze exposed skin.

Rough-looking young men watched them from the neighboring huts as the occasional woman glided by covered from head to foot in a black *burkha,* carrying a load of bread or spring fruit. The village was gray and brown, like the clothing and the countryside and the day. Wake and Rork stood staring at the locals as Faber sat under the lee of a wall and morosely kicked sand against a bush.

"Aye, a day like this makes me miss the West Indies. An' that one's feelin' helpless, for sure, sir," said Rork, eyeing the Frenchman.

Wake walked over to Faber and sat down. "We'll find her, Mr. Ambassador. We'll find her."

Faber looked up, tears filling his eyes. "I will die if we do not. I've lost everything I thought was important to me—my good name, respect from the leadership of France. But all that is nothing. Catherine is my life, my reason to exist. She is all that I have.

He sighed. "It all has gone by, Wake, and now here I am, in the middle of nowhere, melancholy in a God-forsaken place I was sent to because my own stupid pride made me arrogant. I dragged her here, you know. She wanted us to stay in Europe, or maybe go to America, but I dragged her here."

"You were promoted, though. Promoted to an ambassadorship in Morocco from being a consul general in Genoa. That's an honor, sir."

Faber shook his head. "Hah . . . They promoted me up—and out of sight, Wake. I was too unsteady for Paris to keep in Europe, especially after that scene with Moltke, so they sent me to Africa, where the worst I could do is alienate some primitive Arabs."

Against his better judgment, Wake felt sorry for the man. "Morocco is important to France, from what I've been told, sir. I think they needed someone they could trust to be ambassador."

"Paris already had someone they could trust in Morocco, Wake. The commercial attaché is the one with the real power, not me. He does the agreements, socializes with the sultan, lives in a lavish estate. I periodically show the flag from my pathetic office and am expected to know my place. And ignore the whispered insults. No, Morocco was the perfect spot for their purposes—far enough away from the important work and close enough to recall quickly."

"Well, whatever happens politically, you need to be strong now, Mr. Ambassador. For Catherine, if nothing else."

Faber nodded. "Yes, on that you are correct, Lieutenant. All else is minor now to me—she is everything."

They climbed the hill silently, Sohkoor and Woodgerd somber, the guardsmen sullen, Faber still depressed, and the two American sailors confused. Wake hadn't seen a map, and other than the direction of the sun, had no idea where he was and where they were heading.

Rork gazed toward the sunset, a cold red glow between the layers of gray windy clouds. As if reading Wake's thoughts he said, "That's the way home, sir. The ocean is somewhere o'er there. A week o' riding on one o' these beasts, or maybe three times that by foot."

"Let's hope it doesn't come to *that,* Sean Rork."

The top of Tilaal Mumeet was flat and an acre in area, reached as the last of the sun disappeared and the temperature plunged even further. They made camp and shortly thereafter sat around a small fire, drinking a cinnamon tea called *hunja* and eating chunks of dried and salted lamb. Sohkoor sat apart from them, Woodgerd explaining that he was preparing for the evening by eating special a food, called *majoun*. It looked indigestible to Wake, but Woodgerd said it had herbs that would assist Sohkoor in understanding what would happen later.

When asked for details, he simply said, "You're not in Pensacola now, squid. You're beyond the back of the world and there're some things I can't explain. Hell, I don't understand it myself. You'll just have to see it for yourself."

Two hours later, after the final prayer toward Mecca, the mountaintop to their east began to glow as the sky, blown clean of clouds, lightened along the horizon. The group was huddled together close around the fire, except for two of the Arabs on picket farther out and Sohkoor still sitting forty feet way, alone. The glow transformed into amber, then pink and soon the moon peeked up over the jagged landscape, a half-crescent that seemed like you could reach out and touch it, the air was so clear.

Wake saw the Arabs glance at Sohkoor, waiting apparently for him to do something. But the scholar still sat, quietly facing east. Faber, who had been silent since his emotional outpouring to Wake earlier, turned to him, his voice sad and low.

"You were her friend. I will not inquire further on that. But I will ask you if you think she will want to stay with me after this."

Uncomfortable with the subject, for Woodgerd and Rork were next to him, Wake tried to be reassuring. "Sir, she is your wife and respects you greatly. You are the hero of Paris and a man whom France has honored repeatedly. I am sure that this ordeal will cement her devotion to you." Wake steeled himself. It had to be said. "And just so you know, she and I were friends, but not lovers. We talked but never did anything else."

Faber studied Wake's eyes for several minutes, the prolonged silence and pleading look on Faber's face crushing Wake's heart. "I do think you loved her just a little, though. Do not worry—it is not a problem, Lieutenant. What normal man would not fall under her spell? I believe you when you say it did not go further."

Faber looked off for a moment. "You have a wife also? And children?"

"Yes, sir. A boy and a girl."

"And you are happy?"

He thought of Linda's last letter, received the night before he left on this mission. One paragraph telling him they could make it, that she wouldn't let him go. He choked with emotion. "It's not easy to be a naval officer with a family, sir. It's very hard on the family, especially on the woman. But I hope it will get better and that my wife becomes happier with her marriage. I hope it gets better for you too, sir."

"I want you to please call me Henri, for after all we have been through it seems that we share something—a common sadness and a common hope."

Wake held out his hand. "Yes, Henri, I think we do. Please, call me Peter."

Faber exhaled loudly and shook Wake's hand. "Peter, we *will* find her. I have no doubt of that now."

Woodgerd snored abruptly, which made everyone laugh. Rork said, "Well, if the toughest man amongst us can sleep, then methinks we little people can rest easy."

"Good point, Rork," Wake observed. "We should get some shuteye."

Wake tried to settle into sleep, his mind was whirling. He noticed that Faber was not asleep either. Perhaps here's an opportunity to loosen Faber's obnoxious façade, Wake thought. He turned to him and said in a low tone. "Henri, if we can't sleep, we might as well talk. I'd like to ask you about Paris during the German invasion. Is it true you actually flew balloons out of the city?"

Faber regarded him suspiciously. "Why?"

"Because it's one of the great accomplishments in military history and I want to hear about from a man who was there."

The Frenchman shrugged. "Yes, I was on the committee that tried to maintain communication with the outside. I helped to construct balloons and operated one of the last out myself. Actually, we flew many of them out, right over the Germans with their vaunted big guns. It was how we got thousands pages of national documents—treasures, really—and secret communiqués through the siege. And, of course, we used the birds. Pigeons."

"Birds and balloons. Amazing," exclaimed Wake. "But what if they had captured them?"

"We thought of that. The Germans would not have been able to read them—we had them photographed and reduced the images to a tiny size, with many of them on a sheet of paper." Faber was warming to the subject, the pride of his accomplishment obvious. "They didn't look like normal photographs, they looked like dots to the average person."

"I've never heard of that. They used balloons a bit in our war, but not to that extent. Very innovative."

"Oh, the Parisians did far more than that. We sent out many balloons with carrier pigeons who then flew inbound over the Germans with messages from outside. On the ground the siege was tight, but in the air," he grinned again, "it was not so dominated by Prussian metal."

Rork asked, "Didn't they try to shoot you down, sir?"

"Yes, quite aggressively. The balloon I flew out in January of seventy-one had several dozen holes and was deflating slowly when I landed outside the city and beyond German lines. They upended their cannon and fired grape, but by the time it reached our elevation it was robbed of its, how do you say? . . . punch? But it was very frightening, I must say."

Wake had never seen the man like this, Faber's eyes were shining as he narrated what he saw during the famous siege. "We had to be innovative, the Germans were closing the ring tighter and tighter. We used magic-lanterns, semaphore stations, small boys who would hide in containers, and of course, those pigeons, who became the heroes of the city. They carried much of the tiny film documents—almost three *thousand* of them. You know, Peter, they even arranged money transfers that way. Germans like Moltke may boast of their army and the defeat of our country, but they never defeated us in Paris. *Never!*"

Wake could visualize the man at the scene three years earlier, his élan and strength leading the way for a beleaguered people. No wonder they revered him afterward. Faber and the defense of Paris was one of the few bright memories of the war for the French.

"An incredible story."

"Not all was successful, though, Peter. We had failures with some of our ideas, which in retrospect seem ridiculous. We tried flying out five special sheep dogs who would then walk back and return to the city with messages from the outside. They got out but never made it back in. We floated zinc metal balls, *boules de Moulins,* down the river Seine to the outside world, but none made it. We even laid a secret telegraph cable down the river's bottom—a very good idea—but the damned Germans found it."

"Yes, but Paris never was captured," said Wake, "and the German Army never stopped the birds."

"Yes, my friend. It shows what determined men can do, does it not?"

Just then an animal howl rose from the darkness around them. It was Sohkoor, standing at the edge of the firelight, arms raised to the east. Woodgerd spun over, wide awake, one hand on his rifle. He looked at Sohkoor, then the others.

"It's about to start. . . ."

36

Dance of the Dervish

"*Ibn Qamar! Ibn Qamar!*" cried out Sohkoor to the moon. "*Shukran bezzef, lhamdo llaah!*"

"What did he say?" Wake asked Woodgerd under his breath.

Woodgerd wagged his head. "*Ibn Aqmaar.* He's called upon the son of the moon, who comes out very seldom. And he offered thanks to Allah for the arrival of the son of the moon."

"*What* son of the moon? The moon doesn't have a son, or even a moon of its own," said Wake.

"Oh yeah? Look at the moon now, Wake," said Woodgerd. "And I'll be damned if the old sonovabitch wasn't right."

Wake, followed by Rork, stood up and walked to the edge of the firelight, focusing on the white moon, now above the southeast horizon and well into its evening flight across the sky. Wake guessed it was about two and a half points off the horizon, or maybe twenty-five, twenty-seven degrees up. The slightly more than half-crescent was bright white, illuminating the sky and blotting out stars that were close by, except for . . . Wake saw something. Something was close by the moon on the outer side, to the right of it. It was a bright spot, an object brighter than a star. Faber came over and Wake pointed it out to him. Soon all the men were standing there, staring at the moon and its "son."

"By all the saints in Heaven, I never seen the like o' that in all me years at sea," muttered Rork. "Son o' the moon, indeed."

Wake had never seen anything like it either. It was very close to the moon, as if it had risen from the surface and was flying just above it. Wake tried to orient himself to the sky. There in the south, to the right and slightly above the moon, was the constellation of Leo, with its Zosma and Denebola barely showing closest to the moon and Regulus a bit father away and brighter. Over on the eastern side of the moon was the constellation of Virgo, with tiny Spica trying to be seen through the lunar light. Wake understood what he saw in the sky, except for that object next to the moon. He had no idea.

Sohkoor slowly circled now, palms outward, returning to face the moon. He paused, then resumed his turning around, chanting in a low tone that got higher and higher in pitch. The circling gathered speed as the chanting grew louder and louder. The Arab guardsmen grew nervous, backing away from the scholar. One started praying to the east. Sohkoor was spinning fast, the sounds inhuman, his face distorted as the firelight flashed on it, grimacing in pain or ecstasy. Screaming chants into the mountains around them, he whirled faster until he became a blur, the echoes eerily returning seconds later so that it seemed as if there were ten more Sohkoors out there, everywhere.

Sohkoor's unworldly dance and the screaming and the strange lunar object presented an unreal scene in the firelight on the mountaintop, and Wake felt chills going down his spine. He looked around and saw the others felt it too, even Woodgerd the cynic.

"You knew something was going to happen. What the hell *is* all this?" he asked Woodgerd.

"I know that Sohkoor is not merely a scholar of classical knowledge, Wake. He is a mystic, a *sufi*. But he is more than even that, he is one of the *dervishes,* mystics who can predict the future by leaving their worldly bodies behind while in a trance. I saw him do it once before and, God help me, I know what's about to come."

A gasp came from the men and Wake turned to see that Sohkoor, still whirling and screaming, now held a skewer in his right hand. His eyes widened as he spun, a terrible sight to behold. Suddenly he froze in position, silent, the skewer held high, pointed to his face. Wake held his breath as Rork uttered a Gaelic oath.

And then in one smooth motion, Sohkoor plunged the skewer down into his right cheek, so hard that it emerged from the other side of his face.

Instantly, he circled again, the metal needle sticking out of his face, his voice growling louder and louder, a guttural rasping like a lion tearing meat. The trickle of blood coming out of both cheeks was spun away in a streak, so that his face was soon striped red, looking specterlike, the wounds bleeding more with each turn so that drops began to fling around him. Wake felt the blood splatter on his own face and realized that he was now part of this ritual, a blood brother in a bizarre way, and that the image would stay with him for the rest of his life.

Woodgerd, his face bloodied too, got Wake's attention again. "One more thing you need to understand, Wake. Sohkoor is not just a mystic with special powers. He is also the *vizier,* the principal adviser, to the sultan. He is the one man the sultan always listens to, and whose advice he always follows. And that, Wake, makes the man you are watching right now the most powerful man in Morocco—in fact, in this part of Africa."

"It is *Jupiter,* I think," called out Faber, pointing to the moon and its strange satellite. "Yes, it must be Jupiter, right next to the moon."

Sohkoor's spinning was slowing down, no longer a blur of color, but now a man circling, his chant more human now. The soldiers crowded forward. It was all winding down. Wake realized he had been holding his breath and took a deep breath of the cold air. He saw that his hands were trembling. His words to Faber came out in a shaky voice.

"You may well be right, Henri. It probably is Jupiter, that's the right position in regard to Leo. But as far as *I'm* concerned, Sohkoor's correct and tonight the moon showed us its son."

He was abruptly aware that the noise had ended. Sohkoor had stopped moving and was gazing at them, as if noticing them for the first time. The yellow loom of the fire lit him from below as if he were in a stage tableau. He slowly slid the skewer out and carefully wiped it with a cloth, all the while holding them transfixed with his eyes. Then he calmly walked over to the foreigners.

"*Ibn Qamar*, gentlemen. The son of the moon has arrived as I had hoped, as our ancestors had said it would. I will now partake of *kif*, and afterward explain what all of this means. I would kindly suggest, Colonel, that everyone be ready to move. Our tasks have just begun this evening."

Wake stared at the holes in Sohkoor's face. They had stopped bleeding.

A few minutes later Sohkoor nonchalantly narrated in academic terms the significance of Jupiter's rare but predictable emergence from behind the moon, explaining that he knew what was about to happen because the scholars of Damascus and Cairo had learned, and maintained the knowledge in great libraries, what the Greeks had discovered thousands of years earlier. He smiled when he said that the Islamic scholars had retained Western science when Europe had forsaken it after the fall of Rome and regressed into tribal barbarity, a comment which Wake saw made Faber twitch but not comment. He said that the trance that he had entered was a mystical communion with Mohammed and with Allah, demonstrating his faith by proclaiming his knowledge beforehand and sacrificing his flesh afterward. And no, he added, it didn't hurt. He was without pain because his faith had over-come it.

Sohkoor then explained that, because of their vast repository of scientific understanding, the foretelling of celestial events was widespread in the Islamic world and that accompanying allegorical legends and tales were used to teach people the guidelines of life, much like the Christian Bible. The arrival of the son of the moon, he said, was a visual fable to teach believers that strange—and apparently impossible—events can come true, that unreachable goals can indeed be achieved.

The scholar then quietly suggested that they all mount their horses and depart, for they had to go into the land of the Tuareg, the Blue Men of the Sahara Desert, and the sooner they got started the better. When Woodgerd asked exactly where their des-tination would be, Sohkoor answered Marrakech, which made the Arab soldiers react with visible concern. Wake later learned that this was because they were coastal Arabs and had heard frightening tales of the desert and of Marrakech in particular. Sohkoor reminded them that Allah was guiding them and that they would be safe, but none looked reassured.

Now the file of men on horses was heading south, bound for a shadowy purple-tinged mountain in the distance that Sohkoor had pointed out to Woodgerd. After that mountain would come another and another, he said, and then they would descend out of the highlands of the Atlas and down into the desert of the Sahara.

As they slowly made their way across the rocky landscape, surrealistic in the moonlight, Wake's mind was still captivated by Sohkoor's performance—the dance, the self-mutilation, the sub-sequent explanation. He looked over at Rork, engaged in a pan-tomime comparison of daggers with a guardsman who spoke no English.

After regarding the Arab's *khanjar* knife, the bosun raised a stiletto and said to the ferocious-looking man, "Aye, now that one's a fancy bit o' metal, but it's too big for a quiet job. Take a sight o' this, boyo. Now this little darlin' can slide *between* the ribs an' into the heart jes' as pretty as you please, with nary a fuss about it." Then Rork leaned over and grinned at the wary Arab. "Perfect for buggers who're close alongside ya."

The Irish bosun caught Wake watching and gestured toward the guardsman. "Thinkin' jes' a wee bit o' deterrence would be a good thing right about now."

Wake turned his attention to Faber. After his reconciliation with Wake, in which no accusations had been made between them, it was as if any unspoken fears or grievances had been forgiven. Faber seemed calmer, more human, to Wake. It was an immense relief.

A notion suddenly hit Wake. He examined his pocket watch. It said a quarter till midnight. The talk with Faber and Sohkoor's subsequent trance had been about two hours earlier. He leaned over in the saddle and asked Faber, "Henri, what day is it?"

Faber pulled his chin, then said, "It would be the twenty-seventh day of April, Peter."

"No, I mean what day of the week?"

Faber started to answer, then paused and looked at the back of the scholar riding ahead of them with Woodgerd. When he did speak there was reverence in his tone. "*Mon Dieu* . . . it is *Tuesday,* Peter. As Sohkoor predicted days ago, I feel changed."

Wake wondered aloud. "It's beyond strange, gentlemen—it's positively crazy. Here we are, in the middle of who knows where in Africa. A mercenary, a diplomat, and two sailors, heading off in the dark of the night toward a den of thieves."

Rork chuckled. "Aye on that, sir. An' we're bein' led by a whirlin' dervish o' a mystic man, jus' like the days o' old. If this ain't a test o' faith, I don't know what is!"

"Yea, though I go into the valley of death . . ." offered Wake.

"My thoughts exactly, Peter," agreed Faber. "My thoughts exactly."

37

Into the SaHraa

It took them five days—from sunrise to well past sundown each day—to go one hundred miles through the mountains. It was cold during the day at that altitude and freezing at night, and Wake struggled to continue, his stamina drained and his previous confidence in the expedition waning rapidly. The horses were exhausted, the lowland soldiers jumpy in the claustrophobic ravines and passes, and the foreigners worried, including Woodgerd, who had never been this far from the coast and was by this point was completely reliant upon Sohkoor for all decisions.

Only the scholar seemed tranquil, periodically reminding them all that Allah was in control and they were merely executing his will. That mantra was wearing thin on Wake, who was tired of religion and mysticism being the center of everything around them.

At Ouaoumana they came down to the southwest out of the upper elevations of the Atlas, following the valley of the Oued er Rbia, a seasonal stream that was flowing with the spring rains onto an undulating plain that Rork said reverently was as green as Ireland. Pastoral scenes were everywhere they looked, with flocks of sheep and solitary shepherds on the broad fields and little hamlets tucked into clefts of hills. Women could be seen washing clothes in streams. It got warmer and sunnier. The air smelled of flowers and hay and animals, and the horses seemed almost happy as they walked without effort on the nearly level track. The change in scenery from the stunted alpine forests to the cedar and oak groves and wheat fields improved all the men's outlooks too—until Woodgerd, looking at a hamlet set into the short cliff, thought aloud.

"Damned good defensive positions, not that you squids would notice," he opined to Wake, then wondered aloud where the local warriors were. Faber offered that perhaps this was a pacific area, with no need of warriors. Rork repressed a retort when Wake eyed him.

Sohkoor shook his head. "No, there are warriors. These are all Berbers, some of the finest warriors of all northern Africa. They knew we were coming and are out there, all around us, watching us. As long as we keep moving through their area they will never approach. Or even be seen by your unaccustomed eyes."

"Do you see them, Sohkoor?" asked Wake, swiveling in his saddle and examining the hills. "I don't see anything."

"Sometimes, Peter, a rock is not a rock. Look there, at the top of that far away hill. That is an old faded goat skin, gray like a rock, but with the flesh of a man under it, watching us."

Wake scanned the hill, but couldn't see which rock Sohkoor was talking about—there were hundreds of outcroppings. They all looked like natural rocks to him. "All right, if you say so."

Sohkoor smiled. "You have a sailor's legs and stomach for the sea, my friend, necessary things to survive. But here, it takes the eyes of *saqr*, a falcon, to see what is around you. To see danger. Falcons are very important to us in this land and the Berbers are renowned for being the best of the best falconers. The sultan has several on retainer for hunting at each of his various palaces."

"You never cease to amaze me, Sohkoor."

"Oh no, Peter Wake, my Christian friend, it is you who are the amazing one. Your American eyes are wide open to new things, not blind as some from other continents have sadly been."

Wake took the compliment with a smile and said thank you in Arabic, "*Shukran*," which caused Sohkoor to look aloft as he rode ahead and cry, "*Shukran bezzef, lhamdoo Llaah, haadha MaseeHeyy hasan!*"

Wake turned to Woodgerd. "What was that all about?"

Woodgerd harrumphed. "Well, I'll be damned. He never said that about *me*. Sohkoor just talked to God and thanked him for you, a good Christian."

"You've only been here about three months and you already speak the lingo pretty good, don't you?"

"Yeah, well, that's one of the few things I can do well in life. Got a good ear for picking up sounds. I'm not fluent, mind you, but I can understand the gist of a lot of what they say here, as long as it's in Arabic. Berber's pretty much lost on me. Arabic is an absolute necessity in this land. Already saved my life once, when I first arrived. But that tale's for another time."

Wake was thinking that over when Woodgerd offered some advice before he too rode forward. "Wake, you can be an open and nice American all you want with these people, just be ready to gut 'em like a fish when the time comes. 'Cause I can assure you—it will." The colonel's eyes narrowed. "And when I'm needing help in gutting you damn well better not turn naïve on me."

As Woodgerd trotted ahead, Faber regarded the colonel's back. "He is a realist, not an idealist like you, Peter. I know that kind very well, for I am one too. He survives danger, but he does not sleep well at night."

"Well, I'd fancy doin' both!" interrupted Rork, attempting to lighten the moment. "But no's the worry, sir. With a bit o' the Sainted Isle's luck, a month from now we'll be in a tavern tellin' o' this little adventure."

Just then Wake saw a rock near the crest of a nearby hill

move its position ten feet uphill.

"Sean, I'm not sure the Sainted Isle's luck works here."

The green plain gradually sloped down, the men shedding layers of garments as the temperatures went up, until one afternoon a soldier pointed to the southern horizon, a brown line stretching across in front of them. *"SaHraa!"*

Sohkoor cantered up from the rear of the line. "The western edge of the great desert is ahead," he announced. "What you call the Sahara. We are getting close. Now the difficulties come. Be very aware of our surroundings and notify me instantly if you see something unusual."

Sohkoor continued up to Woodgerd at the front and Wake muttered to Rork, "This whole damn place is *unusual.* I'm pretty tired of this."

"Aye, me too, sir. Been nigh on three weeks an' no end in sight. Worse'n bein' stranded in Liverpool! Now there's a hell o' a place for a sailorman. Did ya ever hear me tell o' the one-armed Liverpoodlian girl I fancied? No? Well, this is no dung, I tell ya. There I was, mindin' me own self late one evenin' in a pub . . ."

Rork's tale went on for an hour, during which Faber and Wake were joined by Woodgerd and Sohkoor in laughing uproariously at the bosun's calamities and highjinks in one of the roughest seaports in the world. Wake suspected that a least half of the story was fiction, but loved the bosun for telling it. Their minds were kept off that brown stain on the horizon that was growing larger.

They stopped at a pathetic hamlet of wattle huts squatting along the river where it turned from southerly to due west. It was inhabited by scarecrowlike people on the verge of starvation, whose haunting sunken eyes watched their every move as the men made camp. Sohkoor went into one of the huts and spoke with the elder, the *al-akbar*, then emerged and told the men to rest for the night. They would depart before dawn. From that point on they would be moving south through the lands of the desert Arabs—the Tauregs.

Wake noticed that for the first time Sohkoor seemed more than merely alert, he was nervous, and that the soldiers' evening prayers were much longer, more plaintive, than before. And he heard in Sohkoor's prayers the same beseeching tone—begging really. Wailing filled the dusk, and a feeling of dread swept through Wake, chilling him far more than the onset of the evening cold. He looked over at Woodgerd. The colonel, with a lopsided sneer on his face, meticulously cleaned and oiled his revolver. Wake pulled his Navy Colt out and did the same.

The occasional stunted bush was the only break from the shale rock and sand for the next two days except when a caravan of overloaded swaying camels heading north from Marrakech came over a low hill. Sohkoor spoke with the leader while the soldiers inspected the cargo unenthusiastically for contraband, but found none.

"They don't want to find any," said Woodgerd with a sigh. "Don't want the locals upset. These soldiers are as tough as you can find on the coast, but out here they're as scared as any white man."

Sohkoor watched the caravan head off, glanced grimly at Woodgerd and said, "*Talaab ShayTaan. Ams,*" at which the colonel grumbled a foul expletive.

Seeing Wake's expression the colonel explained, "*ShayTaan* is the Devil and the *talaab* are his students, his disciples. It's a fanatical separatist sect that's far apart from true Islam. Renegade criminals who use the name to scare people and justify their banditry. They were seen by the caravan yesterday."

Wake glanced south over the featureless desert. "Down that way, where we're heading?"

Sohkoor came over, followed by Faber. "Yes. Toward Marrakech. They may well be the band that has the hostages."

Everyone glanced at Faber but no one spoke. A moment later Sohkoor said, "*Yalla*" and they mounted their horses and silently plodded southwest again. The mountains they had left behind days ago were now a distant smudge, shimmering in the heat.

They saw the palm groves first. Scattered strands of palm oasis—Sohkoor explained they were called *waaha*—were strung in scraggly patches along *wadis* that had a thin mush of watery mud like a stream in the early spring. Their palms' thin fronds looked anemic to Wake, who remembered the lush coconut palms of the Caribbean. But compared to the incessant brown of the desert anything remotely green was a welcome sight to him.

Then they saw caravans in the distance drifting northeast toward the coast, two weeks distant. Finally, with Woodgerd's binoculars, far away on the horizon they saw tan minarets and low walls against the powder-blue sky, with beckoning palms wisping up here and there. Woodgerd muttered an oath, then sighed as he handed the binoculars to Wake.

"Marrakech. Fabled crossroads of the caravans from Timbuktoo, Senegal, and Fés. Where anything—and anyone—is sold."

Focusing the lens, Wake saw a tall minaret, much larger than the others. When asked, Sohkoor said that the one–hundred-fifty-foot-high minaret of Marrakech's famous Koutoubia Mosque was built six hundred years earlier as a sister to the Giralda minaret at Sevilla in Spain. The largest in Africa, it was a source of pride for the kingdom of Morocco. Wake looked again, realizing with a shudder that even though he was a thousand

miles from the Alcázar, he was looking at a duplicate of the cathedral of Sevilla's tower, built by the same people at the same time.

38

Marrakech

It took two saddle-sore and sun-seared days to reach the city's walls, the Koutoubia Mosque's minaret growing with each hour. As they arrived under a glaring sun before the battlements, the huge tower inside dominated the scene, reminding all around Marrakech of the dominance of faith in their lives. Marrakech, the scholar explained, was an ancient settlement whose name was originally a local term for "walk fast," meaning to get inside to the safety of Islam before the pagan tribes outside could get you.

Though its glory days were long gone, Sohkoor said that it was still an imperial city and that their great sultan, Hassan, had chosen it to be his place of coronation the previous year. It was a mystical place, he said, describing it as the burial location of the seven saints of the Moorish people; an oasis of safety for the desert Arabs; one of the imperial cities of antiquity; a crossroads of caravans from east, south and north; and the meeting point of black Africa, Arabia, and Europe.

An officious fat man stopped them before they entered the city. His *ugal,* the black cord circle worn over his *kufiyya* head-dress, was decorated with gold ornaments that symbolized his status as the taxman of that entrance. All who entered paid tax on man, beast, and cargo. He stood a hundred feet before the walls, exchanged prolonged greetings with Sohkoor, and for all the world appeared jolly and hospitable. Sohkoor walked back to where Woodgerd and the others stood by their horses.

"He does not know of my position or yours, Colonel. Our tale here is that we are a band of caravan guards come to Marrakech to meet up with up employers. Please keep your uniforms covered securely."

Sohkoor waved to the taxman, then turned back to them. "He wants a bribe, which I will pay. That will gain the evidence against him, and thereby seal his fate. By tonight, when sun goes into the western ocean, that man will make his own payment in pain and the bribe he won will seem paltry."

Moments later, paid and happy, the tax man smiled and beckoned them onward with his right hand, through the Bab Debbagh gate, where Wake was immediately nauseated by the rancid stench of the tanneries all around them.

Holding their bridles, the column moved through the city on foot, squeezing into the increasingly narrow streets. A swirl of sound and motion enveloped them, overwhelming after the quiet of the desert. Wake was startled by the sudden whacks of the tanners as they slapped their hides, the cries of "*barak, barak*" by camel men as they warned others to get out of the way, the brain-spearing high-pitched wail of school students in a *madrasa* as they sang the praises of Allah, and the constant odor of excrement.

Sohkoor stopped, gazed at the sky, then called for them to gather around him. "We go to the *souk* by the Jewish Mella, just north of the Kasbah fortress. I must meet a man there. Then we will go to the quSoor Bou-Ahmed, the palace of Sidi Ahmed ben Musa, the vizier of Marrakech. He is the final stone to be overturned, for he knows, or can find out, anything that is happening regarding the ShayTaan bandits and the hostages."

Woodgerd harrumphed. "I've heard of that slimy son. He's in the know because he's getting *bakshish* from everyone in the

Medina of Marrakech, Sohkoor. And whatever you ask him he'll pass along to the other side. Including the fact that we're here."

"They already know we're here, Colonel. The ShayTaan gang has spies in Marrakech. They are watching us from the rooftops right now. They will gain nothing from our conversation with the vizier, but we can gain something from the vizier about them. He is a practical man and will not go against me. But first, the souk by the Mella. It is always better to get as much intelligence as possible before the action, is it not?"

Rork and Faber both looked up at the roof lines and fingered their hidden pistols. Wake thought he saw a head dart behind a wall above them. Or maybe it was his imagination. I'm getting too jumpy here, he told himself. Calm down. You must keep calm.

Their route to the Mella was through half a mile of winding alleyways, Sohkoor turning here and there into tiny alleys with no markings, until Wake lost all sense of direction. Finally, with the shadows darkening their way, they arrived at the Mella, which Wake recognized by the balconies set into the walls. They turned left into the copper *souk*, where chattering men were clanging away on metal plates, forming them into bowls and platters, while others were chiseling designs on copper. The scholar led them down an alley six feet wide, turning left into one even narrower but just as full of people. The sky was closed out. Wake felt claustrophobic, the dusty stench-laden air making breathing difficult. He steadied himself and kept walking even as the horses balked and had to be forced forward.

Then they burst into a relatively open space perhaps fifteen feet in width. Wake saw the sky and took several deep breaths in relief. Sohkoor stopped at one of the small doorways set into the wall, holding up his hand and giving his reins to one of the Arab soldiers as he addressed the group.

Sohkoor bid them to stay put for a moment while he went forward to find his informant. He warned them not to stray— they would get hopelessly lost in seconds among the maze of passageways. Then he was gone, disappeared into the swarming mass of men and animals constantly moving through the tiny arteries of Marrakech. Wake had no idea which way he went.

Wake asked Woodgerd what he knew of Sohkoor's influence in the city. The colonel shook his head as he eyed the crowd.

"Don't know, Wake. I've never been here. But I do know that Sohkoor has influence everywhere in Morocco, especially in the imperial cities. I wouldn't underestimate him. At all."

Faber asked, "What do we do now, Colonel?"

"Nothing. We wait until Sohkoor tells us what to do."

The sky was graying above them when the shadows took over their waiting place. Lanterns came on in the sellers' stalls, the business of the copper *souk* continuing in the dimly lit gloom, the sounds of flutes and stringed instruments periodically overcoming the hammering of the craftsmen.

Wake and Rork stood together, backs plastered against a wall, watching the comings and goings. From the top of the minarets, *muezzins* started to call the faithful for evening prayer. Their wail rose above all other sounds of Marrakech. Soon silence came over the city.

"Come, we go now!" said Sohkoor as he appeared out of the darkness two hours later. "*Yalla!*" he said to the Arab guardsmen and strode away down a different passage, pulling his horse behind him.

As he led the column he explained to Woodgerd, within the others' hearing, "My man says the perpetrators of this crime are here in the Medina, watching us. They are definitely the ShayTaan gang, renegades from the Taureg Blue Men, with thirty men under arms. Our enemies are confident that we are but a token force wandering aimlessly about on a search. They do not know that you, Colonel, and I, are here."

Sohkoor paused and smiled. "If they did, they would flee, for they would know the great sultan was about to smite them. We must make haste to Ahmed ben Musa and find the final key to our puzzle."

"What about that taxman?" inquired Woodgerd as he squeezed his horse through a particularly narrow stretch of the passage.

"I have notified the Pasha of Marrakech of the man's transgressions. He will be ruminating his mistakes in the Kasbah as we speak. I also sent word to the Pasha of our mission, so that reinforcements will be available."

Woodgerd grunted. "I'll believe that when I see 'em."

The palace of Sidi Ahmed ben Musa, vizier to the pasha of Marrakech, was a grand mansion of three floors that overlooked lush gardens fed by underground water channels from artesian wells. It was entered through a nondescript door in a mud wall outside the central Kasbah fortress. Once inside, visitors were greeted in a garden of orange trees. Beyond lay the ornate main house, with dozens of rooms for the vizier's four wives, twenty-four concubines, and dozens of children. Sohkoor and his foreigners went through the door into the garden, the troops staying outside the wall with the horses.

After preliminaries, they were ushered through three different archways, one squared, one curved, and one latticed, and into the main hall. Led across a central plaza with fountain spraying, they entered the debating room, with walls of incredibly delicate latticework, ceiling paintings, and alabaster carvings.

Wake said that the entire place reminded him of the Alcázar, which Sohkoor said was an illusion, since Musa's palace was only a few years old but made to look ancient. The Vizier of Marrakech was very wealthy and had arranged for the finest artisans in the kingdom to recreate the grandeur of the imperial city's past. He pointed out the calligraphy on one wall, above an archway with a Star of David etched into it. The inscription, Sohkoor said, was the epic tale of Shaherazade.

As two old men played lutes quietly in a dim corner, servants brought them tea and little cakes, fawning especially over Sohkoor, who stood silently, waiting, while the others sat back on giant stuffed couches upholstered in yellow silk. With the sound of a gong, the scholar was shown into another room, leaving the others behind.

Faber, shifting from side to side, sat next to Wake and Rork. "I feel we are close to Catherine. I am so very nervous, Peter. This incessant searching and talking and waiting is making me go mad. She is close by—I know it."

"Henri, keep calm," said Wake. "We'll only make it worse if we do anything without Sohkoor's guidance."

"Yeah, Faber," rumbled Woodgerd. "I've got enough friggin' problems without you going off half-cocked on us. We have to be smart about this."

Rork nudged Wake and whispered, "Some o' these lads ain't servants, sir. Those in that dark hallway o'er there got hard eyes. I know that look. Soldiers."

Wake glanced at the hallway where two tall square-shouldered black men stood, each pulling out a large scimitar cutlass and laying it across his chest. Both were intently watching the foreigners.

"Senegalese," said Woodgerd. "Good warriors. Extremely strong. Fearless. Not related to anyone in the kingdom, and therefore completely reliable as personal bodyguards. Sultan Hassan keeps them at each of his palaces. They're his inner guard and sworn to him entirely. I suppose this Musa fella must've bought some of his own."

Rork wasn't impressed. "The way they're eyein' us, I'm a wonderin' if they're part o' the bandits."

"No, the bandits are renegade Tuareg. Different color and

culture. Those Senegalese are devout Muslims. The bandits are anything but Muslim."

Suddenly footsteps echoed fast along the tiled floor and Sohkoor appeared, his expression drawn. He didn't break stride. "We go. Now."

In the garden he turned to Woodgerd and Wake as they reached the doorway in the perimeter wall. "The bandits tried to sell the hostages today at a *caravanserai* near the Mella for a thousand Spanish dollars. They were refused and left. The vizier thinks they are somewhere in the area north of Djemma el-Fna, the great market square of Marakech, but no one knows exactly where. They will be trying to get out of the city in the dark, I believe."

"How does he know all that?" asked Woodgerd.

"Because he buys and sells slaves—on the side, as you Americans say—and he is the one who refused the offer," answered Sohkoor. "He said the price was too high for such dangerous items."

Wake was stunned. He thought the vizier, as a government authority, was above trading in slaves. "Damn. I didn't think they still did that, officially."

"*Officially* they don't, squid," growled Woodgerd. "But in this part of the world rules are made by the guys with the most muscle and broken by the guys with the most money."

The colonel asked Sohkoor, "What does he know about us?"

"Everything. And it was not I that told him."

Sohkoor pulled and pushed the door, but it wouldn't open. Woodgerd swore an oath and tried, but it was stuck closed. Wake tried kicking it outward, but the solid oak door didn't budge.

Then Rork put a hand on Wake's shoulder. "Ah, gentlemen. Look behind us."

They turned around, looking back across the garden.

Faber was the only one to speak. "Oh, *mon Dieu.*"

In the flickering torch light of the garden Wake saw twenty giant Senegalese standing in a line across the patio, massive arms holding huge scimitars that mirrored the golden torchlight. Half a dozen smaller blue-robed Arabs stood to one side, rifles aimed at the center mass of each of the five men at the door.

39

Dance of Death

They stood there stunned until a previously unseen man in saffron *jellaba* robes approached from the side of the garden and told Sokhoor in Arabic, and the others in German-accented English, to put their hands up. He carried himself with confidence, snapping his fingers for the Senegalese to come forward, search, and tie them up. Their hands intruded roughly everywhere, yanking out knives and pistols, money and watches, dumping them in a pile on the ground.

There was a gasp from the tall black men when they saw the naval uniforms under the Americans' robes, but the Arab leader in yellow just smiled knowingly. "Ah, yes, the Americans, who want Morocco to be protected from the greedy Europeans. We knew you were here with Sokhoor. You are so stupid. Why are you even here? To assist the French? They despise you. To assist Sultan Hassan? He laughs at you even as he takes the trade tribute from you. The Germans are the ones you should be assisting, but your British masters won't let you."

Wake tried to bluff the best he could. "I am Lieutenant Peter Wake of the U.S. Navy and I *demand* to talk to the vizier, and to know your exact name."

"You will talk to no one and do nothing unless I permit you. You do not impress or intimidate me. Be quiet and listen."

Then he said to his other prisoners, "I am Falah. Do exactly what I say and you people will not be hurt. In fact, we want you to stay healthy."

Sokhoor's immediate protests were cut short in Arabic by Falah. Whatever Falah said, Wake saw that it dejected the scholar, who visibly deflated. As each of them had their hands tied tightly in the front, Woodgerd stood grimly silent, eyes switching back and forth from Sokhoor to Falah. Faber began to speak, but stopped when a Senegalese cinched the knot tight and made him gasp in pain. Rork's eyes flared. Wake leaned over and whispered, "Now Sean, let's play this one calmly. We can always kill them later."

"I'm memorizing the bastards' faces, sir, so I kill the right ones later." He tilted his head toward Falah. "An' *that* sonovabitch is at the top o' the list."

"Good plan, Rork. Just please be calm now."

Woodgerd asked the scholar, "What did that man tell you? And just who the hell *are* these men?"

Sokhoor nodded to the black men and sighed. "The Senegalese are the vizier's. The Arabs are ShayTaan Taalib renegades. The vizier is a hostage to this also, evidently. The bandits have his family somewhere. And there are a lot more of the bandits than I thought. I am sorry, Colonel. Our own men outside are already dead. They resisted and were cut down."

Woodgerd hissed a foul oath, then asked, "What's next?"

"I do not know. Just do as they say, all of you, or they will kill you now without hesitation," warned Sokhoor, as the group was pushed across the garden. At the palace they were shoved into separate rooms, told to sit on the floor and guarded by two of the stone-faced Senegalese.

Wake was led to a mosaic-walled room, dark red tapestry adding to the gloom, and flung onto the marble floor where he was forced to kneel in front of three short reed baskets on a rug.

In seconds two men in the indigo-dyed robes of the Tuareg sat down by the baskets opposite Wake. Their attention was on the baskets and one of them pulled out a flute, from which scratchy notes pealed high and low, repeating faster and faster.

Falah came in and stood to the side, his eyes locked on Wake's. The smallest basket moved slightly, catching Wake's attention. Something inside it was jiggling the loosely woven top, which was now sliding up and back. Falah's doomsday voice matched his sneer.

"Lieutenant Wake, of the American Navy, you really should be honored. Your earlier impertinence has earned you a great distinction. You are about to go through one of our quaint African tests of manhood.

"If you fail, you will die painfully and we will use your body—and its unique wounds—as a vivid incentive for the French to pay our ransom for their meddling missionaries. If, against all odds, you somehow succeed, you will become highly valuable to me, for the mysticism attached to your success will have tangible rewards. It is, as I understand you Americans say, a winning situation for us. Oh, and of course, if you try to flee, the Senegalese behind you will slice off your head. Their master has been persuaded to assist us and told them to follow my orders."

Falah's arrogance had Wake seething in anger, but he controlled his tone. "Well, you've got me curious, Falah. But maybe we can dispense with all these theatrics and just use some common sense here. There's no reason for you to hold *us*. You made your point—"

"No, Lieutenant Wake, I haven't. But I soon will."

The small basket tottered again and a thick head poked out. In seconds, its body followed, a six-foot-long yellowish-brown snake with a squared pattern along its length. It came out of the small basket and dropped onto the rug, then slithered over in the direction of the flute. Wake noticed that the second Arab was tapping his foot hard against the floor. The snake was following the vibration. The man rose from his squat, reached over and in one smooth motion he scooped it behind the head and walked toward Wake.

Wake's biggest fear was snakes. His service in Florida during the war had shown him what they could do. The snake man stroked the snake, murmuring to it as he carried it forward.

The screeching of the flute rose as the Arab reached out for Wake, who suddenly felt the tip of a Senegalese cutlass begin to slice into his back. The snake, its tongue flicking, was wrapped around his neck twice, ends dangling down his chest. Wake felt his heart pounding in his ears. He dared not move or speak. The thing was moving slowly, squirming as it examined its new perch.

The doomsday voice started up again. "Our very own vaunted Russell viper of North Africa, Lieutenant Wake. A beautifully efficient machine of death. So similar to your diamond-back rattlesnake, but without those ridiculous warning rattles. The Russell doesn't let you know when it will strike, which is an admirable trait. *Never warn your enemy*, Lieutenant—it's a silly notion of romantics who have never fought to the death."

Wake saw the other two baskets move, lids sliding back. A snake came out of each basket, these snakes brownish-black with no pattern. Instead of dropping to the floor, they stood up, their glistening bodies supporting them a foot high out of the basket as they rotated their heads around.

Falah sauntered from the side of the room and stood in front of Wake's view. "Ah, now here are two of my personal favorites, African cobras. Not as efficient as the viper around your neck, and certainly not as colorful, but more artistic in their actions. I know you will agree, Lieutenant, when you see their dance of death."

Wake struggled to stay still, the heavy viper around his neck remaining docile, but his eyes were on the cobras. Seemingly urged on by the flute, they slid out of the baskets and toward the American. One of them, the smaller cobra, slowed and lay down in a coil, but the larger one, at least five feet long, continued forward. The Arab tapping his foot moved around behind Wake, then gently unwrapped and removed the viper from his neck and placed it back in its basket.

Sweat poured into Wake's eyes as he finally took in a breath. It took every ounce of discipline not to burst into tears with relief. Then Falah's sarcasm sent another wave of fear through Wake.

"Very good, Lieutenant. The viper was not agitated. Didn't even smell your fear—most unusual. Not many men could have done that. Congratulations to both of us, your value to me just went up and you are still alive."

Another movement drew Wake's attention and he involuntarily turned his head to look, then was unable to turn away from the sight. The cobra closest to him was rising up again, this time only a foot in front of his knees, as the flute's melody slowed and became more lilting, more sensual.

The snake rose up and up, until its head was almost level with Wake's. The black eyes were watching him, measuring, while the shiny skin behind the head began to flare into double and triple its size. The cobra started weaving back and forth in time with the music, its tiny black eyes never leaving Wake's, the body getting closer and closer.

Wake was on the verge of screaming as he recalled Falah's earlier words. The dance of death, he called it. An incarnation of evil, the snake was hypnotizing him, controlling him. Wake knew he had to stop this. But how? He forced himself to think, to work out what to do. The snake was always watching his face, locked on his eyes. That was something important. As if it was searching. For his eyes?

Wake forced himself to keep his eyes still and slowly turned his head to the left. He kept his gaze downward, hiding his eyes from the snake undulating in front of him. He was dead if he made a break for it—the Senegalese's blade point in his back was penetrating the skin, he could feel the blood running down his spine.

Wake waited for the bite.

It seemed an hour, but he knew it must have been only minutes, before the flute man said something in an angry tone. Wake could hear slithering in front of him but didn't dare look. The man behind him tapped louder.

Rapid Arabic snarled from Falah with fear obvious in the replies from the snake men. What was happening? Wake kept his breathing shallow and waited. Abruptly, the music stopped and he heard footsteps on the marble fading away, the Arabs plaintively explaining something to Falah. He allowed his right eye to glance at the cobra—it was on the floor by his knees, coiled several times upon itself, head toward the basket.

Falah called out from somewhere near the door. "You passed the test, Lieutenant Wake. You successfully faced down a viper and a cobra. Your value has now reached the highest level for an infidel. I must admit that you fascinate me."

The snake men lifted the cobras and placed them in the baskets, then scurried out of the room, leaving Wake still kneeling with the Senegalese behind him. He felt the blade withdraw and come to rest across his neck. He collapsed on his side, tears and sweat mingling on his lips, chest heaving for air, clothing soaked with sweat.

Wake mumbled a prayer of thanks. He had always considered himself a Christian and attended church on the holy days. But he'd never felt it enter his soul, until now. Now he wept like a baby as he said thank you.

He rolled over and found the black guards in the exact same position, still standing above him with the razor sharp scimitars, one of which had a dark stain. He looked up at their faces and felt his hope disappear. The dark faces still watched him, devoid of emotion, and he knew it wasn't over.

An hour later Falah came into the room, surveyed him curled on the floor in the torchlight, and left without a word. At a shouted order from outside the two guards lifted Wake from the floor and trotted with him out into the night, where a line of five wagons waited, each with a large crate on the bed and a team of worn horses in trace. One of the Senegalese lifted Wake into the air and threw him headfirst into the crate of the second wagon, the other slamming the door.

"Welcome home, sir," an Irish lilt muttered from the dark. "It ain't much, but it's ours."

"Rork! Oh God, am I glad to be back with you." Wake moved to relieve the pain in his shoulder. "What's going on, Sean?"

"Not even a wee clue, except that none o' them bastards seems a bit bothered by this. Seems like jes' another day to 'em."

"Just what I was thinking—"

A woman's scream pierced the air close by, followed by a commotion and stream of desperate French from the same voice.

"Catherine? Catherine, are you out there? It's Peter. Peter Wake!"

Another crate was slammed shut somewhere back down the line of wagons, then a frightened female voice. "Peter! You are here to save us! We are here in a box, save us!"

Wake's eyes were getting accustomed to the dim light coming through the slats of the crate. Rork, two feet away, cocked an eyebrow and gave him a rueful look.

Wake sighed and called out. "I'm in a box too, Catherine. Are you hurt?"

"A little. Oh Peter, I am so frightened . . ."

"Stay strong, Catherine. Henri is here, somewhere. He may be in a box too. He came to search for you. We all did. Just stay strong. We'll all get out of this."

The sound of a scuffle, then a crate being shut, was followed by German-tinged English very close to the crate. "Oh yes, Lieutenant Wake. You will all get out of your boxes when you reach your new home. I hope you enjoy the journey." The tone lowered to almost a hush, the humor in it brutally sinister. "I must say thank you. Your new *master* in Mali paid a lot of money for you, double what it was before you passed the test."

Wake slumped against the side of the crate, strength draining away with the realization of Falah's meaning when he had said his value has risen. Rork let out a long breath.

"Oh sweet Jesus, sir. We're bound for the middle of Africa as *slaves*."

40

Shay Taan Taalib

A sharp pain cut across Wake's back as he crashed against the
side of the crate. He opened his eyes to jarring light, gradually taking in the scene around him. The wagon was still jumbling over the rough roads as it had been for hours, but now there
were shafts of sunlight through the slats, proving to him it wasn't
some horrid nightmare. It was all too real.

They were in some type of animal crate. Wake guessed it was
for goats by the layer of feces in the straw. They were both still
bound behind their backs, hands swollen and dark red, with
bruises everywhere. Rork had a gash above a closed right eye,
matted blood covering half his face. They went over another rock
and Wake bounced his head into the splintery wood above,
swearing and rousing the bosun slumped in the corner.

Rork leaned up, his lopsided grin looking idiotic with the
mangled face. "Pretty bit o' a mess, ain't it, sir? Even the bloody
English wouldn't do this to a poor Irishman. Of course, there was
that time—"

"Sean, you're cut bad over the eye, but it looks like the bleeding has stopped. Hurt anywhere else?"

"All over, sir, but that's cause o' this crate an' these here lashin's. No other cuts. Where are we?"

Unable to see forward, Wake peered out of the side and back slats to the flat brown terrain around them. They were on a track through shale rock desert. He counted at least three other wagons behind them, guessing that Catherine was in the last. He wondered where Sokhoor and Woodgerd were.

"I don't know where we are, Sean, but let's think this out. The air is still relatively cool and the sun is low, so I think it's morning, maybe around nine or so."

"Sun's on our bow, sir, so we're headin' east."

"Right. And we're moving at maybe two or three knots. It was around nine o'clock yesterday evening when they got us. They kept us for about two hours, then got under way in these damn carts, so that means we've been going for ten hours, more or less. Made maybe twenty miles, maybe more, but probably only twenty when you count in the slow traffic in the city. I remember a lot of stops and starts when we first started out. So we're twenty miles east of Marrakech and heading further east."

"Aye, sir. So what's out east o' Marrakech?"

"Well, let me remember the map I saw in Rabat. There're some mountains that divide the desert about fifty miles away. I think Berbers live there. Beyond them to the east is nothing but wasteland—the main Sahara—for two thousand miles to Egypt. Mali is a thousand miles to the southeast."

"Wait a minute, sir. I thought we were in the Sahara already an' that's where the Blue Men live—an' also those bastards what captured Miss Catherine and the missionary people."

"We were in the Sahara, but just on the edge of it."

Rork let out a gasping whistle. "Sweet Mary, mother of Jesus, if that journey we already made afore Marrakech was jes' a wee bit o' the friggin' desert, than this ol' bosun wants no part o' the main affair. I venture it's time to end this, sir. Now."

"I'm for that, Sean. We need to get out of this while we're still near Marrakech. It's the last city for a thousand miles east or south. Now, how to we get these bindings off?"

Rork fell over when the wagon lurched, grimacing in pain when his head hit the side and started bleeding again. He sat up and looked at Wake from his left eye.

"Aye, that's it, sir. These boards are rough-hewn, with plenty o' sharp splinters. We use 'em to cut this here old hemp. Jes' hold the lashin' against the splinter an' let the bouncin' o' the cart do the work, sir."

"Damn, Sean, that just might work."

It did work, but it took hours, until the sun had reached its zenith and the fetid reek of the crate's prior inhabitants was gagging them both. Amid shouts of orders and threats to the prisoners—Wake still couldn't think of himself as a slave—the wagons had halted to feed and water the horses from skinbags and bales piled atop the crates. A wooden cup of filthy water was carefully wedged between the slats into the crate. Wake saw the man was an Arab wearing faded blue. The Senegalese were no longer around.

"My hand's free," uttered Rork as he fell back in exhaustion. "Oh, God, that feels good," he said rubbing his wrists while he lay on the floor of the crate.

Wake was still trying to saw through his own rope. "I think I'm almost through it."

Rork crawled over and fiddled with Wake's binding. Blood was coagulated all over the bosun's face and he looked and smelled awful, but Wake loved him when he heard Rork say, "There, it's . . . cut through. You're a free man, sir!"

Wake let out a sigh of relief as he massaged his own hands, feeling the blood pricking him with little points of pain as his hands came back to life. Both men lay there, panting in the heat and letting their limbs regain sensation. Finally Wake said, "Very well done, Sean. Now we've got to get some slats undone and get out of this dog box."

"Aye, aye, sir. Let's check all o' 'em for the weakest."

The familiar voice of Falah came down the line of wagons. He called out to the people in the boxes.

"You will all be fed at the next stop. I'm afraid we don't have enough for more than one meal a day for the slaves. Not quite the quality of food that you've all been used to, but it's an acquired taste, I'm told. By the time you reach Timbuktoo you will appreciate it."

A growl emanated from Rork. "I got dibs on that bastard, sir. He's the one who told those black monsters to pound my head open, an' he laughed when they did it."

Wake couldn't help a chuckle. "Gee, Rork, he's the one I wanted. But since you're my best friend, I'll let *you* kill him. But you'll owe me."

"Much obliged, sir."

Falah stopped next to Wake's wagon and looked in at the Americans, who had resumed their previous positions and were moaning in pain, which wasn't faked.

"It appears my Yankee friends are not enjoying the journey as much as I had hoped. Perhaps their new master and home will be more to their liking than traveling with the *ShayTaan Taalib*."

"Who are you, Falah?" croaked out Wake, watching the other man's eyes examining him through the slats. "From what I've been told, this isn't what Islam teaches. *ShayTaan Taalib*—the Devil's Disciples? That's not Muslim."

"Quite right there, Lieutenant Wake. But then again if you know what our name means in English you know that we do not pretend to be Muslim. And who am I? I am Sheik Falah bin Ali bin Abdel Musa, of the dreaded Blue Men of the desert, the Tuaregs. I am the leader of the clan of the Devil's Disciples and we wreak havoc among the two-faced believers of the books. All of them—Jew, Christian, and Muslim. None of you matter to us, except as prey. Like a mouse to a falcon."

"The Tuaregs are Muslim, though, so you're no Tuareg. You're a renegade."

"You've been told that, I see. I revel in that term, for we are free while the others have become vassals of a corrupt society and sultan. Not to mention the French, who are slowly but surely taking over everyone's freedom. Call me what you will—bandit, renegade, monster—but I am free and you most certainly are not. I will die a free man and you will die a slave. A white slave in black Mali—one who has passed the test of manhood, but has failed the test of Africa. You underestimated us with condescension. What a fitting end for you."

"Your name. The vizier in Marrakech . . ." Wake was having trouble breathing in the suffocating dust.

"Ah yes, my decadent cousin, Ahmed, vizier to the pasha of Marrakech. We share the name of our grandfather and our German educations, but that is all. Grandfather believed in education. Studying in Berlin and Hamburg allowed Ahmed and me to understand how Europe operates. I learned that lesson well. Ahmed did not. He came back and wallowed in his decadence."

Wake coughed. "He's part of this?"

"In his own weak way. We have a mutually beneficial relationship. I allow him to live in his depravity and he facilitates my activities."

"You *are* the devil, Falah."

"Thank you, Lieutenant. That was the most complimentary thing you could tell me. I must go now. As I said before, your . . . lunch . . . will be served at our next stop. I hope that you enjoy it."

As Falah walked away, Wake shook his hands free and leaned over to his friend. "Tell you what, Sean Rork. You'd better kill that sonovabitch fast when we get out of here, because if you don't, he's mine."

"How many are there, sir?" asked Rork as they worked loose the fourth slat on the right side of the crate. He started on the slat next to it.

"I saw five wagons and I see two men guarding each, with some riders out there somewhere. So that's ten men on the wagons and maybe another ten riding horses. The riders will be scouting to the front and flanks. I think the ones we have to worry about first are the wagoneers."

Rork stopped his work. "You and I can take the two on this one, sir, but what about the others?"

"We've got to get to the rifles on this wagon. If we can do that, then one of us can go free the others while the other holds the guards at bay with the rifles. I know it's thin, Sean, but how's that sound?"

"A whole lot better than bein' a slave in Africa!"

By the time they stopped for the next break, the two men had loosened ten of the slats, practically the whole side of the crate. They resumed their poses when the line stopped, Wake's heart pumping hard as he watched the bandits assemble around a cooking fire. By a stroke of luck, the loosened slats were on the side away from the fire.

"We're in luck, Sean. They're all around that fire. I don't see many rifles over there. That means there must be some weapons back on the wagons. We'll sneak out of this gawdawful contraption as far as we can without them seeing us, grab the rifles, then shoot. We both shoot a volley, then you continue firing while I go free the other prisoners."

"No disrespect, sir, but you know I'm a bit stronger. So I'll be the one to go an' get our friends out while you stay here an' take some shots at those buggers."

Wake shook his head. "No, you've always been a better shot and I can run faster, especially since you got that head wound. Besides, you don't have to hit them, just keep shooting and scare them."

Rork held up a finger. "Well now, I hate to disagree. But really, an Irishman can be as quick as a colt when times demand it. You should stay here an' shoot, sir."

"Damn it, Rork, I cannot believe that you are arguing with me about who's going to get to shoot the friggin' rifle while we're cooped up in a goat box in the middle of nowhere in Africa on the way to be slaves to some savage sonovabitch. Good God, man, just follow the damn order. Discussion's over, Bosun."

Rork cast his eyes downward and coughed. "Aye, aye, sir. But I was jes' thinkin' that—"

"No, dammit!"

"Yes, sir . . ."

The drivers of the wagons were starting to ladle mush into bowls while other bandits were lying on the ground with their *kufiyyas* drawn over their faces. Snoring and subdued conversation were the only sounds Wake heard and he wondered where Falah was.

He nudged Rork. "Ready?" The bosun nodded.

They eased the slats off and Wake slid his head out, craning around to see in all directions. To the front, the direction he couldn't see before, he saw a line of mountains with a valley cleft in it. In front of the mountains, about a mile away, he saw a group of horsemen trotting their way.

There were no other horsemen around the camp, so he surmised that was the mounted guard of scouts and flankers. Almost all of the wagoneers were over by the fire, except for two or three resting under the shade of the wagons. He wondered if there were some under his wagon.

Moving slowly, Wake tried not to make any motions that could catch the eye of the bandits. He hung down and looked under the wagon. No resting bandits there. He lowered himself to the ground and crouched between the crude wheel and the wagon side as Rork made his way forward to the driver's seat.

He saw Rork smile, then hand him a rifle. It was a muzzle-loader, apparently without a round in the barrel. The bosun handed down some powder cartridges and bullets from a belt pouch on the seat. Trying to control his breathing, which he was sure could be heard by the bandits forty feet away, Wake slowly loaded the powder cartridge and ball, then slid the wadding and ramrod in. Slowly he cocked the hammer and put a percussion cap in the action. Rork, crouched behind a hay bale on the wagon, was doing the same.

"Ready?" Wake mouthed. Rork nodded and laid his rifle over the seat, drawing a bead on the bandit standing closest. Wake used a spoke of the wheel to rest his barrel and picked another man as a target. A bandit by the cooking fire glanced up. Wake shifted his sights onto the man.

Then the man pointed at the bosun and started to open his mouth.

"Fire now, Rork."

The blasts came out together, felling both targets. Rork, reloading quickly, got off another shot twenty seconds later as the bandits were scrambling to find cover. Wake was already running to the next wagon behind, where he found another rifle, which he loaded faster than he had in his life, calling out the sequence as he remembered Gunner's Mate Durling doing with his sailors during the war.

Swearing foul oaths while fumbling with the cartridges, he got off two shots, one of which went into the face of a bandit climbing up from under the wagon. While Rork kept firing, Wake took the man's khanjar knife before going around the back of the wagon and grabbing the back panel of the crate, yanking it open. He reached in and cut the bindings of Sokhoor and Woodgerd, who then used it to sever the ropes tying the others inside.

Woodgerd emerged shakily, followed by Sokhoor, who yelled something in Arabic as Wake ran to the next wagon. Another three men fell out of the crate, missionaries, one with a clerical collar. The bandits were returning fire now. Out of the corner of his eye, Wake saw the horsemen riding fast, a dust cloud climbing into the blue sky behind them. He didn't have much time. They were getting close. Woodgerd was shooting, Sokhoor loading a rifle, but the missionaries were disoriented.

"Grab rifles and shoot them!" he bellowed at the missionaries.

He saw Rork standing on top of the second wagon now, calmly marking his targets, shooting and reloading. A bandit came charging around the next wagon, khanjar in hand, shrieking at Wake. The man raised his knife, ready to plunge it down into Wake, when an invisible punch doubled him over and knocked him down. Blood spread in the middle of his robe as Wake kicked him in the face and wrested the knife away.

The next wagon had no rifle on the seat. Wake jerked the door open. A man tumbled out and he cut his bindings, then handed him the knife to free the others who were crawling out. Wake heard the wailing of women above the gunfire. He raced to the last wagon and saw one of the horses in front drop, screaming with a hole in its head, the other horse panicking and skittering around trying to rear up while still in the traces. The wagon skewed and leaned over, hanging precariously for a moment before crashing on its side. The crate rolled off, resting upside down beside the wagon, the women inside shrieking. Wake was frantic as he looked for the latch.

"Catherine! Are you in there!"

With all the confusion he didn't hear the riders sweep around the line of wagons behind the crouching hostages. With Falah leading, they fired a volley into the wagons from fifty feet away.

It felt like a red-hot poker had been rammed into Wake's right side.

He doubled over. Wake knew it was a gunshot wound in the right side of the chest, then his mind blanked. The noise of a thousand bees filled his ears and his eyesight dimmed into a blur. He was aware of motion swirling all around him but couldn't focus. He tried to call for help, but nothing came out. He straightened up but a blaze of pain filled his lungs and he collapsed next to the crate, deaf to screams of the women trapped inside.

The horsemen had ridden through the wagon line slashing at the missionaries before emerging by the campfire on the other side, where Falah was rallying his men for another attack. Through the blur Wake saw Woodgerd yelling something to the hostages-turned-riflemen, while at the front wagon he saw Faber, in a blood-soaked white shirt, shooting at a blue-robed figure in front of him.

Seeing the Frenchman brought Wake's mind back. Catherine's face was in the crate. Her mouth was open, saying something. He rolled over to the crate and willed himself to crouch up, groaning with the pain. Grasping the latch he pulled it open with his weight as he fell back. The women inside pushed their way out of the box—the first two were shot instantly, dropping as they tried to stand with their hands still tied behind them. Catherine fell out and he knelt there, his head roaring while he fumbled with the rope. He was failing and he sobbed for God to help free her as he lost control of his body and hit the sand.

Wake lay there, clutching his chest tightly, feeling blood leaking out and foam coming up in his mouth. He felt a hand on his face, a soft hand. Catherine's tears were dripping onto his cheek, and she was beseeching him, but he couldn't understand her sounds—or even move.

Wake slowly began to hear the women screaming as his eyes started to focus. His senses were returning. He was about to speak to Catherine when a shadow came over him and he looked up. Falah was mounted on a horse, standing tall above him, circling a scimitar over his head, eyes wild in rage. The man's voice was the thunder of hell as he rallied his men for the final kill, screaming. *"ShayTaan Taalib!"*

Falah glanced down and saw the American by the horse's hooves. Their eyes met and Falah smiled. A strange, bizarre smile. Wake saw a revolver come out from Falah's robes, his mind registering that it was his own navy issue Colt, immediately understanding Falah's expression. The revolver swung around and aimed down at him.

This is it. I'm dead, Wake realized. Here, now. In this far-off, empty place in the middle of nowhere so far from home.

The revolver's muzzle exploded in a blast, but Wake never heard a thing.

41

Kiss of Allah

But something was wrong. He could see Catherine, so he couldn't be dead. She was still bent over him crying, her face grimacing in horror as she gazed off somewhere. He was light-headed, drunklike, the scene around him unfolding like a play in slow motion and he was the audience. It was all so very curious, illogical.

"I'm supposed to be dead," Wake croaked aloud to himself.

The pain was real, though. And the sights around him. Catherine had gore all over her dress, the red splatter contrasting with the blue gingham. Henri Faber was there now, an arm around Catherine. Both were staring at Wake, their concern obvious, saying something he couldn't make out. And there was a lump or rock beside him on the ground.

But no, it was Falah. The maniac, or what was left of him, was sprawled on the sand, his sightless eyes bulging out of the mangled meat of his face. The Colt was still in his hand and Wake reached over to pry it loose. He had to get that Colt. It was issued to him. The ringing in his ears faded and he heard sounds now as he pulled those grimy fingers off the pistol grip.

"Peter, can you hear me?" he heard Henri Faber yelling from only a foot away. "It is done. Finished. They are running away."

Wake got the Colt free and held it in a shaky hand, rolling to the left as he felt another shadow cross over him. He raised the revolver to fire at the attacker, understanding at the last second that it was Rork, looking gaunt, utterly exhausted. The bosun knelt down as Wake let the pistol fall.

"Neither o' us win the bet, sir. That bloody bastard was nailed by Henri here." Rork opened Wake's shirt looking for the chest wound. "An' jes' afore he would'a put paid to my old friend Peter Wake."

Rork found the wound, his probing sending a wave of fire back through Wake's chest. "Looks like we both owe Henri a bit o' rum sippers at our next liberty port. In fact, I'd make it gulpers."

Faber and his wife were holding onto each other, crying with in relief. Rork rolled Wake over, searching for an exit wound. As he was turned, Wake saw Woodgerd warily kicking dead men, rifle aimed at their torsos, one of the freed missionaries picking up the weapons strewn about. Sokhoor, haggard and blood-stained, walked over to them holding his arm. He spit at Falah's body and ground his sandal into the head, uttering something in his language. Then he stormed off, deliberately doing the same to each of the dead bandits.

"What . . . happened?" Wake asked Rork.

"Buggers ran off, they did, sir. Devil's Disciples my arse. Didn't much like hot lead or cold steel, by the looks o' it."

Rork pushed a rag into the hole in Wake's chest. The bosun reached around and put another into a place in Wake's back, where sensation was now returning, searing in intensity. Wake had never seen his friend look so serious, so grief-stricken. He suddenly comprehended that it was because of *him*, and a wave of shame came over him.

"I'm sorry, Sean. I got myself shot and let you down."

Rork stopped, tears filling his eyes. "Ah damn you, Peter

Wake. Damn you all to hell an' back. 'Tis not a thing to apologize for, ya bloody fool. Good God above, you're sounding like some sort o' snotty midshipman."

Rork wrapped the makeshift bandages around Wake's abdomen. "Now jes' lay there for a wee bit an' we'll get ya to stop filling the damned desert with officer's blood. Unbecoming, it is, sir. Bleedin' like this in front o' the men. Won't do, sir. Won't do a'tall."

"How bad is it?"

"Thumped on the noggin, ya was. Concussed, I'm thinkin' but that's nary a worry, you bein' an officer. Shot in the chest too, ye was. Through an' through, so if we keep that clean an' let it drain, no fever inflammation. But you'll have ta keep the pressure on these wounds, though. We'll do a fancy turn o' sewing an' stitch ya proper-like later, when we get somewheres safe."

Woodgerd limped over, a gash across his thigh oozing over his trousers. Everyone Wake saw was wounded, even Catherine had a cut on her arm. The colonel looked down at Wake. "Well, Rork, our sailor boy here gonna live?"

"Yes, sir. The lieutenant will be right as rain in no time, Colonel. Jes' gotta let him rest a bit."

"He'll have to rest while riding a horse, Bosun, 'cause we're getting out of here. Right now."

"Wait."

They turned to see Sokhoor, looking like the specter of death itself with his arm now hanging, trudging toward them holding up his other hand. "I have something for Lieutenant Wake. To make the pain go away a little." The scholar leaned down. "Here, Peter. Try to eat this. It will dull the pain so you can get on a horse." It looked like crumbled spinach to Wake.

"Kif hash," said Woodgerd with a nod. "That'll do the trick all right."

Wake was able to get some down his throat, flushed by water from a skinbag. He lay there for a few minutes, regaining his senses, while the others gathered weapons, food, and water for the journey. When they came back over to him he was feeling slightly stronger.

"I'm ready to ride. Just help me up."

⁓

Rork rode next to him, steadying him as he swayed. While they rode, the bosun told Wake what happened at the end of the fight and why he was still alive.

"They was chargin' an' yellin' to beat the band, they was, sir. Hellacious wailin' o' some kind. By that time the women you freed had opened up the crate with Sokhoor an' the rest o' the missionary menfolk. Ne'er saw clergy so violent as those boyos there," Rork gestured forward where several of the missionaries were riding. "Took on those horsemen barehanded. Lost a bunch o' them doin' it, but they slowed the buggers down an' we got about five o' them nailed good with the rifles."

"And Falah? I saw him about to kill me."

"Bastard was shot nice an' clean by that Froggie diplomat, sir. One shot, in the head. Wish it were me, but I was busy by me ownself. When the other bastards saw their lead devil, or whatever they calls themselves, fall down dead, they had a change o' heart an' took French leave on the double quick. Bound off to the east an' those mountains—might be in that Timbuktoo place by now for all I know. "

Rork paused, embarrassed. "Oh, beggin' your pardon, sir. I suppose we shouldn't be sayin' *French leave* anymore. No sir, not after what I saw these Froggie lads do today. Ne'er knew the French could fight like that. An' they're God preachers, too!"

"Everybody wounded?" asked Wake as he started counting the survivors.

"Everbody that lived. Couple o' the ladies and several o' the men didn't make it." Rork put a hand on Wake's shoulder. "But your plan worked, sir. An' more's alive than woulda' been on that voyage to slavery."

"Now we just have to get to Marrakech and the protection of the pasha."

"Aye, sir. I'd rather see Key West coming o'er the horizon, but any port in a storm, eh?"

The fire was kept dim that night. Sokhoor warned that the *ShayTaan Taalib* might have reinforcements, find them, and finish them off. Wake huddled under a *bournous* and blanket. He'd been eating the hashish all day and evening to dull the throbbing waves of pain that swept through him without warning. Rork, Sokhoor and a couple of the missionaries were out on the perimeter on guard. Others around the fire were lying still, some moaning in pain.

On the other side of the fire Catherine lay on her side, Henri behind her, his arm resting across her. Both were asleep, folded into another completely, their faces calm. Wake thought of Linda in their bed in Pensacola. Of his children. His life back home that was so distant from this harsh world. It was like a dream.

He studied Woodgerd, who had just finished cleaning a rifle. The man's eyes were sunken and grim, but still determined. Wake suddenly wondered if the soldier had another side.

"You ever have a wife, Colonel?"

Woodgerd stared at the coals. "Still do. She's back home."

"Why'd you leave her?"

"Money. No work for a man without honor who's been cashiered from the army. Why hire you when there's all those heroes coming home? Had to leave. Only one thing I'm any good at and that's soldiering, so I decided to go to Europe for a year or so. That was eight years ago. Money was good so I stayed. She comes over sometimes. I go back sometimes."

"But you found enough work to make it worth it?"

"Hell, yes. They didn't care anything except that I was a veteran, seen the elephant in combat. I'm good at training and commanding and I don't run off. The Piedmontese paid me pretty good. Then the Venetians. Then the Greeks. Egyptian Khedive for a couple of years. And now the Moors. The friggin' sultan pays me better than any of 'em."

"And you send it home to your wife?"

"Yep. What the hell am I gonna spend it on around this place?"

"When do you think you'll go home?"

"Contract's over in six months. Going home then. Might stay back there this time and curl up with the woman for good. How about you, sailor?"

Wake thought about that. "Don't know. Depends on this," he pointed to his chest. "My assignment is for another two years. If this doesn't heal, I'm sent home on half-pay. They won't take me back on active service if I leave wounded. Too many officers in good shape to let me back in. I've got to heal up."

"If I were you, I'd take the half-pay and go home to my wife and family. Do something else for a living."

Wake huffed with a sour laugh. "Well, you've got some company on that idea, Colonel. My wife wants me to quit the navy. Or she'll quit *me*." His voice faded. "Might already have. I'm not sure I have a home to go back to."

Woodgerd pursed his lips and nodded. "Yeah, I've heard that too." He paused, then said, "Aw hell, call me Michael. After the mess we've been through, we should be on first names. Besides, I'll damn well admit it, you're a pretty tough fighter too, Wake. Never thought I'd say *that* about a sailor squid. If it weren't for you leading the way back there and busting out of the crate at the beginning, we'd all be slave meat for some bastard in Mali. Imagine that, me a slave in Africa?"

Woodgerd's expression made Wake laugh, which made him hurt. "Michael, call me Peter. You're not so bad either, for a hidebound soldier. Guess we both have woman trouble. Going to have to solve *that* mess sooner or later."

"Yeah, well, we need a little more luck, yet. We ain't home safe, not by a long shot." Woodgerd sighed as he leaned back on his good elbow. "At least we had some luck today. That was looking bad there for a while."

"It was the kiss of Allah, gentlemen," uttered Sokhoor as he entered the glow of the fire. "Not luck at all, but the gentle kiss of Allah, which he bestowed upon us today."

Woodgerd grunted but Sokhoor ignored it and continued. "Allah gave you wisdom, Peter, in planning and leading our escape from the boxes. He gave you strength, Colonel, in fighting those Devil's infidels who outnumbered us so fearfully. When it appeared as though you, my dear friend Peter Wake, would die at the hands of that blasphemer Falah, Allah gave the gift of true sight to our dear Henri, so that in the midst of that chaos he could end the threat to your life. And now, Allah gives yet another kiss of healing to you, my friend. He smiles upon you, Peter, for you are a man of peace in your heart."

"Thank you, Sokhoor. And I do thank God."

The scholar sat down next to Wake. "Allah has shown his mercy upon us all and has helped us smite those heathen monsters, those defilers of my blessed and merciful faith. Let us be thankful to the God of us all—of Abraham, Moses, Jesus, and Mohammed."

Seeing Wake's reaction, Sokhoor touched his shoulder. "Oh yes, my friend, please know that Jesus, whom we call Isa—peace be upon him—is one of our most beloved prophets. He is smiling tonight, Peter, for one of his flock has been saved."

Sokhoor raised his hands to the black sky and chanted in Arabic.

After a pause he bowed to Woodgerd. "And if you would be so very kind, Colonel, please relieve me on the guard. It is time now for your turn. It has been a very eventful day for me and my body is weaker than my soul."

The colonel groaned as he stood. "Better weak than dead."

42

Peace be upon you

They rose before dawn and slowly helped each other's battered bodies get up into the saddles. The line of riders plodded away from the sky lightening in the east and toward Marrakech. Woodgerd had suggested a circuitous route, to foil any pursuers. But Sokhoor pointed out that all of them were wounded and needed medicine, and that two of their number—one of whom was Wake—were critically hurt. Time, he said, was of the essence. So they stayed on the main track northwest, everyone gazing at the horizon and expecting the enemy to attack at any time.

Wake, empty of strength, dehydrated and without any more hashish, willed himself to keep going, a mile at a time through the dust haze and suffocating heat. That night, as he shuddered in the cold and watched the woman he had almost fallen for that night at the castle in Porto Fino curl up with her husband near the campfire, he thought of Florida and his own family. He slid into sleep and reveled in the cool ocean breezes of his past, his dream taking him back to stolen nights with Linda at Useppa Island.

Seeing his friend's expression, Rork told Woodgerd and

Sokhoor that Wake's mind was likely far away in a nicer place with the woman he loved. The scholar said that was the very best medicine.

The next day they neared the southwest gate of the city at Bab al-Ahmar. While still some miles away, Sokhoor hailed a man from among the gawkers who had gathered around staring at the bloodied column of foreigners and told him to take a message to the Kasbah of Abdel Aziz, Pasha of Marrakech. Sokhoor told the man to say to the officer of the guard that *Mu' al-Lim Sokhoor, Vizier al Hassan, SulTaan al-Maghrib,* was entering the city and required assistance immediately.

"We will have help soon, God willing, my friends. This time we will be entering the city officially, as the envoys of the great sultan of Morocco, and our reception will be far different. Our danger is over now," the scholar told his companions as the walls came into view, with the great minaret towering above.

An hour later, after threading their horses through the growing throng of curious onlookers, they arrived at the giant gate, just as a troop of imperial cavalry lancers came thundering out and whirled from a column to line abreast, rearing their horses. The wild-eyed commander trotted up to Sokhoor and waved his right hand with a flourish, proclaiming loudly the gratitude of Pasha Abdel Aziz of Marrakech for the safe return of *Mu'al'Lim Sokhoor,* the Grand Vizier of the Sultan of the People of Morocco, Hassan the Beloved, Lion of the Atlas, and Protector of the Faithful. The procession proceeded into the city, a no-nonsense lancer beside each survivor to steady them and shoo away the curious.

Wake was glad for the cool shadows in the city and concentrated on not falling out of the saddle, for he wasn't sure how much longer he could hold on. The wounds were leaking and each jolt opened them up further. They rode past the Jewish Mella and the crashing salute of guards into the ancient Kasbah of the city's pasha, where non-Muslims were rarely permitted.

Abdel Aziz personally greeted them in the courtyard, snapping out commands to minions while grooms held the bridles. Some of the survivors fell off of their horses into the arms of servants. Wake was gently helped down to a chair, then carried inside on the shoulders of four men. Rork got the same treatment, managing a grin and "nicely done, lads," as he was taken, by Sokhoor's direction, to the same room.

Sokhoor then examined Wake in detail, nonchalantly explaining that he had studied medicine at the university in Damascus under the great Islamic physicians. After an hour of probing and palpating he announced the bullet had entered between the fourth and fifth rib, creased the right lung—by the grace of Allah it missed the heart and aorta—and exited between the third and fourth rib in the right posterior quadrant. There would be no surgery if there was no great inflammation, and Wake would definitely heal.

Wake's eyesight and hearing returned and three days of rest and attention by Sokhoor, assisted by the pasha's personal physician, enabled Wake to have the strength to stand. Every movement caused sharp pain as he walked the passageways in the Kasbah, determined to regain his mobility. During these days attendants bathed his wounds frequently, alert to signs of a dreaded mortal infection, but none appeared.

The following day he was greatly curious, for Sokhoor mentioned, as an aside during a conversation, that the vizier of Marrakech, cousin and covert supporter of Falah, had died abruptly of unusual causes. It seemed his heart had somehow "failed." The mansion and grounds were immediately seized by the Pasha of Marrakech, looted of anything of value, and the twenty-four concubines, four wives, and dozens of children were expelled and told to head east into the desert. When asked for details, Sokhoor simply shrugged his shoulders and said it was God's will and man's mystery.

Messages arrived from Sultan Hassan that was he coming to make sure all was as well as possible, and at the end of the first week, the survivors were assembled in the main *durhbar*, or meeting hall, of Hassan's personal palace in Marrakech. It was even more opulent than the palace at Rabat, the senses enchanted by lush fabrics, delicate perfumes, quaint stringed music, exquisite mosaics, and the most attentive servants Wake had ever seen. The former hostages were allowed the unheard-of honor of sitting down in audience before the great sultan, arranged in two rows of chairs.

Hassan, robed in golden silk, sat on a raised throne of cedar wood. Translated by a monotoned courtier, he was solicitous regarding the well-being of the missionaries, inquiring as to their comfort in detail. He apologized that this tragedy should have happened within his kingdom and the land of Islam. Then he edged forward, his tone softened as he looked into their eyes.

"I know that Mu'al-lim Sokhoor, my personal vizier, scholar, and emissary, has explained to each of you that the people who attacked you are not of our faith. You must know that we of Islam respect the People of the Book, Christians and Jews, as we respect ourselves. And that the teaching of our blessed Prophet, Mohammed, my direct ancestor and guiding spiritual mentor, expressly prohibits such actions as those which the devil's animals had done to you, and others before you. The *ShayTaan Taalib* are not of any faith, but are followers of that monster of death, the Devil."

Hassan straightened in the throne, his voice rising. "The remnants are being hunted down like the dogs they are, as I speak, and will be *smitten*," a fist smashed down on the side table, "from the face of this earth."

The missionaries sat there and listened vacantly but said nothing. They had seen too much, their friends and loved ones humiliated, tortured, and killed, and they themselves horribly maimed. Of the original twenty-one Christians who were captured, only fifteen had survived the *ShayTaan Taalib*.

Catherine cried quietly, and Henri Faber gripped his wife's hand, stoically watching Hassan. Woodgerd, dressed in formal uniform, stood with his arms crossed behind his back near the sultan's dais, staring impassively at the audience. Rork, next to Wake in the back row, watched intently but displayed no reaction.

Wake was mentally perusing the potential political repercussions of the missionary tragedy when he heard Hassan call out his name. Startled, he looked up and saw Henri Faber stand and approach the dais.

Rork touched his shoulder and whispered, "Come on, sir, they want us both up there, front an' center."

The three of them were joined by Woodgerd. Sokhoor appeared from behind the dais with a shadow box and held it for the sultan. Hassan looked each of them in the eye and boomed out an imposing phrase in Arabic, which was translated, "And now, by the authority granted me by the grace of Allah the Almighty and Merciful, Mohammed the Wise and Compassionate, and the Faithful of Islam, I present to each of these men the highest decoration of the Kingdom of Morocco, the Order of the Lion of the Atlas. May all men know of your courage and accord you the respect it deserves."

It was a golden medallion, embossed with the likeness of a Barbary lion and suspended by a green and gold silk ribbon. Hassan pinned the first on Wake, clasping his hand and saying shyly in English, "Thank you." The others received theirs, and the audience, led by the sultan, burst into applause.

"Well, I never . . ." Wake said to Rork beside him, who answered with a laugh, "Well, sir, now you have!"

Hassan held up his hand and the room instantly was quiet. "And now, may each of you feel the healing touch of Allah upon you. May you always remember the peace of Islam and the gratitude of the faithful. May your lives know joy and your families know the blessing of children. May you remember my kingdom—the land of the Atlas, the Sahara, and the Ocean—with memories other than pain. Thank you. Thank you. Thank you. Peace be unto you for the rest of your days."

"Guess you'll be a hero back home now, Peter. They might

even decide to keep you around," said Woodgerd under his breath.

"Maybe. And you can charge double for your services, Michael."

"Nah, already tried. Sonovabitch said I'm under contract. Can't raise my fee."

After Marrakech, Rabat seemed dull, but that was fine with Wake. There was one thing at Rabat, though, that brought life back into Wake's body more than all else—the smell and sight of the ocean. He was stronger now, taking long strolls and even pushing himself up off the floor with his arms. It had been more than a month, and his wounds had closed, the muscles still sore but gaining strength. Now that he could, Wake reveled in breathing in the thick sweet air deeply, filling his lungs as he walked the ramparts of the royal palace overlooking the old fortress by the river's mouth, with the sight and sounds of the sea before him.

The American ambassador, Pickering, had met them as soon as they arrived. He explained he had sent messages off to Washington and the American fleet in Europe advising them of the hostage situation's outcome, but the only reply was a terse telegram from the admiral's staff at Genoa: "No warship available. Arrange fastest transport to Genoa for Wake and Rork."

Since commercial traffic was nil at that moment, the quickest transportation heading toward the Mediterranean turned out to be HMS *Doris,* which the British ambassador said would be visiting the port sometime in early June. The Brit offered the Americans a ride, saying the Royal Navy would be proud to convey the heroes to their own fleet.

Wake was more than ready to leave Africa. He wanted to return to his own people. Recuperating in luxury, the decadence and boredom bothered him. But not Rork, who proclaimed that now he knew, "how that tough ol' soul, the Bishop o' Waterford, must live, amongst splendor an' glory. Aye, sir, the life o' the idle an' fancy rich is for me. I could get used to *this*."

The regimen included diplomatic functions among the small international community, and Wake saw Henri and Catherine Faber often. Henri was quiet about the ordeal he had gone through, refusing to describe it even when pressed by the others over brandy. He would simply thank God for their deliverance and hug his wife. He was very friendly to Wake each time they met and on several occasions they exchanged knowing glances, then nodded without words.

Though he was certain she wanted to, Wake and Catherine never spoke alone. He was afraid to allow that to happen. He knew he did not love her, and that she did love her husband. But Wake still felt a pang of hurt, which he couldn't explain and made him feel guilty. So he stayed away from her except for public events.

May turned into June and the heat of the desert overpowered the sea breezes. Wake remembered the overland journey through the vast wastelands shimmering in the heat of April and couldn't imagine what they must be like in June. His uniform, a new one courtesy of Sultan Hassan, was growing too warm for long walks. He lost track of the days. Wake looked out at sea and longed to be free.

Then, one morning he heard a shout of joy in Gaelic followed with, "By all the saints, ain't she a pretty sight!" and Rork burst into his room saying the *Doris* had just steamed into the open anchorage.

It was an emotional sendoff at the dock. Sokhoor was there representing Sultan Hassan. Standing next to Woodgerd was a company of infantry and troop of cavalry rigidly in formation, looking their most resplendent. Most of the foreigners in Rabat showed up. Pickering was there, frail next to the others as he handed over some mail to Rork. He wished Wake luck and thanked him once again, saying that the American reputation had been immeasurably boosted in the Arab world by his actions.

Woodgerd came up and quietly said something to Rork, who roared with laughter. Then the colonel offered his hand to Wake. "Peter, I hope we meet again, in far better circumstances and far nicer surroundings. Rum's on me."

In spite of his initial dislike, Wake had grown to respect the man. He hoped that they would meet again. "I'd like that, Michael. And yes, the rum is definitely on you."

Wake had been searching but didn't see the Fabers. As he was about to step down into the launch he suddenly heard Catherine call to him. "Wait one moment, if you please."

He turned and saw the two of them. She stood there, her beautiful hair done up in the twist he had remembered, and it was all he could do to take his eyes from her as Henri shook his hand.

"Thank you, Peter. From the core of my soul, thank you. For all that you have done for Catherine and for me. You will always have a friend in each of us."

Then Catherine rushed forward and kissed him, her husband subtly turning to look at the warship offshore. Her sad eyes, those beautiful sad eyes he remembered from Martinique, were glistening, almost breaking his heart, as she brought her mouth to his ear. "Peter, forgive me. Someday you will understand . . ." she said, then returned to Henri's arm.

Rork tugged at his sleeve. "Time to shove off, sir. Royal Navy's waitin' for us."

Wake looked at the launch's boat officer and crew, immaculate in their blues, and realized he was returning to the world of the sea. His world. The world he had dreamed of in the desert but thought he'd never see again.

Then Sokhoor stepped forward and held both his shoulders,

embracing him and kissing each cheek. The scholar had tears running down his face.

"Peter, we will meet again in heaven, my dearest American friend. For remember this, we are all the children of the God of Abraham and our greatest rewards are not of this world, but the next. It has been an honor for me to be your friend and to have you as mine."

There was so much Wake wanted to say but didn't know how. "Sokhoor, you have taught me so much. About Islam. About life. About God. Thank you my friend. Peace be upon you. *Shukran, Sahdeeq.*"

Sokhoor looked skyward, then touched his chest. "*Wa Àlaikum as-salaam wa-raHmat ulaahi wa barakaatuh.* And peace upon you too, as well as God's mercy and his blessings."

As they clasped hands Sokhoor said, "In gratitude, Allah will soon show you a magnificent cosmic celebration. It will come when you are far from here, Peter. When you see it, rejoice and think of the true peace of Islam, of our beloved Sultan Hassan, and of the things that you have accomplished and have learned, here in my land. And perhaps, God willing, you will kindly remember me, too."

Sokhoor paused, looking into Wake's eyes. "And when you see what Allah has sent you, that which has troubled your heart will be gone." He held up a hand. "Oh yes, I know you have had tears inside. But all will be better."

Wake tried to speak but the scholar shook his head. "Now the time has come for you to go forth, my friend. It reminds me of another old Roman saying—*Porro et Sursum.* Onward and upward. Goodbye, Peter."

As Rork steadied him down into the boat, Wake felt his throat swell while his eyes filled. Sniffling, he choked out, "Under way, Rork. Get us under way, now."

The oars dipped and pulled, propelling the launch quickly away from the dock. Rork was violating naval tradition by sitting in the stern with an officer, but he didn't care. He knew his friend needed a steady hand right and whispered, "All right, sir?"

Wake muttered yes and looked aft at the people on the dock. They were waving and calling out good luck in three languages. He waved back.

Wake stared for a long time at the scene astern of them—the brown mud huts in front of the gray stone fortress with the green banner of Morocco flying overhead in the blue pastel sky, the lusty singing of the beach fisherman as they hauled their catch ashore, the plaintive wail of the *muezzin* atop the minarets calling the faithful to prayer.

Africa had almost killed him, but he was incredibly fascinated by it all—like the beautiful snake that had almost killed him. He let out a long breath.

"Peace be unto *all* of you. *Inshallah*."

43

Allah's Gratitude

June 1874

At Malta they saw HMS *Lord Warden* and Wake was pleased to learn he and Rork would make the passage to Genoa aboard her, for she was still flying Admiral Drummond's pennant and Pete Allen might be aboard. His hope was justified when he climbed through the entry port and heard the Royal Marine exclaim.

"Well, the Devil couldn't kill him and God doesn't want him, just yet. You consistently amaze me, Peter Wake. I've been hearing outlandish tales about you and Rork. We must immediately repair below so I can ply you with spirits and get to the absolute truth of the matter, which, knowing *you,* will be more farfetched than the rumors." He gave Wake a hearty handshake. "Damned glad to see you, old son."

It was an easy passage with nothing to do except think as he lay in his berth. Wake spent most of the time thinking about Linda and his children, going over in his mind again and again her letters and his replies and wondering what the fleet mail would have for him when he arrived. Would she tell him it was over, practically if not legally? She was strong-willed and had already endured ostracism during the war, he knew she could handle the kind associated with an estranged marriage.

Would she understand his need—which even he couldn't justify but knew it was part of his soul—for the sea and for the navy? Would they keep what they had started during those dark days of the war, when everything, and everyone, was against them?

He grew more fearful and withdrawn the closer they came to Genoa and the certainty of his finding out her decision.

Unlike his first arrival, it was sunny when they glided up the bay into Genoa. Colors he hadn't noticed before, red roofs, flowers, the green hills, gaily welcomed him, complemented by saluting guns echoing off the hills. A heartfelt goodbye to the officers and men of the ship culminated with Allen's farewell. The Royal Marine knew of Wake's fears for his marriage.

"It'll be all right, Peter," he said with concern. "It will get better, my friend. She'll still want you." Then he laughed. "But God knows why, for you really are bloody daft!"

The farewell to the *Lord Warden* was more emotional than their welcome back aboard the *Franklin*, anchored three hundred yards away. They came up the entry port and reported in to a drowsy officer of the watch, who advised Wake that the admiral was busy but left word that he would see him later. Rork allowed a grunt of disdain at that, excused himself, and went forward to the petty officers' mess. Wake went aft to the cabin he hadn't seen in months. After the initial reception he wondered if he even had a cabin assigned anymore.

It was still the smelly domain of the surgeon, who grudgingly allowed him in. Filled with dread, Wake went to the purser and asked for his mail but was told there wasn't any. Depressed, for that surely wasn't a good sign, he returned to the cabin and listened as the blowhard surgeon waxed on about the privations of naval medicine, each breath reeking of medicinal brandy.

That evening at the wardroom mess it got no better. Wake felt all eyes on him, but no one asked any details of his assignment, the purser saying he heard it turned out fine and the executive officer remarking that independent duty was just the ticket for escaping the boredom of flagship billets. The surgeon opined that it "must've been damned tough in a Mohammedan country, what with the lack of decent rum, or even any rum at all." That got a round of guffaws. By the time dinner was over Wake was disgusted by the company and not in the mood to remain. He asked the executive officer for permission to leave and took a walk on deck.

In the three days since his return Wake had only spoken once for any appreciable time with Captain Staunton, the squadron staff captain. Staunton was noncommittal about Wake's staff work, saying he should recuperate and that they'd done without him for three months so they could do without him a few days longer. He warned Wake about bothering the admiral, who was busy with Spanish chaos, wounded Greek pride, German machinations, and whining Ottoman Turks, "not to mention our damned American diplos ashore. They think we serve them. God help us."

Frustrated and worried, Wake went forward and found Rork. Normally he wouldn't have asked his friend about the situation—it was a breach of custom and would put Rork ill at ease—but Wake was at the point of real worry. Something was very wrong.

"Have you heard anything about me or you in Morocco, Rork? Nobody's talking to me and it's as if they're ignoring me because they think we've done something wrong. Damned if I can figure out why they're acting this way. And no letters from Linda. There is something wrong here, Rork. Good God, I can't even get in to see the admiral, my boss!"

Rork's reply had a serious tone, which didn't ease Wake. "I think it'll be jes' fine, sir. Ye've nary a thing to be sorry for or worried about. They're probably jes' restin' ya, sir. They've gone light on me ownself too. You know how the bloody navy goes, sir. Hurry up an' wait. Then they'll bash ya for bein' so damned lazy. Part o' the job."

Rork put a hand on Wake's shoulder. "Steady on, sir. Your good lady will do you fine. She's a bright girl an' a fine lady. Ain't none better that I've seen, an' I've seen plenty."

Wake knocked three times on the door, then entered Admiral Case's great cabin after the Marine guard announced him from the passageway. After a week of nervous waiting, he'd had a summons from the admiral on this Sunday morning, just before church services on the main deck were about to commence.

"Lieutenant Wake, reporting for duty as flag lieutenant, sir."

Case, reading glasses perched on the end of his nose, spun his swivel chair around and calmly studied the officer standing tall in the prescribed manner, three feet in front of the desk. Staunton got up from the chart table against the bulkhead, nodded quickly at Wake, and departed silently.

"Stand easy, Lieutenant," Case said tiredly. "I have read your report of the events in Morocco with interest. I'm also told that you seem to be healing well from your wounds. You've been back now for what, a week? When will you be ready for full duty?"

"Right now, sir."

"Hmm. And your bosun?"

"Right now, also, sir."

"Hmm. So by five days from now you'll both be ready for an assignment? I have a job for you and I don't want it fouled up."

Wake expected some questions about Morocco, possibly a compliment or a concern. Something. But Case was acting as if Wake had just come back from a bar fight ashore in Genoa. Scrutinizing the man's eyes revealed nothing. They were ice blue and unblinking.

"Fully ready, sir," Wake replied, evenly.

"Very good, Lieutenant. On next Friday evening I want you to be my personal aide at a big soirée at the French Consulate. Everyone of import will be attending and there will be no room for mistakes or failure. This is a social event of the highest occasion and I want everything done right. Bosun Rork will be in charge of transport. Understood?"

"Yes, sir. Are we guests or hosts, sir?"

"Guests. I want my senior staff and all ship captains there, on time, in full dress uniform, sober and ready to converse and impress the diplomatic corps of Europe. You will be in charge of making sure that they all get there, behave, and depart without untoward incident. I'll repeat that, Lieutenant—without untoward incident. You have a reputation for somehow getting involved with, or creating, unusual incidents. I'll have none of that at this function. Welcome back to the fleet, Lieutenant Wake, and your *staff* duties. Your wild adventures are over."

"Yes, sir."

"Very well. Make it so. You are dismissed."

"Aye, aye, sir!"

Wake paced the quarterdeck for an hour afterward, watching the bumboats and coastal cargo boats making their way in and out of the docks while analyzing the brief one-sided conversation with his commander. Did Case disapprove of his actions? Was he jealous of Wake's "adventures?" Was the admiral in trouble because of Wake's decisions?

He grew angrier as he paced. Wake decided he had no idea what the admiral thought of his actions in Morocco, but it was apparent the man wasn't enthusiastic about them. He had, in some unfathomable way, made the admiral uneasy by his actions in Morocco, but couldn't figure out how or why.

He stretched, his abdominal and chest muscles throbbing, and grimaced. Amazing, he thought cynically. Amazing how what seemed like a victory in Morocco could be viewed ambivalently in the genteel ambiance of Europe. And now he had to ride herd on American naval officers like some sort of school chaperone. Case appeared to have glee in his eye when he talked about that. What the hell has our navy come to? Wake asked himself. And me? I've become a nursemaid for grown men.

Then he saw the surgeon waddle up on deck and start toward him. The sight of his foul cabin mate made him groan again. It was going to be a very long tour of duty.

The French were doing this up right, Wake thought as he shepherded his charges—all of whom outranked him—through the gilded doorway into the grand salon of the French Consulate, where a line of plume-hatted dignitaries stood waiting to be fawned over. He had made sure the American naval officers were all in full cocked-hat and sword, heavy dress uniform, precisely on time and, especially in the case of the surgeon, clean and sober.

Rork's transport, by launch and landau, went without mishap, and now there were nineteen American naval officers arriving resplendently to represent their country amidst the colorful arrogance of Europe. Strom was there with his lovely wife Christine, the American consul general acting surprisingly pleased that Wake had returned.

"Glad you're back, Peter Wake. Been dull around here without you!"

Wake had been worried about Strom's reception and was relieved. The consul general's brow furrowed. "Seriously, son, I'm glad you got through that mess in Africa and are recovering. Relax and enjoy yourself this evening."

Davis the assistant consul came over right afterward, one eyebrow raised, and wagged a finger. "See, Peter, I told you he liked you. In some ways you remind him of himself in his younger days. He was worried as hell when he heard what happened to you in Morocco."

Over the string quartet in the corner, Wake heard a staff pound onto the polished marble floor three times, then an imperious French voice call out something unintelligible. Wake did catch the *"etats unis"* part though.

"Rear Admiral Augustus Ludlow Case! Commander-in-Chief of the European Squadron, United States Navy . . . and his officers . . ." repeated the major-domo in English.

Case moved along the reception line, smiling and nodding while blissfully mangling their language, which made even Wake, with his rudimentary grasp of French, wince. As the mere flag lieutenant, Wake didn't even join the procession—he had read the protocol rules the day before and junior officers never were introduced to the upper classes at such affairs. But after the senior Americans had gone through, a gold-bedecked French admiral beckoned him over. It was Admiral Geaugeard, head of the *Conseil d'Marine* and a senior officer in the French Navy.

Wake glanced nervously at his boss who had seen the gesture. The admiral eyed him with a bemused expression and nodded to go ahead. With that tacit approval, Wake greeted the Frenchman using his own atrocious French, *"S'il-vous-plaît, excusez-moi, mon excelencie, pour mon frances c'est très mauvais."*

Admiral Geaugeard laughed uproariously, saying in very good English, "Lieutenant Wake, it doesn't much matter if a naval man speaks the language of these," he disdainfully looked about, "diplomats very well, as long as he can and will do his duty—killing his country's enemies. And from what I have heard, Lieutenant—" He looked at the Lion of the Atlas medal on Wake's chest, "that is something you can do very well."

Wake stammered for a second, then blurted out, "Ah, *merci beaucoup,* sir. I just do my duty as best I can."

Geaugeard put a hand on Wake's shoulder. "Enjoy the evening, Lieutenant. We are delighted you are here. I think you will have a good time."

That confused Wake, who wasn't used to any, let alone foreign, admirals being so hospitable to him. He said thank you again and went off to the foyer make sure all was well.

As Wake asked the servants to take out some finger food to Rork and the American bluejackets waiting in the street, Captain Staunton summoned him from across the crowded room. To his consternation, he saw Rork standing next to the captain, looking uncomfortable. Enlisted men, even senior enlisted men like Rork, were not customarily allowed inside officers' soirées, and Wake knew instantly that something was up. A myriad of potential problems, topped by something the shore party had done, probably to or with a French female, entered his mind. But no, Staunton was smiling, so it couldn't be that bad. Wake had never seen Staunton smile.

"Lieutenant, I'll need you in a moment," said the captain as he turned toward the entry. Wake was about to ask the bosun what had happened, when Rork also faced the doorway. The major-domo's staff pounded once, followed by a deep bass announcement.

"Consul General et Madame Henri Faber, de le consulat de la France avec le Sultan du Maroc."

Henri Faber, with Catherine looking exquisite in yellow silk, swept into the reception line, greeting familiar faces, all of whom had gossiped about them months earlier when Faber had been dismissed from the post in Genoa. Wake had no idea they were in Genoa. He felt an odd sense of relief when he saw Catherine so obviously happy on her husband's arm. A moment later they both embraced Wake and Rork.

"We have been recalled to France temporarily, Peter," explained Faber. "Then we go to another posting. This time as *chargé d'affaires* at the embassy in America, of all places. Can you believe it, my friend? Such good fortune!"

"What wonderful news, Henri. Then your leaders are . . ." Wake didn't know how to phrase it delicately.

"Still angry with me?" offered Faber, who shrugged. "Oh, maybe just a little. But we French, even the weak-willed ones in charge, don't like those arrogant Germans. My outburst has mostly been forgiven. Besides, the situation in Morocco came out well and they think more kindly of me now. Another chance at my career, it would seem."

His eyes went to his wife. "And with my personal life also, Peter. The past is, as you say in English, long gone."

Wake was happy for them, but there was certainly more to the story and he wanted to hear about it. "Congratulations to you both. Tell me—"

Rork interrupted with a harrumph and inclined his head toward the entry again. The major-domo was banging his staff again as Wake muttered, "All right, Rork, one minute. I was just—"

"Sir, look at the doorway. *Now.*"

Wake was suddenly aware that the ballroom had gone quiet. No music, no chatter, even the clattering of champagne glasses had stopped. A huge grin was spreading across Rork's face but his eyes were misty. Wake glanced around. He saw Bishop Ferro there in the corner, waving to him, grinning like a maniac. Everyone in the room was grinning.

At him . . .

"Madame Linda Wake, l' épouse de Lieutenant Peter Wake, de la Marine Americaine," the major-domo boomed out, then repeated it in English.

Wake wasn't listening anymore, for there was his Linda, more beautiful than he had ever seen her, like a queen in a gown of navy blue, with sapphires set in gold across her chest, on the arm of a French naval officer. The crowded drew apart, opening a path for him as Wake, eyes filling, covered the sixty feet in a trance, his mouth opening but no words emerging. It wasn't a dream. It was really Linda.

Just as he reached her, a deafening crescendo of applause rose. The two of them held a kiss, folding into each other, caressing each other's face, crying in disbelief and joy.

"How did you . . . ?" he choked but couldn't finish. It had been so long, so very long. Linda anxiously touched his chest.

"We'll talk later, Peter. There's a lot to tell you. But first let me tell you I love you. I always have and I always will."

The applause was fading. Someone was approaching them. Wake didn't care.

"I love you, too, Linda. I was so scared that—"

"Don't be scared. We're good, dear. We're very good."

It was quiet again in the ballroom. Several people were next to him, but Wake only saw Linda.

"The children? Oh, God, our children?"

"They're fine. I brought them with me. You'll see them tonight. Later."

"No, we'll leave now. I want to see them."

Linda gently caressed his cheek. "No, not now, dear. There is something we need to do here first. The admiral will explain."

Wake turned to see Admiral Case standing with the French admiral. Rork came forward and hugged Linda, the two sharing a conspiratorial wink. Wake suddenly realized it was all planned. Everyone knew. Case was beaming at him. The crowd was pointing and smiling. Catherine and Henri's faces crinkled in delight.

Admiral Geaugeard walked to the center of the ballroom and held up his hands. He spoke in French, then translated his words into English. "My dear friends, distinguished guests, colleagues, welcome to this honored occasion. It would appear that our guest of honor has been deceived completely—though benevolently, I can assure him. I now call upon Rear Admiral Case of the United States Navy to introduce our guest of honor."

As the applause began again, Wake felt his knees go wobbly. He looked around him. Linda was shining with admiration. Rork was laughing. Case was calling him forward. The Royal Navy contingent, spurred on by none other than Wake's friend Jackie Fisher who had arrived unnoticed, was cheering. The American officers were whooping and hollering. Wake walked unsteadily forward toward the French admiral.

Case bowed. "Admiral Geaugeard, we of the American Navy are honored to be here, guests of the Republic of France, humbled by our magnificent surroundings, and enchanted by your hospitality. And now, may I present *Lieutenant Commander* Peter Wake, of the United States Navy!"

Pandemonium broke out one more time. Wake stood there, confused over Case's mistake on his rank, until he saw Linda walking forward with new epaulets. They were promoting him? He didn't know why. This was a promotion party? A surprise promotion party put on by the French? That wasn't logical.

But it was true. He was promoted. After all those years. Case, assisted by Rork, undid the pin clasps of his decade-old epaulets, tarnished from salt air and rough wear, and removed them from his shoulders. Linda handed the admiral the new ones with the golden oak leaf in the center. A moment later they were secured—Wake could have sworn they were heavier than a lieutenant's—and Linda reached up and kissed him.

But he still wondered why all this was taking place at the French consulate? Nothing was making sense. Admiral Case whispered for Wake to close his mouth and stand up straight— he wasn't a junior officer anymore. Geaugeard spread his arms and called for silence.

"And now that Lieutenant Commander Wake is properly attired, we may proceed with the most important—" he bowed toward the Americans, "from the French point of view—aspect of our gathering here this evening. Lieutenant Commander Peter Wake, please step forward."

A nudge from Admiral Case got him started, and Wake stepped two paces into the center of the room. Admiral Geaugeard's tone deepened.

"Innocent citizens of the Republic of France, Christian missionaries who had ventured forth into the wilderness to bring healing medicine and knowledge to the world, recently found themselves victims of terror by merciless brigands in the wastelands of northern Africa. . . ."

As the admiral went on images appeared in Wake's mind—that initial audience with Sultan Hassan, the whirling dance of Sokhoor in the firelight on the mountain, trudging across that empty shimmering desert, the eyes of that cobra during its dance of death, the suffocating heat of the slave crates, and the red-hot pain in his chest as he was shot by Falah's men. He knew his hand was shaking and hoped it didn't show, that Linda couldn't tell. The French admiral mentioned his name.

" . . . and when Lieutenant Peter Wake offered his services to assist in the search, little did he know what it would eventually cost him in blood, horror, and pain. He received grievous wounds while leading the captives' escape and fight against the Devil-worshiping fiends that were transporting them into slavery. But the result was most certainly worth his sacrifices and travails. For most of the hostages, including two Americans, were rescued, and one of them, the lovely Madame Catherine Faber, is here today."

Catherine came forward and kissed him on both cheeks, the guests gushing and clapping. Wake gritted his jaw, for he knew he was losing control, as he almost had at the goodbye at Rabat. Here were the two women of his life, one his love and the other his dear friend. It was almost too much for him. Henri came up with Rork, who put a steadying hand on his shoulder.

Geaugeard continued. "So, by the authority of the President of France, I have the privilege of bestowing on a son of America—the republic which showed the people of France that liberty and equality were indeed the rights of man—the highest honor that France can bestow. This is the honor first established by that most sainted son of France, Napoleon Bonaparte, on the nineteenth of May, in the year eighteen-oh-two, and it is still the award to which many aspire and all respect."

He paused for effect. "And now . . . I hereby proclaim that Lieutenant Commander Peter Wake, of the United States Navy, is awarded the *La Légion d'Honneur,* rank of *Chevalier!*"

An honor guard of French naval officers marched out to the beat of drummers, wheeled right and stamped to a stop before Wake and the admiral. With a clicking of heels and a flourishing salute, the senior officer of the guard presented Geaugeard with a blue-satin-lined shadow box, then carried it for him as they both stood before Wake.

The admiral held up the medal for all to see, eliciting a hush from the crowd. The white-enameled cluster star, on the center of which was embossed *Honneur et Patrie,* was below a blue-enameled oak wreath, the entire medal suspended by a red ribbon. Linda held her breath at the sight and Catherine cried. Wake was speechless.

"This medal, long known for its value among brave men, hereby welcomes another to its brotherhood of honor." Geaugeard pinned it on the left side of Wake's uniform, above his medal from the sultan of Morocco.

The crowd thundered its approval. Wake knew he had to say something, but he wasn't prepared, couldn't even think straight. Besides, he felt that he didn't deserve it. Sokhoor and Faber and Rork, yes, but not him. All he did was get shot.

He managed to get out, *"Merci beaucoup. Merci."*

The musicians struck up an old French army marching song, *La Marseillaise,* since the Franco-Prussian War the new anthem of the republic, and the French in the ballroom sang it lustily as people closed in around Wake, shaking his hand, offering congratulations, patting his shoulders, asking questions in half a dozen tongues. Wake tried to be polite and answer, but there were too many people and his wounds began to ache, then throb. He became separated from Linda and the others, finally seeing her in the distance talking with Catherine. They were standing closely, speaking intimately.

Someone shuffled Wake over to a flag display where he was

presented to a new dignitary and a photograph was taken. A moment later a champagne flute was put in his hand and he was expected to give a toast, but only said *"Merci"* again, to wild applause. Music started and a woman asked Wake to dance, a man asked him to dance with his wife, but he just wanted Linda. He needed to have her close. Then Admiral Case asked him to come to a quiet corner, for there was another matter they needed to cover.

Rork cleared the way with his body toward an alcove, where Wake and Case sat on a couch. The admiral was concise. "Your work is done with this squadron, Peter. You and your family are going back home to America. You've been overdue for shore duty for sometime. That's being rectified by the powers that be in Washington. In fact, that's where you're heading, Commander—Washington Naval Yard. Seems that you're wanted there."

"Sir, all of this. I don't know what to say, Admiral, except thank you."

"No, son, it's I who gets to thank you. You went into a terrible situation, endured unspeakable experiences, and came out with victory, making our country smell like a rose. You gained us prestige with those Moroccan Arabs, and gratitude with the French—not an easy outcome in the very best of times. Hell, Wake, you even made *me* look good on this."

"Admiral, I thought maybe I'd done something wrong. And now all this. And Linda. Did you know she was coming, sir?"

Case grinned. "Of course I did! Why do you think we had to delay this shindig? She was late in getting here and that set us back. She's been heading here for two months, since we got word you survived and were coming out of the desert. Hell, half the naval know-it-alls of France came here tonight, just to see the grand surprise. We did get you, though, didn't we, son?"

"That you did, sir. That you did. I had no idea." Wake abruptly remembered the snickering in the wardroom, Rork's odd expressions. "Rork! The bosun knew too?"

"That he did, the old rascal. The Irish make great conspirators. I'm one too, you know. It's in our bones."

Linda's arm was wrapped around his waist as they climbed up to the seat in the open carriage for the ride to her hotel. Wake had no clue as to how she had paid the way to Europe for herself and the two children, and he didn't ask. That could come later. He just wanted to revel in the magic of her being there with him, on the other side of the world.

"Happy birthday, dear."

Wake shook himself out of his reverie. "What?"

"Peter, it's June twenty-sixth, your thirty-fifth birthday. Good Lord, you can't have forgotten that!"

He had forgotten completely. "Thinking about everything else, dear. But it's been a great birthday. Incredible."

They rode along the bay front, dimmed gaslights across the city allowing the stars to show in the moonless night. The warm summer breeze and night sounds of the city accompanied by the horse's lazy hoof beat. Linda snuggled close to him and was so soft. He breathed in her perfume, caressed her hair and let the awful memories of the *Shaa Taan Taalib* and its terror mastermind fade away.

"She's very beautiful, isn't she?"

"Who?" he asked, but he understood her question.

"The lady you rescued, Peter. Your friend Catherine. Who else would I be talking about, silly? She's very nice. We talked and she told me you met her in the West Indies, then she and her husband in Italy, and then you helped to track her down and rescue her in Africa. An amazing story, Peter. She's quite an admirer of yours. Said I was lucky to have a gentleman like you. Described what you went through, but stayed sane and decent throughout it all. She called it 'an affair of honor,' but I got the feeling she meant more than the part in Africa."

His mind went to that New Year's Eve on Martinique. Was

it only six months ago? It felt like a lifetime ago.

"Catherine's a good person and a friend, and yes, she's beautiful. We were lucky to be able to save her and most of the others. Her husband saved my life." He saw Linda still looking at him quizzically. "And yes, our friendship was, and is, an affair of honor. No problem there, dear."

She held him tighter, neither saying anything further. It was such a wonderful evening he didn't want the drive to end, so when they reached the hotel he promised the driver an extra hundred lira to take a slow drive into the hills so they could overlook the city lights below, telling Linda that the children were surely asleep anyway and that he'd kiss them in the morning.

As they crested the top of one of the hills surrounding the city to the north, Linda pointed to the northwest sky. "Oh Peter, just look at that! Have you ever seen anything like that?"

Wake was awestruck. "No. I'm not sure anyone has, Linda."

Low above the Maritime Alps in the distance, across the inky black void just to the right of Cassiopeia and the constellation Camelopardalis, was a brilliant blaze of amber fire covering fully sixty degrees of sky across the northern horizon. It was the most incredible comet Wake had witnessed or heard about—so bright and huge as to be unreal.

Then Sokhoor's final words came to him. "Peter, you're shaking, shaking badly. Darling, are you all right? What is it?"

"Nothing's wrong. Just remembering what a friend told me when I left Africa. He said that Allah would soon show me a cosmic celebration in gratitude and that everything would be better for me. Somehow he *knew*."

Linda held his trembling hands and saw tears in his eyes as he stood and looked away to the southern horizon, over the dark Mediterranean—toward Africa.

"*Shukran bezzef, Sokhoor. As-salaamu alaikum,*" he murmured.

Wake sat back down and told the driver to take them to their hotel. Pulling her closer, he kissed Linda slowly, savoring her taste, her scent, the feel of her body.

"What was that you said, Peter?"

"Just a thank-you to my friend Sokhoor. I asked that peace be upon him."

Wake decided then that Linda never needed to know the horrors he had seen and been through—she'd been through enough herself, trying to raise a family alone, wondering where her husband was and if he was even alive. He thought of Sokhoor again—*Porro et Sursum*. It was time to look forward.

Under the light of the comet Peter and Linda's bodies molded to each other under the carriage blanket. There was so much he wanted to ask, to say, but it wasn't the right moment. Stroking Linda's soft auburn hair, holding her in his arms, he knew everything was all right now. They were going to make it.

Words weren't needed anymore.

Acknowledgments

What an adventure it was to write this novel. After researching the background material for five months, I embarked upon an eleven-thousand-mile trek by ship, car, van, and plane, from the languid tropics of the New World to the urban complexity of the Old World—finally ending up in mysterious Africa. Many people on three continents, eight islands, two seas, and one very big ocean assisted me along the way in English, Spanish, French, Italian, Latin, and Arabic. Here are my thanks to some of those who really went beyond the call of duty.

Thank you to Calvin Kelly and Hal Ulrich, the can-do guys at Computer World on St. Thomas, for efficiently solving my cyber dilemma so I could get this book started.

My respects go to Caswall Richards, one of Antigua's finest sons, for showing me his island and convincing that bus driver to wait for me. The ship wouldn't have waited.

Merci to Audrey Jason, who led me back in time through the interior and along the coasts of enchanting Martinique—where so many cultures have blended so deliciously.

Thank you to the charming Martineve Browne and the imperturbable Steve Bryan, for sharing their love of Barbados' past, its people, and its beauty.

To Susana Pérez, one of Spain's most delightful daughters, *mil gracias, mi amiga,* for immersing me into the magical world of the ancient Alcázar and the cathedral, in the heart of one of my favorite cities in the world—Sevilla.

Señor Tony Muñoz, *el historiador* of Palma de Majorca, gets a thank-you for teaching me who was doing what to whom in 1874 at that fascinating junction of Mediterranean peoples.

My amazing friend, writer Pat Brogan, PhD, gets a huge thank-you for helping me do the eyeball recon, decipher Andalusian dialect, and work out the scenes in Tenerife, Palma, Cadiz, and Sevilla.

Thank you to my multinational shipmates aboard the M/V *Opera* who became wonderful friends and made every day enjoyable. See guys, I really was writing a book!

Anecdotal information on the Royal Marine Light Infantry was graciously given to me by Lt. Peter Sharp Allen RMLI, (WWII), of Great Britain. It is an honor to call him friend.

In Italy, Oswaldo Balicco helped me in Santa Margherita, and Minnesota's Catherine Rose motivated me (and therefore Peter Wake) to climb that damn cliff to the castle at Porto Fino. *Mille grazie.*

Casablanca, Morocco—that chaotic and intriguing cross-roads of Africa, Arabia, and France—is the home of Mourad Djelleb, who knows everyone, and Ouaziz Mostafa, who can arrange anything. Bogart would've loved these guys. *Merci pour l' assistance, mes amis.*

Shukran bezzef to El Harras Hassan, who took me into the secretive labyrinth of the medina in Fez, where it's still the year 1059 A.D. Someday I will be back, *ensha'llaah.*

A sincere *shukran* to some other impressive men in that part of the world who helped me: Historian Noureddine Mrani in Meknes, Sidi Mabab Abdul at His Royal Highness King Mohammed VI's palace in Rabat, Mawad Mohammed in the Kasbah of Rabat, and Elouane Aziz in the medina of Marrakech.

Sidi Goudimi Ahmed helped tremendously with Moroccan history, language, and culture. *Shukran bezzef, sahbi.*

This trek involved daunting logistics in Europe and Africa—but Teresa Lioce of Pine Island Travel planned and implemented them all with calm efficiency. If you're heading out into the unknown, she's the one you want to plan your op. Well done, Terri.

The fascinating celestial information was a treasure discovered by the lovely Nancy Glickman, gifted astronomer and dearest of friends, who patiently explained it all to me. She amazes me. Latin phraseology was provided by Michelle Glickman, 13-year-old Florida State Latin Champion, and her dad, Ron. Father Bill Loughran, Jesuit Vatican linguist, helped on Italian, Latin, and Church hierarchy.

I was graciously assisted in the Paris balloon information by none other than Julian Nott of Great Britain, the premier authority on ballooning in the world, and LTC Mike Woodgerd, US

Army, the lighter-than-air expert for the DoD. In addition, Mike entered the title contest for this novel and beat out 376 other entries from around the world, gaining him the role of a character in the book.

French culture and language was explained with gentle patience by Denise Couturier. *Merci beaucoup, ma cherie. En avant et ascendant!*

A sincere thank-you goes to June Cussen, a writer's dream editor; to Randy White, the premier novelist of Florida and my mentor; and to the other members of the Parrot Hillian Writers Circle: KDN Wehrle, the best critical reader in the world; Roothee Gabay, spirited novelist; and Sheba the Wonder Dog (RIP).

Peter Wake has a support crew in the islands where I live that all sailors would envy: Punkee Moe, Bill and Patti Standing, Annie Wenz and Larry French, Randy and Chris Briggs, Marianne Paton, the Yard Dogs, and Marc and Chris Strom.

To my readers around the world, thank you for your wonderful enthusiasm and support. You keep me motivated and strong.

Onward and upward!
Bob Macomber
Serenity Bungalow
Matlacha Island
Florida

Author's Postscript

The swirling international political climate portrayed in this novel is accurate. Bismarck, Moltke, Verdi, Garibaldi, Gladstone, Disraeli, Sultan Hassan, Grant, Commander Jackie Fisher, and Admirals Drummond, Geaugeard, and Case were all real. As Wake's career progresses so will theirs, and he will run into some of them again.

The ships of the U.S. and Royal navies in the book were real, as was RMS *Trinidad*. Weapons described were real, from the Whitehead and Howell torpedoes to the Gras rifles. The race for torpedo technology was very serious during this period.

Descriptions of the locales in the West Indies, Europe, and Morocco were taken from my personal experiences. The description of the memorable sunset transit through the Straits of Gibraltar is from my voyage.

The Mt. Pelée volcano at St. Pierre on Martinique finally did explode on 8 May 1902, killing 29,000 people—everyone in the city except one prisoner in the jail.

The African cobra test of manhood is only too real—I went through it at Djemma el-Fna in Marrakech. *Never* do this.

The celestial events depicted in the novel were real. Jupiter emerged from behind the moon in late April 1874, easily seen from Morocco and appearing as if it had emerged from inside the moon. The comet described at the end of the novel was real and spectacular. Comet Coggia (Comet C/1874 H1) stunned the astronomic community in 1874. Islamic astronomers were some of the world's very best prior to Europe's surge in telescopic technology.

I did my best to present the foreign languages (Spanish, French, Italian, Latin, and Arabic) accurately in both flavor and fact. Any errors in translation are unintentional and mine.

The mercenary in the novel, Colonel Michael Woodgerd, does not reflect the attitude or actions of the real LTC Mike Woodgerd (USMA), who won the title contest and so became a character. The literary Woodgerd would cringe at some of the adventures of the real Woodgerd.

Sevilla, Porto Fino, and Morocco are fascinating places that my soul aches to experience again. I will. And I urge my readers to visit them also.

I hope readers of this novel will gain an understanding that the three great faiths of Judaism, Christianity, and Islam are inter-related, and that fanatics are not representative of any of these religions. It is my fervent hope that one day we will all start cele-brating our similarities and stop dwelling on our differences.

Peace...
Bob Macomber
Key West
Florida